Adventures in the World of Eä
Out of the Shadows
Book Two: White Flame
N. L. Rose

Image credit: Jessica Kay and Natasha Rose

Copyright © 2022 by Natasha Rose

All rights reserved. Published by Natasha Rose. No parts of this book may be reproduced or transmitted in any form or by any means, electronic or mechanical, including photocopying, recording, or by any information storage and retrieval system, without written permission from the publisher.

For Austin, for being my biggest support and the love of my life, and to my friends who helped me bring this story to life.

Part One

Prologue

Through dusty, dark, and secret passages I ran, lungs burning and sides cramping with each frenzied stride. A single orb of white light guided my way and harsh, ominous fire was closing in behind me. They weren't far behind. I turned sharply, jamming my fist into a notch in the wall, opening a narrow slit. I squeezed through, tearing my long dress in the process, shredding through the layers of airy, flowy fabric.

Tristan! I sent my thoughts to him, including the mental image of the courtyard I could see just out the window and down below. I knew he could hear me, knew he'd come. I just had to get there before they got to me... A long hall sprawled before me, pale creamy white stone walls and floor were pink in early morning light.

Racing footsteps echoed from the passage and spilled into the hall. They were coming through. As I reached the end of the hall I looked back, confirming my fears. One of the men caught up with me. Crying out, I ripped free of his grip but not before I saw the eerily glowing stone in his hand. Together we stumbled down a wide set of stairs into the courtyard. Before I knew what was happening the man was over me, flipping me onto my back and clamping a hand over my mouth. But my eyes weren't on him. They were on the stone in his hand.

"This is your last chance," he offered.

He removed his hand from my mouth and the stone closer to my heart. I looked from him to the stone and breathed in.

1

In a field freckled with golden leaves I stood outside Belleview High with my two best friends and the captain of the football team. It wasn't what I wanted, not at all, but while my two best friends flirted back and forth, I faced the grim reality of forcing interest in Andrew. Other girls would have killed to be going out with him, but I couldn't get past his privileged attitude. Becka tried so hard to arrange this, and it wasn't her fault Mike finally asked her out. He didn't know she'd planned anything.

Becka and Mike deserve this, I thought, breathing in slowly and releasing it slower. They've been pining over each other since middle school. We're all seniors now. I've got to be a good sport so they can have their chance. Smiling as much as was believable I replied, "I'd love to go get some ice cream." Andrew's face lit up.

"Awesome!" He took his hands out of his letterman jacket pockets, keys jingling. "My dad finally restored my Aston Martin. I'll swing her around, so you don't have to walk."

"Thanks!"

This time I didn't have to try to be excited. I have a thing for classic cars, but he didn't notice anyway. He was already jogging to the back of the lot.

"So where are you two going?" I asked, just to stop Becka from blushing.

"Movie and dinner," Mike smiled. "I heard that Mina's Café has the best lobster roll in Maine. What about you and Andrew? Where'll you go?"

I shrugged, "I dunno... maybe the Ice 'n Creamy or Mt. Custard, or maybe that cute little diner over on Wilmington. They've got the best pie..." I immediately pictured a slice of steaming apple, a-la-mode.

"Better pick one," Becka sang, "Andrew's coming."

"Have fun guys," I hugged Becka.

"Let me know how it goes!" She smiled. "I know he's been trying to ask you out for a while, so don't break his heart. Kay? I could totally see you two going to prom together."

She squeezed my hand. It wasn't that I exactly had a reputation for playing hard to get, but I was going on eighteen and I'd yet to date anyone more than a few months.

"I see where you're coming from. I mean... I have to use binoculars, but I can see it," I joked. "Don't you two go nuts and elope and abandon me here, forever alone."

"See you later, Celeste," Mike put his arm around Becka and guided her away.

They were made for each other. You could just tell, and I could tell in the same way as Andrew pulled up to the curb and checked his hair in the visor that he was not my one and only. I sighed, hitched my bag over my shoulder and opened the door.

"Careful!" He winced as I closed the door. A sharp exhale, a tug on his jacket, and then he shifted into drive. I bucked my belt, smoothed the hem of my blue hooded jacket to lay flat. "Someday you'll understand," he said. "This is my baby." He patted the dash and we pulled towards the main road.

"So which dessert place do you like?" I asked.

"Oh, well I don't... but Mike said dessert was your favorite."

I couldn't even respond right away. What kind of person didn't like dessert at all? "We don't have to get dessert." I offered, "What about maybe... hike a trail? The leaves have been beautiful this year."

"I've got a game tomorrow. I should take it easy, so I don't get over exerted. What about we just go see that new Horror movie?"

"Which one?" I asked. I was not a horror person, but maybe it wouldn't be so bad.

"Death House, the one where some patients from a mental institution break out and hide in this boarding school's basement. I've been dying to see that one."

"Oh, sweet..." He failed to notice my fall in morale. "Sounds great."

"You should wear dresses more," he said, noticing I was fidgeting with my skirt. "You've got great legs." He looked ahead with that stupid, cocky grin on his face.

"Thanks..." I mumbled, silently resolving to wear jeans for the rest of my life.

When we got there and took our seats with a giant popcorn and drinks there were only a couple other people in the theater. It slowly filled up so that once the movie started it was mostly full. The last person to find his seat was with a hyper group of college age guys right behind us. I watched him climb the steps one by one, watched the way his eyes scanned the rows until he met mine. It was too dark to see much, but the way he grinned made me tense uncomfortably. I thought I heard him scoff as he looked away from me and his smile grew. To my dismay he sat right behind me.

"Don't be afraid to grab my hand if you get scared." Andrew offered, sipping his drink.

I slid down my seat, hiding in my hood and decided to rest my head on his shoulder. The rest of the lights turned off and music reminiscent of anguished souls started, preceding the opening scene of fog rolling across the rocky beach. A man stood in the surf and then disappeared.

Within the first half hour of the movie I pulled my hood down over my eyes and was clinging to Andrew's arm from then on. I screamed when everyone else jumped, and when everyone else held their breath for more I was watching with one eye, too petrified to look away. An hour in, with an hour and a half left to go, I heard Andrew sigh.

"Out of popcorn already?" I whispered looking over at the empty bucket in his lap.

"Yeah, and it wasn't full to start with," he complained. Without asking I took it from him.

"Let me get you some more," I said and hurried out.

I let out a sigh of relief as the door swung quietly closed behind me and I walked into the clean, brightly lit lobby. The line was only two people long, so before I was ready to face the movie, I was standing in the empty hall with the newly filled bucket of salty, buttery, crispness, staring at the door.

"You ok?" someone asked from nowhere. I jumped, spilling some popcorn. "I see this is not the movie for you," he laughed.

I flushed and cast a side-long look at the guy. First I saw his biker boots, then I saw his distressed jeans, plain red shirt, and brown leather jacket. His eyes were dark, as was his short coffee colored hair.

"Horror's not my thing." I shrugged and looked away.

"I love a good scare. I missed the first half though. My friends didn't want to wait for me."

"Bummer." I feigned a sympathetic smile.

"Vince," he greeted, extending a hand.

"Looks like you're getting a call." I nodded towards the light in his pocket. He looked and slipped his hand inside, lips slightly parted and eyes wide like I'd said his zipper was down.

"Enjoy the show," I said while I pushed the door open and went inside.

He came in and joined the party behind Andrew and me a few minutes later. Was it my imagination, or did the group tense up the minute he sat down at the end of the row? His pocket was still glowing. Someone kicked his seat until the light was gone. Andrew stretched and put his arm over my shoulder. It might be the lamest trick in the book, but it made it so much easier to hide my face in his side as the guys glowered down at me.

I pretty much stayed like that through the whole rest of the movie, and when it was over Andrew and I were among the first few out the door, leaving half eaten popcorn and our two drink cups behind.

"I can't believe that movie." I said as we walked across the lot. His arm was still around my shoulder.

"I know! I've still got goose bumps!" He laughed then dropped his arm and left me waiting at the passenger side while he unlocked the car and got inside.

"There she is!" someone yelled. I looked back briefly as I got in the car. Victor, or whatever his name was, was running this way.

"Who are those guys?" I asked. Andrew backed out of the stall and put his taillights to the group.

"No idea, probably just some guys pulling a joke. Don't let them spook you." He took my hand, and I flinched.

"So what's next?" I asked. He took back his hand, shifting gears.

"What about a party? My friend Jordan's parents have this beach house a little way out of town. I was gonna go later, but I'd love to show you off to my friends." He winked. I wasn't sure if I should be insulted or flattered. Instead I forced niceness to the surface, remembering Becka's plea that I give him a chance.

"Yeah, sure! Let's party it up."

2

It was a lot farther out of town than he let on, like not even in Maine anymore, but down in New Hampshire. Once we were on the highway there was no going back. I sent a quick message to my mom, letting her know I'd be home late. Unlike stereotypical mom's she didn't put a curfew on me, but she did still expect that I show up for school and do my absolute best at everything regardless of circumstance. However, if she knew I was leaving the state she'd be livid.

We rolled up to the house at about quarter to six and there were only about five or six people there, all of whom were locals, so I was forced to follow Andrew around like a lost puppy. By eight thirty about twenty more people showed up bearing a keg and cups, and by quarter to ten I'd taken refuge alone on the beach, walking barefoot in the ankle-deep swell, shoes tucked away in my bag.

After a while, when I was away from the bass beats, drunken shenanigans and could hear myself think again, I laid on my back in the sand. My backpack provided the perfect cushion and the crashing waves played softly, a soundtrack second to none. I closed my eyes, listening until I drifted off.

"Celestial," Someone called my name. I sat up and dusted the sand off my backpack.

"Yeah?" I twisted to see who was behind me. "Victor?" I feigned to remember his name from the theater. "You came to the party too huh? Small world." I got up and finished dusting off, deciding it was time to find Andrew.

"It's Vince, actually," He corrected, walking with me. He pulled something glowing from his pocket, tossing it in the air and catching it like a baseball.

"Do you regularly carry glow-in-the-dark rocks in your pocket?" I asked. *What was he even doing out here?* I wondered, but then he probably wondered about me too.

"This is special," he said in a relaxed, matter of fact, sort of way. "It rips a person's power from their body, and it only glows when close to the person whose it was. In this case..." his voice trailed off.

I turned, heart pounding, breathing slowly as if I didn't want him to hear me. The stone seemed like it got brighter the closer he came, and the faster my heart raced. He lunged at me, nails ripping into my skin as he caught my arm and yanked. I stumbled forward and the stone in his hand touched mine searing like I'd touched something red hot.

"Get away!" I screamed. I felt my heart flutter, and something surge out of me, bright white and blinding. He screamed and let me go.

I snapped awake; another scream caught in my throat. I looked around, alone on the beach where I'd laid down to relax. Faint white light grabbed my attention. I looked down, thinking I'd find my cell phone in the sand but saw my own hand instead, glowing white under my skin and showing the shadow of my bones. It slowly faded, leaving me staring at my hand as if I were having some sort of trip. I rubbed the spot where the stone touched me. It was burning.

I must still be dreaming... It stole my breath to realize it really hurt, and my other arm was bleeding. Sand went everywhere as I scrambled to grab by backpack and get the hell out of dodge. I attracted some wide-eyed stares as I hurried up the steps and into the house, but in the main living area nobody noticed me.

"Chug, chug, chug!" Half the football team must've arrived while I was on the beach because they were circled around Andrew and another player who was pouring beer down Andrew's throat with a hose and a funnel.

"Andrew, what the hell?!" I exclaimed.

The kid who was holding the can and the funnel dropped them both and everyone cheered as Andrew burped and threw his hands in the air.

"I am the keg king!" He slurred and turned to me. "Hey baby! Where ya been?" He stumbled over to me and basically fell on me as he wrapped an arm around my shoulder.

"I just got attacked and here you are friggin' hammered!" I exclaimed, bearing his weight. "Where are your keys? It's time to go." He burped in my ear and laughed while the team set up some girl with the same apparatus and a line of full cups. Patting him down, I felt his keys in his pocket.

"If you wanna get frisky there's a great room upstairs." His face was inches from mine, and I winced from the alcohol reek.

"Come on Romeo," keys in hand and struggling under his weight I guided him out of the house and into the passenger seat.

"I'm in the wrong seat," he started but I slammed the door, cutting off any protests until I climbed into the driver's side. "I knooow," he burped, "you like me, but nooobody touches... my baby... except..." I waited for him to finish but by the time the car was started, and I looked over he was already passed out.

"Lucky for us I can drive a manual," I mumbled and pulled onto the road and away from the party.

*****

"According to his readings, the anomaly manifested in the neighborhood up ahead." A man with short wavy blond hair looked down at the laptop on his lap, currently open on a map with a single pinned location.

"Zach was positive it was Dark magic, and positive it was all the way out here?" the driver of the cruiser asked. His uniform was pressed and clean and the badge looked a little too new. His companion looked a little more broken in.

"Mitch!"

"Sorry, yes. He was positive. "

"And he hasn't been able to trace the point of origin?"

Mitch sighed heavily. "No, just the location of the actual manifestation. Tristan, you know this happens, and, more often than not, has nothing to do with Wes. Why do you assume it's him every time?"

"Don't lecture me," Tristan started, following the curve of the cliffside road. The ocean could barely be seen while the moon slipped behind thick clouds. "We've been tracking him, and tracking him, and the area of interest has been the same twenty miles for months. Why would something happen so far out?"

"You need to keep a level head about this, boss. Let's just play cops and see what happens." Mitch looked down again, opening an instant message.

"Looks like there's a house party not even a mile from the site. Someone may have seen something."

"Where?" Tristan leaned to see the map, taking his eyes off the road for a fraction of a second.

"Look!" Mitch pointed ahead. Both men watched as a car just down the road rolled over the barrier, plunging into the choppy swell below.

3

I screamed and swerved to avoid the figure in the road. Andrew never woke, not when we hit the barrier, not when we flipped, and I realized he wasn't wearing his seatbelt. He lifted out of his seat and ended up in the back. We hit the water. The windshield cracked but held. The black ocean grabbed hold of the car and sucked us down into the darkness.

"Andrew!" I screamed, hot tears streaming down my cheeks.

Not like this! I don't wanna go like this! My hands were shaking, fumbling with the belt. I pressed the button, then again and again but it wouldn't release. Dread poured over me as ice cold water seeped into my shoes and up so fast that I didn't have time to draw another breath before it covered me. There was movement in the back as the engine died and the lights went out.

Andrew flailed around and managed to kick me in the back of the head when the water reached and woke him up. My lungs were burning. Andrew beat on something, trying to get out. I tried the button again and pulled, but it wouldn't budge.

The car groaned as the pressure equalized and the next thing I knew, Andrew had swum up front and gotten the passenger door open. I grabbed for him, letting him know I was still here. He pulled on the strap once, twice, but it wouldn't budge. Bubbles were seeping through my lips and my head was spinning. Andrew tried one more time and then pulled himself through the open door.

My body lurched, basal instinct kicking in. Water came in, burning and filling me up. I felt a shift and the same light from before spread through me, illuminating me from the inside-out. The car shuddered as it hit the bottom. Holding the button down I pulled on the strap with everything I had left. Finally, it gave way and I floated free, finding a tiny air pocket trapped in the back corner of the car.

As I took in the last little bit of air the light inside of me faded, leaving me scrambling around in the dark, holding my breath. Immediately I went to the passenger door where Andrew escaped, but found it opened only a couple inches, wedged in place by a sand bar. I went back, feeling my way to the driver's side. I found the handle, but it jammed. My insides were screaming for air, and I forced down the urge to breath in the frigid black water. I turned back to the passenger side, attempting to squeeze through the impossibly small gap.

One arm and shoulder fit through, but that was all I could manage. I went back in, searching for one more air pocket. I found one but it wasn't enough. Everything around me was getting lighter, I could see again. My body felt like lead, heavy and uncooperative as I tried to maneuver. Something hit the car, moving it several feet. The light was bright now, just outside the car, then in the car. I thought I saw a face and for a moment I forgot where I was. Then I tasted salt, felt the water burn its way down my throat and the light went out.

*****

Mitch dragged Andrew out of the water and onto the rocky ledge where they parked the curser, and once he knew the kid was okay, he put him in the back with a blanket. Mitch was surprised the guy made it to the surface, as intoxicated as he was. He winced as the kid emptied his stomach. Meanwhile Tristan resurfaced, gasping for air.

"There's someone else down there. I'm going back down!" He called. Before he dived a translucent bubble grew around his head, sealing in the air and glowing softly for light.

Almost three minutes later he resurfaced, head still protected by the glowing bubble.

"I've got her!" he called. Tristan struck out towards shore with the girl in his arms and then handed her to Mitch who pulled her onto the shelf and leaned over her.

"She's not breathing," he said, beginning to sweep her long brown hair out of her face. Tristan climbed out of the water while Mitch saw her face and immediately put his mouth over hers, forcing air down her lungs.

*****

A modest one room apartment was dark except for the two red wax candles that lit themselves when the other lights flickered and went out. Vince stood in-between them at the head of a table and waited for the lingering whispers of the summoning to quiet.

"My lady, to what do I owe this pleasure?" He looked down into a bowl of water, obscured by wispy black mist that flowed over the rim and cascaded over the edge of the table, shading everything beneath it.

"We are not well pleased," the crackly voice of a woman rose out of the mist.

"My lady," Vince tried, but her voice drowned his out.

"Enough! If you do not acquire her soul, I will devour yours and get the girl myself! Our master is weary of your prolonged failure." Vince nodded. He had no doubt the witch could see him.

"I attempted to take her through dream sending, but she slipped out of my hands, literally," he explained.

"If I do not have her soul by the birth of the new moon, I will come for you," she warned and then the mist that was so active and flowing before was starting to recede.

The connection was broken when the candles died.

"New moon..." Vince muttered as he crossed the short space to the only window and parted the binds with his fingers.

Less than three quarters and weaning. He turned and pulled his phone out of his jeans pocket and held down the two key until it rang.

"Wes, change of plans. Do you have all the ingredients for the tracking spell?"

"No, but I'm closing in on a few of the rarer items," he answered.

"How long?" Vince didn't need to turn the lights on to know where he'd hung his keys. He crossed the room, snatched them off the hook, stepped outside and locked up.

"Optimistically? I'd say a week."

"We don't have a week. We have four days. We'll get the stuff, find her, and be ready to portal back to Parna before Saturday. I'll be over in ten." Vince hung up and jumped into a discrete black Sudan and peeled out into the night.

*****

I came to on my back, puking water out of my lungs. Strong hands shifted me onto my side as I choked and sputtered for air. I swallowed gaping mouthfuls of air and the burning throughout my body started to pass. I whined and whimpered, reaching for the intense pain splitting through my scull on the side of my head, not yet registering where I was or how I got here. A pair of hands held my head.

"Tristan! Backup is on its way, and Danny managed to procure an ambulance. What's her status?"

"Conscious and breathing." Came the reply. "Celestial?" I cracked my eyes open, vision blurry. I felt like the world was spinning around me. "Hey, hun, come on," he encouraged, cupping my face. "Let me see those eyes." He pried one open and shined a light in it. I winced away, eyes watering from the sting. The pain was sobering. The other officer jogged over to us.

"Where's Andrew?" My voice was horse but otherwise alright.

"He's fine, drunk as a fool, but otherwise fine. I'm surprised he could swim," he reassured.

"My head..." I groaned.

"That's the alcohol telling you 'You shouldn't have been driving'," the other guy said.

"I don't drink," I argued. "Someone was standing in the road. I hit the barrier and went over." I sat up.

"We need to test your breath for alcohol any way," the blond officer was saying, handing me the breathalyzer. I gave a good puff of air, and they deemed me sober.

"Mitch, I think that's Danny and Chloe." Tristan pointed.

"They must have opened the doorway." Mitch's voice was too soft for my ringing ears to pick up. He stood and jogged towards the flashing lights speeding towards us.

"What's your name?" I asked, fighting the overwhelming urge to lay down. He just looked at me for a long time, the both of us dripping wet.

"Tristan," he finally said, "the paramedics are here. I'll ride with you and your friend to the hospital where we can call your families."

I swayed, losing my center of balance as the pain in my head sharpened. Tristan grabbed my arm, maneuvering me so that I was now in his lap with my bleeding head getting wrapped in a dry jacket that had been discarded an arm's reach away.

"I need you to stay awake until we can get you to a doctor. Can you do that?" He asked, the makeshift bandage in place. With me in his arms he got up, walking me to the ambulance. Mitch opened the back door and pulled out the stretcher. Tristan passed it, stepping up into the back, depositing me into a chair, and strapping me in.

"Sorry. There's only one stretcher and your friend's got dibs since he passed out again."

A girl climbed in behind us, wearing scrubs and had her hair pulled back into a sloppy bun.

"Oh Celeste!" she exclaimed, eyes shining, "I'm so relieved-"

"Chloe, stop" Tristan cut her short, shaking his head. "She doesn't remember us."

"What's going on?" I asked, head feeling heavier by the minute. "Who are you people?" I whined again and rested my forehead in my palm.

"Help Mitch with the other one... I'll get her head patched up..." Chloe and Tristan traded spots and he hurried to Mitch to lift Andrew onto the stretcher. Chloe on the other hand took the jacket off my head and clicked her tongue.

"It's pretty bad, isn't it?" I asked.

"Stitches for sure, but we're just going to clean and wrap it for now." She pressed a square of gauze to it while she rummaged through a drawer with her other hand. "Tell me about yourself," she said. She slipped on a pair of gloves and the guys slid Andrew into place inside the van and strapped him down.

"...My head's... pounding, and.... my eyes sting. Do... Do I have a concussion?" I asked. The words came out slow and thick, slipping away from me. Mitch jumped out and closed the door.

"You guys ready back there?" The driver called back to us.

"Take us to the nearest hospital, Danny," Tristan replied, hooking Andrew up to a machine to monitor his vitals. "It's just a precaution," he said when he caught me watching and went back to work without another word.

"Where are you from?" Chloe asked.

"Um..." I paused, having to process through the pain, "Portland."

"Maine, right?" Tristan asked, looking up.

"Uh, yeah. I live there with my mom."

I leaned back when Chloe was done wrapping my head and closed my eyes. I managed to stay awake through the trip to the hospital that was almost right on the state line, mostly because Chloe kept trying to talk to me, asking me questions about my life.

If I had brothers and sisters (I didn't), if my mom was married (she wasn't), and a slew of other questions. Tristan asked if I was dating Andrew and seemed a little too relieved when I said no and tensed back up when I added that we had in fact been on a date.

"Worst date ever," I said, looking down at Andrew and wishing I were the one passed out and oblivious.

"I can see that," Chloe snorted.

Tristan gave her a look and she shied away, climbing out when Mitch opened the back door. With Tristan's help I was ushered inside and into an examination room and a paper gown and an itchy blanket to keep me warm. I spent the next few hours going in and out for scans and blood tests before Mom arrived with Andrew's parents.

4

Both Andrew and I were released from the hospital Saturday afternoon after an anonymous patron offered Andrews parents the full sum of the Aston Martin's worth and an added, undisclosed amount of money to settle out of court. I tried to ask mom more on the car ride home, but she clammed up, saying that was all she knew, and I better count my lucky stars; but there was something else that came to her attention while she was at the hospital.

"Celestial, that officer that pulled you from the water claims he knows your birth parents." Mom broke the long-standing silence, setting a mug of hot cocoa in front of me. Our Kitchen table sat six people, max, and was positioned in front of the bay window offering a view of the front yard. I sat at the head of the table, watching mom sit at the other end.

"How?" I asked, ignoring the steaming beverage.

"He's a close family friend, I guess. He called them after you were checked into your room. Stephen, I think that's his name... Anyway," mom went on, "Stephen came to the hospital and I consented to let them take a little extra blood from you when they were checking for alcohol in your system."

"And?" I leaned forward.

"And it was a match. Look, Celeste," mom scooted to the seat next to mine, "I know we never really talked about things, and I should have asked if you wanted to be tested or not, but I want you to know that it's your choice if you want to have them in your life. I have Stephen's number, but I wanted to talk to you about how I was able to adopt you." Mom slid a folded slip of paper to me, leaving it beside my drink.

"When I adopted you, there were no records for you anywhere. You just sort of appeared in the nursery and nobody could trace you. At the time, I was on the state's adoption waiting list, so when they weren't able to find anything on you, they called me."

"How could there be no papers?" I asked. "I thought you couldn't take a baby from the hospital even if it was yours without proof?"

"Yes, but you were just there! None of the doctors remembered delivering you, and there were no reports of anyone off the street leaving an infant in their care. I talked to Stephen and his wife. I think her name's Katherine?... Well, I guess you'd been taken from the nursery by a nurse who'd been let go that day. She was never found, and neither were you."

I stared down at the table and the neatly written number. I didn't move to take it, and I wasn't sure of what to say. Eventually mom started talking again.

"They asked to see you, but I told them I'd talk to you and give you the number. What do you think?" she asked.

"I think..." I stopped, unsure of what I thought. Outside a car pulled alongside the curb. "Who's here?" I asked.

"I don't recognize it... Oh, I know!" mom exclaimed. "Officer Thompson, the one that pulled you from the car!" She got up and sure enough it was him climbing out of the driver's seat bearing a bouquet of flowers.

Mom ran to the front door, opening it before he even reached the porch. I got up and crossed the kitchen to the hall and tried to creep up the stairs, embarrassed that I was still wearing "borrowed" scrubs from the hospital. I made it to my room before Mom called my name. Leaning on my closed bedroom door I closed my eyes, remembering clearly the strange glow from under my skin. I rubbed the bandaged scratch and felt warmth spreading out of my heart. I fled to the bathroom, thankfully connected to my room, and gawked at my reflection. Some sort of light was making me glow from the inside out.

"Celeste?" mom opened the door and I pressed the lock to the bathroom. She jiggled the handle. "Honey, Officer Tristan came to see you. Can you come down?"

"I'm not up for visitors!" I called through the door, pulling down on the collar of my shirt to see the glowing better.

"Celeste, I know you're tired but just come down for five minutes."

Mom's tone wasn't a question, but I was relieved when she walked away. Eventually, just like before, the glow went away, but I could still feel the cause of it, this warm and constant sensation around my heart. It was ten minutes after mom told me to come down that I did, dressed a little better in low-rise denim jeggings and a warm, peach pink knitted sweater.

"Sorry to keep you waiting. I wanted to get cleaned up."

I lingered in the hall outside the kitchen. Tristan sat with a mug in his hand at the end of the table, and mom drinking my hot chocolate at the other end.

"Honey look what Officer Tristan brought for you!" Mom held up the bouquet, a small bundle of calla lilies. "They're her favorite," mom added.

"Thank you very much," I took the bundle from mom then found a vase and arranged them carefully inside. "Did the station send you to check in, or..." I left the question open-ended.

"No, nothing like that. I just wanted to see how you were doing. You were pretty shaken by the accident, and I was worried." He looked up at me, half smiling.

"She's as well as can be expected." Mom answered before me, "the flowers were a very lovely gesture, were they from you or the family?" She sipped my drink and watched him with a critical eye.

"From me, but your family is so relieved to know you're in safe hands," he said to me ignoring mom's scrutiny. "The shop had another arrangement that I almost got instead. I'm glad I picked right."

"They're beautiful, thank you." I smiled but couldn't help the little color that rose into my cheeks from the way he kept his eyes on me. "Did you graduate from Belleview? You seem familiar," I asked, trapped in one of those moments where you could swear you'd just run into an old friend who'd been out of contact for a long time, and could no longer remember their name, or where you knew them from.

"I had some friends who graduated there last year. Maybe you saw me around."

"I thought you've been with the force for a while?" mom asked.

"I went through training right when I turned eighteen. I graduated from the academy and high school at the same time last year. I got special permissions for high performance."

"Where did you go to school?" I asked. He finished the last bit of his drink and set the mug aside.

"Private study at home. My parents got to know yours through my home-study program, so I know your parents and the twins pretty well."

"Twins?" mom asked, grabbing my drink and his and taking them to the sink. "Celeste, why don't you sit down?" Mom took the vase from me and nudged me towards the table. I sat, noticing Tristan's eyes were blue for the first time, like bright moon light on the ocean.

"Yeah, Zachary and Destiny. They're your younger siblings, fraternal twins. I think they're turning sixteen next summer."

"Not much time in-between Celeste and a set of twins." Mom commented over the running tap while she rinsed the mugs.

"They were a surprise," Tristan shrugged. "They're cool kids, and they're in the same private study program I was in, but at an accelerated rate. They graduate in March."

"I see who got the smarts," I joked, then yawned. "Sorry," I said, "It was a long night, and we just got home. I'm bushed." I tried not to but yawned again.

"No, don't apologize," Tristan was quick to respond, "You must be exhausted. I should let you rest," he stood, politely pushing in his chair. "Maybe we could go for ice cream some time to figure out which group you know me from?"

"Aren't you and Andrew dating?" Mom asked. I let out a short breath.

"No, we are not. Last night was the first, and forever the last time I will be going out with him." Mom huffed but turned to the sink. I followed Tristan out of the kitchen and picked up a pen and tucked it behind my ear. "I'll walk you out," I said, holding it open for him.

"That kid didn't seem worth your time," he said as we walked down to the curb. "But I promise a much better time than a keg-er." He pulled his keys from his pocket, flipping slowly through them.

"You beat him when you said ice cream, oh, and when you saved my life. We'd both still be in the car if you and your partner hadn't been around to see the accident. Thank you," I looked up to his face, noticing that his eyes were a brighter blue than I'd been able to see in the kitchen. His hair was a very complementary cool dark brown, and short, but long enough to allow it to have plenty of body.

"I'm just glad you're ok," he said.

"So, how's about a number I can call so we can meet up?"

"It's not a return-favor date, is it?" He asked, "I've got a strict, no-pity-date policy."

"No!" I laughed, "Besides, you're the one who offered dessert. Don't offer treats to a lady unless you plan to stick around. Number?" I asked again pulling the pen out from behind my ear.

Smiling he took the pen and my hand, writing his number on the back of it.

"I'll get my new schedule Monday, but I'm generally available on the weekends since I do a lot of weeknight shifts."

"Sounds good." I looked down at my hand, feeling the tingling sensation from where his hand held mine. I stepped back.

"Get some rest," He unlocked the car and pulled open the door. "I'll be waiting for your call, so don't leave me hangin' too long."

"See you later, Tristan. We'll talk soon." I promised. I walked back to the house, pausing in the doorway to wave as he left.

Mom pronounced me grounded until further notice the minute the door closed behind me. She didn't need to explain what with me going to a party out of state where there was alcohol without her permission.

"Stephen's number is on the fridge when you're ready to give him a call," she said.

"Thanks," I nodded and then climbed the stairs to my room, closing the door, and climbing into bed and pulling the covers over my head.

I laid there thinking. I'd fallen asleep on the beach. I remembered that much, but I woke up after that Vince guy attacked me. I remembered clearly seeing a hooded person in the road. Who was it? Why couldn't the police find any traces and how could nobody else see them? I was passed by a lot of cars before the sighting. You would think one of them would have seen and reported something. Then there was the glow. How was any of it possible?

I fell asleep still feeling the warm light and slept through the rest of the day. It wasn't until mom came into my room Sunday morning that I woke up. She forced orange juice, over-easy eggs, and toast into me before she would let me go back to sleep. I napped off and on all day and slept through fitful nightmares of Vince chasing me across town with a posse and that burning white stone. I woke up in a panic when he caught me at the end of the dream, then was sent into a frenzy when I saw there was blood all over my pillow. I dashed to the bathroom to find red smeared all over my face and into my hair.

Rationalizing that I must have bled through the bandage, I steamed myself in the shower, scrubbing until the water ran clean. Mom was already gone to work, but she left a note taped to my door that I had the option of staying home from school, and the backup cell phone was on the table waiting for me, since the other, with all my school supplies, were at the bottom of the ocean.

I almost considered going but decided in the end to stay home. Ever since I woke up I felt eyes on me, and I couldn't put aside the irrational fear that Vince was going to get me if I went to classes. By the time I double checked all the locks in the house and tucked the old flip phone into my pocket I wanted to go back to bed. My head was throbbing, and the mysterious glow was back.

Going into my bathroom I closed the door and locked it just in case mom came home to check on me unexpectedly. Leaning over the sink I studied my reflection. The glow was radiating from my heart and lit up veins as it traveled up my neck, and face and into my eyes. My pupils were blown, so dilated light burned them like staring at the sun. The pain mounted. I clenched my eyes shut tight, trying to block out all the light.

The pain grew and just when I thought I couldn't take it anymore it was gone and I was on the ground, dreaming that I was hiding behind an overturned truck in the middle of the road.

*****

Tuesday morning, I met up with Becka in front of the school by the flagpole, wearing the newly washed sweater and pants from Saturday and a comfy pair of sneakers.

"Why did I have to find out about the accident online? Why didn't you call?" Becka smothered me, hugging me until I peeled her off. She linked our arms and deftly guided us inside. "I can't believe you would make us worry like that! The whole school thinks you're at home in a coma, and Andrew isn't helping things." She went on.

"Andrew's just mad because he was too hungover to play in the game," I retorted. The ground floor common area was crowded with groups all trying to fit in a little social time before the first bell. Circling around the outside of the room to the stairs we headed up to English together.

"And you ran his precious off a cliff." She jabbed. "But I'm glad you're not really in a coma. Mike and I were worried when you didn't show up yesterday."

"I'm feeling better, but the stitches itch like none other," I complained. "And" I dropped my voice, "I keep having nightmares about this guy I met at the theater when I went to refill Andrew's popcorn."

"Random, but ok. I'm all ears." Instead of sitting in the front like usual I pulled her with me to the back corner where we could talk. Mr. Jenkins welcomed me back to class and then flipped off the switch and turned on a blurry VHS version of Romeo and Juliette.

"We're watching this today and Thursday. On Monday you're all expected to turn in a typed, five paged short story of your own versions of this classic tragedy." Ignoring the whining he sat at his desk and kicked up his feet, reading by the dim light cast through the small rectangular window in the door.

Through the movie I told Becka everything and then after class we went into the restroom, and I showed her the glow and the scratches and burn.

"Dude, you're like a friggin' mutant right now." She reached out, touching my hand and tracing the outline of my skeleton.

"Thanks," I mumbled.

"So, you haven't said anything to anyone?" she asked, watching the glow recede up my arm to hide under my sweater again. I shook my head.

"You're the only person on Earth who would believe me. Everyone else would just probably want to study me. And what if my birth parents found out and they didn't want me anymore? What if the feds took me and somehow Stacey was blamed?" Becka gripped my arms and shook me.

"Chill, light bulb. I can see it through your sweater. Nobody's gonna disown you or take you away, 'cause I won't say anything, not even to Mike," she added. "I gotta get to class before I'm marked absent. Figure out how to snuff your candle and text me if you need me. You have my number in that brick, right?"

I pulled the flip phone out and handed it to her. "Care to update my antique?"

She ended up being late to her next class, and I ditched mine completely. However, I did manage to get the glow to turn off in time for third period after lunch. Becka and I walked to our classes, parting ways at the stairs. She went down and I continued to World History. In this class we had assigned seating, but luckily I was in the back corner under the window. I prayed the glow wouldn't come back, and if it did, that the light from outside would be enough of a cover.

When the bell rang I pretty much ran to my next class even though my head was starting to hurt again. I walked in and right to my desk, front and center.

"Celeste! How are you feeling?" Mrs. Fenway looked over the rims of her glasses at me, stacking a pile of papers neatly on her desk. "Are you ready for the test?"

"... What test?" I asked, completely blind sighted.

"I told the class about it on Friday. It's for chapters five, six and seven. Are you ready?"

"Oh..." I paused. I read the chapters last week but hadn't given a second thought to it since then. I was also pretty sure she hadn't said anything. "I guess so. Can I retake it or is this a one-shot deal?"

"One shot deal, but why don't you come in during your homeroom tomorrow? I know it's not as much time, but I've extended the same offer to Andrew because of the accident."

"Right," I sighed and cracked open the textbook left on the desk from the period before. "My book is at the bottom of the ocean," I said as the room started to fill. "Can I borrow this one?"

Andrew was late, as usual, and walked by me without so much of a glance. Mrs. Fenway got up, passing a stack of papers to the head of each row. I handed the stack to the girl behind me and stared blankly at the open book for the rest of the class.

5

"Celeste?" Mom knocked and opened my bedroom door, letting herself in. "You've got company downstairs."

I was on my bed in a tank top and flannel pajama bottoms, still looking down at the textbook, pretending to study. Since getting back home I'd gotten better at starting and stopping the light at will but had only felt confident enough to change out of the sweater half an hour ago.

"I'm not feeling up to people. I've been having lots of headaches."

"It's your parents, and that cop. Come down and meet them." I watched mom with a dumb sort of shock, and I tried to play cool as that warmth around my heart started up trying to light a spark.

"Give me just a minute to find something a little nicer to wear," I stalled. "I don't want to be in a tank top for our first meeting." I explained. Mom nodded, but her face was blank, expressionless. She just sat there, quiet and staring into space. It was then that I noticed she wasn't blinking either.

"Are you ok?" I asked, getting up.

"Just fine sweetie," she said, just sitting there.

"Could you step out so I can change?"

Mom didn't nod or anything, just got up with a strange sort of stiffness and walked out into the hall. Something felt wrong, some twist of nature. With her back to me I saw the crimson stain saturating the back of her sweater. My insides churned as if I were about to be sick. I went to the door about to call out for her, but stopped short, choking on the words. I could just barely see over the railing to the living room below and it wasn't Tristan I saw. Vince and his group from the theater were huddled in the living room. I closed my door before they caught a glimpse of me while mom just stood in the hall like a mannequin.

Standing in the middle of my room I tried to catch my breath. I went to the window, seeing no other vehicles out front but mom's Jeep and Harley and a black car across the street that shouldn't have been there. My parents and Tristan weren't here, but maybe Tristan was close, I hoped. Thankfully, the number was saved in my phone. It only rang once before he picked up.

"This is Tristan," he greeted.

Afraid someone would hear I locked the door and then went into the bathroom, locking that one too. "Hey, it's Celeste," I said.

"Celeste, hi!" I could almost hear the smile on his face. "I was thinking about you, actually. I just got off my shift." My heart dropped into my stomach. The final confirmation that something incredibly awful was happening.

"So, you're not with my parents in my living room?" I asked, trying not to cry as someone tried the knob, rattling my bedroom door.

"No... but I am just outside of Portland. Is everything ok?"

"Celestial, open this door!" mom screamed, and I cried out a little when she started kicking it.

"Something's wrong with Stacey! She tried to lure me downstairs, and now she's trying to break down the door! She's not herself at all and there's blood on her clothes!" I cried. The bedroom door slammed open, shaking the walls from the force of impact, making the mirror fall off the wall and shatter. I screamed and jumped away.

"Get that girl!" This time it was a man's voice.

"I'm on my way! Is there a way out of the house?" Tristan asked. I could hear voices in the background.

"Not unless I want to jump out the window..." I went to it, sliding it open and looking out. Not far from the window was a drainpipe, but it was too far to reach. Something hit with massive force, cracking the door, but it still held.

"I'm ten minutes out. Back up will be there in five or less. Now, is there any way out? Can you hide?"

I looked down. The strange light was glowing brighter by the second. *If only I could shut it off or go invisible or something!* I whirled around as they started up on the door again, making serious progress. They struck again. I screamed and dropped the phone. The screen shattered and went dark. I closed my eyes and braced myself for the onslaught of Vince and his friends.

"I don't see her!" someone charged into the room right passed me. "The window is open!" He added, "She must have climbed down."

"Then get moving, Wes." An old woman, dressed all in black and as if she were from the Middle Ages, stepped into my room and Vince followed from behind her. "We need her light. She cannot be allowed to escape again. If I do not have her by dawn..." She trailed off and turned to Vince. He dropped to one knee, bowing his head. "If I don't I'll be taking the gift from one of you. I may not need her to restore General Algoroth to power, but capturing her essence is essential."

"Yes, my Lady."

Vince stood and the others gathered behind him coming from the hall and the two friends left the bathroom, in total making nearly half a dozen people. The old woman raised her hands, thick dark smoke coming out of them, cloaking everything in darkness. I froze in place, too terrified, and stunned to move.

When the smoke cleared, everyone was gone, and flashing police lights danced on my bedroom walls. I looked in the mirror, not seeing myself when I should have. Another light obscured my vision, my own. My hands flickered, and so did the light from my chest. The light flashed and then faded, leaving me fully visible.

"Mom?" I crossed the threshold to where she lay on her side, blood soaked back facing me. Dropping down I pulled her into my lap, knowing she was already gone.

*****

True to his word Tristan arrived a few minutes later. Police were crawling all over my home, pawing over everything and asking more questions than I was prepared to answer. How could I answer? It was absurd that some old lady and a bunch of men just disappeared in a cloud of smoke while I just stood there like the invisible man... or woman, and that they did what they did to take away some funky light inside me.

Even though Tristan came, I only got a glimpse of him before I was ferried away in the back of a cruiser to the station. It wasn't until midnight that I was released into the custody of Tristan and Mitch for them to take me to the home of my birth parents, whom the officers were still trying to contact.

"Are you sure you're alright?" Tristan asked again.

We merged onto the highway, heading towards the border. I stayed quiet in the back seat, staring down at my hands, wondering how it was all possible. If it weren't for the thick sweater I pulled on before leaving the house everyone would be able to see the glow. It was a miracle they hadn't noticed yet.

"We're sorry about Stacy." Tristan pressed. "If you need to talk about anything..." I looked up and our eyes met in the rearview mirror. I pulled my knees into my chest covering the glow a little better and hiding my face.

"Thank you," I managed.

Vince's face flashed behind my closed eyes, and then I saw the face of the old woman, this time darkened by a hood. I sat up in a flash, chest glowing brighter, showing obviously through the sweater. I wrapped myself in my arms and chewed my lip. The hooded person on the road, could it have been her? So far, she was the only person who could disappear I knew existed, and something about what I just saw looked so much like the person I tried not to hit.

I supposed that if I could glow and go invisible then she could vanish into thin air or in smoke. I took a deep breath and forced the light off. My chest was warm, buzzing and the power was pushing to break out again. I did my best to keep it down, along with the lump in my throat. Nearly forty minutes later we were still on the road.

"Where do they live again?" I asked.

"West Plattsburgh," Mitch answered. "It's almost a 6-hour drive, so let us know if you need to stop."

"I didn't realize it was that far away. Tristan, I thought you lived by them?"

Tristan glanced back at me. "I live in Augusta now, but I grew up as their neighbor. I am actually trying to get transferred to their county to be closer to home."

"I see."

I watched the dark countryside pass by in a blur and the car fell back into silence except for the police radio. Eventually I fell asleep, dreaming in cycles about Vince chasing me through old stone passages, then out of the theater, on the beach and in my home. I watched him walk to the door and stab Stacy in the back before doing some weird chant while his friend sent a light like mine into her and sending her to get me. Others came inside, opening some sort of portal in my living room. The woman in black walked through, smoke trailing behind her. She turned away from Vince and his friends and looked right at me.

I woke up in a panic, sucking in air like I was about to scream. The sun hadn't yet poked over the treetops yet, and so things were still dark. Despite the early hour people walked passed the cruiser and into a convenience store. Tristan sat in the passenger seat, fast asleep and lightly snoring. The driver's side door opened, and Mitch climbed in.

"Morning, Princess, wanna get out and stretch your legs?" He asked.

"That'd be great."

He came around and let me out and I went inside and strait to the bathroom, which was surprisingly clean for a gas station. Finally, alone, I made the light shine, practicing a few times turning it on and then off, just to make sure I had control. A few minutes later I was back in the cruiser beside a bag of teriyaki beef jerky and a bottle of water from Mitch. I slept the rest of the way, only waking when Tristan opened the door and shook my shoulder.

"We're here," he said, helping me out.

6

We were in front of the biggest "house" I had ever seen, as were the other homes around us. This neighborhood seemed to have emerged from nowhere. Even in my state of distress I gawked out the window at this beautiful home. The yard was the most eye-popping feature. Bushes with pink, yellow, and white roses lined the whole front of the crème-colored brick house. There was a cherry wood deck that wrapped all the way around to the back of the house, and a large willow tree waved at us, tall and majestic from the center of the yard surrounded by green grass littered with little yellow leaves.

The house had several large windows framed with white shutters. One window on the bottom floor had a set of potted herbs growing on the sill. Next to the window were some wooden lawn chairs and a small table, all of them matching the deck to a tee.

"Welcome home, Celeste." Mitch joined us outside the car.

"Everyone is inside and excited to meet you, if you're ready." Tristan took my hand. I smiled but let go. I didn't want to be clingy, even if I was scared to meet these people, and was glad he wasn't as shy as I was.

"Let's go, I guess." I followed Tristan into the house and Mitch was right behind me.

"We're here!" Tristan called out. Silence greeted us. "I guess they're not all here."

"I'll go find them." Mitch offered and went up the staircase.

From what I could see the entire main level was oak hard wood floor, a very classy and timeless look. It was mostly open, with a kitchen tucked in the corner of the house that was separated from everything by a half wall on one side and a peninsula on the other. A dining table and chairs had been set up alongside the half wall, giving the illusion of a formal dining. We passed the kitchen and dining area to a well laid out living room.

"This is nice," I offered, just to break the awkwardness and sat on the tan microfiber sectional.

"It is," he agreed, "Down the hall behind the stairs there's an entertainment room and powder room. Would you like me to grab your things from the car so you can freshen up?"

"If you don't mind. Thank you." Mitch came down while Tristan was outside, followed by the girls from the ambulance, Chloe, and the driver, Danny.

"How's those stitches?" Chloe asked.

"Fine," I mumbled, nerves getting the better of me.

"We all got to be family friends through Tristan," Mitch explained to answer the questions written across my face. "They invited us all over for dinner today to celebrate your homecoming."

"That was nice of them." I offered.

"Nice of who?" Tristan asked from the doorway with my duffle bag.

"Of Stephen and Katherine to invite us to dinner tonight," Danny answered.

"It should be a nice little get-together." Tristan paused by the stairs. "Where is everyone?" he asked.

"Zachary and Destiny are in class, and Stephen and Katherine are both out running some last-minute errands…" Danny answered.

"In that case, why don't I show you your room, Celeste? We have a bit before the twins are back so there's time for you to unpack and unwind." He watched me expectantly as I nodded to the others, crossed the room, and climbed the stairs, arms folded, and lips sealed.

"You're just down here," he said.

I stepped aside to let him by. Taking in all the pictures of my new family and expensive looking paintings, I took it all in. Halfway down the hall I stopped and caught my breath.

"What?" Tristan asked from down the hall.

"Where is this?" I asked.

Behind my reflection on the pristine glass was a painting of a White stone place, adorned with towers upon towers, marvelous stained-glass windows, exquisite gothic architecture, luxurious gardens, and an iron gate wrapped entirely in ivy vines encircled it all. The Palace seemed so vast that the tallest spires weren't in the picture at all. It looked like something out of a fairy tale book, and yet it seemed so entirely familiar, like Tristan.

"Oh, Destiny painted that. She won a contest and got to study abroad in Europe. I'm not sure which country that's in. Pretty, isn't it?" I could feel him behind me, warmth coming off his body and greeting mine like it had happened a hundred times before.

"It is, and I've got to figure out where I've seen you before. It's driving me crazy."

"I'm sure you'll figure it out, but first why don't you get settled? You've had a long night."

By the hand, he took me to my room, the last one in the hall, and set my bag inside. I went in, sitting on the queen-sized canopy bed, thumbing the fabric that came down like blue gossamer clouds.

"Tristan?" He stopped in the doorway, looking back at me. "Thank you for everything, I don't know if I could have dealt with all of this without you."

"I'm here any time, Celeste. If you need anything I'll just be downstairs."

I nodded and he closed the door giving me my privacy. My sneakers hit the floor with a dull thud as I slipped them off beside my bag. The oak floors against my socked feet was a bit of a chill, but pleasantly refreshing. The room was much bigger than I was used to, even with the queen bed. Floor to ceiling French windows overlooked the back yard, and to the woods in back behind the whitewashed fence.

The room was bright and airy, but with the blinds down and curtains drawn it was almost dark as night. Letting my guard down tears fell freely, shaking my shoulders and making it hard to breathe through the pit in my stomach. Still in my pajamas from last night I slipped under the down comforter and pulled it over my head.

Before long I was sleeping hard and dreaming I was inside the palace from the painting. I was running from Vince and his gang. Hindered by a long dress, Vince caught me, and we wrestled down a flight of steps and held the glowing white rock over me.

"This is your last chance," He warned.

Even without the stone touching me I could feel it pulling on the light inside me, trying to rip it out and burn me up. I breathed in and thought of Tristan. I called for him and I knew he'd be coming, but was it already too late?

"Join with us or meet your fate." Vince lowered the rock, and it felt like my heart was literally on fire. "Answer me!" Vince screamed, and someone from his gang sent a surge of shocking power into me. I bit my tongue, but the scream came anyway.

"No!"

My light exploded out of me in white-hot rage, scorching the stones and everyone in the courtyard. They screamed, but Vince held tight. Putting everything I had into the light, it wrapped around me, and his hands slipped right through it. I departed, leaving only a blackened courtyard and Vince behind, his loyal men writhing in agony on the ground in my wake.

The next thing I knew I was standing in a vast field; thick fog was everywhere, and I could hear the rush of a stream or river nearby. Tall grasses expanded farther than I could tell and seemed to never end. The fog seemed to be the source of light all around me, well-lit but surprisingly gentle on the eyes.

"Welcome, Princess." Came a voice from the mist. I spun around, my light glowing involuntarily. "Now, now," a man stepped into view, dressed impeccably in a hand tailored suit. "There's no need to be frightened. I don't bite… much" He smiled, bearing long canines and his golden yellow eyes seemed to flash.

"Your assurances are not very reassuring." I stepped back, creating a safer feeling space.

"Child, if I wanted to harm you I would have done so already. No, that's not why I'm here. I often come to this place to think. Why are you here?"

I paused. That was an excellent question. Obviously, I was still dreaming, or I wouldn't be here, but why was I dreaming this at all?

"What is this place?" I shifted, moving as he did to keep an eye on the strange glowing eyed man.

"This is Death, dear child. Which is why I am puzzled to find you here, since you are obviously not a spirit."

"Ha, ha. You're hilarious." I folded my arms. "If this is Death, then why are you here?" I asked back.

"I have my reasons." He evaded, watching me like a cat watches a ball of string. "You intrigue me, Princess. We will meet again, but first perhaps you should learn how to keep your Gift in check before you kill us both."

"What?" I asked before I could stop myself. The stranger just laughed.

"Your light," he reached out to me, taking my hand, "is called the Gift, and I can tell that yours is particularly powerful. Be careful my dear, or someone could get hurt, like that Stacy woman did." I blanched and ripped my hand out of his, backing away.

"Who the hell are you?" I demanded. "You're one of Vince's loser friends, aren't you?" Again, he just smiled.

"Princess, I am Algoroth, and I am much more dangerous than that little idiot could ever hope to be. Go now. It's time for you to wake up. Your brother and sister are home and waiting for you to join them in the entertainment room." He took a step back into much darker fog, fading away. "I will be seeing you very soon, dear," He promised and was gone, and I found myself standing in the middle of a small living room with Vince and his friend Wes.

The clock chimed the ninth hour and Wes's body dropped to the ground, the last of his light draining out of his eyes and into the stone in the old Witches hand. The light attempted to pass from the stone and into her, but she deposited the stone into an orb of darkness, keeping the power contained within.

"Your friend's Gift will be rewarded as his name is praised in the Dark One's new age."

"Yes, my lady," Vince looked down as his friend was carried away. "I will find her, if it's the last thing I do," He swore.

She dropped a teardrop black diamond pendant onto the ground in front of him. Avoiding touching the stone itself, he grasped the thin silver chain and stood.

"This is more than sufficient to capture Celestial's light. Once you have it..." She trailed off, opening the black portal behind her, "Our King wishes to instruct you further." She went back into the portal and was gone, taking Wes's Gift and the darkness with her.

I woke up in a panic and made it from the bed to the hall bathroom in two seconds, locking the door behind me. I screamed when I saw myself in the mirror. Red, all I could see was the crimson dripping from my eyes and into the sink. To turn the sink on and splash my face repeatedly was my first instinct. The bleeding hadn't stopped yet when there was a knock on the door.

"Celeste, are you alright?" It was Tristan's tired voice, then someone else's.

"I sensed necromancy. Something's wrong." It was another guy, but his voice was unfamiliar. One of them tried the knob.

"Celeste?" It was Tristan again. Thinking fast I turned the water off and pressed a wad of tissue to my eyes.

"I'm telling you!" the guy said again, "I felt necromancy-"

"Zach keep your voice down!" I could barely hear Tristan hush him.

Hands shaking, I opened the door, keeping the wad pressed against the one eye that was still bleeding.

"My eyes are bleeding." I pulled the wad away, checking to see if it had stopped yet. Disappointed I turned back to the bathroom and threw it into the waste bin, then splashed my face one more time.

"What did you see?"

I turned away from examining my eyes in the mirror. This, I assumed, was my newfound little brother. Not that I couldn't have guessed it without seeing pictures of him and his twin in the hall.

"Excuse me?" I asked, gathering another wad.

"Well, you're bleeding so what was your vision?" he asked as if this were something he saw every day.

I looked to Tristan, at a loss. "Hi... I'm Celeste. You must be Zach," I extended my hand in awkward greeting. He just gawked at my hand until I dropped it. "So... I'm assuming you've seen this bleeding before. Wanna fill me in? Is it like some funky genetic thing?"

"Are you kidding me?" Zach huffed and stormed into my room, muttering under his breath.

"What's his problem?" I asked, tossing the wad into the trash, and checking to make sure the bleeding was really stopped, and my face was clean. Something crashed in my room, followed by more of his muttering. "What's he doing?"

Tristan made it into the bedroom before I did but I still managed to see Zach looking through everything, the empty closet, the empty dresser, under the bed, the mattress, the pillow.... He turned on my bag next, dumping it all onto the bed.

"Are you crazy?" I rushed him, shoving him away from my belongings and the small picture frame of Stacy that he almost dropped on the floor. "What are you doing? I've heard of nosy little brothers, but this is ridiculous." I rippled a pair of my socks from his grasp.

"I know there was a manifestation in here, and I know you're involved." Zach jabbed his finger at me.

"Zach I've explained this several times. Your parents get it. Destiny gets it. Why can't you? Lay off and wait downstairs." Zach glared Tristan down before he stormed off.

"Manifestation?" I echoed, turning to Tristan. "What's he talking about?" Tristan ran his fingers through his hair and rubbed the back of his neck, breathing out slowly.

"I'll go talk to him... He gets very, uh, stubborn, but he means well." Tristan followed Zach's trail and left me severely confused and alone in my new room with a pair of unfolded socks in my hands. I lay on the bed, trying to block out the yelling from downstairs, but eventually gave up and went out to the hall to listen.

Not long after, Stephen and Katherine arrived home to Tristan and Zachary arguing and everyone else but me trying to bring some sense into them, but from my view at the top of the stairs it looked like they were all a little kooky. Destiny was crying, Danny and Chloe were trying to convince Tristan to leave Zach alone, and Tristan was arguing some weird thing with Zach about dark magic or something. Mitch looked like the only sane person, just standing there with an arm around Destiny.

"What's all this?" Katherine set down her purse by the door and Stephen hung his and hers jackets on the rack by the door.

"There was a manifestation in Celeste's room, and I just don't believe she's innocent!" Zach yelled. "She goes without a trace, and only now appears after so long, *and* she remembers nothing about Eä or us? She's been at three manifestation sites, all with the tinge of Necromancy! Nobody else sees this as a red flag?"

"Mitch, Danny, Chloe, would you mind taking the twins to Hathor's?" Zach was about to protest but Stephen cut him off. "Son, I'll join you in a minute. Just go."

Danny and Mitch led the twins outside, leaving just the four of us in the house. I remained where I was, studying my biological parents from a distance, imagining I could hear Stacy crack a joke about how proper they looked. They talked quietly as if I weren't there at all, asking Tristan to explain, which he quickly did.

"She really remembers nothing?" Katherine asked. "Nothing at all? What about her Gift? Does she still have it?"

"Remember what?" I asked from the top of the stairs, but they kept right on talking. "Hello?" I called down a little louder, but it was like I wasn't even there. The grandfather clock in the living room chimed half past nine o'clock, and Stephen asked where I was.

"Locked in her room." Tristan answered, "I can't get her to come out."

I turned and went there myself, though the door opened easy enough for me, what I saw inside froze me mid-stride. Algoroth, the man with the glowing yellow eyes, was in there, holding me by the throat and dangling the black diamond pendant over my heart.

I woke up, chest burning and my light glowing like the sun. As fast as I could I changed into jeans, sneakers, and a warm hoodie before running like some psycho downstairs and into the entertainment room where I found Zach, Destiny, Danny, Chloe, Mitch, and Tristan.

"Tristan, I really need to talk to you," I blurted. Warm wetness dripped from my eyes, painting my cheeks, and splattering on to my hoodie, which thankfully was dark grey, so it was hard to see the blood.

"Zach call your dad." Tristan said before moving cautiously towards me. "Take a couple of deep breaths, Celestial. We'll get you taken care of, but you need to get a hold of yourself."

Air burned its way down into my lungs, like that stone was still inches away from me, still trying to suck out my light and set my insides ablaze. Without warning pressure mounted in my head behind my eyes. I cried out and dropped to my knees, smearing the bloodied tears on my face with my hands.

As if I were watching a movie projected into reality in front of me, Tristan picked me up and carried me to the nearest chair. His hands were pressed against my shoulders, keeping me in place, and everyone was arguing amongst themselves, not listening to me at all. In my last dream, it was about half after nine that I found Algoroth in my room, and sure enough it was almost that time again.

"There you are, Princess." I whirled around, staring up at those golden yellow eyes. I looked down as he reached out to me. The black pendant hung loosely in his grip.

"There is no place you can run that I cannot find you, and trust that anyone who gets in my way will perish." Algoroth's glare cut deep into me, ending the scene abruptly.

Just like I'd seen, Tristan carried me to the chair, set me down, and kept a hand on my shoulder. *What was happening to me? What was this light and how were they not as freaked out by it as I was? Why were these dreams coming to me? And how on earth could I be hurt in a dream and still hurt when I woke up? Was this all real, or was it all inside my head?*

"You can't seriously still side with her." Zach said, breaking the silence. "She's playing us! Didn't you feel the power coming off her? And bleeding like that only comes from one thing, dark magic."

"Dude, she doesn't remember! How could she do anything like what you're saying? She can't even control her light!" Destiny argued.

"I'm with Des on this one, Zach. You weren't there when we found her, or when she went missing, and I don't see her presenting a better case for herself."

"You didn't see how she went missing either! You got there after the fact!" Zach spat back.

I rolled my shoulder and Tristan let go of me. I could feel the blood still dripping, and cringed, but at least my head wasn't hurting any more.

"Zach find a room and chill out! We will get to the bottom of this, but we don't need you flinging accusations around."

"When she turns on you don't come crawling to me!" Zach seethed and stormed out of the room.

It was then when I watched him storm off I caught sight of the clock. So far pieces of these dreams had proved entirely too accurate for my comfort. None of it seemed possible, and yet Stacy was gone. There really was a light inside me that seemed to be some sort of power. They, and that Witch, Vince and everyone was calling it the "Gift". If all that was real, then there was a probable chance that this Algoroth person was on his way here now. Everyone was still arguing, still fighting, and we only had minutes left. Destiny waved a hand across my field of vision.

"Eä to Celestial," she called to me. "Do you have anything to say at all, or did you lose speech with your memory?"

"That's the first thing you're going to say to your sister who's been missing for almost two years?" Mitch spoke up.

"We'll have loving family reunion later, when Zach doesn't want to rip out her throat," she dismissed.

"Uh..." I paused. "Where did Zach go?" It was nine thirty. Algoroth should be coming after me by now. A nauseous pit opened in my stomach, and I got the vibe something was going down in my room. "Zach?" I called out to him, with no response.

"No offense, but do you really think he's going to answer you?" Chloe asked. I'd forgotten she was still here.

"I think we've got more problems."

I bolted from my chair and to the living room. When he wasn't there I raced up the stairs. What if he went into my room to look through my things like in my dream, and Algoroth found him? My Gift flared at the thought. At the top of the stairs Tristan caught my wrist and I felt a surging panic to which my Gift reacted.

Tristan cried out and stumbled on the last step, letting go of me. I hurried down the hall. I didn't have time to spare. I found the door already wide open and a doorway of darkness forming behind Zach. He didn't see it. He was too busy pulling drawers out of the empty dresser. He looked up, startled to see me, then went pale and slowly turned to face the darkness, and the man coming out of it.

"Hello Princess." Algoroth stepped through the doorway and Zach backed into the dresser.

"Zach, run you idiot!" I rushed into the room and grabbed him, shoving him towards the hall. Zach collided with Mitch in the doorway. Algoroth snickered.

"I told you I would find you. Pity you didn't make it more of a challenge."

"Seems I'm just one big disappointment lately." I took a backwards step towards the others.

"At least you managed to warm up your Gift for me." He smiled and dangled the pendant in the air between us.

"Who are you?" Tristan asked pulling Zach behind him. A pale golden light flowed from his heart to his hands, gathering into an orb in each hand. "And why have you come here?"

"Captain Tristan, I am the Dark King's servant, General Algoroth, and I'm sure if your little cherub could remember, she would tell you more. Alas," he smiled, bearing his fangs, "we must be going."

"Liar, General Algoroth died nearly eight hundred years ago!" Tristan raised his hand as if to throw the orb.

"True enough, but thanks to a noble, willing sacrifice I'm back in living flesh."

Algoroth didn't hesitate like Tristan had. He gathered dark red power in his hands and hurled it passed me and catapulted everyone in the doorway into the wall behind them, but he wasn't expecting me to do the same to him. Stunned he stumbled back, but not as much as I hoped for. Tristan and Mitch were already climbing back to their feet.

"Celestial down!" Tristan ordered. I felt the heat from Mitch's power as it sailed over my head as I dropped to the ground. Algoroth was ready. Like it was his own he caught it and snuffed it between his hands.

"No more nonsense!" Algoroth growled and grabbed a fist full of my hair, pulling me to him and held me against him. He wasted no time in enclosing us in a dome of power and pressing the pendant to my sternum. Power like white hot fire poured out of me and into the stone. Burning tore through my veins and threatened to burn me up from the inside out.

"You might have been able to kill then reincarnate yourself to escape your fate for a time, but now your soul and the future of Eä is in the Dark King's hands!"

As I lost strength and feeling he lowered me to the floor. I quickly went limp, only able to stare up at the top of the dome in agony. Lightning rippled across the outside of the dome, striking harder and faster each time. Everything was growing darker, and the sound of running water drawing closer. Just as I was about to be swept away the dome broke, and the lightning crashed down on the general's head. His hand slipped and the stone's connection with me was broken, leaving only a sliver of light within me.

"You're too late! Her Gift is mine!"

He held the glowing stone over his head, disappearing through the darkness with his laughter ringing in our ears. Someone dropped down beside me and then everything faded away.

Part Two

7

The doorway closed behind Algoroth, leaving him in the comfort of the living darkness that surrounded him. The only spec of light was that of Celestial's Gift, just barely contained within the diamond, not even giving enough light for him to see the chain attached to the pendant. He breathed in the familiarity of it all, savoring the way the vapors of darkness cooled him to the core, as they'd done the first time the Witch brought him here to take the blood oath.

He walked the lonely halls, tracing the ancient runes with his fingertips. He spent years studying old manuscripts but had yet to master the language of the ancients. It was his joy in past lives to learn from his predecessors, spanning back nearly five thousand years before his birth. The Witch knew eons of knowledge, and more besides. As he was passed the scrolls and the codex to begin learning her native tongue, it was all destroyed and his life with it. Now was the time to begin again. He entered a vast space and stopped on the threshold, waiting to be invited.

"The girl still lives?" The Witch's voice echoed across the stillness.

"No, my Lady." Algoroth entered and bowed low. "I carry her Gift within the pendant. There is no way..."

"Fool!" She stood swiftly and green and purple fire rose out of trenches of oil lining the edges of the room. "You captured her Gift, but you failed to bring me her soul. I need her here alive!"

His knee hit the stone floor with a thud. "Please accept this pendant and permit me to depart to complete the task wherewith you have given."

The Witch crossed the room slowly, bare feet slapping the floor. Long flowing robes danced behind her like snow dust in the breeze. Boney, pale fingers stretched out and then wrapped around the light and took it from him.

"No." She bade him rise with a gentle touch to his cheek. "First we must make the other preparations. Vince has proven his usefulness and paid the blood oath. Go back to Earth. Find Vince, and then I want the two of you to return to your castle. Once there, we will start gathering my children. The girl's time will come."

"May I inquire as to her significance?" Algoroth asked.

"It isn't her the master is concerned with, but her progeny."

"Perhaps we should dispatch her siblings as well?"

The Witch shook her head. "They matter not. Only Celestial carries the lineage of the first born in her veins. Now go! There is much to be done." He bowed, kissing her hand, and disappearing into a vapor of darkness.

*****

A week later Vince and Algoroth trotted along a seldom used gravel road, Vince on his gray and white horse and Algoroth on his tan and white splattered one. Throughout their trek to the western mountains, the thick pine tree forests had gradually given way to the grasslands, only dotted here and there with a few lonely pines now.

"So, tell me," Algoroth looked over to Vince who had been silent for most of their time together. Vince looked over to him, listening carefully. "Why did we trade in the automobile for horses the other day? It seems to me that if we hadn't we would be halfway there by now." Vince's horse neighed and shook its mane as if in agreement.

"The technologies of the other world only work close to the palace, where the doorway to Earth opens." He answered, stroking the horse's neck. They rode for a few more hours in silence, covering miles of road, before Algoroth looked suddenly back. "What is it?" Vince asked.

"We are being pursued, undoubtedly by the Royal Guard. We must make haste."

Algoroth kicked his horse's sides and the beast lurched forward into a mad gallop, but Vince caught up with him easily enough. The horses left a cloud of dust in their wake. However, by the time the dust had settled, and the tracks were getting distorted by the wind, the Royal Guard was still miles away.

The two men raced down the gravel road until the horses were ready to collapse from exhaustion. Dismounting, they led their horses over and down the side of a grassy hill and through a little grove of trees. Once behind the hill and trees they were well hidden from the road. They used their powers for everything from warmth to shelter, and while Algoroth watched Vince with his Gift he became increasingly impressed.

"It must have been a challenge to take your friend's Gift," said Algoroth as they were mounting their horses as dawn broke the next morning.

Vince sat atop his horse and led the way out of the grove. Usually, Fairies would be swarming around the morning dew, but at the ending of winter they were nowhere to be found. Except for maybe a rare few who were brave enough to face the bitter cold that would continue to intensify. He watched the faint blue glow of a fairy slip silently out of the grove, heading the way they had come.

"Extremely," Vince answered, turning his attention back towards the road.

Algoroth looked up towards the sky, only half listening to Vince. There were no clouds in the sky, but a chilly wind blew at their backs from the east. He sensed storm clouds.

"What are you doing?" Vince asked, watching Algoroth remove all the supplies and baggage off his steed. "If we don't get going now we may not be able to find shelter from the storm before it hits us."

"I think you are right. However, I would much prefer to fly to our destination. It is too cold for my taste, and I want to be warmed by a fire with a book or two to read."

"Fly?" Vince watched as Algoroth finished unloading the horse and then continued to remove all the riding gear. "How are we supposed to fly?" He asked.

"Have you ever ridden a dragon?" Algoroth looked back over his shoulder at Vince and grinned.

"I thought they died out."

"Maybe so, but a little necromancy comes in handy for many things, not just for the raising of dead men, but creatures as well."

With the horse fully unloaded and all the riding equipment taken off, Algoroth drew symbols in the air, then he pulled a curious looking flute from his bag and entered the land of the dead.

A damp mist curled around his legs as he went in. He knew this place all too well. He walked to the banks of the river and watched the current begin to pick up. Holding the flute out in front of him, he studied it like a child would regard a toy he hadn't seen in years. The carvings on the wooden instrument were of excellent quality. Placing the flute to his lips he played a simple tune, summoning the beast.

"Nightfang, bring your mate and come to the river to cross." Algoroth waited for only a moment before something began to appear through the mist on the other side of the rising river.

Vince sat on his horse and waited back in the land of the living. His ventures into necromancy were primarily just practice with small animals or spirits of the dead to bring back as servants.

He never kept the servants for long though. He didn't like having them around, as irritatingly clumsy as they were. He liked his solitary time.

Bringing back Algoroth had been his first real challenge and had not been won without a struggle. It was only after he traded Wes's life for Algoroth's that the Witch had allowed him to absorb Wes's Gift. Now his next challenge was to raise an army. He figured the lesser dead would work. They wouldn't be as smart, but they could be more easily summoned and commanded. Vince jumped off his horse and held the reins as Algoroth came back into life.

"Hold on tight to your horse," He called back to Vince.

The doorway closed and a black mass, almost three stories tall gathered in front of him where the doorway had been. Algoroth turned to face it, his hands glowing dark red from his power. The mass slowly formed into the shape of a dragon, its wings outstretched and eyes glowing orange with a black slit for the pupil. As soon as it appeared it began to solidify.

The long, spiked tail formed first, slashing the ground. Then the claws, feet and legs formed. The body formed slower, each scale, color shining in the morning sun, developed one by one. And last of all the head and neck formed. Six-foot long fangs protruded from the beast's mouth, and a stream of smoke, barely visible, was coming from its nostrils. Stripes of white, orange, and dull red were painted down the side of its face, neck body and wings while the rest of its body was black as ink.

As soon as the dragon had fully formed another began to appear at its side. This one was not as large and didn't take as long to form but was equally impressive. It measured a head shorter than the first but was thin and agile. The legs were lean and muscular. Its eyes locked with Vince's. They were a startling shade of the purest light blue, and the white skin of the dragon was speckled with the same blue, and patches of gold. It spread its great wings and stood on its hind legs, revealing a dark blue stripe along its belly. As it came back down it locked eyes with Vince again and came forward.

"Don't move. She's testing you," Algoroth said.

Sometime during the transformation he'd gotten onto Nightfang's back. Vince stood his ground as the dragon came closer. Without another word his dragon leapt into the air, grasped Algoroth's belongings in its talons, and soared into the west, leaving Vince and the other dragon to bond. The dragon came closer and sniffed Vince, and then huffed and stomped a foot. The ground shook and Vince lost his balance, but only for a moment.

"I do not like you." The dragon sent its thoughts into Vince's mind. Irritated, he looked at the ground and stepped back. "However," she continued, "I will let you ride me for the time being, because my mate wishes it of me." She ended.

"I thank you, great she-dragon." Vince bowed.

She huffed again, and smoke filtered out through her nostrils. "Do not make me change my mind," She warned menacingly. "Now send the horses back the way you came, that they may be cared for and nourished by those on your trail."

8

I peeled my eyes open to a dim room. Sheer blue drapes enclosed my bed in a canopy, effectively giving the illusion that I was alone until my vision adjusted. To my right an armchair was no more than a couple feet away, and the in-home nurse nestled in it snored softly. A dark-screened phone sat loose in her limp hand. To my left was another chair, identical to the other, where a man had pulled it close and slept leaning over the side of my bed. His face was clear to see since the drapes were behind him, and because of the pictures all over the house and the strange dreams I knew I was looking at my father.

I didn't dare move to take his hand or let him know I was awake. My whole body was on fire and my chest felt like someone smashed through the bones and ripped everything inside to shreds. Where I'd felt the strange new light, there was now only a sliver of it left, leaving a gaping empty weight with nothing to support it. I tried to breath in deep, but my chest ceased, heart stopping pain cutting deep into my lungs and muscles.

I didn't know he'd been holding my hand until I squeezed his, gasping for air, only to have my chest cease up again. My face was soaked before I knew it and no sooner than I'd uttered my first cry and squeezed his hand he and the nurse were awake, and the room got brighter and brighter until I was forced to close my eyes. Each of them held my hands, resulting in a strange warmth creeping through my veins and soothing the crushing fire until I could breath.

"Hush, hush baby." He wiped away the tears and came onto the bed, cradling me in his arms as if I was a small child. "Daddy's got you." He soothed, stroking my cheek. "Amber, page Dr. Stein and if you could get Katherine?" From the corner of my eye, I saw her nod and leave the room with the door wide open behind her.

"Dad?" I asked, still trying to catch my breath.

"I'm right here, baby. You're safe and sound." He held me tighter and I returned the gesture, slipping my arms under his into an embrace. "I was so scared when you went away, but you're back now, and not Vince, not Algoroth, or anyone else will take you."

"Celestial?"

Dad and I looked up to a woman standing in the doorway in a long robe and fuzzy slippers. She came in and pulled back the canopy. Shoulder length nut brown hair, hazel eyes, high angular cheeks... It was like looking at myself aged twenty years and my long locks chopped off. Dad let me slide off his lap and onto the bed where mom swooped down and wrapped her arms around me.

"Hi mom," I sniffled, holding her just as tight. When she let go I swayed, dizzy and starting to hurt again. Each breath hurt more and more, but I tried not to let that show. She sat and cupped my face in her hands, studying each detail.

"You're so pale," she whispered, more to herself than anything else. "Honey," she looked to dad, "Did you and the nurse give her any healing?"

"First thing, dear." Dad confirmed. "Do you need more?" he asked me, putting a hand to my clammy forehead.

"I don't understand..." I winced, clutching at the collar of my gown. My chest was on fire again, threatening to burn me up.

"Watch," Dad told me and took my hand. A light inside him lit up, just the way mine did, and spread through his chest, down his arm, his hand, into me and up, again soothing away all the hurt.

"Do you have the light too?" I asked mom. Face scrunching like she might cry, she just nodded. "How long was I asleep?" I asked, thinking it better to change the subject even though I had so many questions.

"It's November third, so a little over a week." Dad answered.

"I guess I have no excuse to be so tired then." I joked. Mom's face just turned sour, and dad sighed. Amber knocked softly on the door, alerting us to her presence.

"Dr. Stein is on his way. He's asked that I take her vitals and update her chart." She came to the bedside.

"Of course," Mom cleared her throat and came around to stand by dad.

"Ok, Celestial, I'm Amber and I was your nurse through the night. Some of these questions will be repetitive, but just humor me." She picked up a stethoscope, ear thermometer and a strange looking flat crystal.

"Ok…" I hesitated.

"Hold this," She placed the crystal in my hand. It looked like someone sliced off a piece of a geode crystal rock and polished it. "Take deep breaths. Let them out slowly." I did and she slid the icy surface from over my chest to my back. "Good, very good. How's the pain? What are you feeling?"

"My chest feels like it's on fire, but it's not as bad as before."

"Any improvement is good," she smiled and made a note. "Ok so how tall are you?"

"Five foot four."

"Weight?"

"One seventeen-ish."

"Age?"

"Seventeen,"

"What?" Dad scrunched his face as if I'd spoken in Latin. "No, you're almost nineteen." He insisted.

"And unless I slept for two years I'm positive I'm still a minor." I insisted right back.

"I think this is what Tristan was talking about," Mom stroked dads' arm, and taking his hand.

"When's your birthday, and what time?" Nurse Amber asked.

"June twenty-first, about seven in the morning." I looked to mom and dad to see if they would contest anything. Other than exchanging glances they said nothing. Amber sighed.

"There's definitely some discrepancies... I'll leave this here for Dr. Stein and give you some privacy."

She closed the door this time and left us, and I don't know what she was thinking would happen, or what I was expecting, but mom and dad talked quietly, and I stared down at the blanket. This was all so strange but still undeniable. Algoroth's voice played in my head. I'd killed myself to resurrect myself. How was it possible? How could any of this be possible? What did all these strange people want from me?

When the doctor came, he examined me, took the crystal, shaking his head and invited my parents to talk with him down in the foyer and insisted I go back to sleep. I lay down in the dark room after they turned off the lights and left me. I thought back on all the strange dreams, especially the one where Vince and I were fighting, and I burned up myself with my light. Was that what Algoroth was referring to? But then how could I reincarnate myself?... Unless I didn't really die and used the light to do some kind of life-swap or age reversal thing.

I rolled onto my side to face the windows. None of it was logical, and yet here I was. Stacy's gone because of me and this funny light that Algoroth stole... I should have let Vince take it, I cursed silently, slamming my fist down on the bed. If not for the light she'd be safe, living the life she was meant to live, and nobody would have to baby-sit me. Tristan told Zach there were things I didn't remember. Maybe I really did live another life. Maybe there was more to this puzzle than the pieces I held.

I rolled back over to see the time on the bedside clock, glowing on the table. If things were normal I'd be getting up for school in an hour. I pushed the blankets off me and got out of bed, wobbling with each step. I checked the drawers, finding the clothes I'd salvaged from home and more besides. I selected an old t-shirt, my hoodie and a pair of boot-cut, dark-wash jeans, ankle socks, and my sneakers. Maybe if I could get some air I could clear my head.

I opened the door, expecting to find the dark hall empty, but down by the bathroom Destiny and Zach argued quietly. I walked out into the hall, floor squeaking underfoot. They shushed abruptly, turning my way like deer in headlights.

"Uh… Hi," I nodded awkwardly. "Guess after sleeping for a week I've finally had my fill." I joked. They said nothing, made no indication that I'd said anything. "How are you?" I tried again. Destiny had been folding her arms, but she dropped them with a heavy sigh.

"I assume you're fine now?" Zach asked, his hands shoved into his slack pockets as he leaned back against the door frame.

"Uh… No, but I can't get back to sleep." I answered honestly.

"So, what did you give the Dark's most famed general?" He leaned off the door sauntering over to stand close, looking down his nose at me. His own light glowed beneath his skin, giving an eerie, Halloween-ish glow, like a bright flashlight pressed into someone's palm.

"I didn't give him anything, thank you very much." I stepped back and into the doorframe of my room, my heart was pounding, each beat burning more than the one before. I could feel the sliver of light within me trying to grow to fill the void, but it couldn't.

"Why don't I believe you? Oh wait, I know," He gripped my arm, keeping me from going back into my room.

"Zach stop!" Destiny hissed.

"If you wanted to hurt Algoroth you would have. You've got the most powerful Gift this family has seen in centuries. I don't believe that you just forgot how to use it, or that you've just conveniently forgot about us."

"Zachary Andavir let go of your sister!" Dad charged and pried us apart. "I know what you think son, but it isn't so!" Dad let go of me, but held onto Zach, his voice gaining volume and gravel.

"It's fine," I piped up, "He's just worried-"

"Celestial shut up!" Zach cut me off, "Don't try to get back in my graces. I'm not so easily won over." I could have sworn there was fire in Zach's breath but when I blinked it was gone.

"Go to the Palace!" Dad boomed, thrusting Zach down the hall and through an archway made entirely of light.

"What is that?!" I exclaimed. I'd dreamed of it but hadn't believed it would be real.

"That's the doorway into Eä, where we're from. This Palace," Destiny touched the painting, "Is in Caleath, our home, your home too..." Her voice trailed off before she looked up at dad and back at mom behind her, then at me. "You really don't know us anymore, do you?" She asked.

I shook my head, "I don't. I'm sorry." I gripped the neck of my hoodie, as if it would help snuff the fire in me, burning within the empty. "If it helps," I panted, using my doorway as a crutch, "I might remember one thing... I don't know. Maybe it'll make more sense to you than it does to me."

"Tell us!" Zach popped back through the doorway of light, and it faded away.

"Uh... Alright." I licked my dry lips and bit the inside of my cheek. Zach's enthusiasm fell, but he still looked at me expectantly. "So, I don't know if it's really a memory. I dreamed it, and it seems like something that already happened, but it doesn't make a lot of sense to me."

"Do you want to sit down?" Mom asked, squeezing passed Destiny, Zach, and dad. I let her guide me to the armchair where the nurse had snoozed, and everyone followed us into my room. "Just tell us what you saw," she said gently after I sat down.

"So, it starts out where I'm wearing a long dress and heals and I'm running from Vince down a hall in that palace," I gestured to the painting in the hall. "At the top of the stairs he tackles me, and we fall down the stairs. When we got to the bottom he pinned me down and pulled out this glowing white stone," I closed my eyes, wincing, but trying to keep a mostly calm exterior. "Vince said I could join them or 'meet my fate'. I said no and sent out my Gift. Vince let go and then it ends..." I trailed off.

Did I even know what it felt like to die? Could I take what Algoroth said for the truth? Did he even know? I dropped my head into my hands, beads of sweat running down my forehead and neck, making my hair cling uncomfortably in places. My whole body was shaking.

"I heard Algoroth say that you killed and reincarnated yourself." Zach said, "Is that true?" I glanced up at everyone and shrugged.

"I don't know. I suppose anything is possible, but I don't know why I would do that or how..."

"If it is, you have a big, broken law to account for."

"Zachary, please!" mom exhaled.

"Well necromancy is a capital offence, isn't it? I can't think of any other way she could have done that."

"Unless she didn't bring herself back to life, just used her Gift to maybe give herself a new one." Destiny theorized.

I shrugged again. My hand gripped the material over my chest so tight my knuckles were turning white, and with my eyes clenched shut I didn't notice everyone staring at me. I did notice the pressure mounting behind my eyes.

"I think... I should go back to bed... I'm getting a headache." I panted.

"Ok, sweetie." Mom squeezed my hand and stepped away so dad could help me into bed.

*****

Tristan paced the length of the kitchen, rubbing his thumb along the stubble coming in on his chin, thinking deeply while everyone else debated. It was obvious to everyone that Celestial wasn't faking her memory loss, and even Zach had to admit she was more than a little clueless. The question now was, did they bring her back to Eä, back to Kings City in Caleath, or was it safer for her and everyone else if she remained here? Wards were up, so there was no chance of anyone, other than household members, getting inside uninvited.

"But" Katherine argued, "The wards are stronger in Eä, and she will need to come home eventually. Your father and I can't rule Caleath effectively from here, and it isn't safe to be opening the doorway so often."

"Maybe you're right," Stephen leaned back in his seat at the table. "We'll have to explain it all to her sooner or later, and I agree that traveling between worlds needs to be as low as possible. When she wakes up again, why don't we move her back into her old room to finish her recovery?"

"She's going to need a lot of help, and have a lot of questions," Destiny added, "Shouldn't someone stay with her?"

"Tristan and his team are still assigned to her. We'll leave that the same." Tristan nodded from the kitchen. "Unless of course there's still a conflict of interests?" Stephen directed his inquiry to Tristan.

"Not right now, your majesty, but if she wanted to, or remembered..." Tristan cleared his throat despite his cool demeanor he felt his cheeks heat.

"You would like to pick up where you left off?" Katherine finished for him. He nodded.

"Danny, Chloe, Mitch, I still want you guarding her. She knows your faces, and I don't want any information leaked into the public yet. Destiny, Zach," They both looked to their father, giving undivided attention, "I want you to work with them. Learn what you can about the manifestations, and anything you can about Vince and Algoroth's plans. The fate's only know what they have in store..."

Katherine's tablet on the table beeped, reminding her to check the agenda. "Oh, Honey, we've got to meet with The Lord and Lady from Parna in about ten minutes for the luncheon. I guess they are pressing to go back tomorrow." Blacking out the screen she slipped it into the bag at the side of her chair, ready for her to grab at a moment's notice.

"Did they say how Princess Scarlett is holding up?" Zach asked, tapping his fingers on the table. He tried and failed to not look anxious.

"As well as can be expected, son. If you want to write to her, I'll make sure they have it to take with them before they leave."

"Thanks mom," Zach nodded. "I'll get it to you."

"Well, I guess we're off. Contact us directly if anything comes up we need to know about." Stephen rose and pushed in his chair, then Katharine's chair when she was up. "Tristan, would you walk with us a minute?"

Promptly following them down the hall and into the entertainment room Katherine opened the door to Eä, glowing white in all its majesty, stirring the air softly.

"What can I do for you, your majesties?" Tristan lowered his gaze, remembering his place.

"At ease, Captain." Stephen squeezed the young man's shoulder. Tristan relaxed, but not much. It wasn't easy to be at ease in the present company. "Thank you so much for the use of your home through this ordeal. I know it's been difficult, housing your team here, and my family, from time to time."

"It's an honor to serve my country, my King, my Queen," Tristan bowed.

"Son," Stephen's let the formality out of his tone, "Take leave for a week or two, you've more than earned it. I'll make sure the staging is gone once Celestial is moved back into her old room."

"Thank you," Tristan made to bow again, but Stephen stopped him. Confused, he looked up at his King.

"I want you to know that you still have our blessing with Celestial, for what that's worth. Your father would be proud of the man you've become."

At this Tristan swallowed hard, emotional and at a loss for words. Instead, he shook their hands and watched as they passed through the light and the doorway shrank closed behind them.

Back in the dining area the others talked quietly amongst themselves. Mitch hung back, waiting for Tristan. Meeting him halfway between the hall and the living room the two wandered around to the back of the house and onto the wrap-around porch. The sun was still high for late in the afternoon, but it was surprisingly cool. Frost covered the blades of grass and fallen leaves unlucky enough to be in the shade.

"So, what's your assignment? Are you still assigned to Celestial?" Mitch asked, sliding the glass door closed behind him.

"I'm on leave for a while. I get why they still don't want me being head of her security."

"Conflict of interests," Mitch quoted. Tristan nodded, leaning on the rail. "Do you think you two will get back together? I mean... No offence but I don't know if I could handle her baggage. You pretty much have a free pass since she doesn't remember."

"I know you're my best friend and all, but I'd never tell anyone to date you. Her 'baggage' isn't her fault, and besides, what if her memory does come back and we're not together? I can't leave her like that. I don't want to leave her."

"Just make sure you know what you're getting into, man." Mitch slapped his back. "Before you know it, you could be King one day."

"Shut up." Tristan play shoved him. "I never want to be King, and she said she didn't want the crown, so that's why we worked before. We both just wanted normal, happy lives, you know?" Mitch leaned on the rail next to him, both men looking out over the lawn, watching birds dart in and out of the wood behind the house.

"So... if you're on leave, does that make me boss?"

"Yep," Tristan popped his lips on the "p" sound, letting out a long breath after. "I'm gonna go sit with her for a while." He decided.

"See you later." Mitch stayed where he was while Tristan went back into the house, rubbing and flexing his fingers to warm them up.

*****

I walked a long path, winding along the mountain side in a dried-up canyon. The sun sinking low in the sky made it hard to tell exactly where I was going but eventually I reached a bridge that let me into a valley, tucked back behind miles of mountain trails fallen into disrepair. Hiding in the brush off to the side I watched the creatures down below.

Tall, scaly skinned, pointy eared goblins raced around, lighting torches all over the valley, making it all one big orange glow by the time the sun set completely. In the back, fortified by stone walls and a heavy drawbridge a castle loomed in the distance. I seemed to float there through the camp, passing more goblins, and even giants, trolls, and men with wicked tattoos on their faces. I passed through the walls as a ghost, floating on until I found Algoroth, Vince and the old witch standing on a high balcony, overlooking the camp.

"More are coming from the southern borders, out of Nule. They've taken extra care not to draw attention from the dwarves or the elves. Our spies report they are unaware of the movement." Vince didn't seem to be talking to anyone, but the witch nodded, a slight smile on her weathered, old lips.

"Soon they will march into the heart of Caleath to open the doorway to Earth. Those pitiful humans... soon they will taste real magic, and the rest of Eä will belong to our King."

Algoroth turned to the witch, dropping to his knee, and taking her hand. "My lady Caoranach, one who graces the presence of Darkness, when do you wish them to depart?" She took back her hand to stroke his cheek, a tender touch.

"Not until the southern division arrives and the Dark Warriors have been summoned. Without them they may rival our numbers. Everything must go as he commanded."

"And what of the princess?" Algoroth gazed up at her and the dark power radiating from her eyes.

"She will be in Eä soon. Leave on the morrow, and remind Vince," she gripped his arm and her voice changed, as if it were never her speaking but the rumbling voice of a man, using her body as a marionette. "I need her alive for the ritual."

9

    Tristan's leave was cut short when a report came that Vince had been spotted with someone of Algoroth's description entering Caleath's western grasslands... and the rumor that they were on dragons didn't help anything. To me, everything was still so new, and I wasn't sure how I felt about any of it. Tristan had spent every day with me once I woke up and we moved into the palace, but as soon as he left everything felt colder and more unfamiliar. I also learned that it was his house we had been in, not my parents. Apparently it paid well to be a personal guard for the royal family and helped with military progress too.
    Zach still didn't trust me but was obligated to try and help me control what little of my power was left since mom and dad had a country to run, and traitors and a legendary murderer to capture. Destiny was easier to be around, but I was still uncomfortable during our history lessons in the palace library every afternoon. My parents theorized that learning about where I was from and reconnecting with my light and old life might jog some repressed memories.
    More than a month passed with little progress. My power grew closer to what it had been, but it still felt raw inside and I struggled to control it. None of Caleath's or Eä's history jogged old

memories, and I wondered if what I'd dreamed was really a memory at all. I read somewhere about death whispers, the last waking memory of a person's previous life. I kept this idea to myself, unsure if the idea of reincarnation was something I put stock in, or if there was something else to blame for my amnesia and the age gap.

Whatever the case, and whatever Tristan and my family believed, Zach was convinced I was faking it. His training sessions were getting more and more brutal, and I'd cried on more than one occasion of overexertion. Each time he pushed just a little bit harder. At five this morning he dragged me out of bed and outside the city limits to the forest and a run-down, beaten sliver of a trail he claimed I used to run every day. It was barely light enough to see, but he still hadn't brought any flashlights and never bothered to fill me in so of course I wasn't prepared either.

"Are you sure I used to come here?" I asked through cold gasps about a mile and a half into our run.

The rising of the sun hadn't done anything for the temperature. White wisps of air trailed and faded behind us like smokestacks from a locomotive. It was just the two of us, no soldiers, and no guards. He looked back but didn't answer.

"What does this even have to do with my Gift?" I asked a little while later.

"A healthy mind and body are key," he answered, as if it should have been obvious. "And you have been slacking since you went to Earth." Zach slowed enough to let me catch up.

"Whatever," I huffed. I pushed on, sweat dripping down my face and back and legs. "If you're planning to ditch me in the woods or run me to death and leave me to die," I panted. "There's a lot easier ways to kill someone than that."

"You would know." He slowed down to a stop, breathing hard but not nearly as hard as I was. I bent over, leaning my hands on my knees while I tried to catch my breath.

"What are you talking about?" I looked up at him to find him grimly looking down at me.

"I am so sick of watching you pretend you don't know." His whole body glowed beneath his clothes, barely contained rage triggering his power. Steam rose from him and into the crisp air. I stood up fast and backed away, hands out in front of me. "I was with Tristan when we discovered your security team had been murdered. Then you had the audacity to call to him for 'help' on the other side of the palace, so we came running only to find you missing and more bodies and learned later that more traitors had attacked mom and dad's security team while we were busy chasing your cry wolf!"

In my haste to back up I tripped over a tree root, falling onto my backside. I backed away as he advanced, until I was stopped by the tree behind me. He stood over me as he pulled his Gift back into his heart.

"What are you going to do?" I asked as calmly as I could. "I don't remember what you're talking about, and the tiny bit I dreamed about I already told you. Even if, somehow, it was my fault, I wouldn't know. You're so convinced it's all my fault," I stood slowly, as if he might pounce any minute, "so what are you going to do? Better do something while I can't fight back, because when I can, I will."

I looked him in the eyes, fighting every instinct I had to duck and run. "Zach, I don't know who I was, but I know who I am now and I'm not capable of what you're accusing. If you think I did, fine. Believe it. Try and prove-"

"I SAW YOU WITH VINCE!" he bellowed over me. "I saw the two of you together the night before the attacks. I never told Tristan because it would destroy him to know that you and Vince were together behind his back. I know you two were behind it all!"

I paled and the world seemed to stand still, frozen around Zach and me.

"I don't understand. Tristan and I were together, but I was with Vince? That's insane."

I looked down at the subtle glow in my chest, which flowed through my veins and into my fingertips. The light was still shamefully dim in comparison to what Zach seemed to expect of me.

"You and Tristan were engaged. I don't know how long you and Vince were doing what you were doing." He looked down and ran his fingers through his hair. Releasing a long breath, he sent his power to his hands and walked up to me. "I thought if I could prove it with hard evidence it might be easier to swallow for everyone."

He looked down at me, waiting in the defensive for me to say or do something. I couldn't. It was as if all air was frozen in my chest. I forced in a deep breath through my nose and out again through my mouth. He believed the deaths and betrayals were my fault, so then why did he say he'd train me?

"But you haven't found anything. You only know what you saw." I said as I realized it. I brought my gaze back to his face and saw the hurt there, and wondered what he saw in mine, if he could tell now that I really didn't remember. "There has to be a reason," I breathed. "I just don't think I'm capable of doing something like that."

"You did, even if you don't remember." He stepped away and back onto the trail. "I am going to find out why." Without saying anything else he turned and jogged off, not bothering to wait for me.

"I am too." I said to the forest before following him.

*****

That afternoon in the palace's library with Destiny I listened to her read out of an old book about some invasion that took place a thousand years after what she explained as the "Rebirth of Eä and the Light." Up the winding staircase by the back wall, along the railing to the loft high above us I let my eyes wander, feeling drawn over and over to find out what was up there even though Destiny had told me a hundred times.

Destiny dropped the thick, leather-bound volume on the table and huffed, "You're not even listening. Do you want to remember? Do you want to get better? Do you even care?"

Without meaning to I smiled and continued to look up towards the loft for a second. When I finally looked at my sister, I got up.

"What's so funny?" she finally asked.

"This," I laughed as I said it. "It's been a hell of a day and I'm really frustrated." I walked over and picked up the book she'd been reading out of, opened the cover, and flipped through the aged parchment pages. "This isn't helping." I put it down.

"You haven't really tried." She folded her arms and set her tone.

"I've memorized and read everything you asked me to, Destiny, but I still don't remember anything. Maybe it's time to try something different."

"Like what?" she let her shoulders fall, and her tone revealed how tired she was, not that the dark circles didn't already testify.

"Tell me stories about us growing up. Let's explore the palace, the city, the woods. Something has to jog my memory, right? If not then maybe we can find out how Vince's uprising happened."

"Where do you want to start?" She unfolded her arms to slip her thumbs into her pockets.

"Tell me about you. I wanna know every scraped knee to your first kiss. And while you're at it, why can't we go up there?" I nodded to the loft.

"It's not like we can't, I just don't want to." Her eyes grew wide and lips thin as moisture built in the corners of her eyes.

"What happened?" She stiffened under my touch, so I withdrew and watched her wipe her eyes.

"Dustin, he was my boyfriend. He got caught in Vince's cross hairs. They killed him up there."

"Des..." I went to comfort her, but she stopped me with one look.

"I don't want to go up there."

She stood there like a stone and said nothing else while I gathered the books and put them back on the cart by the stairs.

"Let's keep the history to three times a week, and the rest of the time let's just get to know each other again. I'll tell you about my life on Earth, and you tell me about growing up here. Deal?" She sniffled and walked slowly towards the door and into the hall.

"I'll run the idea by mom and dad when I see them tonight."

I stood by the stairs in dumb silence, alone for pretty much the first time all day once she was out of sight. Everything that happened this morning with Zach, and now with Destiny, was all so heavy and weighted me down. Without really deciding, I turned and walked up the stairs, one step at a time. Perhaps if I could find out what happened that day everyone could heal.

"Where are you going?" Zach called up to me, shaking me out of my thoughts. I stopped and looked down to where he was in the doorway.

"I wanna see what's up here." I continued climbing.

I was halfway up already and almost at the top when I heard Zach's shoes on the wood steps ascending after me. I reached the top and I wasn't sure what I'd been expecting, but there was literally nothing up here but a table and some chairs. There were no lights up here, just a few candelabras fastened to the walls. None were lit, so the only light up here came from the massive window down on the main level of the library.

Once I was up there I felt I wasn't where I needed to be, but needed to be somewhere deeper in. I followed the call to the candelabra in the corner. My hand moved on its own pulling down on it until I heard a click and then a grinding sound. A plume of dust shot out of the ground as the wall seemed to remove itself. I jumped back and found Zach right behind me.

"We're not allowed in there," he said.

I turned from him and back to the tunnel. Now that the dust was clearing there was something familiar about it. I went to investigate, but Zach gripped my wrist. I didn't fight him. I didn't want to give him another reason not to trust me, but what was down there?

"This is familiar," I said as I glanced back at him.

"Not surprising," he let go of me. "You used to sneak into the passages all the time. Sometimes we'd go together and play hide and seek from Destiny."

"I think this is the tunnel from my dream. I think this is the one I used to try to get away from Vince and his guys that day." I said the words as they occurred to me. I stepped towards the tunnel and Zach followed me in.

"Are you ready to find out whether you're guilty or not?" I looked back at him, scared but determined. I needed answers as to why Vince and Algoroth were after me and why it looked like I was masterminding a rebellion against my country.

"I have to know."

Zach lit the way with his power, and the wall closed behind us when he pushed in a brick directly behind the candelabra I'd pulled. It took a minute for the dust to settle again, but once it did we moved on in the direction my dream had taken me. I opened the passage to the hall outside the courtyard, just like I remembered, and explained the dream to Zach along the way. Instead of following it to the courtyard Zach suggested we take the tunnel a little farther.

The tunnel opened to the hall outside the courtyard, the hall where my siblings and my bedrooms were, twisted down into the kitchen and then ultimately came to a dead stop in the cold storage room, a level above the dungeon according to Zach.

Quiet and contemplative we made our way to my room. Both of us declined dinner. I wasn't sure why he did, but I had a headache from hades from all the dust. Zach sat with me for a few minutes, sending his healing power into me to try and clear the headache away, and when that didn't work he left to find mom and dad.

"Maybe you just need more practice healing," I teased to ease the concern off his face before he left.

"No, I'm as good as any medic in this city. Your Gift is blocking me from healing you for some reason. I'll be back."

I nodded and laid my head down on my pillow, wincing as he closed the door behind him. I could hear him jogging down the hall until he got too far away. I rolled towards the window, watching birds land on the balcony railing outside until the light became unbearable. My lids slid closed and before I knew it the heaviness in my mind went to my body and I was asleep and dreaming.

I was back in the hall, just outside my door, ready to go inside. Tristan stood with me, smiling, and looking down at a ring on a very significant finger. He didn't say anything, just leaned in and kissed me. The dream had control of itself, and I kissed him back.

"Just think," I whispered as our lips parted. "In a year we'll be married and have our own little home."

He kissed my forehead with a smile on his lips then said, "It can't come fast enough, love." Without meaning to I yawned. "I think I should let you get some sleep."

"Breakfast tomorrow?" I put my hand on the door handle, letting the weight of my hand do all the work. It fell and the door swung open.

"I'll come by your room at eight." he confirmed.

He kissed my cheek before heading down the hall and I went into my room. A few minutes later, as I was pulling bobby pins out of my hair there was a knock at the door. Thinking it was Tristan I went to answer.

"Vince?" I didn't hide my surprise. "Is everything alright?" As I asked this I recalled that he'd been my head of security for the night.

"Yeah," he nodded and rubbed the back of his neck. "Look, I know it's late, but can we talk?" I stepped out and closed my door. He sighed and started walking. Curious, I followed him. We walked together through the palace, saying good night to Destiny and Zach along the way. They were dressed up just as nice as I was.

The palace was quiet, most everyone was sleeping or getting ready for bed and the only people in the halls were the night guards, Vince, and I, and I sensed someone was following us, someone who forgot how to erase his shadow when he went invisible. I let Zach follow us into the hall outside of the library.

"Vince what's going on? What did you want to talk to me about?"

We came to a stop outside the doors. Vince opened them and went in, the lights still out. Hesitantly I followed him inside. Zach stayed in the doorway.

"Celestial..." He came to me, speaking low.

As he came closer I stepped back and back until he had me pinned against the wall by the door. Before I could push him off, before I could say anything he slid his hands from my hips to my face and kissed me. When he pulled away I was so stunned I didn't even notice that Zach's shadow was gone.

"Well," he said louder, "now that he's gone let's get down to business."

He came at me again, but this time I sent out my Gift, burning his hands where he touched me. He shoved me into the wall, ignoring the pain. Wes came out from behind a bookshelf with Dustin, and a few others, all closing in around me.

"Get away!" Power surged from me to Vince, catapulting him away from me. "Zach!"

I screamed his name, but Wes was beside me in the blink of an eye with his hand and a rag over my mouth, cutting off my cries and filling my lungs with some strange chemical. Wes brought me slowly to the ground and through my fading vision I watched, stuck in weak, tingling limbs, as Dustin came towards me with a dagger and an empty vial.

The next thing I knew I was waking up on the floor of the library loft, arm slit. My light went to heal without much effort from me. In moments, my mind cleared. Though it was dark, I heard voices around me, deep enough in discussion that none noticed me. From my place on the floor, I held still and listened.

"In about half an hour they'll find her missing. When they do I want you all in position. With our coup, and our brothers in Parna, we'll hold the power over both doorways."

"Earth should succumb fairly easily," Wes mused.

Vince paced. He held something in his hand. I couldn't make out what it was until he walked over to the railing, peering over the edge in the creeping dawn. It was the vial Dustin had been holding before he attacked, and now was full of crimson. I pressed my lips into a thin line and willed my stomach to uncramp at the sight of it.

"It appears Tristan the Gallant found out early." A man from my security team said, reading off his phone. I recognized him as the newest member, someone Vince had recommended to my parents who had come from a long line of Caleath's military men. In fact, as it grew steadily lighter I remembered that my whole security team was here except for maybe a few people.

"It's time to prepare the stone." Vince came to the table and dropped a smooth black stone into a bowl and poured the contents in with whatever else was already in there. It sounded as though he'd dropped it into a pond. "Give the signal to Fin. Once the King and Queen are out of the way start on the twins."

Vince pulled the bowl between him and Wes. Golden light flowed from Wes into the bowl and the two of them started chanting low and quick, words I'd never heard before, in a language reminiscent of the elfish tongue. When they were done the concoction bubbled onto the table and floor, some kind of black toxic ooze. Nevertheless, Vince reached in and removed the stone, glowing white in his palm. He turned slowly to me.

"Seems someone woke up early," he said with a twisted grin, "Dustin eliminate the twins now." Vince's smile turned dark as he came towards me.

From where I lay I could feel the strange, powerful magic pulling on my light. Dustin stood from the table the same moment I jumped to my feet. It was all too much, and I didn't need to see the black metal knife in his hand to understand everything that was said and what "eliminate" meant, but I did see it. Dustin barely had time to blink before daggers of my light tore into his chest and into his heart. His eyes never closed and none of the other guards stepped in to protect him, or one another as I tore through them with my blades of light.

Bodies on the floor, only five of us were left alive in the room out of the ten or eleven that there had been. Wes hurled fire, cutting off my escape to the stairs. My only option now was the labyrinth of tunnels hidden between the palace walls. Glowing light surrounded me, then through me as I became translucent as a spirit. I dimmed the light once I passed through the wall and became whole again, leaving only enough light to make my way through. Explosions erupted behind me, casting my shadow ahead of me with the orange glow. Acrid smoke tinted the air and cascading footsteps followed in my wake, catching up quickly.

From there it all happened exactly as I remembered, and when the blinding white light tore out of me and where the dream ended last time, a new one started taking shape out of the brightness. The white light remained bright, but the walls faded away, revealing a vast blue sky and miles of forest beneath, stretching farther than I could see. I looked down, finding my wrists bound together with rope woven of light and spun gold. The rope coiled around my wrists, bound my arms to my sides and secured me to the saddle on the winged beast I rode, seated behind Vince.

I was already bleeding when I jolted awake, breathing in great gulps of air as if I were starving. Strong hands gripped my arms, softer ones brushed hair out of my face, and someone called my name.

"Celestial," Mom crooned, smoothing my hair. I looked over at dad, holding my arms and restraining my Gift with his own. His neck and face were damp, and I hadn't even realized my Gift was doing anything. I pulled it all back into my heart and he released his hold on me, panting as he did.

"I thought she hadn't made progress with her Gift, son?" Dad looked back at him, standing between the bed and the door.

"She hadn't," he said flatly, narrowing his eyes at me. "Unless our walk today jogged your memory?" he asked, folding his arms as he came over to us.

Mom wiped my face free and clean of every trace of the vision, the evidence left in the waste bin under my bedside table and in my oversized pupils. They were slowly returning to normal, so I ignored the sting from the lights.

"We jogged too hard," I said, still winded, and more than a little frazzled. I closed my eyes, seeing all the people and their lives I'd taken to break up their coup and protect my family.

"What?" He asked, moving in. Mom stood up beside dad and let Zach come in a little closer. I remained where I was, seated on the bed, halfway under the covers, and wishing I could pull them over my head and forget everything I just saw, and everything that happened.

"Mom? Dad? Can I talk to Zach for a minute?"

They exchanged nervous glances, but they relented, "We'll be waiting in the hall." Dad gave Zach and I a stern look before going to the door. Mom was slow to go, watching the two of us with worried confusion, but eventually left the room with Dad.

"What's going on?" Zach walked over to the balcony doors, pealing back the thin curtains to look outside.

"What you saw with Vince and I that night, I wish you would have stayed just a few minutes more, then maybe none of this would have ever happened." I dropped my head into my hands, wondering how it all came to this. What signs might we have missed that could have prevented their ambush? Why was it my Gift they needed?

"What happened?" he asked, dropping the curtain, and coming to sit on the other side of the bed.

"Somehow we all missed signs, red flags... Vince knew you were there. That's why he kissed me. He wanted to get you to leave without letting you know he knew you followed. Once you were gone I was going to confront him but Wes and Dustin and everyone ambushed me, knocked me out with chloroform."

"Dustin?" Zach echoed, shocked to hear the name.

"Yeah. He was part of the coup." I nodded. "Zach... All my guards aside from Danny and Chloe and Mitch were in on the coup. When I woke up I was in the library loft. They'd taken my blood and done some ritual, so they could use a stone to contain my Gift. I don't know why they want it, but the minute I heard that they were going to kill our whole family I lost it. I am the one who killed Dustin and the others." I confessed.

I forced down the emotions rising to the surface, reminding myself it was over, and they couldn't hurt my family anymore, and that Vince and Algoroth were in the west desert somewhere far away from me. Visions couldn't always be right, could they?

*****

Once mom and dad and the twins knew everything that I'd seen things were even more tense than before, and despite everyone's effort I remembered nothing else new. During the rest of the week there were no nudges to explore locked rooms, no more flashbacks of things long past. However, I dreamed every night about riding captive with Vince and his dragon. It was always the same dream, over and over, night after night.

The only thing I made progress with was my Gift. Seeing myself use it in those dreams seemed to unlock something, something wild and powerful. When December hit all my training and tutoring came to a stop as it seemed the people of Caleath celebrated Christmas, something they adopted from Earth almost two hundred years ago. Along with their normal duties mom and dad attended charitable events every day, some they organized and others they didn't but wanted to support.

Zach and Destiny were also busy in the city and those close enough to visit in a day. I wasn't allowed to leave the palace. Mom and dad said it was because my power was so unpredictable, but I knew they wanted the guards to keep an eye on me and report anything "unusual". The only person who was outwardly pleased with this was Zach. After we talked he decided he still didn't have enough evidence to trust me since he couldn't trust my word alone. Destiny avoided me whenever she could, "just to keep out of the drama," she claimed, but it still hurt.

In one of the palace's many living rooms I laid on my back on a charcoal sofa, tossing a little orb of light into the air and catching it over and over like a baseball.

"Who wants to go out for hot chocolate?" I asked. Danny lifted her face off her fist and her elbow off the little table by the door where she'd been sitting with Mitch.

"I'll call the kitchen and have them bring you some." Her voice was thickly coated with boredom from long hours of monotonous "princess sitting".

"Never mind." I sighed and tossed the orb again, imagining it really was a baseball. I closed my eyes and caught it, pausing at the feel of hardened leather and thick stitching.

"Celeste, you know we can't take you out. The press hasn't seen a glimpse of you for going on three years. Imagine the mob they'd be to get to you." Mitch chimed in, but I barely heard him, more fascinated with my creation.

"Hey look what I made!" I sat up and lightly tossed it to him. He caught it with unenthused ease, and looked it over, still not impressed when he looked up and tossed it back to me. I sulked, disappointed.

"Sorry." Mitch scooted out from the table, chair legs scraping the floor. "It's just that the last time you said that you'd made the most epic sword ever."

"Oh." I sulked.

I waited for someone to say something else, but nobody did. Eventually I got up and they followed me around the palace, wandering aimlessly until Zach and Destiny came back home and gave my three guards a break. Des and Zach walked me to my room, neither speaking to me. Since we were on the other side of the palace it was a long awkward walk. When we finally did reach my room, I put my hand on the handle and turned. Before I could open the door all the way Des cleared her throat and put her hand on mine, pulling it shut again.

"We need to talk." She took her hand back and folded her arms.

"What about?" I looked from her to Zach and neither of them looked very happy. "Is everything ok? You guys seem a little off..."

"It's just been a busy day, but everything's fine. Mom and dad called, and they want you to come with us to an event." Zach sported a lopsided grin that seemed more than out of place. I paused. Something felt just wrong, but I couldn't place why. I shrugged and smiled.

"I have been going stir crazy in this place. Where is the event? What are we doing?"

"We'll be out in the woods outside the city. It's a snow day type thing for the kids and a booth to collect donations for toys for the outlying towns," Zach explained. "Your coat and stuff is in the car in the garage." He added.

"Oh, So I don't need to grab anything?"

"Nope," Destiny shook her head. "We have to get a move on though or we'll be late."

From my room we practically ran to the garage using the tunnels that were allegedly off limits. The jeep we piled into held no plates and was a little more covert than I imagined the twins using. And where were their guards that followed them everywhere? I patted my pocket, ensuring my new cell was still there. Alone in the back seat I typed a message and quickly sent it off. The reply came a few minutes later and not from the person I'd been watching.

"We're still at the soup kitchen. Why?" Des' reply made my stomach drop, just like when Vince attacked my house and used Stacey to get to me.

We slowed, approaching the traffic light that was changing from yellow to red. My seatbelt made the faintest of clicks as I unfastened it. The moment we came to a stop I opened the door and flew out of the car, sprinting down the street as fast as I could. The cell was already dialing, and I heard the first ring as I put the phone to my ear.

"Celeste what's going on? You knew we'd be here a couple hours." Destiny answered the phone in a huff.

"SOS!" I panted. "Your and Zach's evil doppelgängers are trying to abduct me!"

"What?" She sounded far away. "Me and Zach's what's are where with you? I'm so confused." Destiny pulled the phone away from her ear, but I understood enough words not to be surprised when Zach came on the line.

"Where is the soup kitchen from the corner of Westshire Lane and Jennings Road?" I asked, risking a glance back to the intersection I was running from. Though the light was green the Jeep just sat there, still running. I caught a glimpse of the copies as they got out of the vehicle, realizing I was gone.

"Too far for you to go on foot. Why aren't you with Mitch?" Zach asked in his best dad voice.

"You and Des came to get me, but it turned out that it's not actually you guys and I don't know who they are, but they look and sound like you and they're trying to take me out of town, but I jumped out of the car and now they're after me."

I didn't breathe through the story and looked back again, seeing not Zach's doppelgänger but Vince and beside him was a creature that was molting Destiny's face as it lagged. Zach said something, but I didn't hear it.

"Get me the hell out of here! It's Vince and a friggin' zombie!" I screamed into the phone. I turned back around to run and collided with someone, someone who was ready for the impact. Knocked to the ground, I landed on my side and dropped the phone.

"I guess I shouldn't pursue a career in Hollywood." Vince laughed and picked up the phone, putting it to his ear. "Hey, look kid. Your big sister has decided to take her life in a different direction, so just let her go. I'm sure you'll have a nice family reunion on the other side of the river soon enough."

He took the phone away from his ear, sending power into it and destroying it. Dropping the remains, he crouched over me. People were starting to take notice of us, gathering around us. He lashed out, grabbing a fistful of my hair and pulling me to my feet and creating a barrier between us and the citizens, brandishing a black knife in his other hand. He brought it to my neck and the crowd went quiet, unsure what to do.

"One scratch from this poisoned blade will paralyze you. If I actually cut you your heart will stop in three minutes." His breath was hot on my cheek, the knife cold on my neck. "So be a good little princess and cooperate."

"What do you want with me?" I leaned as far away from the knife as I could but between it and his grip on my hair I didn't get very far.

"It's not about what I want, it's about what he wants, and he wants you." I grimaced at how close he was and how much I knew he was enjoying this. "I wanted you too, but you chose that errand boy Captain over me." He hissed.

The crowd was growing restless, and some were starting to recognize me. I looked around, hoping to see maybe a way out of this or to think of something, but my mind was blank.

"While we wait for our ride, maybe we'll be able to hear the twin's screams from here." Forgetting the knife, I struggled against him. He only held tighter. "Careful, I almost cut your beautiful throat." He slid the blade along my skin, not breaking it, but I felt the coolness drag along, threatening death.

"Leave them alone and I'll go with you," I blurted, panicking.

"Really?" He lowered the knife slightly.

"I will go wherever you want!" I squeaked as he brought the knife close to my eye. A shadow passed over us. Vince looked up and smiled before he kissed my cheek.

"Hold tight, Celestial. Our ride is here."

His light wrapped around us, wound through us, and lifted us up, going higher until we were high above the city, and I could see the dragon soaring towards us with zombie Destiny on its back. The next thing I knew we were sitting on its back and the zombie was falling to the pavement below. Vince pulled out his own phone and dropped it too.

"You'll never win this," I promised, watching the golden rope appear around my wrists.

"Darling," he said, "I already have."

10

By the time it grew dark, and Vince was too tired to keep me awake, we landed in a meadow miles away from any towns, farms, or villages. Once we were on the ground the dragon lumbered off through the trees, curling up with its back to us and if it weren't for the trees rustling in its breath I wouldn't have been able to tell it was there. As if being tied in his unbreakable rope wasn't enough he secured me to a tree mere yards away from the dragon.

"Try to escape and I'll have her burn you to a crisp and I'll only heal you enough to keep you alive."

"How can you tell it's a she?" I asked trying to distract him while I sent my Gift to my hands, trying to break the bonds.

Instead of answering he walked to the dragon and rummaged through a pack that was strapped to her back, returning with a thermos, and sleeping bag. The bag he tossed away into the snow but the thermos he kept. Positioning it at my lips, he waited for me to drink.

"I'm not going to kill you," he scoffed. "If that were the plan you never would have left that courtyard." I kept my lips pressed together. No way on Earth or Eä was I going to take him at his word. "Drink."

He pried the rim through my lips, splitting my lower lip in the process and almost chipping a tooth. Losing patience, he yanked my head back and poured the concoction down my throat. Whatever it was, it burned like liquid ghost peppers and tasted like motor oil and copper. My Gift flared before it dimmed and Vince let me fall to the ground, convulsing while the poison did its work.

Ignoring me, Vince set up camp for the night which was rolling out the sleeping bag and starting a very small fire. He curled up and watched me writhe in anguish. My face felt like my bones were melting and restructuring, then my hands and ears started to burn simultaneously while my top canines started to grow from my gums, becoming slightly more prominent. I knew this when I bit my tongue and my mouth filled with blood from the puncture.

When it was over Vince just laid on the other side of the fire and grinned. My hands came to my face as my first instinct and before I could rub away the ache left in my cheeks; I saw shiny black nails with florescent purple moons. Either my skin was pale against the change or my whole complexion was paler. I stared down at my hands, each detail so clear and precise it was like someone implanted magnifying glasses into my eyes and night vision to boot.

The fire was brighter and colors more vivid than I could have imagined and everything else looked so sharp, so clear I could make out minute details passed the small ring of light the fire produced. Finally, I felt my face. Nothing really felt different except my cheek bones were higher and more prominent. Next, I felt my ears, elongated, and pointed tips. I spat the remnants of the poison and blood out onto the ground then ran my tongue over my teeth.

"What did you do?!" I sat up, still looking around and getting a headache from all the new levels of detail and brightness of the night. Even the stars were luminous, more like lights I could touch than distant suns for other worlds.

"Dark elf looks good on you. Makes you exotic."

He winked, grinned that stupid, cocky, crooked grin of his and rolled over, snuggling into his sleeping bag while I sat in the snow. I grabbed a handful, noticing that it was cold, but the temperature didn't bother me like it should. Making as hard a ball I could I chucked it at the back of his head. It exploded before it passed the fire.

"Nothing gets passed me," he yawned.

"Nothing gets passed me," I mimicked, "because I'm Vince, the murderer of friends and man without a soul," I went on. "I recognize your power. You took your friends Gift, didn't you?"

He burrowed deeper into his bag and snapped his fingers. Out went the fire. In the dark everything took on an eerie, serene, crystalline beauty from the snow and moon and stars. It would have been awesome if not for the monster to my left and the dragon to my right and my headache coupled with the dizzy, queasy aftermath of the poison.

"Why change me?" I asked, disturbing him again. He didn't answer, but I expected as much.

He woke before dawn and kicked me in the ribs to rouse me, though I didn't remember falling asleep. It wasn't long after we were in the air again that I was already back asleep.

I dreamed a pale green light hovered behind a tall pine on the edge of a platoon of goblins which had migrated out of the valley where Tristan and his team believed Algoroth was taking refuge. Tucked away in the back and carved into a cliff side was the ruins of his castle, where he forged his battle plan to try and conquer Caleath many hundreds of years ago.

But before Algoroth there was another, more powerful Dark wizard and while Algoroth studied this infamous mage, he could never compete with his wrath and brutality. It was this mage that the goblins were talking about around their campfire, roasting the legs of several antelope they'd torn to pieces on their venture into the grasslands where Tristan and his team caught wind of them.

The green glow softened until it was almost undetectable and what was beneath it was visible. A fairy wearing a pink rose peddle tunic and ivy leaf trousers. Her auburn tresses were shorn to shoulder length and curled out at the ends. Butterfly wings fluttered to keep the frost away while she listened.

"Do you know the origins of the castle ruins?" a tall but thick goblin asked in a deep throaty voice. The others around him looked and waited. "There's a whisper in the stony crags surrounding it that the original owner was one mightier than General Algoroth and who held audience with the Darkness." This goblin stood, animating the story with facial expressions and compelling tone. Everyone including the little fairy listened on the edge of their seats.

"Not long after our mother created us out of the muck and shadows there arose a warrior so gifted in the art of Necromancy and Dark wizardry he threatened to upset the balance of power between all Eä's nations. It took the greatest and best of the Gifted from all the nations to stop him and his undead army. Though he was defeated it is said that his soul could not be contained in Death, so great were his powers. Those who defeated him destroyed his body and sealed him away within the depths of a cave deep beneath the castle ruins."

A figure emerged out of the back of the group, startling everyone. Algoroth laughed and warmed his hands at their fire.

"A master storyteller you are, Commander. Would it please you to serve under Malthor the Necromancer, Master of the League of Shadows?"

The goblin bowed his head and dropped to his knee; dry skinned knuckles clenched over his heart.

"Nothing would please me more than to serve the League of Shadows."

All the goblins murmured their unanimity. The fairy held her breath and kept her wings still, running the risk of them freezing together. She peeked through the branches, hoping to get a clear view. Algoroth smiled, fully exposing his fangs.

"Agreed, comrades. Prepare yourselves for his arrival." He announced. He turned towards the trees and stretched out his hand.

The fairy caught her breath. His blood red power coiled around her and pulled her out into the open. Goblins shrieked and cursed, raging at her discovery. Algoroth's power pulled her nearer until he gripped her in his fist. She trembled, terrified as he leaned his face a few inches from her.

"Mayla of the Inner Forest Clan, inform your Captain that Parna will cease to be a nation long before Malthor begins to crush Caleath."

His release was so sudden that Mayla almost hit the ground before flying away as fast as her wings could carry her. Her heart was pounding. Not only was there a conjoined army of tens of thousands of goblins, trolls, and men, but they were also planning to restore Malthor. She pushed harder. If he knew they were stationed nearby, he certainly wouldn't let them expose their location or battle plans. Mayla was left with the uneasy clarity that ambush was probably already under way. She just had to get to Captain Tristan before they did.

*****

I was slow to wake up. As I did I blinked the vision away and let go of the saddle to wipe the streams of blood off my face before it froze. Mayla. She seemed familiar. I must have known her in my previous life, I mused. Something about that seemed to feel good to the point that I believed we might have been friends.

Vince steered the dragon west and into the setting sun. We'd flown all day without more than a couple stops to relieve bladders. Up ahead, plumes of thick, dark smoke rose from the side of a mountain range. Leaning over the side I could just make out a small group riding away from the smoke and another, larger group riding towards it but they weren't on horses but wingless dragons.

I squinted to see it better and a name surfaced from the depths of my memory. The creature was a drake, and the ones riding them were goblins.

"Who is Malthor?" I asked.

Vince glanced back at me, meeting my eyes for the first time all day. He turned back and continued to guide the dragon towards the valley I'd dreamed about twice now. He hadn't spoken to me since transforming me into a dark elf, a move I didn't quite understand the reasoning for. Even still, it didn't sit well knowing I was a pawn in their game.

It was late when the dragon landed on the edge of a precipice beside an ancient stone castle. Algoroth was there to meet us and laughed when he saw Vince pulling me around like a dog on a leash.

"Well done," Algoroth clapped and took me from him. "I am impressed you made the journey before the new moon tomorrow night."

"As I said I would." Vince scoffed in his usual arrogant way.

"Prepare yourself," Algoroth dropped the friendly façade, "Lady Caoranach is expecting you in the great hall."

Vince sauntered off, head high on his shoulders and Algoroth watched the dragon pick off loose blue and gold speckled scales. He reached down and picked one up, holding it up in the light before passing it to me.

"These are the rarest and hardest materials known to man. Count yourself lucky to even look at one."

I slipped the scale in my pocket, without thinking much about it when he turned and pulled the rope, taking me through a crumbling archway. Inside was as I'd dreamed. It was in better repair than the outside led you to believe, but there were still cracks and drafts everywhere. We descended countless flights of stairs until I was sure we weren't in the castle anymore, but deep within the mountain itself. After what felt like an eternity he opened a door and shoved me into a pitched dark room before leaving without a word. I sent out my Gift, lighting up the place.

More than a few skeletons, humans, and other creatures besides, crowded the small cell. Hanging from the ceiling in the middle of the room was an iron bird cage, housing a very familiar green glow. I put my light out to see her better.

"Mayla?"

I went to her, seeing the dark green on her back where her wings should be. She turned to look at me, confused. I moved in closer so she could see me, and her gasp was enough proof for me that we used to know each other.

"Princess Celestial?" she covered her mouth with her tiny hands.

"I guess whatever Vince did to me is pretty bad?"

I touched my cheek, wishing I had a mirror. It was strange not to know what I looked like.

"The only reason I knew it was you was being able to see your inner light! You're a dark elf! How? When? Why?"

She came to the bars of the cage looking into my eyes, taking it all in. I shrugged and sat down in the thick dust.

"I honestly haven't got a clue why they want me or why they did this." Mayla was quiet. "What happened to your wings?" I finally asked.

"Ice, but they'll be back in a few days." She said flatly. "Tristan said you lost your memories, but you seem to remember me okay." She changed the subject.

"You were in a vision I saw this afternoon. But I saw Algoroth let you go?"

"I was but goblins got me after I split from Tristan to warn your parents... So, you don't remember me?" she asked in a small voice. It broke my heart strings.

"Maybe if we stick together we can get out and you can tell me stories about before all this. You do seem familiar, and I'm bound to remember something sooner or later." I tried to sound confident and cheerful but really I wanted to lay in the dust and scream.

"If we're going to do something we better do it fast cause I heard them talking about trying to raise Malthor on the night of the new moon."

I groaned loudly, "Crap. That would be tomorrow. Algoroth and Vince were talking before they brought me inside."

"Celestial that's why they brought you here." Mayla poked her head out through the bars to look down at me. "They think they can take your Gift and your soul and use them in a spell to break him out of his prison and give him new life."

"Why am I so lucky?" I sulked.

"There's something else they're plotting, and I don't know what it is. It's got something to do with your bloodline…"

"How do you know all this? Does Tristan?" I laid back and a plume of dust clouded around my head. I fanned it away.

"No, I learned it after I was captured. Goblins are big gossips."

"Did they gossip about a way out of here?" I asked without much hope. Mayla laughed, and it wasn't the sort that brought smiles to other people's faces.

"At least in this dire situation you haven't lost your sense of humor," she replied.

"Yay."

I looked at my hands tied in front of me as my Gift brightened up the space. I grimaced at my now naturally black nails and hoped I could be put back to normal. My Gift burned around the rope, fueled each time I thought of Vince and all he'd put me through. Behind closed eyes I imagined my light burning through the gold and setting me free. When I looked down, I chocked back a frustrated cry. As hot as my wrists were I was going to burn my hands off before the gold.

"No luck?" Mayla looked down at me, head poking through the bars.

"No." I sat up again and sent out an orb and made it float to the top of our cell. "But really we should figure a way out of here."

With the room now lit up we both looked around. Grey, grey and more grey. All around us was nothing but stone blocks and bones and chains. Even the door was made from dark grey wood. I walked to it, feeling it, knocking on it, testing it.

"If the palace had doors like this nobody would ever get in."

"Celestial..." Mayla complained, pulling at her hair. "Time to get serious!"

Despite the burning and the sting from before, my light was in my hands once again. Palm pressed over the lock, power like molten lava poured out of me, melting the lock. My hand burned while the lock melted, but rather than stop I clamped my mouth shut and forced more power out. When the door swung free I stopped. My hands were red, swollen and blistered in some places, and some of those were bleeding.

"You did it! Now get me out of this cage so we can get out of here!"

"Let me fix my hand first..."

I looked down at it. There was more of my light shining through some parts than others while I tried to remember how I'd healed myself in my dream. I closed my eyes tight, imagining my hand, whole and perfect, with normal pink nails to boot. I felt my power working, felt the fibers of my skin and tendons weaving back together until my Gift eventually just pulled back and went dormant. Upon investigation my heart sank. My hand was healed but my nails were still black.

"Better?" Mayla asked, head tilted to the side.

"Yeah," I sighed. "Let's get you out." I made towards her cage, but when I did Mayla screamed. I turned and heard the sickening crack on my scull before I felt it and lost consciousness, never seeing my assailant.

11

The last of sweet, crisp, golden, bubbling nectar passed through my lips, smooth on the way down. It wasn't often we served Fairy food at our galas but tonight was a special night and who didn't like a delicacy from the Fae Queen? It didn't alter perceptions or inhibitions like earthly legends claimed, but it was freaking delicious and made everything else taste like dirt. Tristan held my hand while people danced and socialized around us. I heard my name and Tristan's which wasn't surprising. It was our engagement party after all.

Despite that, unease prevented me from enjoying it. I smiled, graciously shaking hands with the Duke of Nule after Tristan. Even though I was used to crowds, used to being over stimulated, everything was just too loud. My eyes watered and burned when I looked up towards the chandeliers. That meant only one thing.

"These drinks always make me want waffles," I cut into Tristan's conversation with the duke, rubbing my temples even though I knew it wouldn't take any of the pain away.

"Waffles?" he repeated.

"Fresh ones," I confirmed.

"With ice cream?" he asked, confusing the duke further. I nodded, seeing the realization cross his face. Nobody else knew what this meant. Nobody else but him would understand why it was needed. Not my family. Not my guards. Only him.

"Well, I better get back to the old lady," the duke nodded awkwardly and slipped skillfully back among the guests.

He guided me through the people. Though I tried to keep my head down to block out the light people still found my gaze and moved back to let us by.

"Tristan," my hand slipped out of his and everything around me shifted and faded until there was nothing left that looked the same.

In the valley outside Kings City endless lines and rows of soldiers surrounded the city, becoming the only line of defense between whatever was coming and the capitol of Caleath, and the doorway into Earth. The wall was all but gone, rubble piled high in places and scattered in others. Even though I couldn't see through the fog and the smoke into the city I got the distinct impression it was empty. This kind of knowing only came in visions.

Time passed. The sun was rising and falling faster than I could count and then the army moved. Zach led them; stopping before they reached the edge, ready to face the hordes racing through the trees. I saw the men's rotten faces before they entered the valley. Zach raised his sword. The vision ended there, sending me back into the gala, falling into Tristan's arms and waking up simultaneously.

I woke on the ground confused. Where was Tristan? Where was I? Then it all came back to me when I saw Mayla in the cage a few feet away and Vince stirring the contents of a cauldron over a fire of purple and green flames. The vision... I forced my thoughts through the fog in my head and the headache from whatever knocked me out. The vision must be a result of whatever Vince and Algoroth and the Witch were up to. I struggled to sit up, between my spinning head and the gold chain binding my wrists.

"Good evening sleeping beauty," Vince chirped without looking up.

I looked from him to the rest of the room, taking it all in and hoping to find an exit strategy. My hopes fell as suddenly as they'd risen. There was only two ways out, one was jumping over the railing and falling heaven only knew how far down, and Algoroth was guarding the other. I looked up, unable to see the stars in the black sky above us because of the glare from the fire and because the moon was overshadowed, making the night darker than most.

A void opened between me and the fire, the same doorway of darkness the witch had opened in my old bedroom the night Stacey died. I held my breath, waiting for her to come through the void that seemed to pull all the warmth from the room, and sure enough she did. She set her cold eyes upon me, closed the void, and turned to Vince.

"Let's hope your assumptions prove correct."

She turned from him, not bothering to acknowledge his bow or notice as he backed away towards the edge of the room. Beside the Cauldron was a silver goblet. The witch looked to Algoroth, then to me as she picked it up and moved slowly closer.

"This would be a great time for you to use your Gift Celestial!" Mayla yelled at me from across the room.

I sent it out but before it reached my hands pain shot through my entire body, making me see stars as Algoroth's power immobilized me from behind. The witch grinned, showing her rotten teeth, all filed to sharp little pinpoints. My Gift pushed against Algoroth's as it was forced back into my heart.

"Don't worry little fairy," the witch crooned, "all I want is a little blood, and a bit of her soul." She reached into her robe, pulling out a long black metal dagger and surged forward, plunging the blade into my heart, and carving up. A ruby on the hilt of the dagger lit up. Her smile spread across her face. "Well, well. Your intuition was right, Vince."

"Celestial!" Mayla screamed.

Blood poured from me into the chalice while Algoroth kept my heart beating and blood pumping as the witch tore me open. My Gift, now exposed, made her wince, but she pressed on. Filling the goblet, taking a sip. She passed it off to Vince, grinning at me while her skin shifted and tightened until she looked as young as I was. All of this I watched frozen within myself, unable to move or look away while Algoroth had control of me.

Chanting words, I didn't understand she cut deeper then slowly pulled out the blade an inch at a time, drawing out the source of my light, my soul. Once it was free the whole balcony seemed to become bright as day. She slashed it, cutting through and fragmenting it. Vince came to her side, holding a pendant identical to the one Algoroth had used on me before. All but one small fragment of light went into the stone. This sliver she collected into her palm, closing her fingers loosely over it before depositing it back into me, and then loosely closing the wound with a power of her own.

Algoroth kept control of me, keeping me conscious and on my feet. The witch waited until Vince emptied the goblet and dropped the pendant, stirring counterclockwise seven times. Leaning over the bubbling brew, she called out into the night.

"Malthor!" She called once. The ground shook and I could hear in the distance loose rocks tumbling down the cliff face. "Malthor!" She called again and the fire went out. Now the only light was mine within the cauldron, and it was slowly dimming. "Malthor!" She cried into the night one final time and the Darkness closed in around us like a living thing.

Everyone held their breath as we plunged into pitched darkness. The fire slowly returned, burning blue, orange and yellow instead of purple and green. Someone new stood across from the witch, someone cloaked in wispy shadows and a long black cape.

"Receive this soul and serve the Darkness," The witch stretched out her hand and he leaned closer over the cauldron, allowing her to deposit another one of my soul's fragments into him. "All hail the League of Shadows!" she cackled into the night. "We have returned!"

That was the last thing I knew before Algoroth released me to my own strength. I dropped to my knees with the rest of them, though I kept falling. Mayla was the only one standing, though none of the others cared. Malthor crossed the balcony to her, collecting the cage and then coming to me as I fell back onto the ground, gasping for air and finding none. He bent and touched my heart where the witch had cut it through, healing only my heart.

"Caleath and Earth are mine." He smiled and set Mayla down beside me. "Take them back to Kings City." He stood swiftly and turned to Vince. "I want a challenge before I burn this country to ashes."

I saw Vince's mouth move, but his reply fell upon deaf ears as the pain from losing my Gift and most of my soul broke through the shock. He came, slung me over his shoulder and picked up the cage. Everything else was a blur, how we got through the ruins, when we reached his dragon and when we started flying. All I knew was the dragon's talons kept me from plummeting hundreds of feet to my death.

We didn't fly long, just long enough for the valley and the castle ruins to be lost from view. At the base of a forest, we landed. The dragon all but dropped me, and Vince dumped Mayla out of the cage and onto the ground beside me.

"Let's see Caleath's warrior princess now," he scoffed. "Not killing you is the only mercy I want to offer, but the others don't want you dead."

He pressed his palm over my heart, reopening the wound, and then sent his power into me, healing me better than Malthor had, though not much. I felt my remaining sliver of light begin to grow and he must have felt it too because he pulled back, scowling. "You can get yourselves home if you can get through the gate. Oh, and don't bother planning a wedding. Tristan will never make it out of Parna alive."

He climbed back into the saddle, leaving us on our own. I closed my eyes, hardly feeling the snowflakes settle over me, or the layer of snow I lay on. Within minutes of his departure, I lost consciousness and the light snowfall increased with the winds creating all the conditions needed for a blizzard. Unable to wake me, Mayla found refuge from the storm under my sweater and wrapped up in the bottom hem of my shirt.

*****

I woke up in a panic, in my own room, lit by a soft pink nightlight plugged in beside my bed. I touched my chest where the witch stabbed me, finding no scar, no pain, and my light and soul were completely intact. How? I wondered. Breathing slowly, I took a look around the room, forcing myself to chill out. I was safe, at least for the moment and I was home, but how? I wondered again.

My eyes adjusted quickly, letting me see the little vanity set up by the French balcony doors. Even from here I could see the flower stickers all over the mirror, and all the plastic beauty items scattered all over the surface. They were mine, I remembered, from when I was a little girl. Tossing the covers aside I went to it, picking up the old familiar things, touch memories coming back to me of when mom came and played dress-up with me the day before.

I looked into the mirror at myself, seeing not who I knew myself to be, but the little four-year-old me from which the memories came. The realization made me smile, a bit relived I didn't have to face reality yet. I went back to bed, climbing in and pulling the covers to my chin. Without even thinking about it my Gift came out, lighting up the room as if it were the middle of the day.

There was no pain, in fact there was a sense of relief, as if I'd been holding my breath and only now inhaled. Using it felt good, not like while Zach was training me or in the dungeon... I laid down, not turning the light off. What had I even been doing awake when this really happened? My mind went to the vision I'd had at the gala. That wasn't the first time I'd had that vision, but this, the time I was in now, was!

The door cracked open, and someone looked in. I was shocked to find a six-year-old version of Tristan looking in on me.

"You should be sleeping," he said.

"So should you." The reply was automatic. "Why are you up so late?" I asked.

"My mom and dad let me stay up until nine thirty on weekends," he smiled proudly. I remembered my bedtime was eight o'clock. I turned my head to check the time.

"You just have a little while left." I sat up.

"Go back to sleep before my dad comes back. He'll have to tell your dad on you," Tristan warned.

"I can't," I said sheepishly. Tristan rolled his eyes but waited for me to tell him why. "I can't because I had a scary dream and I think it was of the future."

"You can't see the future," he insisted, coming all the way into the room, and leaving the door cracked open. He stood in front of my bed, hands on his hips.

"But it wasn't a normal dream. I could feel things, like I was awake. It was..." I stopped there, my little four-year-old mind at a loss for words.

"Should I get my dad?" he asked, stepping back.

"No!" I didn't mean to yell, but I did. "Don't you know?" I asked, quieting down again.

"Know what?" he asked hesitantly, but he stayed where he was.

"My mamma taught me that visions only come from Dark magic... from witches. I don't want them to think I'm a witch. I don't even know how I could see it." Tristan was quiet for a few seconds, thinking, before he came over and sat on the bed with me.

"Maybe it was your Gift. Yesterday my mom told me the story of how Queen Sagan made the Gift. Mom said that it was made from the Dark and the Light, so maybe that's how come you dreamed the future. I've heard some Gifted people can do it."

I curled into a ball, holding my knees close. I was still thinking things over when Tristan slid off the bed and crossed the room to the door.

"I won't tell anyone your secret, not unless you need me to."

"Thank you," I smiled shyly, hiding in the blanket. "Wait," I stretched out my hand as he turned to go. More power went to my hands, I made a single white rose. I looked at it and then looked at him, who was standing there with his chin on the floor. "Give it to your mom for me." I held it out to him, and he crossed the room to receive it.

"What are you doing in here son?" His dad startled us both, standing in the doorway.

"I had a bad dream, and he came to talk to me," I said.

"What about?" he asked, walking up to Tristan.

"Waffles," Tristan said quickly, clutching the rose.

"Waffles?" he asked, looking from his son to me, one eyebrow arched.

"They were gonna eat me!" I lied. Tristan giggled.

"Did Tristan help you feel better so you can go back to sleep?" He asked.

"Yes," I yawned and laid down, and Tristan reached out, pulling the blanket over my shoulder.

"Good night Princess," He and his dad went to the door, closing it behind them.

Once it closed I reigned in my Gift and the room was dark again. Even though the room was warm I started shivering, feeling a cold that came from my core and out until my fingers were burning and my toes were numb, the light was changing and the walls fading into nothing. Pale morning sunlight shined down on the glittering snow dusting my body.

"Celestial!" Mayla hovered in front of my face, using very small wings, even for her. The pain came flooding into my consciousness, making my eyes water. "Don't cry!" she begged, shivering. "It's going to be ok... somehow." She looked around, though there was nothing much to see and nobody around to help.

"You're wings..." I paused there, trying to breathe through the burning in my chest.

"They grew back a little," Mayla dismissed. "Can you walk? We've got to get out of the open. This is not good! Nobody can see you like this! Can you heal yourself? Do you remember how?"

I didn't get up, despite her urgency. "No," I winced. "I don't have enough of my Gift left to do anything."

"If someone finds you here, looking like a Black elf, they will kill you without thought, and they would be following the law."

"Vince said he turned me into a Dark elf," I said dumbly.

"There are a few different kinds of Dark elves. You are a Black elf, which means you being in Caleath has broken a centuries old treaty that forbids communications between Black elves and us." Mayla explained, watching me continue to lie on the ground.

"Go to the palace without me." I watched her face go from shock to denial and then to anger, but she said nothing while I tried to sit up. Ice that had formed on my shirt from the blood cracked and brushed my bare skin underneath my shirt, making me colder. "You're faster," I said, wrapping my shaking arms around me in a futile attempt to warm myself.

"I can't leave my best friend here," she replied indignantly, "besides, it would be treason to leave you here to die. I can't do that to you." She landed on my lap, knees shaking, and arms folded. Though she wasn't flying she kept her new wings moving to keep them from freezing off.

"I can't go. I have to find Tristan before he gets to Parna."

"He'll kill you when he sees you! It doesn't matter what country he's in!"

"But what choice do I have?" I moved, attempting to stand. I got unsteadily to my feet, with Mayla flying before me, talking in circles about how big an idiot I was. Once I was on my feet and not likely to fall over I looked her dead in the eye.

"Mayla, listen." I tried to sound like when I knew the power my position as Princess offered me. She stopped talking but wouldn't look at me, choosing instead to close her eyes. "Look, I don't want to do this alone, and maybe I might have a shot of getting Tristan to listen to me if you were with me, but someone has to warn my family. Malthor is coming, and there's too many lives at stake for me to ask you not to deliver that message." Mayla finally opened her eyes, looking like water filled marbles.

"But you're my best friend. I don't want to say goodbye."

"Maybe it won't be forever," I tried to sound hopeful, but winced. My chest hurt so much. "I was cursed with magic," I went on, "maybe there's some magic that can change me back before I find him."

Part Three

12

The first few weeks on my own were miserable. I wandered around in a pained daze for a week, just trying to get my bearings. Unlike what I told Mayla, I held no hope that I would find someone to fix me before I found Tristan, so I set out to find him. Even if I didn't talk to him right away I had to at least figure out where he was. I was almost spotted a few times but learned quickly to stay off the road. If I could see the road, travelers and soldiers could see me. The next thing I learned was that I could go two weeks without needing to eat, and three without sleep, and subzero temperatures weren't enough to kill me. All helpful things, but the most useful thing I discovered was my new inhuman speed. One afternoon I was running, trying to keep warm and cover as much ground as I could when I unexpectedly came on a new road, and I wasn't alone.

A thick hooded jacket covered the man enough to where I couldn't see his face when I came alongside him and his horse at a full gallop. We matched speeds, though I nearly tripped over myself when I realized how fast I was going. The man pulled his reins, taking control of his horse I accidentally startled. I didn't stop, didn't dare, not with Mayla's warning playing on repeat in my head.

That night I also discovered I could move much more quietly when I tried, and to my shame this was learned sneaking a loaf of bread out of a bakery, and lifting a long black hooded coat, tan trousers, leather boots, and a plain white shirt out of the shop across the street. Alone, trapped with night terrors and inescapable pain, starving, scared and now stealing... If there was a rock bottom, this had to be it, I thought. What would Tristan think of me, seeing me so low? I ached to see him, but what Mayla had said... terrified me even if I never said it out loud.

Hidden behind a fence a mile from the shops I devoured the bread before I changed clothes, leaving mine buried in some snow to be found by someone in the spring. These new clothes weren't the best fit, I had to admit, looking down at myself, but I was significantly warmer and blended in better. The dragon scale remained in my old pocket. Not that a dragon scale wasn't cool, but all I saw when I looked at it was Vince's stupid face. I pulled the hood over my head, and turned to look at myself in a darkened, dirty window.

Though I couldn't see the details of my face, I did see that the hood shadowed me enough anyway so I could walk the streets. I looked so... strange, for lack of a better word. My face was dirty, clothes crisp, hair a little more than tangled, and not to mention the dried blood on my face from seeing flashes of visions that seemed to come in no order, and about no particular thing. Visions of a hearth where pastries cooked, then an elf on a bridge, a boy playing on a boat, guards running through a castle... all just snippets, and I hadn't bled after all of them. I couldn't remember what that meant.

Setting my thoughts aside and taking a deep breath, I stepped out into the open. One little boy looked my way but quickly followed his mother out of sight. I sighed, hands in my pockets and walking lightly. Though I knew from vague memories where Parna was, I still wasn't sure where exactly to go, or where I even was. I'd been traveling west since Mayla left, and figured that was still my best bet, but there had to be a shop around here with maps, right?

I looked around, wandering up and down the roads until one shop looked promising, Dane's Maps, Atlas, and Books.

I peered inside through the foggy glass and seeing nobody inside figured it was safe enough. If it weren't I could grab a map and book it, I figured, chewing the inside of my lip as I turned the knob and went inside. A little bell over the door jingled, alerting anyone inside to my presence.

"Welcome!" came the voice of an older gentleman. I heard shuffling footsteps and a third thump in rhythm with his steps.

"I'm looking for a map of Lyonshire and Parna." I called back, though a little nervously. "I'm traveling..." That was a normal request right? After not talking to anyone for almost a month my social skills were more than rusty.

"Well, you're in the right place," he came out from behind a door, bearing a stack of books so tall he couldn't see over it. "Let me just put these down over here..." he went into the next room over, mumbling something about glue and parchment.

I moved through the store's entrance. Each wall was filled with stacks of books from the floor to the ceiling, clearly not what I was after. The next room looked promising. Stacks of scrolls and tables filled with globes cluttered the room. It was clear to me that the man must have organized the shop himself.

"So, you're traveling?" he said, coming up from behind me. "That's wonderful, just wonderful. I traveled across the sea when I was a young man, went with my sweetheart to Old Wilden. There's a fine bakery there that I've never been able to find the likes. So," he paused, picking up a scroll, opening it and scanning it quickly before rolling it back up. "What kind of map do you need? Geographical, topographical, a road map maybe? I can't promise it'll be the most accurate for Wilden, that place changes all the time! I hear they have what's called a skyscraper now! Do you know what that is?"

He finally stopped talking and turned to me, finding me hidden behind a scroll that was far from what I needed, unless I planned to head north to the Islands of Ire.

"I've actually been to New York City, once when I was little. I've never felt so small before." I answered, hoping I wasn't sounding too awkward.

"Wait.. you mean on Earth?" he exclaimed, gathering more maps into his hands. "How did you get into King's City without the guards spotting you?" He asked. I felt my heart drop into my stomach and my whole frame went rigid. "I know your kind when I see you." He said, his voice taking on a different tone, though non-threatening.

"And you're still talking to me?" I rolled up the scroll, doing my best not to tear it with my fumbling fingers.

"A customer is a customer, and you're a different sort. Usually, your kind just walk in and take what they want and vanish. I must thank you for not doing that, but you can't stay long. I don't want that kind of attention. I run a respectable shop, and I won't have you ruin my reputation."

"I wouldn't dream of it, Mr..." I paused, and he didn't answer, just looked down at me through the bridge of his nose. I cleared my throat. "So... anyway, what's the best route to Lyonshire from here?" I asked.

"Just head west over the mountains, cross the ocean and there you go." His tone was getting short.

"Right... Look can I just see a map and I'll be on my way?" I folded my arms and held his gaze.

"You're unarmed." His arms scanned me up and down.

"... As far as you can see..." I answered evasively, backing out towards the entry. Honestly, I was unarmed. I didn't dare try to use my Gift. I hadn't since Malthor's return.

"You're elf magic won't work in here. The whole place is warded... If I turn you in I'll get a nice sum." He followed me, standing up straighter, setting aside his cane and somehow looking much, much stronger. "Lucky for me they don't need all of you."

"I'm just gonna keep wingin' it..." I spun around and dashed for the exit, hurrying down the road before he could call for guards or do whatever it was he wanted to do.

I ran until I reached the edge of town, about to cross over the bridge. I slowed, boots ticking the stones. The metal buttons on the hooded coat clinked, cold and unforgiving against the stone ledge I leaned over, looking down into the dark rushing waters. Other footsteps moved behind me. I tensed but ignored them, letting them walk up to the ledge beside me and lean against it, casually looking me over and eating something. Steam wafted into view, and then the smell. Beefy and savory... A meat pastry. Onion, garlic, several aromatic herbs I couldn't identify... My mouth watered.

"I doubt your bread was better than this," the man said, mouth half full, "and thank the light you ditched those clothes. Any longer in the same outfit and I would've had to rip them off you."

I turned my head, looking over in disgust. He shoved the last of the pastry in his mouth and chewed noisily while he brushed the crumbs off his shirt. I paused... this was the one from one of my visions. Clearly I was not a threat to him, but it was just as clear that he could be a threat to me. His eyes were human enough, but long, pointed ears, and sharp canines marked him as an elf, what kind I wasn't sure. I turned my face back to the water, tamping down my panic.

"That shop owner could have killed you. Be more careful who you trust." He snickered, shaking his head, and folding his arms.

"How long?" I asked cautiously, still trying to keep calm.

"How long what?" He reached towards my hood then thought better of it.

"How long have you been following me?" I stepped away, turning to fully face him. He was armed literally to the teeth, a sword on each hip, knives strapped everywhere, armored gloves, bow, arrows, and a spear strapped to his back and needles to keep his long hair pulled back. "And how did I not notice?" I'd meant this last part to be internal and flushed when I realized I'd spoken out loud.

"I, and any other fae, can see through the curse. Because of my long-standing friendship with your family, I'll take you to Parna.

But Princess," He lowered his voice and closed the space between us in a breath. "How did you become this? Last I heard on the wind you had been reunited with your family."

He linked arms with me, but none too gently ushered us back into town. Stunned, I let him lead me on. While I didn't remember him, it seemed familiar that my family was on friendly terms with elves.

"It's a long story, which would explain why I have to ask who you are?" I finally answered him after we were inside a small home, lit only by the fire in the hearth.

I didn't notice his hair was white until he sat across from me, other than that, there were no aging characteristics about him. Nervously I picked up the pastry and took a small bite, ignoring the fact that this was the hearth, and these were the pastries from my other vision.

"I'd just pulled those out of the oven when I saw you run past my window. I knew if I didn't follow you I wouldn't catch up with you for a while, and even dark elves need more than bread."

"It's delicious, thank you," I said, going in for another bite.

"I am Lord Moset, brother to the Emperor of the Light Elves within Alfheim."

"Where is Alfheim?" I asked, careful not to slaughter the pronunciation.

I was sure it sounded familiar, and more than sure Destiny would have drilled me on it. For the past several weeks I'd been more focused on healing and getting to Tristan than remembering the makeup of Eä.

"To the east of Caleath," he answered. "We share the Blue Mountains."

I finished the pastry and sat back, not full, but satisfied. It was wonderful to have hot food in my stomach again. Moset peeked through the drawn curtains and out onto the dark street.

"Are you expecting someone?" I asked, hoping to sound friendly.

"I am, actually, someone you know well. You're just ahead of Commander Tristan, by some miracle." Every muscle in my body tensed. "I've arranged for him and his highest-ranking officer to stay with me tonight and tomorrow so they can restock before they head to sea."

"Then why did you bring me here?" I nearly knocked the chair over jumping to my feet. "Unless you have a cure-all for death I'm screwed! The moment they see me I'm dead!"

"Calm," he put out his hands and I knotted mine. "If he or any of his officers were to find you on your own they would execute you immediately. You are my guest, for now, and as I said I will escort you to Parna."

"So, they can't hurt me?" I asked, wrapping my arms around myself.

"I am going to try to persuade them not to."

All my manners out the window, I groaned loudly and ran my fingers through my hair, gripping it at the base of my scalp. Moset ignored me, crossing the room to the hearth and pulling another tray of pastries out of the little brick oven and putting them on a cloth on the table.

"There's a washroom if you go into the next room and up the stairs. Get cleaned up and try not to worry, Princess." He kept working, pulling out plates and utensils, cloth napkins, lighting fresh candles and filling the lamp with oil to brighten the room.

"Thank you."

I turned away and followed his direction. A bath was just what the doctor ordered, and honestly I did not want to be in the room while Tristan and Moset argued over me. Either it would end bad and bloody, or Tristan would tolerate my presence until we were out of the country.

I climbed the stairs and looked around. There were three halls I could take. I headed down the widest one that ran the length of the stairs and tried each door, but one was a closet, and the other was a bedroom. It wasn't until I'd looked in every room that I finally found it, tucked in the back corner.

The washroom was small. Just a manual water pump, a tiny hearth to heat water at and a tub I wouldn't be able to stretch out in. Though the water was near freezing I filled the tub just enough and went to town, scrubbing every inch of myself with the only bar of soap I could find, then dabbed what looked and smelled like olive oil on the ends of my hair to help the comb through.

I was fully dressed and draining the tub when noise exploded from downstairs, and a stampede rushed up the stairs and through the door. Tristan wasn't heading the pack but bringing in the rear and keeping Moset back. I froze, backed against the tub staring down the blade at my neck from a familiar looking soldier.

"Kind of short for an elf," Tristan mused.

"Commander, she is not a threat. On my honor, you can trust her." Moset was still trying to force his way into the room, but Tristan wouldn't budge.

"Officer Sean, carry on," Tristan ordered. Sean, the man holding the blade, came to memory, on a beautiful lake with our friends, food, and volleyball, before Vince betrayed us.

"Hands behind your back and kneel slowly." Sean's voice was clear, but I'd barely put my hands behind me when he knocked my legs out from under me. My cheek smashed the side of the tub. Blood gushed everywhere from the split. They ignored it, moving fast to bind my hands and drag me down to the front parlor room in front of the hearth.

"You are making a grave mistake," Moset warned, kneeling beside me. I wasn't sure how he got passed Tristan and Sean, but he was there, cupping his hand over my cheek. "I promised to escort her to Parna."

"And what makes her so important she can break the treaty?" Tristan demanded.

Moset looked down at me, then back at Tristan. "Nothing, Commander, but she was brought into Caleath against her will on her travels and I only recently recovered her."

My head throbbed and the room seemed to tip one way then the other as it became brighter, and I had to close my eyes.

Flurries of movement rushed around me, men screaming, arrows and blasts of power flying through the air. When my vision cleared bodies laid around the cart I was chained to, and Tristan was the only one besides me still standing. He turned to me, fire in his eyes and gripped my shirt collar.

"Why leave you alive?" he raged. "Why kill all my men and not you? You of a cursed and filthy race? You're in cahoots with them... you have to be!" I made to deny but he shoved me into the side of the cart, pinning me against it. "We will make it to Parna, through the doorway and back to Kings City, and so help me you will hang." Breathing out in all his furry he released me, stalking off to drag his men to the side of the road. The vision ended, bringing me back to the present with a single bead of blood tearing from my eye.

"Princess what did you see?" Moset was holding me while Sean and Tristan both stood at the ready, swords drawn and pointed at me.

"There'll be an ambush for you and your men, somewhere outside of Parna," I panted, speaking directly to Tristan.

"Who are you and why should I stay my sword against the kind that killed my father?"

"I am nobody." I winced as I sat up and gently pushed Lord Moset away with my shoulder. "So, kill me if you like."

I remained seated staring up at Tristan and fighting the urge to cry and tell him everything. He wouldn't believe me, not now anyway, not while I looked like this. He stared down his blade at me. I closed my eyes, waiting for the strike. Instead, a moment later he tore out of the room, hissing as he left. Sean remained, just as stunned as the rest of us.

"Where is the ambush supposed to be?" Sean asked.

"Not sure. It was on a dirt road in some back country. I just know you hadn't reached Parna yet..." I trailed off into a pause, picturing the country, everything I could see. "I think," I said as I opened my eyes, "it's outside of Caleath. The terrain is too different." Sean stepped away and his eyes gravitated from me to Lord Moset and then to the pastries laid out on the table.

"It must be somewhere in Lyonshire. If it's not here, or Parna, that's the only other kingdom we'd pass through on our way."

"As I will be escorting her out of the country anyway, I offer my services to aid in your men's safety."

"I don't think so." Tristan stood on the threshold, arms folded and staring daggers at me. "As of this moment she is under the arrest of the Imperial Army of Caleath and will remain with us as our prisoner until such a time as her sentence can be carried out or your story proves true."

Moset's eyes narrowed but he didn't say a word and remained where he was when Sean pulled me to my feet.

"May we hold her here with us until our departure?" Tristan didn't sound like he was expecting a no but waited for an answer.

Finally, Moset nodded and composed himself, shoulders and arms relaxing while retaining impeccable posture. "I would prefer that, Commander. I'll show you both your rooms and let you decide in what other room she'll spend the night."

I almost sighed but didn't get the chance before Moset was on the move and Sean was hurrying me out of the room and up the stairs after the Elf Lord and Imperial Commander of the Army. I stumbled more than once on the way up and chalked it up to the fact that my eyes were still stinging from the light and my head and face were throbbing. Perhaps there was more to see, I mused, or I had a concussion. Tristan's room was the first off the stairs, not huge but a queen-sized bed and an already lit fireplace looked inviting. Sean's room was one down from the washroom, and was almost identical to Tristan's, except the bed was a full and not a queen. Both rooms sported matching wardrobes carved out of a fine dark hardwood and a matching end table and desk.

"There's one other room available which is the smallest guest room at the end of the hall." "She'll stay here, where she can be properly watched," was Tristan's automatic response.

I glanced at Sean who looked as uncomfortable as I felt but simply straightened his shoulders and nodded, "Yes sir, Commander." Moset sighed.

"Take a short rest, get something to eat, grab your things. I'll stand watch until you're done."

Dismissed, he relaxed and cast me one long sidelong glance before he left the room and another look from Tristan to Moset left us on our own. Howling wind whistled passed the house, filling the silence between us, but it wasn't loud enough to hide the scrape of Tristan's sword against the sheath.

"Only a select few people know the protocol for finding one of you in our lands. The royal family, their advisors, and the highest-ranking military personnel. Moset must know, or he wouldn't be trying so hard." Tristan stood taller and secured his grip. "Regardless of if you were brought here willingly I can't break the oath I made to my king."

"I respect that, but you need to listen to what I have to say before you... follow through." I said, understanding him a little too late.

The chair scraped against the floor as I tried to sit straight and shift to face him. His face was a fresh canvas, or it would have been to someone who didn't know him at all. Feelings surged, making my voice tremble. While he was calm, I knew he didn't want to lift his sword, even to a black elf.

"I was taken from my home to Algoroth's and cursed with a potion that turned me into what you see. While I was there I learned that their army, the one you sent Mayla to warn the king about, isn't our only problem." He narrowed his eyes, raising the tip of his sword at me, coming close.

"How do you know my messenger?"

"She was there in the castle with me, and she can witness to my words." I carried on, despite the sword and that he was about to speak, "The witch, the one Vince and Algoroth serve, used me in a ritual to bring someone back to life. His name is Malthor, and he plans to bring more forces to their army and there's another part of their plan... I'm not sure what, but... I know it's nothing good."

When I was done the blade was much too close for comfort. He leaned in, studying me. I met his gaze, remembering that night after the gala outside my bedroom... The last time I could really look him in the eyes. I breathed steady. Feelings aside, I had to survive this before I could think about anything else.

"Where are you from?" he asked, stepping back.

"Kings City," I tried to relax.

"Who took you from your home?"

"...Vince. He's also the one who cursed me."

"There's a lot of people in this world who go by Vince. How do you know I know who you mean?" His sword was up and ready again.

"He used to serve as a palace guard and staged a coup to overthrow the royal family."

"Alright but why would he take you? What makes you so special?"

This time I paused. The only way to answer this was to tell him who I was and if I did there was no way of telling how he'd take it. "I don't know," I answered honestly. "Mayla overheard something about my bloodline, but we don't know why that would matter to them."

Tristan watched me closely for a minute until his gaze went to the window. He just watched, quietly chewing the inside of his bottom lip, and furrowing his brows together in thought. He didn't lower his sword. Neither did he bring it closer to my neck.

"I suppose you haven't recognized me yet?" I asked when he still didn't move. I held my breath while he brought his eyes to mine and lowered the sword just a little. He studied me closely.

"I imagine if you were really a black elf this confrontation would have been drastically different. I've never known one to be compliant or so calm... I assume if I'm supposed to recognize you, that we know each other. Tell me what I need to know." The sword clinked against the scabbard as he slid it inside and dropped his hands to his sides, waiting for me.

"You can trust Moset, so take his word. I'll tell you everything that happened when this is all over. Don't undo the bonds, at least until we're out of Caleath. As long as I look like this I want to stay low... I'm sorry you have to deal with me."

"Moset knows something... Otherwise I don't think he'd go out of his way to save you. He risked a lot, bringing you into his home." He turned and walked to the door, pausing briefly to look back at me. "Wait here. I'll be back."

With that he left the room and locked the door behind him. I heard muffled voices but couldn't make out the words. Darkness soothed my stinging eyes, and I watched behind closed lids as the vision finally came. The sound of leaves and the wind running through my hair prompted me to open my eyes. An endless stretch of blue expanded before me, waves breaking in the distance and closer by a few people walked down the beach along the shore, wrapped in scarves and cloaks. Seated beside me on a bench was a little boy, probably no older than six or seven.

"I can't believe we're going to Parna." He said. "Do you think Commander Tristan will let me ride on the same boat as him? How long does it take to sail there anyway? Do we go right there, or do we go through other places first? Will there be Giants? My brother once said Parna has giants..." His questions raced out, uninhibited and with hardly a breath in-between.

Clearly he wasn't scared of me. Did he know who I was or maybe that I wasn't what I appeared to be? At the mention of his brother he paused, looking at me with his big, glassy brown eyes. My heart broke. What happened to his brother? A fat tear rolled down his cheek and I put an arm around his shoulder, drawing him in. He didn't fight me and even leaned into me.

"I'm sure the Commander would love to have you on his ship." I hugged him and he sniffled, using the corner of his cloak to dry his eyes and wipe his nose.

"I hate goblins," He mumbled.

The vision ended there, bringing me back to the mild concussion, throb in my chest, and an ache in my neck. I lifted my head off the back of the chair and rolled my shoulders and my neck, soothing a bit of the discomfort away.

"Oh good, my roommate's awake. Don't expect me to share the bed." I startled and he laughed. "You didn't think we'd leave someone like you alone all night, did you?" Sean scoffed and closed his book, depositing it on the little table beside the bed he reclined on.

"What time is it?"

"Almost dawn," he sighed.

"And you haven't slept?" I asked, trying to ignore the drip coming from my eye that was more than likely blood.

"Not as soundly as you did," he retorted. "What did you see, anyway? And I thought all kinds of Dark Elves were immune to the effects of visions?"

"I saw a little boy," I said shortly, not bothering to acknowledge his other comment.

Sean got up from the bed, bed frame creaking softly at his shifting weight. His footsteps were almost soundless but didn't fall on deaf ears even if I didn't bother to watch him get up and walk over to me, stopping a couple feet away. I stared down at the floor, then at his socks when he got close enough.

"The Commander is in quite a conundrum over what to do with you. Lord Moset claims he knows you but won't give your name, and you told the Commander it was better he didn't know. Why?" He bent down low enough so I could see his face. "Why all the secrets?"

"If Moset didn't vouch for me would I be alive right now?" I asked in return. "Even if I had given you my name, without someone batting for me neither of you would have given me a chance. It would be too unbelievable, especially while I look like this. Dark Elf, human, monster... whatever you think I am. You wouldn't believe me whatever I said anyway."

"True." He consented.

He got up again and strolled to the window, pulling the curtains back he let in the first few rays of sunshine that were making their way over the trees and the rooftops. Streaks of light painted the floor, tinting it red. I followed the beams to the window and while I couldn't see what was outside, the look on Sean's face said it wasn't good. Dropping the curtains, he grabbed his boots and raced out of the room, eyes wide and urgent, and he left the door open behind him.

"What's going on?" I called after him, but my answer was him racing down the stairs and commotion down below.

When after what felt like a long time nobody came back up, I stood, hands still bound behind my back, and went to the window, peering through the small space in-between the curtains. Great plumes of smoke from the forest east of the town filled the sky, blocking out some of the sun, making it seem earlier than it really was. People and soldiers hustled down below, most running west with wagons and carriages, whole families fleeing... But fleeing what? Not willing to find out or wait and see what fate Tristan and Sean had planned for me, I moved quickly, slipping out into the hall and right into Tristan. His sword was out before I could even think to try and go back into the room.

"Get back in there."

I backed slowly into the room at the encouragement of the sword pricking my neck. A trail of blood beaded on the tip and rolled down the blade.

"So, I guess you decided you don't believe me or Lord Moset then?" I tried.

"And why should I?" He sneered and pressed the blade closer, cutting me a little deeper. "Neither one of you are humans, stinking elves the both of you... I should never have been with you. People warned me about you, about how it would hurt my reputation to date the snob princess. I guess you're showing your true colors now aren't you, Celestial?"

"...What?"

I just stared at him, his dark brown eyes reflecting my horror back at me. I froze. Something was wrong. I dropped my gaze to the sword and caught my breath. It wasn't Tristan's face reflecting off the polished metal.

"I can't believe I could have ever considered spending my life with you. Look at what you are now! I bet you wanted this, wanted to break up the kingdom and run off with the enemy."

I took a couple steps back, still too shocked to speak, right as I made to take my third step and he made to follow Lord Moset came bursting into the room, followed by a familiar small green light.

"Commander Tristan, no! Did you listen to nothing I told you last night?" Mayla landed on his blade while Moset rushed in and pushed me back, inserting himself between Tristan and me.

"That's not Tristan." I said, finally finding my voice.

"By the Light..." Moset whispered.

"Guess I can drop the guise now," Vince laughed and glowed briefly before his disguise flickered and faded.

"Why won't you just leave me alone? You've already destroyed any life I could have!"

"That witch thinks she knows better than I do! I was the one who traced your bloodline and discovered your lineage! I'm the one who found Thorkin's world and awoke his power! That Witch is just a pawn in his games and would still be taking her five hundred year-long nap if it weren't for me, and I won't stop until you are dead!"

His Gift shot out of his sword in a blast that swept all of us off our feet. Moset and Mayla were knocked into the ground, and I was blown back into the window and felt the air rushing past me on my way to the cobbled street below. I screamed, closed my eyes, and braced for impact. The rushing air stopped, but I hadn't hit the ground.

I peeled one eye open. Hovering a foot above the ground, I tried to catch up with what had just happened. A couple soldiers stopped and stared but mostly people were running past, one guy even went so far as to jump over me as he raced along, as if I were just something blocking the road.

"You didn't think I'd let you off the hook that easily did you?" Vince laughed, stepping out of Moset's house.

The force that held me suddenly disappeared, dropping me on my face.

"Stay right there!" One of the soldiers stepped up beside me but was looking at Vince. "You are under arrest."

"For which offence, soldier?" Vince mocked, striding forwards. "Maybe the coup I planned? Or was it consorting with the Dark? Maybe murder? Kidnapping the Princess?"

From my stomach I looked up at the soldier and the ones who were gathering around us, surrounding me and Vince. The soldier stayed where he was, but everyone could see he was shaking.

"Perhaps you're referring to the present offence," Vince mused, stepping closer, waving his sword nonchalantly. "You must mean the Black Elf lying at your feet that I brought here."

"All of the above," A new voice came from the crowd, breaking the circle and stepping up to us.

"Hello, Sean, ole' buddy."

Vince bent down and hoisted me to my feet, keeping his sword close to me. I tried to keep steady but was still woozy from the vision and the fall. Noise came from the house. Mayla came swooping down from the window just as Moset slipped among the soldiers and into view. The small gash above his brow was the only indication of his encounter with Vince upstairs.

"Sean don't let him hurt her!" Mayla called to him.

"It's a monster. I think we should be more concerned with the other matter at hand."

"Do you mean me or the Goblins?"

"Both," Sean snarled.

By this time Moset had made his way to Sean, slipping through the ring of soldiers and up to his side. He bent slightly, his face betraying nothing as he whispered something to Sean. Sean wasn't so smooth, his expression betraying everything the elf lord said as his eyes were drawn to me. Our eyes only locked for a fraction of a second before Vince jammed the sword in between my ribs through to the other side, pulled it free and gripped the hair at the base of my neck.

"I'm sure someone will heal you, but rest assured that as soon as Malthor is through with your soul I'll be back to finish you." He promised and shoved me towards Sean and Moset and then vanished.

"Go find Tristan." Moset was quiet enough for only Sean and me to hear as he scooped me up, Mayla landing on my shoulder, and took me inside.

"Everyone get back to getting the civilians out!" Sean barked then sprinted up the road towards the center of town.

*****

Moset rushed me upstairs and laid me on a bed in the back of the house. He and Mayla were talking fast. I tried to focus on them instead of the pain but all I heard was a ringing in my ears. I cried out when Moset pressed his hands over my ribs, two of which I was sure Vince broke in the blast and made worse when he stabbed me. Power came from his hands, spreading through my core and chasing away all the pain as he healed me. When he was done and pulled away I sat up. He looked down at his hands, cringing.

"I'll return in a moment..."

Mayla flew to me as he left, landing on my shoulder, and wrapping her arms around my neck.

"Did you make it to mom and dad?" I asked when she let go and landed in my lap.

"Yes and they were relieved to hear about you. They also wanted me to update them as soon as I found you. I figured I could send someone from my troop to deliver that message. How is your Gift? Are you healing ok? How long have you been here?"

She babbled on, asking her string of questions, and telling me about all she saw on her trip to my parents and on the way here. I listened, waiting for a break so I could get a word in edgewise, but all the words left me when I looked up and Tristan came into the room, pausing in the doorway. It seemed to me that he released a heavy breath, but maybe I imagined it.

"Celestial?" Mayla finally noticed my distraction and turned, fluttering into the air when she saw him.

"Can you give us a minute please, Mayla?"

He stepped inside and out of her way as she flew out and disappeared behind the door as Tristan closed it. I looked down at the massive blood stain and searched for something, anything to say. The bed creaked under his weight and this time I knew I didn't imagine his sigh.

"Moset healed you? You're alright?" He took my hand, intertwining his fingers with mine behind my back.

"Yeah." I spoke soft, too afraid of what he was going to say.

As much as I wanted to return to where we'd left off at the engagement party all that time ago, I was sure this was going to be the part where he told me he'd had enough. I was too much trouble for no return, and he didn't want all the hassle. Besides that, I was a monster now and of a kind that he particularly had grounds to hate.

"Why didn't you tell me it was you last night?" he asked, still holding my hand.

"I just... I wasn't sure what to do." I risked a glance at him. Calm as ever, his face revealed nothing. "...I still don't remember everything yet, but Mayla gave me a heads up about how I might be treated when you saw me, or saw a black elf, anyway." I explained.

"Do you remember more than when I left?"

"A lot more than then, yes, just not everything." I was quicker to answer this time.

I tried to imagine we were back at the palace, that I wasn't a complete mess, and he wasn't doing everything he could to hide what he was feeling. That helped a little, but at the end of the day I was still cursed, and he was still the Commander who was in charge of what was to be done with me.

"Before we really get into this," I started, "I had a vision... There's a little boy out there. I think he's on his own and might be in trouble. I think he's somewhere in town."

"I'll have my men keep their eyes open, but if you're not hurt we have to go. On my way back here, I received word that there's another wave coming behind the goblins. My men will be seriously outnumbered, and the people vulnerable if we don't retreat."

"Better put a bag over my head or something so we don't incite a riot on the way out."

I sighed and rolled my shoulders, letting go of Tristan's hand. Things were getting stiff from having my arms bound behind me for so long. The throb eased slightly but returned quickly. The moment Tristan's hand was free he was on his feet and walked towards the door, his stoic stature made the silence between us heavy.

"I never meant to bring all this on you." I waited for him to turn around, but he just stood there. "I'm sorry for everything."

"You have no idea the position you've put me in, do you?" His face was stern when he finally looked at me. My lips pressed themselves together as my eyes narrowed while I fought the heat rising in my face.

"I'm so sorry to inconvenience you, Commander. I merely thought you'd want to know about the ambush in Parna, or that Vince and his lunatic necromancer dark magic friends are conspiring against you, but apparently I've just put you in a bad position!"

"Celestial, that's not what I meant."

I got off the bed and stood tall, fuming. "I'm so, so sorry to have been kidnapped and cursed," my voice raised as I spoke and stepped closer to him, "Please forgive me for surviving getting my Gift ripped out of me and my soul torn to shreds so I could cross this forsaken country to help you!"

"Celestial-"

"No!" I cut him off. "I've had enough! I didn't ask for any of this! When Vince and his coup buddies ambushed me after our engagement party I thought, 'I have to stop this and make sure everyone is safe.'"

"Celestial," Tristan tried again but I pressed on.

"And since I'm on the subject of us, I'm a monster now, so I can never go home. You're better off without me messing up everything you've accomplished."

I stopped there. It wasn't as if the thought had never occurred to me, but as I said it, it hit me, penetrating through that constant pain in my chest and through to the piece of my soul I still clung to. I couldn't go home, and the man I loved couldn't be mine anymore. I hung my head, fighting the ripples clouding my vision and eventually running down my face. Tristan stepped up to me, rubbing along my jawline with his thumb as he cupped my face.

"You have to pull yourself together." His voice was sweet, which only made my realization hurt more. "We have to go before this town is swarming with goblins. I'm not leaving you here. I'm not leaving you at all, but we have to go, now." We both looked up, startled as the door flew open and Sean and Mayla rushed in.

"Commander, sorry to break this up but we're not just dealing with goblins anymore. Vince and Algoroth are on dragons and are setting the town on fire."

"The town's empty?"

"Yes, sir. It's just us and a couple men. Moset and the rest of the squad are leading the citizens through the mountain pass to the harbor as we speak."

"How many people, including the three of us?" Tristan asked.

"Six, Commander."

"Bring them all in here." Sean was gone without a second glance and before I could ask Tristan what he was doing he'd already gone to the bed and torn a long strip of fabric off the sheet and was coming to me. "I have to do this," he said as he tied it over my mouth as a gag, "Just bear with me, babe please? You were right when you said the people seeing you would incite a riot, but soldiers are worse. Play along?" He pled as he tied another strip over my eyes.

I stopped crying and composed myself just in time for Sean to lead in the men. I wasn't sure who, but someone closed the door. I felt Tristan's grip on my arm, leading me just a few steps. "Men," Tristan called them to attention, hushing their whispers. "Since it's just a small group of us I am going to open a doorway to the harbor town. Once there I'll secure this," he pulled me forward a step for emphasis, "and the four of you will prepare for the rest of the squad and the citizens to arrive. Any questions?"

"Why is it still alive?" one man asked. I could almost see the disgust on his face through his tone. "Don't we kill those on sight?" he went on.

"Saving this one for King's City gallows," Tristan lied. "If there's nothing else we should go."

I felt heat on my back, starting from a small pin and growing until the whole of behind me was warm, though not as if from a fire, but something gentler. Tristan guided me on, moving towards the heat until warm was all around me, and so was the sudden sound of boots on cobbled stones backing away. I wasn't sure how many people were around us now. It was more than a few, judging by the sudden rise in voices around us.

"What's the meaning of this?" Someone came to us, picking at my blind fold though Tristan still held a tight grip on my arm.

"Where is Captain Robertson?" Tristan asked. "Find him and tell him Commander Tristan requires his presence on the docks."

I didn't hear a response, but instead the slap of someone's boots on the road as they hurried off. The people around us spoke softly to one another, most wondering what Tristan was doing here with an elf. I listened a bit more, but luckily nobody could tell what kind of elf I was. Although rumors started through the crowd as Tristan lead me through them that I was dark, judging by the paleness of my skin and the darkness of my hair.

Tristan roughly pulled me along, and I did my best to play along. It wasn't hard, especially since I couldn't see, speak, or use my hands or my Gift, and my head was starting to hurt again. Maybe it was another vision coming. Maybe it was just the bruise under my eye. Either way, I started stumbling long before we reached the docks and the sound of the push and pull of the waves with the slight sway of the dock came to us. I hadn't taken three steps onto the dock before I started swaying.

"You're doing great. Just keep it up a little longer. The captain should be here soon and if he brings anyone with him, I'll send them away. If we're to get you safely out of Caleath, we need him on our side. I can just order him to assist but I don't want to cause any more suspicion than there already is."

I nodded but wondered. What did we need him for? We didn't wait too much longer before he showed up, him and it sounded like a few others. True to his word he sent the captain's men away. While Tristan was loosening the gag, the captain cleared his throat.

"May I inquire as to your prisoner? It's not every day an elf is escorted to our fort."

"She's one of the reasons I requested you to come." The gag fell from my mouth, and I moved my jaw around, stretching and flexing the muscles. It hadn't been in long, but I ached already.

"One of the reasons?" he echoed.

"Yes," Tristan went on, "This is a very delicate situation and is to remain confidential. You are to discuss it with only myself. Am I clear?"

"Yes, Commander." He promised. "Permission to speak freely?"

"Granted, but before you say anything let me explain. The Princess Celestial was kidnapped but is now in our possession, but she was cursed before she managed to get free. Now, I can testify, Lord Moset can testify, and my Messenger Mayla can witness also."

"Cursed how?" he asked, treading carefully.

"She was turned into a black elf." Tristan answered, undoing the blindfold.

I winced at the sudden brightness and the sun stung my eyes. The headache increased, but I tried to ignore it.

"This is the princess?" The man's jaw dropped, looking from me to his Commander and then back at me to stare.

"Yes. I need you to hold her on your ship until my men and I are ready to depart to Parna. There is also a large group of refugees coming here through the canyon right now. Assemble your men and whoever volunteers and help me prepare accommodations for them."

"Yes, Commander, but am I to keep her bonded?"

"Yes," I answered before Tristan. "And I'll play along. We don't want to arouse suspicion. I just want this as quiet as possible."

"Yes, of course, your Highness."

Captain Robertson made to bow, but Tristan reached out and stopped him. Instead, he just nodded his head and took hold of my other arm. Tristan let go, and my shoulders slumped as he walked away. Mayla's wings fluttered, tickling my cheek. I'd forgotten she was even there, but to my disappointment she followed Tristan.

"Let's get this over with," I sighed.

He led me back onto the beach and towards his men who were waiting down the shore. As we approached them I gave a little resistance, as I imagined an actual black elf might and he just paused.

"I'm a black elf. Remember? Treat me like it," I hissed under my breath. He huffed and yanked, now dragging me along. "Better," I whispered.

"Attention!" He called to his small squad, and they stopped huddling together and formed their line, standing salute. "Adams, Greggory, Johannsen, Mitcham," These four men stepped up out of the line, all still in salute. "Assist Commander Tristan with preparing for the refugees and round up as many volunteers from the town as you can to help get things ready. The rest of you," The remaining five stepped up. "Escort this prisoner to my ship. Hold her there. Nobody is to harm it. Nobody is to speak to it. If it gives you trouble, send for me or Commander Tristan. No vigilante justice. Am I clear?"

"Sir, yes sir!" they answered in unison. Robertson pushed me towards them.

"Dismissed. I'll be accompanying them to Commander Tristan in town if I'm needed."

The soldiers escorted me calmly to the ship about a half mile down the beach to the docks, but once we were on the ship and they couldn't see the Captain anymore their attitudes changed, shoving me below deck and passed the sailors.

"I thought we were supposed to kill these things on sight." One of the soldiers grumbled, shoving me onward.

"Where'd you hear that? The official protocol is to hand them over to your superior officer," the man beside him answered, shaking some shaggy bangs out of his eyes.

"Right," the first agreed, "and they are supposed to execute them. What is Commander Tristan thinking?" this last part was whispered to himself, but I felt my skin prickle.

"Questioning your commanding officer, are you?" I snickered, though I wanted to smack him.

The soldier snapped, surprising everyone and shoving me into the wall and pulling a small blade out of his pocket and slipped it an inch into my side before the others mobbed him and pulled him off me. In all the commotion nobody was restraining me. I slipped away from the five unruly soldiers. The one who stuck me pulled free and charged me. I jumped, kicking my leg, and connecting my heel with his jaw. The side of his head hit the wall and the rest of him slumped down to his knees. He spat a mouth full of blood at my feet and the others ignored him, taking hold of me again. I looked down, chin high, and spat in his face.

"That's it!" he screamed and jumped up. "It's a disgrace to allow you on our soil!"

I wasn't sure what his plan was, but as he shoved through his comrades and gripped me by the shirt collar something screamed at me to react. He pulled me towards him and lifted me to eye level, my feet dangling above the ground. I leaned back and then slammed my face down. I felt the crack of the bridge of his nose on my forehead, my knee collided with his groin, and he immediately dropped me and fell to his knees.

Hands were on me again, dragging me away and locking me behind a set of double doors. I dropped down, out of breath and my side burning, and leaned on the door. I wondered for a moment if the moron had punctured my lung but figured I would know by now if he had. I sat for a minute, catching my breath with my eyes closed in the dark, quiet room.

"You have spirit," a deep voice floated from across the room. My eyes snapped open and over on the other side by the closed curtains covering a huge paned window was a man in a red hooded cloak that hid his face. It didn't matter. I knew the voice. Even though I only heard it once, I could never forget. "No hello for the one bearing the rest of your shattered soul?"

I stood and pressed myself to the door, trying the knob. Not that I was expecting it to be unlocked, I was still surprised the captain's idiot soldiers managed to do something right.

"There's someone in here!" I yelled and kicked the door while jiggling the handle as best I could with my hands still bound behind my back.

"Amusing," Malthor laughed and pushed back his hood.

Strolling towards me, he glanced around the room, touching a few trinkets now and again. The room seemed to get smaller and smaller with each stride he took. Though the room was big and there weren't many more pieces of furniture besides the bed, a set of drawers and a small armchair set up in the corner he was coming from.

"Vince was right," he breathed, reaching out to stroke my cheek. "You are quite stunning as a black elf. The curve of your lips and sharpness of your eyes makes me want to see what more you have to offer. Did you know," he went on leaning in and breathing in my scent, still stroking my cheek, "That when two people share a soul both can only live as long as the original host?"

I said nothing, any thought, or words I might have shared were stuck behind a wall of fear. I'd stopped kicking and trying the knob. If someone were listening they would have come by now. My whole body was trembling, and not just because I was terrified. What was left of my soul pushed as if to come out of me and join what he'd taken, while my Gift recoiled deeper into my heart. Whatever he'd done to the power he took from me, it wasn't the same now. Not even close. I could feel how much his Dark malevolence had already perverted it.

"Did you also know," he spoke softly, his breath on my face as he towered over me and leaned his face close to mine, "That Black elves are the most long-lived of all the elves? I've never heard of one to live less than five thousand years. Even your friend Moset, as a light elf, will live only another thousand at most, making him about two thousand and seventy... nine?" he paused, brushing his lips along my jaw while I tried to bury myself in the door.

"Why are you here?" I asked.

"I thought you might want to know why Vince cursed you." He finally pulled away and I felt like crawling out of my skin. I could still feel his touch on my face.

"The longer I live, the longer you live," I voiced. "I will break this curse and get my soul back eventually."

"True loves kiss," he said suddenly, catching me even more off guard. He wandered around the room, opening the curtains and letting light in, smoothing the quilt on the bed.

"What are you talking about?" I asked since he clearly wasn't going to tell me.

"One of the most powerful tricks of Light magic, is the kiss of true love. A soulmate is a rare and beautiful thing, Princess. It can break any curse." He looked up from the bed and grinned at me, chilling my blood.

"Why tell me this?"

"Your Commander is not going to kiss you, Celestial."

"I don't understand," I stepped away from the door now. "Why wouldn't Tristan kiss me?"

"Well, potent black elf venom, for one thing," He walked towards me again. I backed up to the door hitting it faster than I would have liked. "For another, he watched one sink its teeth into his father, or so Vince tells me." He shrugged, reaching out to play with my unruly hair. "Unless he has a death wish, he'll probably never touch you again."

The corners of his mouth twisted up and dark smoke wrapped around him. Just like the witch had done in my room all that time ago, he was gone when the smoke cleared.

13

Tristan had been watching the small, unescorted boy for almost six hours as he supervised the influx of people from the mouth of the canyon into the coastal town. He doubted the boy had noticed he was watching. He seemed so absorbed in looking for whoever he was waiting on that nothing else caught his attention. Eventually he had to check in with the captain on living arrangements for the people but when dusk came and everyone was out of the canyon Tristan went back to find that the boy was still sitting on the top of a stack of crates, head hung and sniffling.

"Hello there," Tristan looked up at the sorry sight. Round, tearful brown eyes, a red runny nose, unruly dirty blonde hair, and a dusty face looked down at him. The lower lip protruding, it started to quiver. "You've manned your post all day long. You must be hungry, eh soldier?"

The boy just nodded and reached down to the Commander. Tristan brought him down, but instead of putting him down he carried the small child. He seemed grateful, resting his cheek on Tristan's shoulder and the top of his head just nuzzled under his chin.

"He went back for mamma and daddy, but I don't think anybody got away." His voice was quiet, but the words were clear.

"Who went back?" Tristan asked.

"Ethan, my big brother. Daddy sent us ahead of them so he and momma could get our horses out of the barn. We got to the city and Ethan told me, he told me to wait for him. He was going to get them and come back for me. I waited until the dragons came and a soldier made me go with him."

To this Tristan wasn't sure what to say. He rubbed the boy's back and held him all the tighter. The ship wasn't much farther, and Celestial would be able to confirm his suspicions. He didn't say so, but he believed the boy was right when he said he didn't think they got away. Goblins were fast and ruthless. Survivors weren't something typically found in the aftermath of a goblin attack.

"What's your name?" he asked after a little while.

"Levi, what's your name?" he asked, sniffling, and wiping his nose on his sleeve.

"Commander Tristan."

"You fought against a small army of trolls in the northern clans all by yourself with nothing but a sword!" Levi's eyes went wide with excitement and wonder.

"Don't believe everything you hear," Tristan laughed, "I had a spear too."

"Whoa!" Levi breathed.

"How old are you?" The ship waited in the water, only a short rowboat ride away from the docks.

"Five," he held up a hand and the appropriate number of fingers before pointing to the ship. "Is that where we're going?"

"It is," Tristan nodded and set the boy in the rowboat where Sean was waiting. "This is Sean, one of my soldiers and really good friend. Is it okay if he comes with us?"

The scene ended abruptly, and I woke to the sun set filling the floor to ceiling paned windows. On the water a little way off I saw them rowing to the ship. While my wrists were still bound, I'd managed to slide them under me and have my hands in front of me again, and that made all the difference when I went to lay on the bed after Malthor left. I hadn't slept long, and I hadn't meant to sleep at all, but the vision forced its way to me.

On the other side of the room, I'd found a little rag and a pitcher of water and was in the process of washing my face when the door clicked open and then shut again.

"I thought you said we were going to meet Princess Celestial." I stiffened where I stood. Not only was it weird to hear the boy outside my mind but what was Tristan thinking? "That's an elf. I didn't think she was an elf," Levi went on, "and I heard she went missing a long time ago. Did you find her? Are we going to see her after this?" My face was clean, so I set the rag down and waited.

"She did go missing and while she was gone, she got cursed by some bad men. We found her and are going to try and break the curse so we can take her home." Tristan walked across the room to me and the bonds around my wrists loosed and fell. "This is the princess."

"Tristan, the sight of me is going to scare him!" I hissed, "Why did you bring him here?"

"Don't worry Princess. I saw goblins and a dragon yesterday. You won't scare me. I can keep a secret too. Commander Tristan said to keep our visit secret."

I ran my fingers through my gnarled hair and sighed, casting a sidelong glance at Tristan. Levi took a step closer but then stopped. I straightened my shoulders, organized all my hair over one shoulder and turned, bringing my eyes from the floor to Tristan and then to Levi. His gasp said it all and I couldn't stop the wince.

"I know," I tried to be cheery, "but hopefully we'll find a cure soon and I'll be back to normal."

"Daddy said Black Elves were the most dangerous, but you weren't born one, so you don't count." He tilted his head up and walked to us, stopping by Tristan, though only an arm's reach from me. "Mama said she was saved from poison berries when daddy gave her true loves kiss before they married. Maybe your true love can fix it."

"That's some impressive imagination you have," I forced a smile and ruffled his hair.

"Hey!" he pushed my hand away, "Mama would never lie to me and I'm not imagining!" Tears came to his eyes and his lower lip stuck out, trembling a little.

"Oh no, no," I knelt down and looked up at him, "Levi that's not what I meant. I'm sure your mother's wonderful. I just meant... well," I paused and looked up at Tristan who seemed just as offended. "I'm poison right now." I said flatly, looking back at Levi. "I won't ask my true love to kiss me because I don't want to chance hurting him when maybe we can find another cure."

"True loves kiss would protect him," Levi was resolute. I smiled and stood up.

"Maybe so," I gave a little but not completely. "Tristan why don't you guys have some fun. I'm sure it was a busy day," I said.

"Go with Sean to get some food. I'll find you in a little while."

Tristan opened the door to let him go out and closed it again after a brief word with Sean. Once the door was closed again he just stood there, watching me. I moved to the window and sat on the little ledge, folding my arms around myself. Who knew just moving yourself freely would be a comfort?

"Thank you for finding him." I said after a few minutes. "I was worried something happened to him." Tristan stayed quiet but crossed the room to me, standing just beside me. Resting his hand on my shoulder he sighed. My hand went to his and held on.

"I know I love you, and I know you used to love me. Has something changed? You say you remember the engagement... I have your ring." I turned away from the window and looked up at him. Something ran down my cheek and I hadn't realized I began to cry. "I'm not saying I'm keeping it." His voice was almost as soft as the touch that dried my cheek.

"How can you still want to be with me after all the crap I put you through? If I could have stopped Vince that morning none of these horrible things would have happened. Levi's family would be okay, and we would have been married by now. Instead, we're at war with a group of necromancers and a witch and I can't go home."

"You don't think the kiss will work because you don't see how I could still love you." Tristan took both my hands and pulled me to my feet and into his arms.

"And the venom." I added. "Even if it did work there's a good chance you'd still get poisoned, and I can't heal you." I echoed Malthor's words to me this morning.

"You won't need to."

He tilted my face towards his and leaned in so closely I could feel the warmth of his breath on my face and the heat from his body against mine. It was all so familiar, so comforting, and so terrifying. My heart was racing, which ached, but I ignored it. I remembered kissing him but even though it was all familiar it was all still new. I couldn't deny what I felt for him. I did want to be with him, today, tomorrow, always.

"Kiss me," he whispered, bringing a hand to my jawline and caressing with his thumb.

"Promise me you won't get hurt." I whispered back. He leaned in closer, hovering his lips above mine as an answer. "Promise me." I said a little louder.

"Promise."

He said it as he kissed me. Warmth spread through me, rushing from my heart out. It seemed to flow right from me and into him. I kissed him, unable to hold myself back and I felt the smile grow the corners of his lips. For a moment, the room seemed to grow brighter but just as quickly it and the mysterious warmth was gone. Tristan kissed me again, and this time I was the one to smile, lips parting to lock with his. The bruise under my eye disappeared and I felt the rest of me returning to normal.

"And you thought it wouldn't work," he teased in between kisses.

"Yeah, yeah."

I would have rolled my eyes if they weren't still closed. He kissed my lips and then my forehead before taking my hands again and grinning down at me.

"Now I get to show you off and have you all to myself."

"I guess I don't have to hide anymore." I added, "I can go verbally assault the soldier who tried to stab me on the way in here."

"What?" Tristan gripped my shoulders and stared down at me, "Why didn't you tell me? I can't allow that insubordination! Who was it?"

Without answering I calmly took his hand and then led him out of the room. A soldier started, obviously not expecting to see the pair of us leaving together and not expecting to see me dressed in bloodied, torn clothes, or looking as unruly as I did.

"At ease," Tristan said as we went down the hall.

He followed, letting go of my hand before we climbed the steps to the upper deck. I paused, looking around to find the man. It wasn't long before I spotted him standing by the railing on the port side with the same group that escorted me to the ship earlier.

"Can I handle it my way?" I asked.

"Technically I can't tell you no, but what are you going to do?"

"Make him feel like absolute scum for attacking me before I toss him overboard."

"After you," Tristan followed a few paces behind me.

"What's his name?" I asked when we were about halfway there, pointing to the man.

"Not sure. They're usually with the captain." Tristan winked at me and charged the group. "Attention men!" All four of them jumped to, standing tall and saluting. "High Princess Celestial wishes to address you."

I stepped into view, trying my best to keep a straight face as I looked them each in the eyes and saw theirs go wide with understanding. The one who stabbed me swallowed hard and later I would swear he went three shades paler. Tristan played his part, standing at the ready and watching me quietly. I wondered if he was having as much trouble keeping it together as I was. I shouldn't have found this so hilarious, but here we were. Maybe all my adventures had warped my sense of humor.

"I just wanted to thank you soldiers for helping me onboard this morning. Can you imagine what would have happened if I'd waltzed onto the ship on my own? I was cursed, but as you can see, I'm back to myself now and let me tell you men one thing."

I paced as I talked, keeping my arms folded and head held high. "Insubordination will not be tolerated on this or any Caleathian Naval ship or from any soldier. Do I make myself clear?" I all but yelled in their faces. They were all sweating bullets and said nothing. "Commander Tristan," I said.

"Yes, your highness," he answered in kind.

"There's no tolerance for disrespecting your commanding officer, is there?"

Tristan cleared his throat, and continued the charade, "None at all, your highness."

"How would an offending officer be disciplined?"

"It's up to the digression of the commanding officer." With nothing left to say I walked up to the man, who now looked like he was going to be sick.

"Name?" I asked.

"Private Adam Danes, your highness," he choked out. I held out my hand expectantly and eyed his badges pinned to his lapel, most of which I recognized from studying with Destiny.

"Give me your knife." He pulled it from his pocket with clammy, shaking hands and handed it over. Pulling it from its casing I saw specks of dried blood on the edge of the blade, my blood. "Private Danes, it looks like you're one pin from a promotion. Is that right?"

"Yes, your highness," he nodded. Everyone on deck was watching us now.

"Not anymore," I took the knife and popped off all the pins except for the least important, the one given at the sign-up office right after enlisting. "Do you care to guess why?" I twirled the knife through my fingers like it was a drumstick.

"My lady, I beg you to forgive me!" He fell to his knees. "I didn't know it was you!"

"That's irrelevant," I snapped, sliding the blade back into the case. "If I ever hear of any insurrection from anyone on this ship I'll strip you of your ranks just like Private Danes here," I said to everyone. "And for the assault... You," I gripped him by the shirt collar and moved in a blur, "Can take a little swim!" In one fluid motion I hurled him over the side of the ship. A second or so later came the splash as he hit the water, then gasping as he surfaced, treading the icy water. "At ease everyone." I leaned over the side, looking down at him. "Someone toss the idiot a rope."

His friends scrambled, finding a sufficient length of rope before throwing it down. I turned and Tristan followed, grinning, and shaking his head as we walked away.

"Commander Tristan, Princess, wait!" I heard Levi call out before I saw him pushing through the crowd.

By the time he and Sean made it to us Adam was on deck again, shivering and dripping in the sunset. We watched him hurry to the barracks below deck. Nobody followed him and most everyone had resumed their tasks, talking amongst each other in amused hushes.

"Is that man gonna be okay?" Levi asked. I sighed and smiled. I didn't want to care but leave it to a child to teach me compassion.

"Would it make you feel better if I checked on him?" I asked.

"Just so he doesn't get sick." He reached up and took Tristan's hand before he put his own thumb in his mouth.

"I'll just be a minute."

"I had some of my men look through the cargo hold for some clothes for you. When your done why not check the room and see what they found?" Tristan suggested.

Smiling I kissed his cheek and went below deck. It wasn't hard to find Adam. I just followed the water trail until I came to a door. I knocked, though it was softer than I'd meant. When no answer came, I tried again, this time the knock could not be mistaken.

"Private Danes?" I called out then tried the handle.

The door swung freely, revealing a long narrow room. One side lined with hammocks and directly across from each one was a trunk, one for each soldier. Not too far into the room a flickering lantern swung gently from the ceiling hook it hung by. Adam was fully clothed in a fresh uniform and bundled in a blanket, his wet things in a heap on his trunk.

"Princess!" He dropped to his knees again when I approached him, and he finally looked up. "I cannot express how sorry I am. Any way that I can make it up to you and Commander Tristan, I will." He paused, sniffling. His whole body was shaking, even his teeth were rattling.

"Your punishment is over and get off the floor. I just came to make sure you weren't going to catch your death. That water is freezing."

"Aye, my Lady," he sniffled and got up a bit unsteadily.

I felt guilty. Sure, I didn't have to care, but he was already getting sick, and it was all my fault. I could feel my Gift in my heart, still raw and still useless unless I wanted to reopen the wound.

"I'll send a healer to you soon. Can't have you getting sick." I patted his arm and turned away, setting his knife atop his trunk before I left him and went back to what was apparently now my room to investigate my clothes situation. On the way I passed the captain and he said he'd look after Private Danes.

Alone I found the situation wasn't as bad as I thought but my options were a little wanting. Still, I had to be grateful. Clean clothes and soon some hot food would be mine. Three dresses and a few sets of underclothes were neatly folded and placed on the bed, along with two cloaks and a corset I had no idea how to put on. Other than the corset the underclothes were easy to change into and fit me better than the pants and shirt I'd lifted. I examined the corset, laced on the front. After a while of fumbling with the strings I gave up and tossed it in the nightstand drawer. I painstakingly tried on all three dresses, glad they all fit but none came up high enough to cover the blaring scar over my heart.

Normally I wouldn't care about a scar showing but not only did I not want to look at it, Tristan hadn't seen it yet. I sighed and pulled a comb through my hair again, staring at myself in the floor-length mirror bolted to the wall across the bed. Really, I looked fine. The dress was a simple long sleeve that buttoned up in the back. It was just like the others on the bed except they were both dark gray instead. It was snug but fit me well, fitted in all the right places before loosening at my hips to a floor length skirt that swished when I walked. The dress was maroon. It didn't matter what color I wore; the scar was the first thing I saw when I looked at my reflection anyway. Putting down the comb on the desk where I'd found it, I grabbed one of the cloaks before heading out. There was no point in making everyone wait when the scar wasn't going anywhere, and we all needed to eat.

14

Outside the windows everything was dark. Inside the biggest room of the inn, it was still quaint with quilts and loads of pillows on the bed and sofa. An untouched pot and cup of tea still sat on the little table from that evening's tea-time after supper. Doilies were all that stood between the pristine surface and the teapot and cups, protecting from rings and sticky spots. The edge of the table itself was carved into the shape of a clamshell while the chips and holes of the body were filled with a blue resin and then smoothed and polished to perfection. The midnight oceanside soundtrack found its way to me even through the closed windows, the soothing sound reminding my body of the feel of the ship as it rode across the sea on our voyage to Lyonshire.

I wandered the room, unable to sleep because of bad dreams. Dark shadows, wicked magic, monsters lurking in Algoroth's castle waiting to be released were all I had dreamed about lately. I could see well enough in the moonlight that lighting the lantern was only an afterthought when wisps of clouds darkened the room for a few seconds. They passed and the delicate whiteness from the full moon gave my shadow life again, growing across the smooth sandstone floors and white shiplap walls. My nightgown flowed around my legs, antique white satin-like fabric hugged my bodice but loosened quite a bit as it came down from my waist and down to my shins. Half inch straps sat on the edges of my shoulders holding up the gown that was more to me like a bohemian dress than a nightgown.

I paced my room, a strange awareness keeping me on the edge of waking and a dreamlike state. Eventually I came to the vanity and sat on the cushioned chair looking into the mirror. My reflection filled it. I looked into my own eyes, seeing black where white should be and my Gift glowing where my green irises and pupils should have been. The sight was terrifying but beautiful in its own right, tiny stars of every color luring my focus into the light. It pulled me in, revealing a dizzying blur of scenes.

Weeks of travel in melancholy weather to a city that seemed to be plucked from a King Arthur tale and a looming castle with a King standing upon his dais while Tristan kneeled before him, and I and Tristan's men stood behind him. The vision sped on showing me things so quickly I couldn't have understood what I saw if I tried. Then things slowed down to real time just long enough for me to see Tristan, Sean and Levi go through a doorway of light and into the grand receiving room of the palace in Kings City. Mom stood alone at the dais beside an empty throne of silver, gold and a stone that glowed purple and red in the sunlight filtering from the open windows. Her somber face sparked into joy when her eyes rose from the ground to them.

All at once the vision closed and my Gift left my eyes, leaving them normal, and flowing back down to my heart where everything felt right except the part of my soul that was missing. Unlike in the weeks following the witch's ritual to revive Malthor my heart didn't hurt anymore, and the giant red scar was now smooth and pink. The pain had eventually faded into a discomfort born from the missing piece of my soul. If I searched hard enough, I could feel how far it was from me, but that knowledge always led to the knowing that the necromancer, the Dark General Malthor, knew where I was at any given time. I refused to let myself linger on the thought because I knew only more disturbing knowledge would arise.

With all of that I hadn't used my Gift other than the involuntary visions that came to me from time to time. This was the first time I'd even bothered to feel my Gift or take notice of it in a couple weeks. Tristan asked about how I was recovering often, encouraging me to talk about what happened to me while I was kidnapped but I never would. Instead, he had to go to Mayla to get her side of the story. He knew everything she did and that was enough as far as I was concerned. *And as far as I can handle*, I thought. Physically I was recovered, but mentally, emotionally... There were some scars that would last a lifetime.

I stood and went to the nightstand and lit the lantern, turning away from my thoughts and shutting out the awareness of my power. Across from the bed were the windows that open like doors to a fenced in patio with a view of the rocky shoreline. Beside them was a screen designating the changing area where the wardrobe was. I went to it and looked through the dresses Tristan bought me when we arrived.

The lilac purple one I chose had a wide, swooping neckline and barely covered my shoulders but sat high enough to cover most of my scar, the fabric resting just under my collar bone. The dress fit much like the nightgown I decided to keep on underneath instead of the itchy shift it came with. The skirt was loose, allowing for maximum movement but would pose somewhat of a challenge not to trip over since the hemline stopped just over my toes. Tristan said that was the modest standard, but I still would have preferred pants. He insisted and I caved. He knew better than I about how I should present and conduct myself. It wasn't like I'd remembered etiquette from my previous life. Though there were things I did remember I still largely identified as the girl Tristan had rescued from the car. It seemed I'd entered a long lull in memories. Nothing new had come to me since before we set sail. Summer was pretty much here, eight months since that fateful car accident and nothing was the same.

The inn was quite peaceful as I left my room and walked the halls, passing Tristan's room, then Levi's on my way to the stairs. I descended silently and went straight to the back door and outside. Cool salty air greeted me in a breeze that pushed my hair behind my shoulders. The sand was cooler than the air, shifting under my weight and squishing in between my toes. The closer I got to the water the louder the waves and the brighter the reflection of the moon across the tops before they broke.

"Hey," Tristan's voice broke the serenity.

I whipped around, bearing my Gift until I saw it was him.

"Sorry," I pulled back my light and turned back towards the water. "I wasn't expecting anyone out here."

My palm went straight to my heart, covering the sting from forcing my Gift out so suddenly. He came over, put his arms around me and pressed his lips to the side of my neck.

"It's still dark, can't sleep?" He asked. His weight and the sound of his voice, he was definitely tired.

"It's fine, you can go back to bed."

"Liar," he breathed in my ear. "What's wrong? You only go for midnight walks when there's something the matter."

"Can't pull the wool over your eyes," I relented and reached up, holding his arms and his rested my head back against his chest.

"Have you remembered anything new? Any progress with your Gift? You seem to be controlling it ok."

"I'm adjusting." I answered vaguely. He just sighed and kissed me again.

"Your stubbornness isn't always cute, you know. Sometimes it's frustrating when you won't accept any help or talk about what happened. Is it dreams or stubbornness keeping you up?"

"Stubbornness, and you think I'm adorable." I answered, letting a teasing smile spread apart my lips as I turned in his arms to face him.

"I don't like seeing you hurt."

"I never hurt with you." I wrapped my arms around his neck.

"Stop changing the subject," he leaned in.

"You love it," I lifted onto my toes and kissed him.

"Ok non married people, break it up!"

A new voice and fast footfall called loudly down to us. We both turned to see a green glow flying towards us and someone jogging along behind it.

"Mayla!" I exclaimed. "You're back!" I only walked a few steps before she was buzzing in my face.

"What am I? Chopped liver?" her companion complained. The voice was familiar, but I couldn't see her face yet.

"Danny, what brings you out here?" Then we both saw the small chest in her hands and the scroll tucked under her arm. "What's all this? Did you just get in?"

"We just rode up and saw you walking out here to her. We came through one of Wilden's doorways and pretty much rushed here. We've been riding for almost a week. How long have you been docked?"

"We reached the shores the day before yesterday. We will ride to Camelot tomorrow to meet with Fangthorn to ask for reinforcements. Is that another order?" He looked to the scroll. Danny nodded.

"Sure is, General Thompson," she grinned and handed him the scroll.

Sending out his Gift he lit up the area so he could read it. When he had read and unrolled it all the way he revealed another small scroll, which he handed to me. Waiting a moment, I watched Tristan finish reading and then clear his throat.

"Congratulations," Danny said and handed him the chest.

"Wow, so you're a General now?" I asked, putting a hand on his back. "I'm so proud of you!"

He couldn't stop smiling as he opened the chest and saw all his new pins and badges. He bent towards me, and I kissed him.

"Thank you, babe." He closed the chest after putting the scroll inside. "Are you going to read yours?" he asked.

I looked down, broke my parents' seal, and unrolled the parchment.

Celestial,

When Mayla returned and said you were safe with Tristan your mother and I were so relieved. Algoroth sent small armies throughout Caleath, burning villages, and raiding everything in sight. We've dealt with them so far, but a larger number of his forces are requiring most of our men in the northeastern border.

Your mother departed after Mayla's initial news of you to request aid from the Elves. She returned last week with roughly ten thousand elfish soldiers who volunteered to protect our capital and the doorway to earth. In addition, your mother and I have instructed Tristan to request aid for Parna from King Fangthrorn, in addition to naval support for us.

We cannot allow the doorways to earth in Wilden to be compromised. We pray this war will end soon, but I believe it will get worse before it gets better. You'll be coming home through a doorway on earth, but only after I give General Tristan the "all clear". Be safe. We know you're smart and resourceful.

Love, Mom and Dad.

I rolled up the parchment and looked back at the shoreline. Across the ocean they could be under siege right now. He hadn't mentioned Malthor at all, which made me worry about what the necromancer might be up to.

"Bad news?" Tristan caressed my chin.

"Just war. You know, invasions, protecting magical doorways, the fate of the world… I'm sure their letter to you was a lot the same." Tristan and Danny exchanged glances, before he handed me his letter. "Are you sure?"

"Just read it. I'll read yours. No secrets."

He handed me his and took mine. I unrolled and read carefully, feeling slightly more ill at ease the farther I went. Then, towards the second half of the letter I felt my cheeks heat up as my father none too gently reminded him that we weren't married and whose daughter I was. Sure, he put in there that they still hoped he and I would get married, but I couldn't help but imagine him haranguing Tristan like an over-protective parent. It didn't get better from there but his none too subtle warnings for Tristan to keep his hands off me finally stopped and dad went on to congratulate him on the promotion before signing off with his official seal.

"Wow," I said as I rolled it back up, letting Tristan put both our letters in his box. "So did you picture him with a shotgun while you read that or was it just me?"

"Just you," he smiled but shook his head and led the four of us into the inn.

I went back up to my room, finally feeling like I might sleep a little, but the second I laid my head on the pillow thoughts and worry crept back into my mind, keeping the wheels of wakefulness turning. The more I laid on the bed and thought about it the more I could feel that part of my soul hundreds of miles away across the sea. While it was unchanged, I was overly aware that Malthor felt my presence and was doing nothing to block me out. The distinct impression came to me that he didn't care if I knew his plans, so I looked, seeing through his eyes.

Blackness was all I saw. Then, after a few seconds I distinguished he wasn't alone. However, his was the only physical body in the area. He was surrounded by spirits of monsters, *a specific kind*, he told me. *Upon the summer solstice, during a full eclipse, I will summon legions of the Droschuil to be one of the forces against your father.* An image conjured of a humanoid creature, tall, skeletal thin, with long gangly limbs and animalistic claws on its fingers. A horrible shark-like mouth with three rows of razor teeth, two slits for a nose and four glowing red eyes burned into my mind. I shot up, opening my eyes and abruptly severing the conscious connection.

We left the inn that morning instead of waiting, though I told nobody of my encounter. I asked Danny if she wanted a day to recoup but she insisted we get moving. Tristan didn't take all his men this time. Only Sean and two other soldiers I had only met in passing, Quin and Connor. Once the eight of us were ready, we bid goodbye to the others who were sailing back with the captain to help fortify the coastal border.

*****

It rained the entire two weeks it took to get to Camelot and the entire time I couldn't stop thinking that I was going to the city of legend while simultaneously ignoring Levi's asking how much farther. In the end and to Levi's further disappointment it was only going to be Tristan, me, Danny, and Sean that would go to the castle and request an audience with King Fangthorn. Connor and Quin instead took Levi to see some of the booths in the market. I was almost jealous. In one of the booths, we passed on our way to the castle they were selling what looked to me like funnel cake. Mayla took a different direction, flying ahead to check the situation in Wilden, Parna's capital.

Once we reached the castle and were permitted to enter, we were escorted by a few guards into separate chambers to freshen up. I wasn't sure about Danny's room but there was a new dress and a handmaiden waiting in mine. She rushed me out of my travel worn clothes and into a quick bath, then a powder blue dress with the longest bell sleeves I'd ever seen. The main part of the sleeve stopped just passed my elbow, but the cream-colored bell trailed down behind my hand almost another arm length. I felt out of place, self-conscious and vulnerable in it. The neckline was lower than I liked but not lower than anything I'd worn before, and the corset was ridiculously snug. Then she turned on my hair, brushing until my head felt raw from the tugging before she swept it all back into a French braid, though she called it something else. I was the last one to rejoin the others in the receiving room, adjacent to the throne room.

"You look beautiful." Tristan took my hand and gave it a little squeeze before letting go. "While we're in there it's probably best if I lead."

"I don't plan on saying anything." I shrugged. "Unless it's to mention our impromptu bounce back to the Middle Ages."

"His Majesty will see you now," a man announced from the doorway, pulling wide and tall carved wooden doors open for us. We entered, Tristan leading me and Sean and Danny following.

"Commander Tristan! Princess Celestial!" A warm greeting floated across the grey stone room from the elevated dais and the man sitting on a golden, jewel encrusted throne.

According to Tristan he was in his mid-twenties, but the thick beard and unkempt hair made him look older. As we got closer, I saw there wasn't much of him that wasn't covered in jewels. His crown, robes, even his tunic collar had sapphires on the neckline. He stood, extending his arms in greeting, and everything glittered. It was hard to notice anything else in the room but him, though there wasn't much else besides tapestries bearing the crest of Arthur Pendragon and the red carpet we walked on that led to King Fangthorn.

"King Fangthorn, thank you for seeing us and for your gracious hospitality," Tristan bowed slightly but after a quick glance behind me I found he was the only one.

"It's my pleasure to welcome you here. I haven't forgotten Stephen's generous support after my wife's passing. Tell me, when did you become a General? Your pins didn't escape my notice, and the Princess! Last I heard you went missing after that awful coup."

He descended the couple steps down to us and shook Tristan's hand, though kept his eyes on me. I looked down, feeling my face flush.

"Thank you, your grace. The promotion is recent, and Celestial's return is also."

"How wonderful, just wonderful. Now, forgive me if I'm being presumptuous but does your visit have anything to do with the goblin migration I heard about from my sailors?"

"To start with," Tristan began. "You learned of the infamous General Algoroth?"

Fangthorn scoffed, "Every school child hears of his demise."

"He has risen and joined forces with a necromantic witch and Vincent, the leader of the coup. They're gathering forces to seize control of Caleath and the doorways to Earth. They may have expanded their aim to other nations besides Caleath and Parna, but this isn't confirmed." Tristan explained and I watched the King for his reaction.

I was expecting shock, or surprise, a raise of the eyebrows, something, but he hid whatever he was thinking well. We waited, silence growing with each passing second.

"I'm aware of the situation," he sighed. "Unfortunately, my knights and their soldiers are tied up elsewhere. Because of Parna's unrest, my men have had to station themselves along the border. The loss of their King and Queen has caused many issues. I must see to that before I worry about what's overseas. I'm sorry, General, Princess." He nodded to me, "Do you have others in your party?"

"Three others, your grace."

I copied Tristan's tone and while I didn't bow my head, I lowered my gaze. Something about the way he looked at me... Obviously he knew more than he was telling.

"Where are they? I'll send my man to fetch them. Rest here. Perhaps over the course of a few days General Tristan and I could come to an understanding." He looked to Tristan and extended his hand.

"We would be most grateful," Tristan nodded and shook his hand.

"Perhaps after Parna has regained control over its people I can help you stop Malthor and Algoroth."

"I see," Tristan narrowed his eyes but bowed his head. "Thank you for indulging us, and the hospitality to say the least. Are you sure we couldn't come to some sort of arrangement?"

"If you'll all excuse me, my knights are expecting me to follow up with them. Their messengers are waiting."

With that dismissal he turned and left the room through a back door while we all went to the great room outside our chambers.

"He's lying." Tristan sat on the stone ledge of a window, looking down at the courtyard. "Sean, do you think you could get to the others before his men?"

"I'm sure I can." He answered from where he stood in the middle of the room.

"Then take them to Wilden. If Celestial and I try to leave too soon it'll be suspicious, and I don't want Celestial on her own while I negotiate. Fangthorn can't be trusted."

"You just don't like how he looked at her." Danny looked from him to me.

"You're right. I don't." He snapped back.

"Are those my orders then?" Sean asked. Tristan nodded and got up to walk over and shake his hand. "I'll get us to Wilden and await your command, General."

"We won't be too far behind. I doubt he'll have an arrangement we will agree on and I'm not wasting more than a week here."

15

It turned out to be five more days of drudgery before the king finally summoned us back to the throne room. There was literally nothing to do within the castle but pace the rose garden maze in the courtyard, or to leave the castle grounds entirely. To my dismay on the third day when we ventured out we learned that the market we'd passed through was just a brief festival and was over. Most of the shops I'd wanted to visit were gone, probably already in the next town over. We did grab some sweet rolls on our way back but that was the highlight of our venture. Tristan led the way to the throne room, and Danny and I exchanged glances when the guard let us in and Fangthorn was standing by the back door amid a few of his knights, all armed and battle clad.

"You're all dismissed." Fangthorn left them, meeting us in the middle of the room as his knights filed out through the back. "I hear you went to the market the other day. It's a shame you came at the end of the festival. People bring trades and treats from all over Lyonshire."

"We managed to enjoy our time out, nonetheless." Tristan smiled politely and shook the king's outstretched hand. "I'm grateful you were able to take some time for us today. We'll be departing in the morning."

"Then I am glad I didn't delay any longer because I do have an idea to propose that may benefit my nation and yours. Perhaps we should sojourn somewhere more comfortable." He made as if to lead us away when he paused, glancing towards Danny and me. "You may dismiss your handmaiden, Princess. She doesn't need to be present for this."

"She is my officer, and I requested her presence," Tristan was quick to recover for me.

"Very well then."

Fangthorn clicked his tongue on the roof of his mouth and turned his back to us, expecting us to follow him through the back.

We were taken through and then down a series of halls that eventually led us outside where a table set for lunch waited for us. Fangthorn came up beside me, pulling out the chair that would put me just beside him. I glanced at the others but accepted the seat, not wanting to be rude. He sat himself and let Tristan and Danny take their seats. Servants bustled about, delivering plates of meat with rolls, butter, cheeses and what looked to me like grapes, and to wash it all down they poured us some sort of malt beverage. I assumed beer by the smell.

"So, General, what areas of Caleath was Stephen hoping I'd send relief?"

Fangthorn used his hands to tear a piece off the meat and pop it into his mouth. He chewed, quietly, waiting.

"King Stephen wanted me to explore a few different options. Primarily, he is concerned about the coastline. Goblins and the like have been exploiting the western shores. He is also concerned about Parna's doorway."

"And?" Fangthorn asked, sipping his drink, and getting a bit of foam in his mustache.

"We sail along the coast, obviously, but another fleet would be most beneficial." Tristan kept his voice level, tone moderate. Nothing about his demeanor was telling.

"I might have a few ships available, and I could deploy more if it were worth my while. We both know Goblins aren't seafarers. Neither are trolls. If they're not an immediate threat to me I'll need some incentive."

His eyes drifted to me while he talked and I felt his gaze, as if it were cutting right to the damaged part of me.

"Such as?" Tristan folded his hands neatly on the table.

"Well," Fangthorn began, "you all know my beloved left this life a couple years ago. As it is, I have no heirs," he said bluntly. "After me who will lead my people? I'll give you all the aid you request, in return I'm looking for a wife."

At this I looked from Fangthorn to Tristan who had lost some of his composure. *Did he want Tristan to find him a wife? What is he thinking?* Tristan cleared his throat and Danny just raised an eyebrow before she tried her drink, watching the pause and silent exchange between the King and the General, while trying to conceal her amusement.

"Your request is wildly inappropriate, to say the least." Tristan spoke boldly, "Second, even if it wasn't, I cannot and will not negotiate such a request. If you'll excuse us, I believe we're done here."

Tristan stood and Danny and I followed. I had barely pushed my chair in when Fangthorn spoke again, "Have a seat. We're not finished."

"Yes we are. Come on Celestial." Tristan remained standing.

Fangthorn took another drink and reached for something within his pocket. He opened a small jewelry box and took something out of it. Immediately I felt a sharp tug in my chest. The white glow coming through his fingers said it all for me, even if the others didn't understand yet. He didn't plan on negotiating at all or sending aid. I pressed a clammy hand over the scar which was now throbbing.

"Does this look familiar to you, Princess?"

He rested his elbow on the table and dangled a pendant just like the one Algoroth used to steal my Gift, except this one wasn't empty. As it dangled above the table it seemed to pull towards me. A bead of sweat trickled down my temple. Within the hollow glass my soul danced and flickered, pressing against the walls to find its way to me.

"What is that?" The edge to Tristan's voice suggested he knew, or at least suspected what it was.

"I'm sure by her reaction you can guess." He smiled and tucked the pendant back into his robe pocket. "Princess, you're the only opinion that matters here. Dealing with the General is merely a formality, one I do not wish to continue. As you are heiress to the Caleathian throne and the only person here within a stone's throw to my class, I will only negotiate with you, moving forward."

"No!"

Tristan slammed his fist down on the table and his Gift flared before filling his palms. Knights closed in behind him and Danny. Swords and spears at the ready.

"Think carefully, young General. Would you attack the one who holds the soul of your one true love?" he mocked.

Danny got to her feet now and slowly walked to Tristan. I wanted to do the same, but everything was heavy, and my heart was in overdrive. Breaths went in and out of me with little to show for it. Sweat beaded the back of my neck and my face continued to pale, the red of my lips quickly turning to pink, to nude and tinting blue. I tried reaching within for my Gift, but it wouldn't budge, frozen like the rest of me.

"Fangthorn, you will pay for this treachery," Tristan warned.

"Fangthorn can't pay for anything. Fangthorn has been dead since before your silly little engagement party. I'm not surprise I was able to fool you, seeing how none of you cared to know the young king or his queen." Green glowed in his eyes and the power went to his hand as it pulled the pendant back out.

"W-who are you?" I panted, still stuck in the chair.

He stood and came to me, hoisting me to my feet and pulled me away from the table with him. Neither Tristan nor Danny could follow, surrounded by blades.

"I am just a humble servant of the Dark. One of the first to fully embrace the Dark King's magic, even before the witch came along."

"Alakai, quit talking and kill those two already." Vince emerged from the hallway with the witch beside him.

Storming towards us, the witch took the pendant and me, retreating towards the hall. Power erupted from Tristan, flinging the table and all the knights away from him and Danny. They charged Alakai who met with equal ferocity. Bolts of green electricity shot from his hands, missing Tristan, and striking Danny. She screamed but the sound was cut off as his hand closed around her throat. Another powerful jolt of power surged into her before he dropped her on the floor to block Tristan's assault.

The witch held me back and both she and Vince watched Alakai block each and every one of Tristan's attacks with a wicked grin. My head was spinning. I'd felt uneasy since arriving but now it was a thousand times stronger.

"Leave it to an Andavir to get woozy around a little necromancy," Vince laughed, watching my condition deteriorate.

Alakai screamed and everyone's eyes snapped back to their battle. Tristan's glowing hands were wrist deep within Fangthorn's body.

"Go back beyond the river, spirit!"

Tristan ripped Alakai from the body and in a blinding flash the spirit and his electric power was gone, leaving Fangthorn's body to drop to the ground.

"I've seen enough," the witches grin curled into a scowl. "You and your friends have been way more trouble than you're worth. This," she held up the pendant, "I will destroy unless your general backs down."

Vince took me from her, and she tightened her knuckles over the pendant, strangling my soul and cracking the crystalline glass.

With each fracture I could feel the shards cutting into my soul. Desperate, I reached out for it, but Vince held me back.

The harder she squeezed the more I could feel my Gift reacting. It wanted out. It wanted the rest of my soul. Doing my best to control its glow I let it seep out a little at a time until it reached my fingertips and I reached to grab Vince's arm across my waist with a burning hand.

His cry startled the witch long enough for Tristan to rush over with his sword made of power. He swung for her neck just as black tendrils of power shot from her body, effectively blocking his attack, but in her distraction the pendant fell from her hand and shattered. Everything stopped as blinding white fire swirled into the air and into me.

16

The moment the light was gone Celestial went limp against Vince and a lock of her hair on top of her head turned shimmering white. Her Gift flared briefly and then settled.

"Kill them all, except the princess!" the witch raged and then wrapped herself in her black power and was gone.

"I've been waiting for that order, but don't worry. I'll look after Celestial."

He laid her down before drawing his sword and stepping over her, sauntering toward Tristan. The General waited for the knights to gather Fangthorn, and barely conscious Danny to move them away before he met his opponent in the middle of the room. Danny, although still disoriented, went to the Princess.

"She was so pleased when I offered up Celestial as a pure Andavir heir, and even more so when I found a second pure bloodline. The One will be reborn into a world we control, and the Dark King will rise again. Now we don't have to deal with her troublesome fiancé and try to keep you alive just for her eventual spawn."

"Shut up, traitor. Stephen and Katherine gave you every opportunity and more and you betrayed them and all of us. We used to be friends but now your just scum." Vince grinned and came forward, running the edge of his blade along Tristan's. "Because of you Celestial went missing for two years and forgot her life. You're the reason for all this chaos."

"All true, and I'm also the one who destroyed Parna. Little Scarlett and Zachary never will see their betrothal come to fruition, I'm afraid."

Tristan swung first. Steering his overconfident opponent towards the corner of the room, but he couldn't break Vince's defense. He swung harder, forcing his way through and knocking the sword from Vince's hand. The tip of his sword sliced through the air, momentum unimpeded by the collision with Vince's blade. Vince screamed and pressed a palm to his bloodied face before he shrouded himself in his power and vanished like the witch.

"General Tristan, we have a pulse!"

Tristan whipped around to find the highest-ranking knight pressing his fingers to King Fangthorn's neck. The King was pale but some of the color had returned to his face. Even from a few feet away it was clear his breath was strong.

"Danny, are you and Celestial okay?" He looked towards the hall where Danny had propped Celestial up against the wall, though she was still unconscious.

"I'm fine, but she won't wake up. I've healed her and there's nothing wrong with her as far as I can see."

"See what you can do for Fangthorn. I'll take Celestial to her room to rest. Come find us when you're done."

*****

I opened my eyes and found myself looking out of a cave, surrounded by Malthor's shadow monsters. The Droschuil waited what felt like forever, but eventually night came and the moment the sun sunk below the mountains and the sky turned into orange fire they went out. Algoroth waited at the bottom of the valley atop his dragon for them while legions of trolls and goblins and men recruited from surrounding countries had already begun the march to King's City. Vince, bearing a nasty scabbed scar that stretched from his jaw, up and across his cheek, in between his eyes and ended just over his brow, waited on the highest balcony with the witch and Malthor.

It was as if I knew Algoroth's plan already and was flying with the rest of the Droschuil as we followed him for days across the Caleathian wilderness, passing and destroying empty towns and villages on the way. Things progressed rapidly, and I just knew it wasn't far into summer. Algoroth's legions arrived not many days after him and the Droschuil. Ready to meet them, my father led his men, riding sword first to drive out the Dark forces.

I woke up briefly as the vision ended, only long enough to discern I was bundled in a blanket and laying in a moving cart, or wagon, or carriage with my head on Danny's lap for my pillow. I was asleep again before I could realize anything else. When I woke up next it must have only been a few hours later. Outside the sun was barely lighting up the road. Inside what I could now tell was a covered wagon I was alone.

I laid there a minute, gathering myself enough to fully wake up and notice we weren't moving and other than my breathing, it was silent. The lack of anything making noise was so profound I wondered if I'd gone deaf until I rapped on the floor of the wagon and was relieved when the knock sounded normal.

"Hello?" I crept out of the wagon. It seemed weird to disturb the silence. "Tristan? Danny?" I called out.

Still the only sound was me. No breeze, no birds, no sound from the horse pulling the wagon... I walked around to the side, where Danny stood looking up at a familiar looking man on a horse, and Tristan was standing next to her, looking like he was about to say something. No words escaped his lips, in fact nothing escaped any of them, all frozen in place.

"Guys?" I hurried over, tapping them on the shoulders, waving my hand in front of Tristan's face and even smacking the horse's bottom. Nothing gained the slightest reaction.

I backed away until my back hit the wagon, panicking and at the same time trying not to panic. I had been sure I was awake when I first opened my eyes. I pinched my arm.

"Ouch... okay," I breathed. The air moved slowly in and out of me, and all I could do was stand there and try to control it and stare at the Knights behind whoever Tristan was talking to.

"Everything will be normal soon enough," came a voice from nowhere.

"Where are you?" I asked.

I scanned the area but there was nobody but the four of us. Just beside me a light appeared and gradually became brighter and bigger. I shielded my eyes with my hands until it was gone, and the light was back to normal.

"Hello Princess. I see you are adapting nicely to your new self." Beside me was now a man. Besides the averageness of his height, there was nothing else I'd mark as ordinary. His shoulder length hair and long, thick beard were whiter than fresh snow, as were the robes he wore. His eyes pierced through me with an intense all-knowing quality and the softest blue irises. In his hand was a tall wooden staff topped with an hourglass that never seemed to fill up or stop flowing. All of this was dwarfed by the fact that I was sure this was not our first introduction.

A scene opened before my eyes. I was home, standing in the palace courtyard watching Vince tackle me down the stairs and pin me to the ground. His accomplices followed right behind and surrounded us. The memory played out but instead of cutting out right when I send out my Gift, it kept playing. Vince and everyone was blown away from me and I, myself was still laying on my back. I'd forgotten the number one rule of using your Gift. Don't use too much too fast. I remembered laying in agonizing pain, chest burning like I'd inhaled fire. None of my assailants moved and I recognized the stillness. The mysterious stranger showed up and pulled me to my feet. He looked exactly the same.

"You have two choices, Princess," he had said to me. "You may remain here and apprehend these Dark servants, or I will give you a new life, a new you. Before you choose, be warned that the choice you make now will seal the fate of not only you, but all mankind."

"How?" I asked.

"Staying now will ensure these men are brought to justice, but because other events never happen, Eä will fall. If you let me erase your memory, who you are, and give you a new life humanity stands a chance to fight for themselves."

"Well, I see how I was manipulated," I mumbled. The man shushed me and pointed back at the scene.

"Why me?" I'd asked, looking at the men laying around us and the scorch marks my power had left on the stone walls and floor.

"Because through you will come the One who was foretold centuries ago to defeat the Darkness and restore balance to the world. It's your bloodline, Celestial Andavir. Now, choose. Time must resume and I will not interfere with mankind again."

"If I let you give me a new life that's humanity's best chance?" he nodded. It wasn't long before I did too, and the scene ended. Back beside the wagon I realized why I knew him, even when that was our first meeting. "You're Father Time." I realized aloud, remembering stories my dad used to tell me before bed. "You said you weren't going to interfere again. Why are you here now? Why am I getting old memories back?"

"To remind you of your choice, and while I will take no further action, my wife wanted to give you some advice."

He turned to the side and a songbird landed on his shoulder then fluttered to the ground and immediately transformed into a woman. Long ash brown hair flowed down her back in loose waves and forest green eyes met mine from beneath thick lashes while rosy cheeks and pink lips against porcelain skin revealed her picturesque, natural beauty.

"I am Mother Nature. This flower I give you is the only way to cure a monster." She smiled at my confusion as she handed me the pale-yellow flower that looked like a cross between a lily, a rose, and a peony. "You'll know when to use the amaranth," she added cryptically before both she and Father Time vanished, and time resumed.

"Fangthorn, we're leaving. We have to get the princess home." It was clear in his tone that his mind was made up.

"Then I'm coming with you. My men can guide the reinforcements."

"No-" Tristan began but the King cut him off again.

"This is where we part, Knights. You have my orders." They turned and left, saying absolutely nothing to their King.

"Oh! Celestial, you're awake!" Danny finally turned her body enough to bring me into her view. "Why do you look like you've just seen a ghost?" she asked, her voice wary.

Instead of answering her, I looked at the flower, the testament to what had just happened, and went to Tristan, took his hand, and pulled him away from the others.

"You look like you're starting to recover. How do you feel? Are you sure you don't want to go sit in the wagon? Danny's right. You do look pale, and what's with the glowing flower?" Tristan kept his hand in mine, though my squeezing might have been a deciding factor and put his other on my waist.

"Um, probably in shock, no I don't want to sit down, and apparently the flower is an amaranth. Long story." I answered in sequence. "Anyway, we need to get home. Malthor's army is only a few weeks away from Kings City and he conjured enough of these shadow monster things to dwarf dad's army, even with the Elves help."

"That would have to be tens of thousands of them. If that's true then I can't bring you to Kings City."

"We have to warn them! I saw dad riding out at the front and I didn't get warm fuzzies like it would go well."

"We will call the minute we get cell reception in Wilden," Tristan promised, stepping closer to me. His hand went from my waist to my cheek where he brushed the white lock of hair off my face. I hadn't noticed it until he moved it, and my heart sank.

"Please tell me I didn't see white hair," I wined and let go of his hand.

"Just that little bit in the front..." Tristan tried to make it sound like nothing, but I pouted while I pinched the lock with two fingers and examined it. "So how did you come by the rarest magical flower in existence?" He dropped his voice to barely a whisper and leaned close.

"Let's talk again later. In other news, why is Fangthorn here?"

"I don't know," he huffed. "There is *no need* for you to come to Caleath!" he yelled.

In the end and after Tristan filled me in on why we weren't attacking Fangthorn, the King could not be persuaded to sail to Caleath instead of accompanying us. He said this way he could begin to pay back his debt more immediately. Since it wasn't really him that betrayed us, I didn't mind him coming. Truthfully, Tristan was the only one, and the two of them feuded the entire way to Wilden. One night, after both men had fallen asleep and it was just Danny and I at the fire, I asked her if she knew anything about it. According to her, there had been a brief conversation between the two about how Fangthorn could see the sense, politically, in he and I getting married. That conversation ended with Tristan punching him in the face. The rest of the trip was highly amusing after that, now that I knew they were literally fighting over me, and that Tristan was just being territorial.

It was a huge relief when we reached the outskirts of Wilden and traded in all the horses and the wagon for a car. Even sweeter was when Fangthorn got all of us rooms at Wilden's finest hotel so we could freshen up. I stayed in the shower for a solid hour just standing in the steamy bliss. When I emerged from the bathroom wrapped in a robe with my hair in a towel Danny was sitting on my bed drinking a cola and eating a toblerone from the mini bar and watching Parna's news channel.

"Want a mountain?" she asked, breaking off a piece for me. I took it and popped it into my mouth, chewing thoughtfully.

"How much do you want to bet Tristan and Fangthorn don't make it to the end of the day without fighting about him getting these rooms?"

"They already did. Tristan accused Fangthorn of trying to impress you. You might want to tell him to back off. He's royally pissing off Fangthorn, and in the end, General ain't no king." Danny flicked another mountain into her mouth and gave me a sidelong glance.

"Yeah, I'll talk to him when he gets back."

I picked up the department store bag and pulled out the clothes Tristan bought me on our way here and went to the bathroom to change. I came out feeling more like myself for the first time in months. "I missed jeans so much!" I sighed on my way out.

"Shush! Look at this!" She snatched the remote and turned up the volume.

"No one knows who the gunmen are, but we have reports that King Fangthorn of Lyonshire and a Caleathian General are within the courthouse as well, though nothing has been confirmed." The anchor woman put a finger over her earpiece, listening intently. "I just received word from our man on the scene that one of the gunmen looks remarkably like Vincent Russo, the man responsible for the failed coup in Caleath a couple of years ago."

"Put your shoes on!" I shoved my feet into the new flats, not bothering with socks or to remove the sticker from the inside.

"Cool it, Princess. You are my first priority," she said as she jumped to her feet to block my exit, "and I'll eat these muddy military boots before I let you leave this room."

*****

Tristan and Fangthorn were laying low behind the back pew in the first court room. They'd stepped inside for a bit of privacy with Councilman Mason Chamberlain, the late king's brother. Before the sudden burst of gunfire from the lobby he had assured them that, however sporadic and unpredictable Parna's doorways to earth were, every precaution was taken to ensure nothing went through them without their knowledge. He also assured them that the betrothal between their Princess Scarlett and Caleath's Prince Zachary was still in place.

The conversation had been brief, and the Councilman excused himself quite quickly after, but Tristan's business in Parna was now complete. Now, if they could get out of the room without getting shot, they had to get back to the hotel for the women and find one of the doorways to Earth.

*****

Danny didn't have to eat her boot to keep me from flying to Tristan, but she did have to lock me out on the balcony. She left the curtains half drawn so she could keep an eye on me and make sure I didn't try to do some crazy stunt like use my Gift to fly or tether down the ten stories to the ground. She had just answered her phone when I saw her look at the door. She crept to it, keeping the phone to her ear, and then looked through the peephole. She said something into the phone and looked back at me, motioning for me to hide behind the curtain. I did but watched through a small gap in the corner. In her hand there was a brief glow that materialized into a colt. Setting her phone on the little table by the TV, she moved back towards the balcony, aiming at the door. I heard the click as she unlocked it and slid the door open and shut, joining me.

"Don't say anything and stay out of sight. I don't know who's at the door, but they're armed." With the sliding door open a little I could hear the knocks on the door, urgently banging. "I'm busy!" Danny yelled, "Come back later!"

Before she could draw her next breath the door burst open, exploding into fragments. Men swept into the room guns first, firing blindly into the room. The balcony shook from the force of the blast, and we could see daylight coming from in between it and the exterior wall. Danny fired back blindly into the smoke as bullets struck the railings around her, narrowly missing.

Another explosion shattered the glass door. As if the balcony was attached as an afterthought it slowly began to pull away from the building. Danny continued firing shots out as if she didn't even notice, but I looked down, seeing a white line hovering two floors down in the air. Three shots were fired from inside and enemies hidden behind a screen of smoke. One struck my arm, the other grazed Danny's cheek and the last went on ahead into the distance. I looked down again, seeing the surface of clear blue waters as the shimmering white line opened to reveal another world.

"Danny!"

Anything I had thought to utter was lost in our screams as the balcony finally detached from the wall and we plummeted through the doorway and into the water.

"Who were those guys?" Danny exclaimed as we surfaced and caught our breath.

"I don't think that's an issue right now," I grunted. I swam one armed, the other cradled into my side where a red haze was steadily getting thicker. "It looks like we're in the middle of the ocean."

"Thank you for your brilliant observation Sherlock. Heal yourself before sharks come please."

"I was waiting for them to come, actually. I've always wanted to pet one," I retorted as I sent out my Gift, using it to push the bullet out of my arm and heal the cracked bone and bullet hole, while she used hers to clean the water. "Any idea where that doorway sent us to? Do you think it will open again?"

"Your guess is as good as mine, Princess. So, I'm gonna try and make a boat, or raft or something. Can you keep the man-eating fishes away?"

"No problem."

I sent out my Gift, a translucent bubble all around us, extending deeper than was probably needed. It took her until almost dusk to construct a small wooden rowboat. It was as we treaded water and kept each other safe, (while I watched her struggle with her Gift) that I realized how special and rare my own power used to be before Father Time took me away from everything and put me into this life. Even if a few memories and even my personality carried over, I was different now. Yes, I remembered those closest to me enough to love them again, and perhaps stronger than before, but everything was still different. Considering I wasn't the same person, why was my Gift and my soul still so important to Vince and the witch he worked for?

If I was going to see an end to all of this, I had to get to the bottom of why they wanted me in the first place. There was the little matter of some prophecy and the "One". If I were to figure anything out, I'd have to start with how that person fit into me and my blood line and why.

Clouds overhead thickened and began to block out what was left of the setting sun. Our Gifts were the only reason we could still see, and the sudden change in light drew me from my thoughts. The small rowboat was as ready as it was going to be, and while neither of us said anything to each other, it looked and felt sketchy as could be.

"I'll keep the sharks and things away as long as I can. Why don't you try to sleep? You look wiped out," I offered after we climbed in and dried off with our Gifts. "Oh!" I wrapped her up in my Gift.

"I'm already wearing a shirt, Princess, so what are you doing?"

I closed my eyes and focused, and a few minutes later let the power on her fade to nothing.

"Life vest," I panted, sweating from the little bit of effort.

"Where's yours?"

"I'll make it in a minute."

Danny stifled a yawn but nodded and curled up with her head on her arm for a pillow. It wasn't long before I could hear her softly snoring over the sound of the little waves around us. To make my own life vest, all I was waiting for was for my strength to recover, but it took everything I had to make hers and then keep up the protective bubble. Over the course of several hours the seas became rougher and the wind grew to howl around us. My whole body ached from the prolonged use of my Gift, but I was wearing a little life vest now too, at great cost to the bubble. Eventually I had no choice but to wake her, just for her to help me keep our rickety boat afloat.

Without warning the waves that had been knocking us around for hours swelled and grew, towering over us like mountains. They bore down on us, pouring over my barrier. The frail bubble of power that had so far kept us safe and dry was thinning with each wave that crashed into it. Glowing cracks began to appear, spreading and shattering the bubble down upon our heads as the monster wave bore down. Water filled the raft, tearing it into tiny splinters and pushing us below the surface before currents took us away.

17

Local police had scoured the building and the immediate vicinity for Princess Celestial and Danny, but both were missing. The only trace left behind was the amaranth now resting safely in Tristan's uniform jacket pocket. The assailants were nowhere to be found. Although they were identified through the hotel's security footage as members of a political activist group nicknamed the "Rebels", it was impossible to tell where they went because of the damage done to the cameras from the explosion. Their leader, Lex, had already released a statement saying they were ready to expel the invaders out of their lands, just like they eliminated the late King and Queen of Parna. This was before the attack...

Tristan hung up his newly acquired phone for the third time in a row with no answer. He hoped Danny wasn't answering because she didn't recognize the number, but there was no trace of his old phone back at the courthouse. Still fuming, he picked up a charred lamp base and chucked it against the wall, cursing under his breath. He went back towards the balcony kicking a small bit of debris over the edge. He watched it fall, expecting it to land amongst the bushes down below, but about a quarter of the way down it was gone in a flash of light. In one swift movement his phone was in his hand again and dialing.

"Sean, I have a lead. How quick can you and Levi get here?"

*****

"This one's breathing! What about that one?"

Someone touched my neck, I roused as we both felt my pulse drumming against the firmly pressed fingers.

"Yeah, I think she's coming to."

Even as the guy checking my pulse spoke I flickered my eyes open. The sun was blinding. I closed my eyes again and the world drifted away as if I was floating back in the boat. Then I was. Danny had just fallen asleep, and I was maintaining the useless bubble we foolishly thought would keep man-eaters and monster waves away from us. After only three of the towering walls of water crashing on us my Gift faltered and the shield shattered. Our raft was broken into pieces and there wasn't even one piece big enough for us to hold onto to stay afloat. I couldn't remember more than five minutes after we were in the water. We were in, trying to stay surfaced, and then a fourth wave broke over us, and I was on the beach, someone checking my pulse.

"Celestial." It wasn't the guy that had checked my pulse. It wasn't a man at all. The more I tried to focus the more it felt like I was still on the water. "Princess, wake up," came the new voice again.

Someone shook my shoulder none too gently and slapped my cheek. I coughed and wished I hadn't. Sea water came up, burning my throat and nose on the way out. Swift hands rolled me onto my side and kept me there until my air way was clear.

"Ow," I wheezed, shifting onto my elbow.

"I frickin thought you were dead! You can't freak me out like that!" This time I recognized Danny's voice.

"I'm a cockroach. You can't kill me," I rasped. My insides and my head screamed at me not to move but I sat up the rest of the way and opened my eyes, wincing from the pain and the brightness. "Where are we?"

"Miami, Florida," the guy who checked my pulse answered. "Do you girls need an ambulance? Are you sure you'll be okay?"

"Know a good hotel?" Danny answered, helping me to my feet.

Water sloshed out of the tops of my shoes and sand had gotten everywhere nobody wanted it.

"Uh, there's a couple about a mile down the road. Are you really sure you don't want an ambulance?" he asked again.

"Maybe a ride would be nice," I tried.

"We came on the bus..." he faltered. "But one comes like every twenty minutes at that stop by the showers. Just go two stops and there will be a few hotels," He offered instead.

The bus stop wasn't too far away, maybe a quarter mile down the shoreline. However, after almost drowning and still in salty, sandy, soggy clothes, it was a tremendous effort to slosh our way out of the sand and all the way down the boardwalk to the bus stop. We could have used our Gifts to dry off and heal our aching muscles, but with our two "rescuers" right by our sides the whole time that was out of the question.

The bus ride, however short, was a slight relief to our aching bodies. We got off at the second stop as instructed and walked right into the first place we saw. Called simply, *Le Hotel,* it wasn't run down, but it was dated, stuck in the early nineties or late eighties. Originally opened to be a comfortable play on French design and the coastal Florida culture, it now looked like Becka's grandmother's living room.

I had no idea where Danny pulled it out of, but her black card got us a double queen room for one night. That seemed to mute all the mumbling about the puddles we were leaving on their carpet and earn instead a false politeness and the offer of a bundle of fresh linens and towels immediately delivered to our room, along with laundry services for our sopping clothes. Once we got to the room she promptly got on the phone and dialed what sounded like a twenty something digit number.

"This is Captain of the Guard Danielle Gianni. The hawk and eagle are flying to the nest, but there are snakes in the grass." Finishing her message, she hung up and flipped through the room service pamphlet sitting on the table by the phone.

"What was that?" I asked, kicking off my shoes and pulling off my dripping socks. She put the phone back to her ear, dialing as she talked.

"I left a message in Tristan's voicemail. I realized on the way here I did recognize some of the guys at the shoot-out. Some were Vince's guys, another was in the alliance, but the one doing most of the shooting was someone I think I recognize from Parna's High Council. I don't know his name... Anyway, since I don't know who else might be with him I was basically saying we're safe and going home, but he needs to be careful. Hi!" she broke off suddenly, "I'd like to order room service please... One of your pepperoni pizza's, the Cuban sandwich, the barbecue bacon burger, crab cakes appetizer, and two orders of fries, and what do you have to drink?" She was quiet for a short stretch and then ordered two sodas with an extra bucket of ice.

"Do you want to shower first?" I asked when she finally got off the phone.

"Princess gets first dibs," she said while she crossed the room to the entertainment center where there was a mini fridge and bar.

Promptly she pulled out two water bottles and tossed one across the room to me. We drained the bottles dry and then I made her shower first. She was quick about it and came out wrapped in one of their fluffy white towels and one wrapped around her hair. I slipped passed her and closed the door to the thickly steamed bathroom. She had already deposited her clothes in the laundry bag given to us at check in and I was ready to put all of mine in there too. Once I did, I slipped the bag outside the bathroom.

I scrubbed all the salt and sand off my body and out of my hair and then just stood in the steaming hot water for probably over twenty minutes. When I finally emerged and wrapped up in the towels my skin was pink from the heat. There were six towels supplied, so I had no problem copying Danny and using two towels myself.

"Hey lobster, come try a crab cake," she greeted me as I came back into the room.

The edge of the bed groaned under my weight, no doubt complaining of its many years of service. Danny had the spread laid out all on her bed and it was a mouthwatering sight. I took the offered cake, and then grabbed a few fries.

"I called your dad while you were in the shower and filled him in. He hasn't heard from anyone since Tristan reported on the attack on our room. I guess Tristan's signal was inadequate. He couldn't even give a full report."

"I hope he's okay. I mean he must have gotten out of the courthouse... Do you know if he's still in Parna?"

"He was when he called your dad, but he said something about a doorway to Virginia. I can only assume he's going there or went there looking for us." I nibbled a fry in silence. So far as we knew Tristan and the others were safe, but I really wished Danny had been able to get through to him when she called. "I'll call Tristan again after we eat. Oh, I hope you don't mind, but I didn't want these hotel people handling our clothes, so I used my Gift to clean them myself. They're in the closet. Oh, and our shoes too," She added.

"You rock," I sighed in relief.

I hadn't relished the idea of a stranger handling my delicates.

For the next hour we stuffed our faces with Danny's room service order while we plotted how to get home. With no mode of transportation, no extra clothes or luggage, it was decided that tonight we would hit the hotel's restaurant for dinner and then again tomorrow for breakfast, shop the boardwalk for an extra set or two of clothes, and then call a taxi or car service to take us to the airport. We called Tristan again but to no avail, and this time Danny left no message. I tried fifteen minutes later and left a short message, nothing more than a "Hi, we're safe and I love you".

After leaving the voicemail I laid atop the plush bed, my mind running over everything before the attack, during it, and after. I played back everything to the present moment. There wasn't anything we could have done differently to avoid being here. It wasn't as if we foresaw them trying to blow us up, and if we had hid anywhere but the balcony they would have.

Snuggling into the down stuffed pillows I closed my eyes and listened to the daytime TV to drown out my worrying about Tristan and the others. The noise did nothing for the rapidly growing headache. However, eventually I must have dozed off because no sooner than the sitcom's theme song rang in my ear, it was suddenly replaced with soft music.

I was no longer laying down but sitting up with a fork in one hand and a knife in the other, looking down at a plate with the restaurant's logo stamped on it. Not that the chicken parmesan didn't look good, but I set the utensils back on the table, leaving my meal half eaten. Intuitively I knew this was a vision. It would happen very soon, potentially even tonight. I could have clued in from the strange clarity of everything I saw, which was better than a dream but worse than actually being awake. Danny sat across the small table from me, casually reading a pamphlet of local must-see attractions. Her plate was speckled with crumbs and a scant piece of crispy fish skin. I looked around the open room, seeing our hotel across the street through the big windows.

"How did you enjoy your meal, ladies?" a waiter asked, surprising us both and carrying an empty tray tucked under his arm.

"Excellent," Danny answered without even looking up.

However, I did. Before I could utter even a startled gasp Vince smacked me across the face with the tray. My shoulder hit the floor harder than he had hit me, but it was still more than enough to stun me. A blur of movement and a quick succession of shots sent the room into chaos as those closest to us scrambled away. I pushed myself to my knees and looked up to Vince. I saw, not him, but the blackness inside the barrel of his gun before he fired.

I woke, flailing my arms in front of me and flinging myself off the bed.

"Get up! Get your shoes on! We gotta go!"

Blood started flowing from my eyes and running down my cheeks.

"What's going on?" Danny followed me into the bathroom and waited while I cleaned up my face and held wads of tissue under my eyes while I waited for the bleeding to stop.

"Somehow Vince knows we're here and he's coming for us. We have to leave."

"How could he possibly know that?" she sighed and huffed, making a noise with her lips.

We both just stood there for a minute until her face drained of color, then dropped in unfortunate realization.

"What is it?" I groaned, dropping the tissue in the waste bin under the counter.

"The only thing I can think of is if Vince somehow got Tristan's phone and hacked the voicemail. They could trace the call here... possibly to the room. It's a long shot, but he's the only one I haven't been able to reach."

Air filled my lungs, flowing slowly, then gliding gently back out while I tried to gather myself.

"So, my dad did talk to Tristan? We're *positive* it was him? Did he say anything about losing his phone?"

"It was him," she confirmed. "After you went missing we were all given new codes to check in with, and we change them after every couple weeks unless we're in the field." She went on, "Your dad didn't say anything about a new phone number, but he did say Tristan wasn't easy to understand, and the report was incomplete because of an inadequate signal."

"We should get going and leave everything here in case they do come. Maybe if we leave clothes behind or something, we can trick them into thinking we'll be back and give ourselves a head start."

I was just thinking out loud, but Danny sighed and took off her uniform shirt, unbuttoning thoughtfully. Wordlessly she went and hung it on one of the hangers and made a point to tuck her boots away too. After a minute her entire uniform was hanging and she'd used her Gift to make herself a new, more casual outfit. She was basic with khaki cargo capris, a white fitted t-shirt, and sneakers.

"My turn I guess..." I sighed.

Unlike her I made the clothes first and then changed before hanging up the old outfit. The new outfit was much more "touristy". A brightly colored sundress, white with watercolor splashes of coral, turquoise, and soft yellow. The sleeves barely covered my shoulders, and the skirt came down just above my knees. I then chose to replace my shoes with white sandals.

"Seriously? A dress and sandals? That's what you want to wear to evade your assassin?" She paused in gathering her wallet and making the room look "lived in" to give me a judging look.

"What? I can run in sandals, and I'll blend in with everyone else."

She rolled her eyes but didn't push any further. Instead, she picked up the phone and dialed the twentysomething digit number for the palace and left another covert message for whoever was on the other end. We made sure to leave the room keys behind, hidden under the little plant by the phone, and fifteen minutes later we were on a bus headed north with nothing but Danny's wallet and the clothes on our backs.

Eventually the bus came close enough to the airport so we hopped off and Danny managed to get us the last two business class one-way tickets to Hartford Connecticut for the following morning, the only flight that would get us anywhere close to getting home. After spending the night in the airport it was a relief when the plane allowed us to board. Every second sitting in the air felt long and arduous. To pass the time, I borrowed the laptop from the person sitting across the aisle from me to check the email I hadn't logged into in almost a year. Over a hundred unread emails, and all (besides some spam) were from Becka and Mike. I felt my heartstrings pull as I clicked on the most recent one. Delivered just this morning, Becka labeled the subject line: Its Wedding Day!

Hi MIA Friend,

Well, it's wedding day! I wish you were here helping me get ready today. I'm sure if you were here you'd tell me how absolutely insane I am for getting married when Mike and I haven't even dated a year. I will state for the record that we have known and cared about each other since elementary school, plus we both graduated this past spring, in case you didn't get that email. In a way I hope I have the wrong email address, or you're stuck in Amish country with no internet. Then at least the silence all these months wouldn't have been intentional. If you've been getting these please come. The wedding is at six tonight, just a little backyard wedding at Mike's house, but it will be fun and cozy. Anyway, I hope that, wherever you are, you are safe and know how much we miss you. BFF Becka A.K.A. Mrs. Michael Danes

I paused for only a second before I hit reply and started typing furiously.

Becka!

I have to keep this brief, but yes. You are insane. Congratulations!!! You and Mike will be awesome! Sorry I dropped off the earth without warning... I have been through a lifetime of chaos since I last saw you. I can't explain any of it now, but I'm on a plane headed to Hartford, and from there I will do everything in my power to be there for you and Mike today. -BFF MIA Friend Celeste

That was the only email I read and responded to before I logged out and gave the guy his laptop back. Since Danny and I couldn't get seats next to each other I couldn't tell her about it until after we landed. When we did finally get off the plane and had gotten our rental car I had made up my mind and would not be talked out of it.

It was a mundane road trip to say the least. We weren't followed and we didn't run into any trouble. We just drove, and drove, and drove. What would have been about a four-hour trip almost doubled because of multiple traffic accidents, construction delays, and long detours to go around closed roads.

I took over for Danny as we came to Maine. When we finally pulled into Portland the wedding was well over and the reception was coming to an end. I pulled up to the curb in front of Mike's house, behind a car full of guests on their way out. Once they pulled out and began down the road I could see a clean white car with "Just Married" painted in white letters on the back window. A few people lingered on the lawn, casually sipping drinks. Some I recognized, others I assumed must be extended family or new friends made since my sudden departure.

"Are you going in?" Danny asked after a few minutes of loitering.

"Yeah, let's go."

She still opened her door first, but after a quick mental push and a long exhale I opened the door and climbed out before I changed my mind. Danny followed but at a distance and stopped at the gate to the backyard, standing off to the side but able to see almost everything she needed to play my guard. I stopped in the middle of the yard, surrounded by soft gold string lights, a few simply decorated tables with white tablecloths, vases of pink and white roses, and little golden beads in the vases. Becka was the real sight to see, dancing slowly with Mike, in a sleeveless Cinderella dress with her hair elegantly swept up. Nobody took notice of me as I crossed the lawn and sat at one of the empty tables, waiting for their song to finish.

"Celeste?"

"Hmm?" I whipped my head to look behind me. *"Andrew?"* I very nearly did not recognize him in his button shirt and tie, hair combed to the side, so different than I last saw him.

"Hey, it is you! I wasn't sure... Haven't seen you around in a long time. I heard about your mom. I'm really sorry."

"Oh, thank you," I fumbled for what to say. The song had ended and Becka and Mike were moving towards the house and the back door that was wide open. "It was nice seeing you but if you'll excuse me... I need to have a word with the bride and groom."

I was already backing away when Danny swept in beside me, reminding me that we needed to hurry. She went back to standing by the gate just as quickly. I sighed. She was right but being torn out of this part of my life was one of the hardest things I'd faced and was still facing. The fact that I'd missed so much and was going to keep missing out was a bitter pill to swallow. The worst of the bitter truths was that Stacey was gone, and my life with my friends here was over.

That reality came crashing down on me as I stepped inside Mike's house, looking at where countless memories had been made. The weight of it sunk down on my chest, making each breath heavy. Though there were a couple people inside, I was still unnoticed. I kept moving to keep it that way. Passed the kitchen and the open living room, I passed into the entryway-family room combo where the stairs to the upstairs were tucked against the wall between the front door and the garage door. Mike stood there alone at the bottom of the stairs, staring down at his phone, scrolling absently.

"Seems like the wall could hold itself up." Mike looked up in a hurry, clearly thinking he had been alone. "Hey, if you don't want people to see what's on your phone you should have picked a different place to scroll." I joked.

"Celeste?" He looked like I just smacked him in the face. "Oh my gosh!" His warm familiar smile spread across his face, and he came over, meeting me halfway and wrapped me up in his arms. "Where have you been hiding?"

He let me go and stood arm's length away while we took each other in.

"Well look at you! You clean up nice, Mr. Tuxedo. Congratulations!" I moved in and hugged him again, though only lightly. "Becka sure wrangled you quick."

"So seriously, what happened to you? When did you have open heart surgery? You just vanished and show up so different? Becka said she emailed you about the wedding but neither of us thought you'd show up."

Ouch, I blanched from the brutal honesty.

"I'm sure you guys don't have time to hear it all, and you wouldn't believe it anyway. I'm fine now, though. I'm sorry for not being able to stay in touch, but I'm so excited for you two. I think you'll be great together."

"Really?" he rolled his eyes and scoffed. "You're not going to explain anything? You didn't even come to Stacey's funeral! We're all actually kind of pissed at you, to be honest. I mean, yeah, I'm glad to see you're alive, but you gotta give me something."

The weight so momentarily lifted crashed down on my chest again and I just stared up at him. My mouth just hung there, gaping open like a fish, even though my brain was demanding myself to say something, anything.

"So, that's how it is? Alright. Well, I just checked our reservation and if we don't check in soon, we'll lose the suit. You should hurry upstairs if you want to see Becka. She's madder at you than I am, so maybe try to be a little more real with her."

I swallowed hard. Tears burned behind my eyes, but I forced it down and swallowed the crushing disappointment of this reunion. He shifted his weight, glancing towards the back of the house. Danny was approaching.

"Hey, done catching up yet? We really gotta go..." she trailed off when she got close enough to see the tension between us and the emotions clouding my eyes again. "What did you do?" She turned on Mike, shoulders squared and eyes begging for a reason to hit him.

"Nothing, Danny. We're done here, I guess. Give this to Becka for me." I handed Mike an envelope I'd made prior to seeing

Andrew. Inside was a check that would make a sizable down payment on any home. I made towards the front door, turned the handle, and pulled it open when I paused and looked back. "Oh, and I didn't have surgery, and I didn't dye my hair. I was abducted. Danny was bringing me home. That's *all* I'm going to say."

I left it at that and left the house. Though I did hear Danny tell him that if she found out he hurt me in any way she would kick his butt. I crossed the lawn and jumped into the car, letting Danny get behind the wheel.

"That couldn't have gone worse," I said once she closed the door. I scrunched my face to try not to cry but everything spilled out anyway. "Just drive," I hiccupped and wiped the tears gathering under my chin.

"I think the bride is looking for you," Danny nodded towards the house where sure enough Becka was hurrying across the lawn in her big, poufy princess wedding gown.

"Celeste wait! Don't go yet!"

I could hear her even inside the car and reluctantly pulled the handle on my door and pushed it open. She stopped a couple feet from the car in the grass and dropped her skirts, breathing hard. I hadn't even dried my face or stood up all the way before she came and pulled me into her, holding on as if that was going to keep me from leaving again.

"You came!" She was crying now too but looked way prettier doing it than I did. "Mike's wrong. I miss you. I wanted you here. Please don't go yet."

"I'm sorry I never got to say goodbye." I was barely understandable, but she knew me best and we'd had more than a few conversations where neither one of us could be understood by anyone else.

"You're not leaving until you have some cake and fill me in on where you've been. I literally was reading your email when I heard you and Mike get into it downstairs. I would have come down sooner, but I couldn't believe I was hearing you. Please come inside. We have so much to talk about!"

She didn't wait for an answer. She pulled me back to the house by my forearm and Danny jumped out of the car. Cursing under her breath and following us, she caught up as we came back into the house. Becka hardly noticed all the people staring at us on the lawn or Mike's calls after her as she marched both of us upstairs.

"Becka we have to go before we lose the room!" Mike called up to us.

Either she didn't hear him or didn't care because she didn't even so much as look down at him over the railing on the way to Mike's bedroom.

"It smells like an old pizza box in here," Danny complained, closing the door behind her.

"Ok, last time I saw you, you were a lightbulb. Now I hear you tell Mike you were kidnapped? You better start talking, now."

For a minute she looked more intimidating than my mom, and Kathrine was Queen of an entire Empire. Danny came up beside me, wide eyed, and grinding her teeth.

"Um," she cleared her throat, "how was our friend a lightbulb?" Danny looked from me to Becka, looking like her head was going to explode.

"When I went to school after the accident, before Stacey was attacked, I couldn't figure out how to turn off my Gift. Becka was the only person I trusted to talk to," I explained.

"Stacey was attacked? Celeste, what happened? One day you're around, and the next you're gone and there's police tape around your house, and a week later all your stuff is being given to charity, and there's a funeral and you weren't there!"

The tears were flowing again as I began to explain, "Our house was broken into, and they killed her. I'm only here because I got lucky. After that I was brought to my birth parents in New York. It all happened really fast."

"Celeste, she can't know about your Gift or anything about us. You know what I have to do, right?" Danny, ever so sensitive, interjected.

"Danny go wait in the car," I snapped. Turning on her and not even trying to stop my Gift from flaring.

"Ok, Lightbulb." Becka reached out, careful not to touch me where I was glowing beneath my skin and turned me away from Danny. "I haven't even told Mike about your glow trick. All I ask is that you don't kill me on my wedding day. Now, that being said... *talk*. I want answers. Why were you guys attacked, who kidnapped you, and what the hell happened to you? I've been worried sick about you."

"That's why I wanted to come." I turned towards Becka, fighting the urge to keep being protective. "I wanted you and Mike to know I didn't just up and abandon you, and I haven't been ignoring you. I just legit couldn't contact you or be contacted until just the other day."

Becka backed up a few steps and sat carefully on the edge of Mike's bed. It was a squeaky, stiff, twin bed that was almost as old as he was and covered by a comforter with cartoon faces so faded it was impossible to tell what show they were from. The skirt of her dress rose like a cloud around her and settled only after she smoothed it with her hands.

"Becka?" Mike's voice called from the hall before he cracked the door open and came halfway in. "If we don't leave now we will lose our reservation."

Her already wet eyes overflowed, streaking her cheeks. Mike went right to her, forgetting about us for a minute.

"Open the envelope," I said to him. He did a double take, looking at me, then the envelope, then Becka, and then back at me again. "I can reply to emails now, and I'll be able to call too. I promise we can catch up, but after your Honeymoon." Mike sighed and stuck his finger in the small opening, tearing the seal before pulling out the check inside. Both went quiet. "Maybe don't worry about your reservation tonight and go somewhere exciting tomorrow instead. Are your numbers the same?" I asked.

"They are, but Celeste we can't accept this! It's way too much!" Becka finally found her voice.

"Yes you can. Call it my penance for disappearing and then showing up and ruining your wedding night."

"We seriously need to go now." Danny grabbed my arm. "Lovely meeting you both. Congratulations. Now, if I don't get her home to her parents before midnight I may potentially be fired, so good night."

We were already in the hallway before she was done talking and Becka rushed after us.

"Wait! Swing by my mom's first! I saved some things from your house before it was sold at auction. I think you'll want them. The box is in my closet."

"What did you save?" I asked, pulling free to Danny's dismay.

"There's a couple photo albums, some of Stacey's books, and some of your clothes. I had to sneak in and out, so I wasn't able to get a lot. I tried to save what I thought you'd want if you ever came back."

"Thank you," I could barely get the words out before I was staring at my feet trying not to cry. "Congratulations again, you guys. We gotta go, but I'll call and leave you a good number for me. See ya."

We were back in the car and pulling out onto the street before I knew it. Per usual, Becka's front door was unlocked so we let ourselves in. We were in and out in less than a minute, and back on the road again. I sat in the passenger seat with the box on my lap in silence. I wasn't crying, but the surge of emotions running through me had rendered me speechless. Danny didn't try to engage with me, but her sideways glances at me didn't go unnoticed. I could tell, without her saying, that she was concerned. At least, now that I remembered better and had spent so much time with her.

Instead of looking through the box I mentally prepared myself for seeing everyone again. Since it was so late I wasn't sure who I would maybe see tonight or in the morning. A large part of me wanted everyone to be asleep so I could sneak to my room in the palace unnoticed. I wasn't sure I could react properly. I should be excited. I should have been feeling anxious to finally come home and to see Tristan and my family again. Instead, all I felt was grief. I missed Stacey more than any of them, and there would be no reunion for a lifetime.

It was two thirty in the morning when we pulled into Tristan's driveway. The porch light was on, but the only light in the house was what looked to be one from the kitchen.

"Ready to go in?" Danny asked, stifling a yawn.

"Yeah," I sighed.

With my box in tow, I followed her out of the car, up the walk and to the front door where she rang the bell twice, knocked, rang again, and then knocked twice.

"Let me take that," Danny gently took the box from me.

We could hear some movement inside and then the door was open, and a very disheveled Tristan pulled me into him, breathing me in. Arms around him, I tried to keep it together, but the dam was crumbling and all the grief I was holding in threatening to break through in a surge. I tried to peel away, and Tristan responded, pulling back only enough to kiss me.

Just as I kissed him back everything I'd been holding in poured out of me, streaming in rivers down my face and leaving me gasping for breath. I fell headlong into the grief that felt as if it was so deep it would swallow me whole. I held onto him as he guided us inside and closed the door behind us.

"It's ok now. I've got you. You're home." His lips pressed against my forehead, voice soft, low, and soothing. "Can you tell me what's wrong?" he asked after a few minutes.

He let go and tilted my face up towards his. I shook my head and stepped back, wiping my cheeks. The box on the table caught my eye, then Tristan's. Arms folded around myself I went to it, Tristan following, never leaving my side.

"Celeste?" He tried again, resting his hand on my shoulder. "Babe, you can tell me anything. I'm not going anywhere. I love you." He tried when I was still quiet.

"I love you too..." My voice was much softer than intended.

On top of the box was a framed photo of Stacey and me. It was the last full day we spent together, on a beach eating lobster rolls and walking along the shore. She insisted we stop and take a selfie, which she then printed and hung in the living room. A week later I rolled the car into the ocean and life changed forever.

"I should take this stuff Home. You know, get it off your table and out of your way." I grabbed the box and fought back a new wave of tears, instead channeling my concentration to my Gift, and opening the door.

"Hold on, babe." He held onto me, hands on my shoulders. "Do you remember our engagement party, and how after I dropped you off at your room and we agreed to meet for breakfast the next morning?"

"Except the coup interrupted everyone's lives." I nodded.

"Right." He came around and took the box, putting it back on the table and I let the doorway close. "I had an ulterior motive for breakfast. I was going to give you my wedding present early, but I never got to."

"What was it?" I asked, drying my eyes, and breathing a little easier.

He stepped into the middle of the house, away from everything and gestured all around.

"I closed on this house the morning of the party and was going to surprise you. It was still technically under construction, finishing touches mostly."

"You bought this for us?"

I almost couldn't believe it, but this was the kind of grand gesture Tristan would have wanted to do. He was a go big or go home kind of guy, after all.

"I did. Before all this stuff happened you always talked about wanting something simpler than living in the palace, but not wanting to be too far from your family. Your dad helped me find the land and agreed to let doorways to and from Eä open here."

"How did I get so lucky to have you? You're too wonderful and so far out of my league."

I went to him and put my arms around his neck. He just laughed and slipped his hands onto my hips.

"There's no way you're out of *my* league. You tell me why you're slumming it with a lowly commoner like me, Princess. The fact is that *I'm* completely out of *your* league."

"Then get down here and kiss me," I smiled, getting up on my toes and waiting for him to meet me halfway.

"Is that an order, Princess?" He leaned in close enough for me to feel the warmth of his breath on my face.

"Uh-huh." I breathed as we kissed.

Being with Tristan improved my mood drastically. We talked for a while, some about Stacey and Mike and Becka, and some about where we saw things going in the future. We looked through the albums in the box and he laughed at seeing me in braces again, and how Stacey insisted I dress up as a bunny for Easter every year until I was eleven. By four in the morning, we both decided we should stop talking and try to get a few hours of sleep. Knowing my dad would be livid if I slept here without us being married, Tristan walked me through the doorway to Caleath and through the palace to my room where I fell asleep on the bed without getting under the covers or changing my clothes, the box tucked safely under my bed.

18

It felt like the best sleep I'd had in years when I finally woke up the next day. Sunlight was streaming in through the windows and the French doors, flooding my room with light and comfortable warmth against the air-conditioned coolness blowing down on me from the vents above. Despite this I still had to unglue my eyes from the crusties the sand man used to put me into a sleep so deep I didn't remember any dreams.

I rose stiff and barely comprehending where I was. *Home, in the palace,* I reminded myself. Everything looked the same. Noting had been moved, nothing added to my room, or taken out. I shuffled across the room to the bathroom, deciding I needed a shower, a fresh set of clothes, and to brush my teeth before going anywhere or seeking anyone out. As anxious as I was to see my family, they probably wouldn't appreciate morning breath and scraggly bed head. However, after freshening up I decided I wanted to wear sweats, a t-shirt that Tristan gave me because it shrunk in his washer, and my memory foam bunny slippers.

I took my time going to the kitchen, walking slowly, and soaking in the bliss of being home. It was almost surreal, being back and this time remembering that this is home, and they really are my friends and family. As much as I wanted to share everything with Stacey it was the best I could do to double back and pull her old Harvard sweater over Tristan's gifted shirt.

All through the palace my mind was buzzing. I was finally in a place where I could fit all the pieces of Vince's twisted plan together. First I wanted to study this bloodline they kept talking about. The kitchen was buzzing with activity when I walked in. Several of the workers went sheet white when they saw me. I tried to ignore it, wordlessly putting on a kettle and rummaging in the pantry until I found the peach herbal tea I was looking for. It wasn't long before the water was ready, and I was on my way to the palace library with the tea's fruity vapors waking up my nose as the baggie steeped.

"Princess!" a familiar voice called behind me, down the hall. I turned just in time to see where the little voice had come from.

"Levi, hi!" My smile was genuine. "How long have you been here?" I asked.

He ran to me, jumping to hug me. I caught him mid jump and hugged him.

"Just a few days," he answered. "Why do you have bunnies on your feet?"

"They're just slippers. It's not real fur, either. Where's Tristan at?"

"He's in war council, in the library. Our messengers arrived this morning with news, but I haven't heard anything else yet." Sean came to us and reached out, ruffling Levi's hair while I hoisted the boy onto my hip and juggling my tea. "We were actually just on our way to the pool for a swimming lesson."

"Fun! I loved my swimming lessons. I learned how to swim with Tristan and his dad." I recalled the memory fondly.

Those were the days that planted our lifelong friendship and eventual courtship. Sometimes I wondered if our dads planned it all, because they had been friends for years before either Tristan or I was born.

"Tristan said the pool is *huge!*" Levi jumped from me to Sean almost making me lose my mug.

"I will probably go to the gym soon. If you guys are still swimming when I'm done I'll jump in with you," I promised.

"Celestial! I thought I heard voices out here." I heard the smile in Tristan's voice before I turned around and saw him standing there in his full uniform.

"I'm sorry If we were too loud." I couldn't help blushing as he stared at me with adoring eyes in my bunny slippers and sweats.

"Sean, Levi, I'm going to have to drag her into the meeting. We'll come find you when it's over."

"Yes, sir." Sean abruptly led Levi away and out of sight around the corner as the boy waved at us the whole time.

"Now, miss pajamas…" he stood behind me and was bent so I could feel his breath on my ear.

"I don't really need to go in there, do I?" I quietly complained. Effortlessly he spun me around and kissed me. "That means yes, doesn't it?"

"We are just about done, but I know your family is dying to see you. Your dad asked me to check and see if you were up when we heard voices in the hall."

"I'm in sweats and slippers," I started to protest.

"And they won't care."

He kissed me again, but longer and deeper. It stirred an image of many similar kisses stolen and snuck here and there around the place before Vince's coup or the engagement party.

"I missed that," I breathed as our lips parted. I stole one more quick kiss before he could pull away and then took his hand.

"Before I forget. That flower, the amaranth that you had, I planted it in a pot for you. It's back at home on the back porch."

"Thank you for keeping it safe. Oh, I still need a proper tour. I don't think I've seen the whole thing yet."

"We can do that," he said as we entered the library.

A massively long oak table and elegantly carved chairs to match dominated the main open space of the room. Tristan and two others made three Generals, of which he was the lowest ranked. King Fangthorn was seated beside them on the same side with Destiny and Zach next to him. In between Zach and seated on the left of my dad was someone I hadn't expected to see. Lord Moset saw me first and nodded in greeting. Mom stood by dad, the two of them talking quietly and looking down at an extensive map.

"That settles it then..." King Stephen stood and let his chair scrape against the floor. "Katherine and Moset will lead the refugees to the northern clans, accompanied by a brigade. Celestial, Destiny, and Zachary will go with Katherine."

"My men are offshore. I ordered them to coordinate with your navy. How else may I be of service, Stephen? Katherine?"

I couldn't help but catch the silent exchange between Destiny and my mom, or that my little sister was holding hands under the table with Lyonshire's king. I looked up at Tristan and he just shrugged.

"They met the day after you went missing and seem to have hit it off." He bent down a little so he could whisper in my ear.

"You may come with us to the Northern clans, if you like. I'm not sure there's much you can do here and most of the fairies, aside from a few messengers, will be coming north so you can still communicate with your fleet." My dad answered before my mom, but Destiny looked pleased at the idea, and so did Fangthorn. That was something I wasn't sure I liked but I had to assume my parents knew what they were doing. "And, generals, go prepare your men as discussed. I'll lead you when the time comes, for now General Thompson and I will assist Katherine with the evacuation."

Mom's face fell, lips thinning into a tight line and eyes watering, but nonetheless she kept her composure and held her head high.

"Eh-hem," Tristan cleared his throat, "a certain Princess finally woke up," he announced.

"Oh!" Mom was already crying as she raced across the room and swept me up.

Dad was slower to come, but only because mom wouldn't budge to let him close until I started to pry her off me. I didn't think I would be emotional but realizing how long we had been apart and how much longer it had been since I really knew and remembered who they were was settling in the more mom tried to hug me. She was already crying, and I was trying not to become a red-eyed, runny-nosed mess. I was not a pretty crier. Unlike Destiny who was wiping glittering teardrops out of the corners of her eyes. Zachary, stoic by nature, was struggling against himself not to rush over like mom had. It seemed the twins had missed me after all.

"We're all so glad to see you, home safe. Your mother wanted to wake you up as soon as she found out you were home."

"I missed you guys," I managed.

"Oh, don't lie, Stephen!" mom said through a sniffle as she wiped her eyes and held my hand with her other one. "I had to stop you from waking her up."

"Ah, well," he cleared his throat and just smiled, moving in for a hug from me. "Can you blame me? We've been worried sick for months and missed you so much."

I held dad just as tight as he held me, maybe tighter but neither of us could be sure. A throat was cleared from the other side of the table. One of the highest ranked generals stepped away from his chair and the other followed.

"With your dismissal, your Majesties, we will instruct the troops on the evacuation and begin organizing the citizens. Is there anything else we can do for you?" They came near but stopped and knelt before my parents. Dad, who still had an arm around me, nodded to them to rise.

"Keep Tristan informed on your progress. I have given him leave for today considering this pleasant turn of events," dad gave my shoulder a squeeze, "but he will be my eyes and ears today. Should you have news or need something, call him first. Thank you, gentlemen. You and all our men and women in arms are truly invaluable."

"Your Highness," the two men bowed and spoke in unison and left the library.

"Welcome home Princess," Lord Moset followed the twins around the table to us, and approached me, taking my hand. "I am pleased to see that you did not let that curse overcome you. Many would have believed all was lost."

"Oh, well I'm just a lucky girl I guess." He followed my gaze to Tristan, who indeed was the only reason I was cured.

"I was hoping I might get to see what you looked like, honestly," Zach teased. "I guess all I can tease you about now is your grandma hair."

"*Zach*," Destiny elbowed him in the side. Fangthorn, still holding my sister's hand, just snickered.

"Ok, so I have to ask," I broke away from dad and mom for a little space. "When did you two decide to pursue that?" I gestured to their interlocked fingers.

Fangthorn smiled, undeterred by my questioning. Setting aside the fact that he was only a few months older than Tristan, something we learned on our trip from Lyonshire to Parna, he looked hardly older than she was. I'd never seen him clean-shaven, and he'd also gotten a haircut. They looked like a handsome couple, but how long had he even been here? I assumed my parents were alright with it, or I doubted they would be so open. Which begged the question, who would mom and dad call upon to be their heirs? I already declined. Zach was already promised to Parna's Princess Scarlett, and if Destiny really did end up with Fangthorn... the crown would no longer be with the firstborn family, I realized.

The crown would either go to dad's little brother somewhere in the northern clans, or it would fall to the Advisors and a new ruling family would rise. The revelation bothered me much more than it might have before Father Time plucked me from my old life and put me in a new one. The Andavir have ruled the Caleathian Empire for nearly a thousand years or more. The bloodline, while not completely pure, was still predominantly Andavir. Perhaps there was more power in us, in our family and genealogy than we even knew.

"I went with dad and Zach to welcome Tristan and Fangthorn back into Kings City. We were introduced and we just got talking and... well, here we are." Destiny's brief explanation didn't make me feel better, but then she looked up at him and he down at her.

Her smile made me realize that I wasn't being fair. She looked happy for the first time since we reunited, and who knew how long it had been before that.

"It's still new," Fangthorn added carefully, "but I am very much enjoying getting to know your sister and your family."

"Perhaps we should all gather in the gardens for some lunch," Mom suggested, chiming in before things got any more awkward.

"That sounds great, mom." I smiled and went on, "I'll meet you out there. I should probably change my clothes first."

My parents agreed and I kissed them both on the cheek before everyone, but Tristan followed them out of the library. Guards allowed the library's double doors to close as they followed the group at a distance, ever present and ever watchful. I went to the table and sunk heavily into one of the chairs and let out a long breath.

"So, Destiny and Fangthorn, huh? I mean, it could fizzle out. It's only been what, like a week? If it doesn't, she'll be in Lyonshire, Zach in Parna..."

"Your parents already know you don't want the Andavir mantle if that's what you're getting at. That's one of the first conversations you had with them when you finally told them we wanted to get serious."

He walked around the table, rolling up the maps my father and the generals had left behind and started laying them into a case he grabbed off the floor.

"I remember," I said through thin lips and chin resting on my fist. "You remember as well as I do that Destiny was pretty eager to step up and was almost further along in her training than I was before the coup. If she marries him it will be the first break with the throne *ever*. In the entire written history of Caleath, the throne has only ever been inherited by a direct descendant..."

I trailed off and he put down the case and just looked over at me, stoic, and contemplative. Sitting up I and putting my hands down on the table and meeting his gaze, I went on.

"I was ok with Destiny. She wanted it. If she hadn't been, I probably wouldn't have been so dismissive. The next in line after me and the twins is dads' younger brother who's somewhere in the northern Clans. He has no kids, never married and dad doesn't have any other siblings. If he won't, or more likely can't take up the mantle, there is nobody. The Advisors would pick up the reins and appoint someone of their choosing. I am not ok with that."

Tristan chewed the inside of his bottom lip, taking in what I was saying. I already knew he had zero interest in being king. I had zero interest in being queen, and still didn't want to... but if it was that or destroying over a thousand-year legacy of an extremely successful empire... I would claim my birth right.

"I doubt your parents would hand Caleath over to Fangthorn if they got married," Tristan added. "What do you want to do?" he asked.

I shook my head, "It's not really what I want to do, but what I should do. It's not really her responsibility to take it up if she doesn't want to. I guess I'm getting ahead of myself. They've only spent a week together."

"He's going with her to the northern Clans when strategically it makes more sense for him to go home. I think he's in it for the long haul. Destiny is encouraging it, and your parents are too kind to refuse anything their children are willing to fight for. Luckily, they like me now, but initially I know your dad was not thrilled with us starting to date. He had someone in mind for you, and let that alliance go because you asked him to."

"He did?" This was something new.

"The son of Ire's Steward, Lord Cromwell, or something. All the guard knew about it. I'm surprised you didn't."

"I had no idea, but it wouldn't have mattered anyway. You pretty much had me from the day we met… Tristan, I love you. You know that."

"I hear a 'but' coming," he frowned, his fists unconsciously clenching on the table.

"But… I can't sit back and let everything fall apart just because I don't want to be queen. I have to be the one to step up if she's decided to step down."

"Hopefully all this is irrelevant because I really don't want to be king." Tristan laughed but there was still an edge to his voice that made me flinch.

Restraining the lump in my chest from rising to my throat took more strength than I expected. I stood and pushed the chair in.

"I'll have to see where she stands, but we should go meet the others. I still have to change."

"Let's go then," he gathered the rest of the maps and papers and closed the case, bringing it with him around the table.

"I'll meet you there. I need to clear my head, and I should probably look a little nicer than just jeans or something. You probably want to think it all over anyway."

Instead of staying to see the contrary expression growing on his face I sent out my Gift and made a doorway to my room and went through and immediately closed it behind me. I took almost an hour changing my clothes and fixing my hair and makeup, and the time did nothing to help ease my feelings. Tristan didn't want to be king, but there was now a high chance I would have to step up to my birthright. It was all I could do to smile and normalize myself with him all through lunch and until mom and dad, Lord Moset and Fangthorn left to begin the evacuation protocol. Not long after they left, Tristan got called by the generals, leaving me at the table with the twins.

"I still can't believe you and Fangthorn are a thing." I said to Destiny as reached for my glass of lemonade and sipped.

"We just got talking and clicked," She shrugged but couldn't hide the subtle coloring of her cheeks. "He's different than I expected, funnier, taller, very sweet. He rescued a baby bird yesterday we found had fallen from its nest." She gushed, and she wasn't even looking at me anymore, but off towards a part of the cement path that ran through some trees not too far away.

"Do you see things getting serious?" Zach asked before I could. "Mom and dad seem to think it's going that way."

She blushed harder and was now obviously avoiding my gaze, nervously smiling, and drumming her hands on the table.

"It's a little soon to say, but he did say, before the meeting, that he wants to come north with us."

"With you, you mean." I didn't say it meanly, but more matter of fact.

"Yes," she finally looked at me through her lashes.

"Can you give us a minute Zach?" Destiny tried to object but he was already getting out of his chair and walking away before she could open her mouth to utter a protest. "Des, you like him a lot already. That's obvious. My question is in the long game. Do you not want to follow mom and dad on the throne anymore?"

"You just don't want to do it. You've never cared about it, or who I date for that matter," she quipped.

"That's not true." I defended, "Yeah I don't want the responsibility, but I do care. Oh, and for the record I just never really liked anyone you dated, but you did so that was more important. Fangthorn isn't a bad choice. He's proven to be a good man and there's chemistry between you two."

"You really think so?" Her voice was small, but she was smiling again.

"As far as I've seen in the very little I've been home," I confirmed. She relaxed a little, so I went on, "So let me ask you again, do you still want to be Caleath's queen?"

"I know I said I wanted it, and have been training for it, but with this war... It's all so much. I told mom and dad I was scared, but I haven't told them I don't want it anymore... yet."

She watched me nervously as she spoke, growing a shade fairer. She held her breath, waiting for me to react. Somehow I wasn't surprised. It would have been too easy for me to walk away from the throne and be simply Tristan's wife. My life was anything but simple, and I should have prepared myself for this. I should have prepared Tristan for this. The throne was something he did not want, and in fact we had only began bonding when I confessed I didn't want to be queen. I was eleven and my training had just begun. It was only etiquette and shadowing mom, but I still fought it. My heart ached to know she felt the same now, and I might lose Tristan because of my duty to my country.

"Are you upset with me?" she asked.

"I can't blame you for changing your mind," I said decidedly. "When were you going to tell mom and dad?"

"I think they kind of already know, otherwise Fangthorn would be off limits as a dating partner. I can tell them soon, before we evacuate, I suppose."

"That's probably best," I agreed.

We didn't talk much longer than that, and I went back to the library, laying out our family tree all the way back to our first recorded king and queen, the first of the Andavir line. Sure enough there were names written above King Ryan, Edward, and Genevieve. Queen Sagan's mother's name was smudged beyond recognition and there was no entry for her father.

I fell back into my chair, my shoulders slumped and just stared up at the ceiling. What now? I needed a way to find out more about their lives. There was something I was missing, something that I either didn't know or didn't remember. I knew their portraits were in the Hall of Honors on the main floor of the palace, a commemoration for stopping the Darkness and beginning the era of peace that lasted until Malthor decided to wage his wars, and then Algoroth after him, and a handful of others. I was grateful the witch hadn't resurrected anyone else but Algoroth and Malthor.

I got up from the table and walked through the library, passed the rows, and rows of bookshelves and found myself vaguely remembering a story dad had read to me as a little girl, before I started training to become queen, when I was still in my first few years of school. I didn't remember much of it, just that she fought the Darkness, or the story's personification, and won, and created the Gift. We all knew she really did create the Gift. Very few people outside the royal family line had it. They were either distant relations to us, or a past King or Queen had given it to them in the same way that my dad had given it to my guards and Tristan. I found the small section in the back on the second level. It was no surprise that all the books were a little dusty. Children hadn't been into the library or the palace in years.

The volume turned out trickier to find than I expected. Not only was it not titled anything I thought it would be, it wasn't even its own book, but part of an omnibus. When I asked the librarian, she simply said that the original volumes of the individual books were all lost over time and handed me the thick volume and offered to have some hot cocoa brought up for me. I gladly accepted both offerings and went back to the table with the book and flipped through to Queen Sagan's story and began to read while I waited for my drink. It was longer than I expected, but I read the first few sections quickly and then skipped ahead until I found the part that I'd started to remember, the creation of the Gift within the Dark world and then how she and the Elementals and the Light forced the Darkness back into his world. I finished as Tristan came into the Library behind the Librarian and my hot cocoa.

"Still slaving away in here, I see. Why don't you take a break and come to dinner with me? Sorry I got called away for so long. The evacuation is getting more and more complicated."

"What's going on?" I asked, putting the book down and accepting the mug piled high with whipped cream. "Thank you," I said to her.

She just nodded and stood back, frowning at all the books and scrolls scattered all over the table.

"We received a report this afternoon that Algoroth is moving his forces faster than anticipated. We thought we had three weeks before he got here but it may not even be two."

"That's not good," I set the mug down, letting the news sink in. "I assume that's what your call was about?"

"It was." He nodded and came around the table to me, leaning over the back of the chair to kiss the top of my head. "I'm not going to let them get to you again."

I sighed. There was so much left to do, so many people to protect and here I was with my nose stuck in books. Not that what I was looking into was worthless, I reminded myself. It was more like trying to figure out their end game, and why they chose me. I was very invested in that last part. If I was going to be effective in stopping them, I had to know not only what they were doing but why. Everything depended on it, and if I didn't want to inherit a broken kingdom we had to stop this now. I reached out and picked up the mug and sipped.

"I think we need to talk," I grimaced. Somehow familiar acrid, bitter notes lingered on the back of my tongue.

"What about?" His voice wavered, and he came around to the side of me as I pushed the drink away.

"I talked to Destiny after lunch," I began and then stopped.

Uneasy churning and cramping assaulted my stomach. I looked at the librarian. Her grin and shiny eyes chilled my spine.

"What's wrong?" Tristan grabbed my arm as I tried to climb out of the chair and stumbled, doubling over as the pain from my stomach started spreading through my whole core and into my extremities, up my neck, and all through my head.

"The Darkness will not be stopped! You will not hinder the King's work the anymore."

The Librarian stepped towards us, and I cried out in pain, unable to send out my Gift to stop it. I tried to remember who she was. I knew her face from before the coup, but who was she? Why would she do this?

"Say back!" Tristan ordered, holding me tight and easing me onto the floor. "What have you done, Leah?"

She ignored his order and walked over, stopping a few feet away as if she just got bored. Reaching out, she picked up my drink and poured it on the floor, watching the drink bubble and steam as it met the wood and spread across the floor.

"I should have joined the coup when Vince asked me. This time when he came calling, I couldn't refuse. For someone who's had so many attempts on her life you're annoyingly trusting, Princess."

"What did you put in her drink?!" Tristan snarled. He held me tighter as I stared convulsing.

"They say it's impossible for a black elf to get into the city, let alone the palace, but if one did manage the feat it would immediately be sucked through a portal back to Alfheim to be tried by the elf King Vesstan."

I caught a glimpse of her wicked grin baring her teeth in-between convulsions, just before Tristan pulled the dagger from his belt and flung it through the air and hit her square in the chest. I closed my eyes after that. Everything was becoming blindingly bright. The potion was working, already changing my outer appearance when Tristan looked down again. The air around us began to swirl, speeding up until I started to lift off the floor. He held me all the tighter.

"Over my dead body you're going to Alfheim."

I barely heard him over the swirling vortex, but I felt his Gift bursting out of his chest and all around us, protecting us from the palace's defense. The wind stopped, and I forced my eyes open. Using only one hand to hold me, he used the other to open Eä's doorway to earth. Before it was even fully formed, he dived through, taking me with him and left the vortex behind. He waited until the doorway was completely closed to relax his hold on me.

"Ouch," I winced, trying to sit up on my own. The cramping all over my body persisted so instead I laid back on him and just let him hold me while the transformation finished. "Ugh... I think that hurt more than the first time," I said a few minutes later.

"We're at the house. It was the only thing I could think to do to keep her from getting swept away to Alfheim."

I looked up at him, confused. His cell was pressed to his ear. I sighed. Sometime between arriving and the completion of the change I must have passed out without realizing it.

"I was able to break the curse last time. In theory it should work again..."

"There's no magic on Earth! Don't try it!" I heard dad's voice blare from the speaker. Tristan pulled the phone from his ear and turned on the speaker. "Moset may know of something we can do. If the magic doesn't carry over into Earth you won't last five minutes before the venom takes you."

"Yes, your majesty. I understand the risk." Tristan said it but looked less than thrilled to follow the command.

"Stay there. We'll be back at the palace soon and we'll go straight to you."

"There's one more thing," Tristan sighed and helped me up.

"What *else* happened?" Dad sounded like he was about to lose his already lacking composure.

"Leah's dead... It was my dagger."

Dad was quiet for a minute. I could only imagine what he was thinking.

"You did what you had to, son. Just keep Celestial safe and comfortable for now. We'll deal with that and then see you soon."

The line went dead, and Tristan tossed his phone onto the table across the room. It slid upon impact and ended up on the floor.

"Are you ok?" he asked.

"I guess," I sighed and rubbed my eyes. Everything still ached, but at least I was in full control of myself again. "Dad's right though. Besides, we do have something else we can try, remember?" I remembered the amaranth. This had to be why Mother Nature and Father Time gave it to me.

"Your flower!" he gasped, palming his forehead as it dawned on him, too. "I planted it in a pot on the deck. Come on!"

Holding my hand, he led me out to the back deck where sure enough there was the pot sitting beside a white wooden bench.

We stopped in our tracks. The single flower he planted was now much, much more. A small cluster of vines overflowed the pot and hung over the edge. There were dozens of little green bulbs dotting the vines. The amaranth was taking full advantage of its new home.

"It did not look like that this morning."

"Seems your thumb is more than just green," I teased. "At least we won't run out of magic flowers now."

"How does this work?"

He knelt by the plant and cupped the mother flower in his hand. It was still glowing, but only slightly.

"Mother Nature didn't say. Maybe I have to eat a pedal or something."

"We could try that, if you want."

"I'd rather do that than put you at risk." I knelt beside him and plucked one of the smooth pedals and looked at the silky, glowing, yellow teardrop shaped pedal in my palm. "Let's go back inside and I'll try it."

Back inside we went right to the couch in his living room. I tried not to notice my reflection in the windows around us. I already knew what I looked like as a black elf, and I didn't care for the reminder.

"Bon appetite..." I popped the pedal in my mouth and the fangs found it first, shredding it. "It tastes like a sweet avocado with the texture of a spinach leaf." I mused aloud after I swallowed.

"So while we wait to see if that helps, what did you want to talk to me about?"

My stomach gurgled, but I ignored it, instead sitting up and trying not to give into the desire to go invisible.

"I talked to Destiny after lunch, about what you and I talked about after the meeting. I mean, I didn't bring it all up, just the bit about what she wants to do."

"What did she say?"

He sat up too but instead of getting up like he looked like he wanted to, he took my hand and waited for me to answer.

"She doesn't want to. She's scared of the war and all that's been going on. She decided to tell mom and dad she's stepping down."

Rolling gurgles I wasn't sure whether he could hear or not became more pressing than the conversation. The pedal was doing something, and it felt almost as unpleasant as the curse. Burning that had begun as a slight stomachache from the aftermath of the curse was now flooding out from my core through my veins giving me a subtle golden glow.

"Let's finish this later," I groaned. "Something's happening."

"Let me see if I can help."

He pushed back his sleeves and sent out his Gift, a steady and gentle flow of his power into me. The amaranth reacted, its power rushing through me and into him. The surge burned but it must have been worse for him. Almost immediately he ripped his hand away, but the golden streaks bolted through him.

As much as I wanted to go to him my stomach lurched. Before I could fully comprehend what I was doing my feet were flying beneath me, carrying me to the kitchen sink where I emptied my stomach. Tristan didn't take long to recover before he was with me again and ignoring his ringing phone that was still on the floor. Everything that I expelled was dark and acrid.

"It's working!" Tristan touched my hand where I gripped the edge of the counter. "Your nails are back to normal."

"That's great," I said unenthusiastically. "I think I need to lay down."

Just outside the kitchen we could hear his phone again, and again he ignored it. Instead choosing to stay with me and hold back my hair while my stomach emptied another round of the black acid stuff into the sink. My whole body ached and burned. I almost wished I'd been sucked through the vortex to Alfheim but at least I could feel the curse being drawn out. Soon it would be over.

A bright light flashed behind us but being the way I was I couldn't exactly turn around to look. Tristan said something, but my sounds made it impossible for me to hear him, or whoever else had just arrived.

"I'll be right back babe," Tristan said into my ears when I was quiet again. "I'm going to talk to your dad. Your mom is right here."

"I'm here Celestial, we'll get through this together." I turned my head to look her way and just as her growing hand was about to touch me Tristan reached out and stopped her.

"The amaranth attacked me when I tried to do that."

"It just has to run its course," I added. "It's gross but I can feel it working."

"Do you want to go into a bathroom?" Mom asked, resting her hand on my arm.

"That might be better," I nodded as I ran the sink to clear away the yuck.

Instead of bringing me to the bathroom on the main floor like I thought she brought me upstairs and into the master bedroom.

"I didn't think Tristan would mind putting you in here. I imagine you will want to rest after everything has been extracted."

Mom sat on the edge of the bed with me, running her manicured nails through my hair and then pulling it all back into a braid. It took three hours for the amaranth to do the job and mom was right. I did want to rest once all traces of the curse were gone, but I wanted to talk to Tristan more. Other than the little while he spent with my dad upon his and mom's arrival, he never left me. Dad came and went, trying to juggle the evacuation preparation and my drama.

"I wish I could just sleep here," I said after dad took mom downstairs, giving Tristan and I a few minutes to ourselves.

"We have plenty of rooms."

"Not what I meant." My head was already on his shoulder, but I snuggled in closer, hugging his arm.

"Oh, I know," he teased, kissing the top of my head. "I don't want to ever imagine my life without you."

This time he reached up, tilting my chin up towards him. I knew what he wanted, but I withheld, instead just feeling the warmth from his breath on my face.

"Does that mean you still want to marry me, even if I have to be queen someday?"

"I would marry you even if *I* had to become queen someday," he laughed but I knew he was still sincere.

"I'll help you pick out your coronation dress," I joked.

"Come here," he closed the gap between us.

"Eh-hem," Dad cleared his throat from the doorway. "The four of us need to have a talk. Let's go."

Mom waved her hand and the doorway opened to the palace and dad followed her through. Reluctantly Tristan stood and holding his hand I followed. The sliver of amaranth that was somehow still in me surged its power through me as we passed into Eä. It flowed through my core and up through my chest and out my head lighting up the room. For a moment, a small spot on the back of my neck burned and then the light and the power were all completely gone.

"I am so done with magic for today," I complained, rubbing my neck.

"Wait, what's that?" Tristan swept my hair away from my neck and I moved my hand.

"What now?"

"What's going on?" mom asked, sounding exhausted.

"She now has a tiny amaranth flower tattooed on the back of her neck," Tristan answered. "Cute." He let my hair fall and I just sighed.

"The white in your hair is gone too," mom added after stepping up to me, examining the tattoo for herself.

"That's good," I chirped, "so what was it you wanted to talk about?"

I took a minute to look around, and of all places, we were back in the library. All the scrolls were still open and scattered, books still sitting on the table in piles. Leah was gone, and so was all the evidence of her betrayal.

"I got another message today that Algoroth has goblins coming from the south and they're only a week away. Kings City and all surrounding will be evacuated by Thursday. Furthermore, I'm emptying the palace too. Not a soul is to remain within these city walls unless it's me or military."

"How did they get so close so quickly?"

"It troubles us too but all we can do for now is to prepare to meet them and make sure our people are safe. Celestial, we're leaving at noon tomorrow. All your essentials are already packed, but you might want to consider if there is anything important to you that you want to bring." Mom was firm.

Somehow, I had missed the memo that I was evacuating too, though it only made sense that the family would stay together as much as possible.

"With all that happened today, there was one more thing," mom went on, but paused, looking to dad to finish.

"Destiny came to us today and has renounced her interest in succeeding the throne, which means that if anything happens to your mother, or me, during this crisis there will be no one to take our place." Dad looked from me to Tristan and then held my gaze. He looked like he was already anticipating my decline.

I nodded, "I know. I already talked to her today."

"We weren't under the impression you changed your mind," mom said.

"You all know I would never turn my back on my family or my country if you needed me, and you do now... So, here I am. I will do whatever is required of me."

"I have something to say here," Tristan jumped in. He squeezed my hand and then looked at my parents. Lowering to his knee, he took both my hands and cleared his throat. "Celeste, I know there's not much time for this, and I know your calling in life is greater than mine. Each time you've gone missing all I could do to move myself forward was believe that we would be together again someday. Now, you are leaving again, and I don't know when this war will be over. King Stephen, Queen Katherine, if I still have your blessing and you're willing... Celestial will you marry me tonight?"

He stood again. His hands were squeezing mine, eyes boring into mine, begging me to answer.

"Tristan, son," dad began gently, "do you understand the responsibility you're taking on, the responsibility she is taking on?"

"You know that I do, and you also know my loyalties to yourselves, your family and this country."

Dad just nodded and then all eyes were on me again.

"Yes."

I barely got the word out before I was blushing and dad whipped out his phone, ordering whoever answered to gather all remaining staff to the throne room, and then called Zach and Destiny and asked them to bring Lord Moset and King Fangthorn there as well.

"So... I *do* have a dress hiding in the back of my closet," I confessed.

"When did you buy a wedding dress, and why didn't I know about this?" Mom looked particularly put out.

"I made it, just a few days after Tristan initially proposed before the engagement party. It was just for fun, and really, I never planned on using it... but I still have it."

"Well, that settles it." Dad clapped his hands together. "Celeste, go change. Tristan, you're already in full uniform so unless you want to freshen up, I will meet you in the throne room." Dad gripped Tristan's shoulder and then gave me a good squeeze before heading out.

"Can I help you into your dress?" mom asked.

"I was going to ask if you would."

Mom smiled at us and left, hurrying ahead.

"What a day," I said almost in disbelief.

I slipped my arms around his neck and pulled him to me.

"I love you." His hand on my waist and one on my back, he kissed me.

"I better go change," I said breathlessly.

"Let's go get married," he smiled.

"Let's get married," I breathed as I kissed him again.

19

Before leaving the library, I grabbed the story book. If nothing else, it would be a good read on the voyage to the northern clans, but I wondered if there might be either some truth to the story or an underlying message that maybe I would only get if I read the whole thing. Also, it would probably help keep Levi from being completely bored on the voyage, since there was no way he would stay here or at the house alone.

Mom already had my iron hot and all my makeup and brushes on the bathroom counter when I arrived. Though it was already ten o'clock, she would not be rushed. Each little chunk of hair she sectioned needed to be sprayed and loosely curled... and then the makeup.

"You don't want too much, but not enough and your features won't be highlighted properly," she said when I complained that it had been forever.

When I finally pulled the dress out and freshened it up with my Gift just over an hour had passed. Mom stood back after adjusting the flowing layers of white, shimmery tulle over the silk skirt. I tried not to look her in the eyes because every time I did my eyes started misting.

"You're nearly perfect. Just two more things."

She walked out of the bathroom and into my room and returned with two small boxes. The smaller, elaborately designed leather box she opened first, revealing a gorgeous glittering tiara.

"This is the oldest family heirloom. It was Queen Sagan's. It was made by the elves." She set it on my head and rearranged my hair before opening the other, plain looking box and taking out a thin veil.

"This was mine. My grandma wanted me to wear hers, but it was completely yellow." She grimaced.

"It's all so beautiful, mom. Thank you for doing this, especially spur the moment."

"Let's take you to Tristan." She placed the veil and covered both my face and the tiara with it. A solitary tear escaped. She was quick to wipe it away and pulled me in, wrapping her arms around me. "I'm so proud of you, of both of you." She pulled away and waved her hand, opening a portal and leading me through by the hand into the throne rooms antechamber where dad was waiting for us.

"Better get up there and tell them to start the music." Dad took me from her, and she hurried off letting the massive doors stay open behind her.

"Thank you, dad. I love you." I wrapped my arms around him, and he drew me in.

"You've been through so much in such a short amount of time. It's about time you have something to celebrate." He paused and we could hear the string ensemble begin their gentle music. "Ready?"

"I am."

Letting me go, he closed his eyes, focusing his Gift and gathering it in his hands until after a moment a bouquet of beautiful white and pink roses formed. He handed it to me and then took my arm guiding me to the doorway where we paused. Straight ahead Tristan stood on the dais, looking down the aisle and when his eyes found me his whole countenance lit up, some from joy and some from his Gift reacting to whatever he was feeling. I understood. It was a struggle to keep mine under my skin, but I was sure I was shining too, and not just from the sparkly tulle.

We walked much slower than I liked, passing beaming faces who whispered their fortune to witness a royal wedding. Tristan waited, with Sean and Zach as his groomsmen. On the other side of the dais mom, Destiny, and Danny waited. Below the dais, standing off to the side, wearing a sharp suit, and holding the ring bearer pillow was Levi, smiling from ear to ear.

We reached them at last and climbed the dais and dad handed my bouquet to mom and then placed my hands in Tristan's.

"I love you," Tristan whispered.

"I love you too," I whispered back, trying not to get emotional.

"Ladies and gentlemen, thank you for gathering to witness and to celebrate this union tonight. I know we are living in a turbulent world, and I know it can be hard to hope in the midst of all the chaos. Tonight, we can set all that aside. Tonight, we can celebrate the hope for the future that this marriage represents, and for the prosperity we will enjoy when all the chaos is over.

"While we hadn't planned on doing this tonight, it has been long anticipated. I have known General Tristan Thompson and his family for his entire life and longer. As was his father, Tristan is an exemplary man, abounding in good works, a strong and kind heart, and a smart and cunning warrior. His father and I often joked about him and my daughter bickering like an old married couple when they would squabble as young children. Little did we know…

"High Princes Celestial Andavir, what can I say that your radiant beauty, like your mother's, wouldn't already tell us? You're strong. You persevere when most would falter or give up entirely. You bring joy, sunshine, and life wherever you go and into each life you touch. You were a wonderful student, graduating a full year early and at the top of your class. You've endured so much in the years following and have become an incredible young woman.

"General Tristan Thompson, do you take my daughter, the High Princess Celestial Andavir of the Empire of Caleath, and heir to the Caleathian throne, to be your lawfully wedded wife before your King, Queen, peers and country, to have and to hold as long as you both shall live?"

"I do," he answered, fighting back tears of his own.

"High Princess Celestial Andavir of the Empire of Caleath, and heir to the Caleathian throne, do you take General Tristan Thompson to be your lawfully wedded husband before your King, Queen, peers and country, to have and to hold as long as you both shall live?"

"I do." My voice was thick as I struggled to keep back the waterworks after such a touching speech.

"Ring bearer, if you please." Dad waved Levi forward and he presented the rings.

Tristan grabbed mine and slid it into place and then I did the same to him. When our hands were joined again, and Levi was standing beside Sean Dad put a hand on mine and Tristan's shoulders.

"By the power vested in me by my father, and his father before him, I now pronounce you man and wife." He let us go and stepped back. "You may kiss the bride."

Undeterred by the eruption of cheering and clapping Tristan moved the veil, revealing both my face and the tiara. Without hesitation he pulled me to him and kissed me like nobody was there as I wrapped my arms around him.

"Now you're stuck with me," I teased as the kiss broke.

"I wouldn't have it any other way," he said as he quickly kissed me again and then waved Levi over and put him on his shoulders.

"For those of you that would like, we whipped up a little buffet in the grand ballroom." Mom announced as her Gift carried her voice over the cheering.

"Do you feel up to food after..." Tristan trailed off.

"Weirdly enough, I am starving. Let's shake some hands, get some food, and then we should go."

"Or... hear me out," Tristan and I walked through the crowd, getting into the anti-chamber before everyone else and paused clear of the doorway. "We greet people out here, say good night to your family, put Levi to bed, and then you let me make you a proper dinner at home, just the two of us. We only have tonight, and I really just want you all to myself."

"I think you've presented a fair case," I turned as people started filing out and plastered on my beauty queen smile and started shaking hands.

"Thank you for letting us be a part of your big day!" one excited guard shook my hand.

"Congratulations, Princess, General," said others.

It took less time than I thought it would before those in the front rows in the back of the line finally greeted us. Fangthorn and Destiny came up together, then Zach with Sean and Levi. Moset trailed behind my parents and surprisingly the other generals were there too.

"Thank you, dad!" I went to him as they exited the throne room. "That was perfect."

"You two deserve better, but maybe when this is over, we can host a ball or something."

"Are you going to the ballroom?" Destiny asked.

"I think I would like to call it a night. It's our last night together and-"

"Say no more," mom smiled, an annoyingly knowing smile that brought color to my cheeks. "We'll see you both in the morning for breakfast."

"Thank you, your Majesties." Tristan and I both bowed but then mom and dad brought us both in for hugs and then led everyone away except Levi and Sean.

"Congratulations, man." Sean clapped Tristan on the back, and I bent down and picked up Levi.

"You look more like a princess now than when we first met, even after the curse was broken. Since you're a Princess, why don't you wear pretty dresses like this all the time?"

"Well, they make doing fun things a little hard. What about you, little prince? Don't you want to wear that suit everywhere?"

Levi made a face that suggested I could go somewhere made of fire and brimstone and I just laughed.

"I'm not a prince," he mumbled, folding his arms.

Tristan reached over and took him and put him on his shoulders.

"You're close enough! Celestial and I and her whole family love you."

"Can a prince do other things or only prince things?" Levi had his arms wrapped around Tristan's head, looking down at us with big brown eyes.

"Well," I said as I opened the doorway to earth and brought us into the family room of my new home. "The prince can do lots of things. What do you want to do?" I asked.

Tristan crossed the room to the stairs, flipping light switches as he went. I followed and Levi seemed to really think about the question. Upstairs I lingered in the doorway to the room I'd used when I first came here after the car accident. Transformed into a boy's room with lots of blues and greys, black and white, it would work for Levi until he was older. The toy chest was open, revealing an assortment of different toys, some looked new, others like what he would have had when he was with his family. Tristan set Levi on the bed and proceeded to pull out a set of pajamas and set them on the bed.

"Can I have help with the tie?" he asked softly.

"I'll leave you boys to it. I'm going to change out of this dress. Can I come say goodnight before you go to sleep?" I asked Levi.

"Do you know any good stories?" Tristan finished unknotting the tie and pulled it free from Levi's collar and laughed.

"She's got loads of stories bud. Now, change and brush your teeth and we'll come say goodnight."

"I'll think of a good story for tonight." I winked at Levi, and we left, closing his door on our way.

"I'm not sure what clothes I have left that haven't been packed. I will have to pop back into my old room and check." I said as I began to raise my hand to open the doorway, directing where it would open on the other side with my Gift.

"A few of your things were left here from before. I stuck them in my closet, but I can't remember if I brought them to the palace or not. Wanna check that first?"

I let the doorway closing be my answer and followed him to the master and sat on the bed while he rummaged through the closet. He emerged after several minutes shaking his head.

"That's ok. I think I have just the book to read to Levi in my old room anyway. I'll be right back."

I was gone in a literal flash, startling a few maids into dropping folded clothes and linens onto my bathroom floor. Wordlessly I helped pick them up again and handing the articles back to the two women and then slipped passed them into the almost empty closet. I'd been left a pair of jeans, a T-shirt, sweater, leather boots, socks, and some underclothes, but nothing to sleep in. I sighed and gathered the bundle in my arms and then went to the nightstand, grabbed the book, and flashed back to Tristan.

"All that was left was travel clothes for tomorrow. Could I borrow something from you to sleep in? I can just wear this to say good night to Levi."

I deposited the clothes on top of the dresser and the boots on the floor of the closet by his shoes. His uniform was already hanging neatly in the closet, while a plain white shirt and some plaid pajama pants replaced them on his person.

"I've got some shirts that will be comfortable for you. What are you going to read to him?"

"When I was looking through this in the library, I found a short story about the creation of the moon."

"That's a classic. Good choice. Ready? I think he's back in his room now."

The story didn't take long to read, but Levi was still almost asleep by the end of it. Seeing Tristan jump into this fatherly role as he pulled the blanket over the boy's shoulders, and how attentive he was on the entire journey, it was difficult to imagine

Levi leaving us. I didn't see it happening, but time would tell if the fairies we sent would find any kin that his parents failed to mention.

"You're going to be such a great dad. Levi seems to think so too. You guys have really bonded," I whispered as we left his room and closed the door. "I wish we didn't have to go tomorrow."

The reality of what was coming was hitting me, and the thought of us separating for any length of time made me want to cry. Behind that, my eyes stung. Or maybe something else was making my eyes sting. I rubbed them and the sensation subsided slightly, but I had the creeping inclination a vision would come my way sooner rather than later. My lower lip trembled. All I wanted was to enjoy tonight before it was over.

"But we do have tonight. Change into something of mine and I'm going to start making us some food."

With that he kissed me and went back downstairs and into the kitchen. With the stinging gone for now, I pulled myself back into being more in the moment and took the opportunity to see what I could do about salvaging this wedding night. I knew most of Tristan's clothes, and all of which would drown me. Standing in the middle of the walk-in closet I looked down at my dress, trying to remember how I'd made it. When that didn't work, I walked out of the closet and sent out my Gift to see if I could imagine it into being like the rose from my childhood. Pain seared in my head and reflexively I pulled all my power back into my heart.

"Baggy pajamas it is," I panted.

I found cotton pajama pants and one of his white sleeveless undershirts and called it good. Because mom tied the lace up my back so tight, and my Gift was currently useless, it took me much longer than necessary to change. The smell of bacon reached my nose before I even reached the top of the stairs. When I entered the kitchen, I could see that he was almost done.

"Breakfast for dinner," I grinned, picking up a crisp strip if bacon, "you remembered."

"I think I'd be in trouble if I didn't remember my wife's favorite meal."

Savoring the initial snap and then the rich savory flavor as I sank my teeth into it, I chewed the bacon. The image before me was simply perfect and I found myself smiling as I watched him move around the kitchen, flipping pancakes, stirring scrambled eggs into fluffy clouds, and buttering perfectly golden toast that seemed to jump right from the toaster into his hands. After thoughtfully and artfully plating up for us, he put the other dishes into the sink. We ate in the living room, snuggling each other with our plates in our laps and then cleaned up the kitchen afterwards. When all that was done it was nearly half past three in the morning and we decided it was time to go up to our room.

Sunlight started streaming through our windows at six in the morning and neither of us had slept. Breakfast at the palace was usually served at eight thirty. We had no reason to assume anything would be different today, so we waited until eight to get out of bed, get ready, and wake Levi. While Tristan was dressed in uniform and I was in the clothes that I'd found in my closet last night, we let Levi stay in his pajamas and slippers. Figuring he could change after breakfast, I put his remaining outfit and shoes in one of Tristan's unused backpacks and brought it, and the story book, with us.

*****

Everything passed in a blur. Breakfast, press address in front of the palace, extremely tearful goodbyes, and an explanation from Tristan about why Levi and I couldn't stay at our house in New York. Apparently, dad was sealing the doorway to Earth and Eä closed, and only he or my mother could unlock it again. If in the extremely unlikely event I was crowned acting Queen over my mom I would be able to open it too, but neither dad, nor Tristan had explained how that worked. All our clothes and other essentials left before dawn this morning, heading the evacuation. We would be leaving in the armored SUV's, mom, Moset and General Hathor, and mom's personal security in one, and the

Twins, King Fangthorn, and their security in another. The third and final vehicle held Levi and I, Sean, Chloe, and Danny. Both Danny and Chloe had been called back from short term leave to resume their places as my security team, and Tristan had appointed Sean as Levi's guard.

As broken hearted as I was to go without Tristan and leave him and dad to thwart Algoroth and Malthor's armies, without going to earth it was our best option to keep Levi safe. We caught up with the wagon train by late afternoon and we were lucky. The SUVs would have only been able to go another half mile before they would have been too far from the doorway to earth and stopped working, laying in the road like toys for a giant. We weren't in the wagon more than an hour before Levi fell asleep in my lap, and soon after I dozed too, too sleep deprived to fight it anymore. The vision that had pained my head, threatening to come since the night before finally came as I was lost to the waking world.

A quick succession of dizzying scenes that barely made sense, I could barely follow it until it finally slowed to a single moment. I stood in the valley outside King's City surrounded by combat, man against troll, against goblin, against other men from faraway lands. One of the trolls swung his spiked mace that was longer than the man was tall. The man didn't stand a chance as he was knocked twenty feet into the air and landed just beyond me, unmoving. The towering creature snarled at me, dragging the mace behind it as it lumbered closer. Without even thinking about what I was doing I blasted it with my Gift and bolted before it could get up and anything else could get the chance to swing at me.

I raced through the battlefield that seemed to stretch endlessly on and on, but really the armies fought all around the city walls in an endless circle. From what I could tell as I ran the enemies had yet to break through the wall and into the city. While this was a relief I couldn't imagine how or why I would be here. I was already on a wagon miles and miles away. The further I got from the wall the less battle was around me. I ran, evading enemies and hoping for a familiar face, but so far there were none. Somehow the vision was pulling me, almost as if by the hand. It stopped so abruptly in the middle of the valley that I nearly stumbled onto my knees. Winded beyond anything I'd ever experienced, I fell to a knee. Luckily, nobody had noticed me yet, all too preoccupied with fighting each other.

"Algoroth!"

The breath I was trying to catch caught in my chest and I whipped around at the sound of my dad's voice. He was no more than eight feet away, sword and shield in hand. Beyond him, but not far, was Algoroth, suited in armor and armed with two long swords spitting fire made from his blood-red Gift.

"There you are..." From where I was, I could see Algoroth sneer and stride forward, letting the edges of the blades drag in the dirt behind him. "These whelps call you king? No wonder they're so weak. How could the heir to Darkness come from weak blood such as yours?" He paused and shook his head and raised his swords. "Never mind. Let me end this."

With a loud cry he lunged forward and swung one sword and then the other. Dad was ready, holding his ground. He raised his large round shield and blocked both swings before countering with his own. The spark of high powered, sudden ferocious melee on the battlefield caught the eyes of everyone around us and everyone aside from me and one other on the other side of the growing circle gave them a wider birth. Tristan stood ready in the open space to jump in at a moment's notice should his king have need. Even though I was out in the open and in plain view he did not see me. I watched my dad's battle with horror. I wanted with everything to jump in and separate them, but a physical force within the vision restrained me. Algoroth swung with blinding speed, drumming dad's sword and making it impossible to do anything other than defense. With no warning Algoroth stopped his assault, flipped himself backwards headfirst, hooked his foot on the edge of dad's shield, and ripped it from his hand, and then landed steadily on his feet again ready and already swinging.

I dived, crying out as the shield nearly flew into me. I landed hard in the trampled, muddy grass, splattering mud in my face and all over myself as I landed and slid a little. Something suddenly felt very different. The cold mud pricked my skin, the sound of battle around and before me was suddenly overwhelming and tumultuous. The colors were no longer vague but vivid. The smell of sweat and blood and earth were everywhere, and the vision's restraint was gone without a trace. Apparently, I was meant to be here at this moment and not a second sooner. The vision ended so suddenly, and I woke so quickly I almost didn't know where I was or who was in my lap.

"Hey!" someone snapped in front of my face and Levi jumped up and out of my lap.

"What's wrong? Why is she bleeding?" Levi's voice was trembling.

"I'm ok, bud!" I dropped my head in my hands, pain suddenly building again. "Take him to my mom." I ordered Sean.

"No!" Levi cried and already his eyes were wet. "I wanna stay with you!"

"Levi, this will pass soon. Go hang out with Sean and my mom and I'll get you in a little while. I'll explain what this is and why it's happening, but after it's over."

"Come on..." Sean signaled the driver and the wagon slowed just enough to let them out.

"Oh man..." I doubled over, seeing scenes flashing across my vison as I held my head in my hands.

I saw a statue of Algoroth. Then Tristan fighting hordes of goblins with our army and Fangthorn's. Before I knew it, it was pitch black inside the palace, except for a solitary, flickering candle. The vision presented my dad, in his bloodied uniform on his bed as if asleep with a wispy thin shroud over him. The scenes ended with more pain than when they started, but I forced myself upright and to open my eyes. The late afternoon sunlight stung but that faded with the headache after a couple minutes.

"What did you see this time?" Danny broke the silence first, but Chloe was staring at me just as intently.

"I don't think our information came fast enough. Algoroth's army is already there, and I don't think the battle is going well. Dad... then Algoroth..." I trailed off, knowing I wasn't making much sense anymore. I looked at the position of the sun and panic raced through me that this vision had only given me maybe an hour's warning. "I have to go!"

I haphazardly wiped the blood from my face but all I did was smear most of it. I stumbled to my feet and that was more than enough of a pause for Danny and Cloe to grab hold of me.

"You're not going anywhere, *especially* not King's City right now!" Danny hissed, keeping her voice low enough that the driver couldn't hear.

"I'm the only one who knows where my dad will be and when he will be there when he faces Algoroth! If I don't step in, we'll lose him!" I hissed back. I was the one gripping them now, my Gift already glowing and begging me to use it.

"You're positive?" Chloe searched my eyes. "Stop the wagon!" she yelled to the driver before jumping out and talking to him in a hush. "Come on." She waved us over to the back of the wagon and we jumped out.

"Chloe, where did the driver go?" Danny asked.

"I sent him to tell Queen Katharine we have to go with Celestial to look into a vision and Levi needs to stay with her for a while."

"Thank you," I breathed a sigh of relief.

"You're not going into warzone without us, and obviously you're going to try and go no matter what we say. We're coming. No negotiations."

"Ditto," Danny chimed in.

"Get swords ready. I'm dropping us into the thick of it." Both unsheathed their weapons, and I wrapped us up in my Gift, using much more energy than I anticipated to get us there.

The massive use of my Gift left a sting in my chest and my head spinning, so it took me much longer than I wanted to recover myself. By the time I did my guards were already fending off a few goblins that dared to come over. I was dripping in mud, and I knew my face was still bloody, but I didn't have time to think about that. Algoroth had already kicked the shield and was gaining advantage over my dad.

The shield wasn't far, an arm's reach. I grabbed it and got up. Dad was out of breath and starting to slip. I raced in, shield first and Gift second and slammed into Algoroth from the side with all my strength and momentum. We crashed, rolling to the ground and into each other and stopping in front of Tristan.

Algoroth was quick to recover but I took a few seconds too long and just as I opened my eyes to see the sky from laying on my back, Algoroth was over me, lifting me into the air with a fist clutched around my throat.

"*Celestial?*" I heard Tristan and dad call my name at the same time, faintly, but it was hard to focus on anything beyond Algoroth choking me.

"Incessant *wench*!" Algoroth howled, "Be gone, and hinder my king's work no more!" He thrust me away, sending me crashing and rolling towards Tristan and my guards who were now with him. Tristan was by my side right away, helping me up. Meanwhile Algoroth charged my dad and the scrape of metal on metal prevented Tristan from questioning our sudden, unorthodox arrival.

"Get back!"

Tristan pushed me away. He held his sword ready and rushed in, blocking both of Algoroth's swords whilst my dad's hit nothing but air and then the ground with a thud. The suddenness of it all made dad stumble back onto the ground, his sword sticking out of the ground. Algoroth's power ripped out of him like a whirlwind, tearing Tristan into the air and back towards me. All I felt was air beneath my feet as I ran to Tristan's side, immediately healing the gash on his side with my Gift as I slid to a stop on my knees and put my hands on him.

Tristan knew he was healed and now that I knew he was fine, we both looked back to my dad, struggling to get back on his feet. Danny and Chloe had been sucked back into battle again, both evading the same massive troll.

"Good riddance," Algoroth sneered.

Tristan and I had already scrambled to our feet and were almost there when Algoroth's swords made contact and one tip fully disappeared through dad's royal seal on his left breast pocket, and the other into his gut.

"*No!*" I screamed and ran full speed into Algoroth again. Though I tried, it wasn't enough to knock him down, but he stumbled away.

I hurled white fire at him, which he evaded and sent a stream of his own power at me. My flaming hands caught it and I almost toppled over but caught myself at the last minute. I pushed back with my Gift, shortening his reach. My chest was burning, my heart was burning, and the more I pushed and fought with my Gift the deeper the burning until I felt it breaching the walls to my soul. I pushed on anyway, feeling Algoroth's Gift strength wavering.

"It doesn't matter what you do to me, Princess. My master has already foreseen his success. The One will come and my master will rise stronger than ever!" Algoroth laughed as my Gift broke his attack completely and engulfed him.

His laughter turned into one long agonized scream as all his flesh and bone hardened into stone until I felt the spark of life within his chest snuff out and all that was left behind was a figure trapped forever as stone. My power put itself out, though my irises and my heart were still glowing when I turned around to Tristan, kneeling with my dad laying on his back on the ground in front of him. I looked around the battlefield around me. It was so quiet I could have sworn I was alone. All eyes were on me, Caleathian and not.

"Algoroth is dead! Unless you want to meet the same fate as your General, be gone!" I commanded for all to hear.

I walked over and dropped to my knees and sobbed into my dad's chest, as unmoving as the statue Algoroth now was. I looked and his eyes were closed.

"Celestial, you have to get up. We have to get you to safety." Tristan gently laid my dad on the ground and grabbed my arm, forcing me to my feet. "Honey, I'm so sorry, but we're not out of the woods yet. They're refusing to retreat." His voice was firm but gentle, reminding me of the gravity of our situation and surroundings.

I sniffled and forced myself to stop crying. There would be time to mourn but it wasn't now. I looked around. It was true. While the fighting hadn't commenced yet, all the enemies were ready for more. They'd come for blood and would not leave until all of ours was spilled. Leaving me for just a moment, Tristan walked over to where dad's sword was still sticking out of the ground and pulled it free. The sword was heavy in my hand when Tristan returned and gave it to me. Deliberately raising his sword high and putting one arm around my shoulder Tristan raised his voice.

"Send these invaders out of our lands!" His voice carried much further than I expected, and our soldiers responded in kind, all crying out with one loud voice in determination before the sound was drowned out in the clash of renewed conflict.

The clearing that had formed was disappearing, and I lost track of Danny and Chloe. Before it was gone completely, I forced my Gift out one more time and sent dad to his bed back in the palace. I was slick with perspiration and tears when it was done. Tristan swung at goblins closing in around us, and I held onto dad's sword, ready for the first opponent.

"Send yourself back to the caravan!"

"I can't!" I yelled back to him as I dodged a goblin's hooked blade. "I'm tapped out!"

I swung, catching the creature across the chest. A few more swings and it went down. Two more replaced it. They raised their swords and one swung for my legs. As I blocked it and made to counter swing, a shadow passed over us. I wasn't going to look, but the goblins did and watched something circling in the sky. It wasn't until they scampered off and all the enemies around us did too that I looked. The goblins cleared away upon seeing the great black and yellow striped creature descending lower and lower. The dragon, easily twice the size of Vince's, was still high above us, but out of nowhere it dropped out of the sky. The beast landed so heavily everything shook and knocked me and many around me to the ground. I searched for Tristan and the others. My guards were close, and Tristan was with them. Somehow, I was the one who had gotten separated.

The dragon tucked in its wings and lowered its head, revealing the rider. I felt my body freeze. I was screaming at myself to run to the others or raise my sword, anything, but none of my muscles would obey. Our enemies cheered as Malthor jumped down to the ground, eyes locked on me. Tristan and the others raced over, all blocking his way.

"I see you did not succumb to the curse. Pity, you were much more appealing as an elf."

Even though the others blocked him from my view I could still feel his eyes on me. I tried to secure my grip on the sword, but my fingers wouldn't move, instead growing limp and dropping it to the ground completely. The rest of me followed as I fell to my hands and knees. I tried to force my will back into my body and all I had to show for it was not lying face down in the mud.

"Be gone!" Tristan stepped towards him, not yet aware of my struggle.

"Stand down, child. I'm sure you wouldn't want to be responsible for any harm to come to the final shard of your little wife's soul. Besides, this is no place for a princess." He pulled a small glass vial, with my soul shimmering inside, from his pocket.

I thought my soul was back to normal. I never imagined or felt that anything was amiss, not until now. Just by holding it and the sheer force of his will, I was completely helpless. Everyone looked back at me, clearly not expecting me to be on my knees. Tristan made to go to me, but Malthor clicked his tongue.

"Let's not make any sudden movements. I have her. This spec, this infinitesimal piece comes from the very center of her soul. It's no surprise she didn't know I had it, but as you can see, even a piece the size of a grain of rice can wield great power. Now," he strode closer to us, and they all stood their ground. "All of you stand aside or I'll have to dispose of the most vital part of her."

Even with the threat they didn't move. Grunting in annoyance he flicked his wrist, and I lifted off the ground and his free hand caught me, holding me in place by my hair.

"Your general is dead. We will drive all your forced from our lands. This isn't a war you can win, no matter what you do to me," I said through gritted teeth.

"Clearly," he smirked, looking at the men around us, exhausted, bloodied and bruised. "My king must now favor me over that self-worshiping fool, oh the folly."

I paused, "I thought Algoroth served you?" It was as if I had no filter, and he was shedding me of any sense.

At this he genuinely laughed, and the sound gave me chills, "In a way, but no. We serve a far more powerful being than I could ever compare with. The Darkness is infinite and eternal. Even if you do, by some miracle, win this war, Thorkin will rise."

There was a name I knew. So, my other idea was right. When they said Darkness, they did mean the literal eternal being of the dark... I caught the fraction of a second where both Danny and Chloe's faces showed pure panic at the idea. While Tristan was more composed, I was sure he was thinking the same thing as me: that we needed to destroy this monster before it was too late. Malthor put the vial away and I felt my control returning. I stumbled a little as I got my strength back and he started pulling us backwards to his dragon.

"Let me go!" I thrashed and pulled, trying to get free.

He only held tighter and slipped his other hand onto my hip and bent low to whisper into my ear, "I hear the entire palace is empty. I think it's time you and I got better acquainted."

I couldn't hold back my own look of panic as I fought harder, kicking and pulling and even forcing my Gift out, burning him where he touched me. Clearly not expecting it, this time he let go and I ran back to Tristan and picked up dad's sword, ready to help defend us.

"Enough of this!" he howled. "You're coming with me, Princess. I want a personal tour of my new palace."

Sending out his power, smoke billowed out of the ground and around him and I, transporting us onto his dragon. Seated behind him I tried to send out my Gift again, but his hand was on the vial, controlling me again. His massive dragon roared and spread its wings. Leaping into the sky, Tristan and the others faded from view and before I knew it, we were landing in the gardens behind the palace. The dragon was large enough that we were able to climb off his back and onto the balcony of my old room.

"Recover your strength, Celestial. I'm keen to see what your power can do now that you turned my only competition into stone. Our faceoff is inevitable, and so is my victory. Don't worry, Princess, when I win against you, I will be a merciful lord and husband."

His hand was still on the vial so I couldn't move away as he came and held me and kissed me. With his lips on mine he popped open the vial and the final piece flew freely back into me. The moment I felt his control was gone I sent out my Gift, but he was already moving, perched atop his beast. It sprang into the sky and was gone.

20

Despite dad having sealed the doorway between worlds all the power still worked within the city. However, inside the palace was dark, every window shuttered tight and only emergency lights were left on. I left my room and walked the halls to the royal suite. I knew what I would find when I opened the door, but I still vainly hoped that maybe dad would be waking up and stretching as if from a nap. It wasn't so when I entered the chambers and went into the bedroom. He lay on his back, hands resting at his sides, just like I'd imagined when I sent him here.

It felt like my boots were made of lead, thumping louder than the pounding in my chest as I crossed the room and dropped to my knees at his bedside and grasped his hand. While my chest still burned because I pushed my Gift much, much too far, it was healing at an incredible rate now that I had the last sliver of my soul back. I wasn't sure I believed there was nothing else missing, it felt like there was a gaping hole in my chest, but I knew that, more than anything else, was grief rising to the surface.

Feeling I had just enough strength, I sent out my Gift again and closed my eyes. I recalled a passage of dark magic I read whilst searching for answers in the library. This particular magic wasn't magic so much as it was a way to use your Gift to cross the bridge into the realm between the living and the dead. Technically, it was a form of necromancy. What I was doing could get me banished, exiled, or executed if I were caught, but I needed dad to know I did everything I could.

I felt with my power, rather than saw the portal open and pass over me. When I opened my eyes again the palace was gone, replaced by the vast mist filled field that I'd first dreamed of Algoroth in so many months ago. In front of me was a swift river, the river only the souls of the dead could cross. I paused. It hadn't been as difficult as I imagined or as the description had made it seem. I looked up the river, flowing endlessly down. I followed the flow with my eyes and was surprised to see someone coming towards me out of the mist.

It was a woman. Skin so pale it was almost blue, hair black as night, and wide dark brown eyes gave an almost inhuman beauty. She wasn't exceptionally tall, though she wasn't as short as I was. Dressed in white robes she approached silently. When she was only a few feet away the air around her hand started to glitter and there materialized a scythe.

"There has been far too much interference with my souls. State your business Celestial Andavir, and perhaps I will allow you to return to the living once more."

I felt a bit of the color drain from my face but did my best to remain composed.

"My father... I wanted him to know I did everything I could, and that I will continue to try and do right by our family and people."

She watched me, her face revealing nothing and definitely no compassion. After a while, just when I thought she might swing her scythe, she merely stepped up to me and rested her feather light hand on my shoulder.

"I understand your wish for closure. I know it was Algoroth that sent Stephen here, and that you in turn avenged him. Princess, I will allow you to see your father one last time," she paused.

"Thank you!" I made to bow my head, but she stopped me.

"On one condition. Malthor's abominable demons don't just kill their victims. They devour souls, the souls I was created to protect here. If you want to see him, you must send Malthor here and use your Gift to erase his existence completely. I cannot destroy souls. You, however, can. I know the origins of your power and if I heal your soul completely you can do what I ask now that it is intact."

"How?" I asked in disbelief, almost thinking she would tell me she was joking and to get lost.

"Kill him in Eä. Then you must cross seven of my rivers and find him and use your Gift upon him until there is nothing left. I will accept nothing less for payment. I would not ask if I did not believe you could do it. Anyone else I would have reaped already."

"Giltinė! Stop harassing the poor woman!" someone yelled from across the river. Another woman was there, and somehow, she struck me, as if I'd seen her before.

Lady Death touched the blade of her scythe to the water and immediately it stopped and dry land rose, allowing this new person to cross. She too had long black hair, and exceptionally pale skin, but her eyes were a striking grey, like storm clouds, and she was nearly my height.

"Oh!" she beamed as she came ashore and saw my face. "I know you! You were the little girl who made the rose with your Gift! Well, I guess I don't know you, but I did see you make the flower in a vision, so that has to count for something."

I wasn't sure how to respond. Not only did she look familiar, but she looked like she lived a thousand years ago based off her clothes. While Lady Death looked like a normal person, this woman was clearly a ghost, transparent and noiseless as she walked. Perhaps all spirits looked like this.

"If you're done, maybe you will fetch her father."

"Yes ma'am." Then the woman was gone and a moment later my dad replaced her.

"Celestial? No, you shouldn't have come here! You know the penalty for doing this!" he hissed at me.

"Dad... I just... I wanted..." I lost the words and hung my head doing my best to keep back tears.

Unlike the woman that was here before he still had substance. He pulled me in, hugging me like I was five again and I gladly buried my face in his shoulder.

"I think I know why you came, sweetheart. My death was not your fault, and you aren't responsible for my choices. I called him out, and I lost. I should *not* have been so foolish."

"Dad I killed Algoroth," I confessed. He was quiet and just held me. "And... I just promised I would take care of Malthor too. I'm going to do everything I can to protect our family and our people."

"I don't suppose my Lady would rethink asking her to do this?" dad asked Lady Death.

"That was my condition. She accepted," She answered bluntly.

"Do you know anything useful about him that might help me defeat him?" I asked her.

She sighed as if there were a thousand better things she could be doing right now. I didn't doubt that there were. She was Death and King's City probably required her presence, no matter how much I wished it didn't.

"No," she finally answered, "but come closer and I will heal your soul. That alone will give you an advantage. His is so cracked and splintered I doubt if he can feel it anymore." She sneered but gestured me forward.

The closer I got to her the colder the air became. Standing right in front of her, I couldn't distinguish the puffs of air escaping me and the mist around us. Her fingertips traced the scar on my chest, hidden under my filthy shirt but somehow, she still knew exactly where it started and stopped.

"I can't erase the scar, but your soul will be as if you were newborn. When this is over you will be back where you came from."

"Thank you," I choked back a protest as I looked back to dad.

The moment I felt something rush through me everything became impossibly bright, forcing me to close my eyes. With the flash all the cold and her touch were gone and when I opened my eyes I was back in dad's room, looking down at him. I sat at his bedside, unable to move until well after dark. Eventually I knew what I needed to do first, and that was to tell the generals of his passing, and that I would be here in his stead, since I was now tasked with stopping Malthor myself.

"I love you," I whispered before going.

The walk through the palace was long and far too quiet. There should have been people in the halls, out in the courtyard and all around but everyone was either long gone or out fighting for Caleath's survival. My blood boiled. None of this should have ever happened. It was my responsibility to stop Malthor, and if I could do that, I could banish the demons he summoned and end this insane war. But first...

I reached the front of the palace and paused. Finally, I could hear voices, though it was faint. The massive, thick doors were to thank for that. Clicking the latch, I shoved one of the doors open just enough to pass through. The sight I saw was not what I was expecting. The tip of a sword in my face was the first thing, and the second was the familiar face behind it.

"Stand down, Mitch. It's just me."

"Princess, what are you doing here?" he exclaimed and lowered his weapon. "I thought you evacuated with everyone else."

"I was forced to come back, but I need the generals. There is something they urgently need to know."

"Tristan isn't back from the front yet, but the others are here. I'll be right back."

He ran off towards the gates, and I tried to ignore the soldiers who couldn't keep from staring, no doubt wondering why I was here and why I was a complete mess. One of them slowly approached me pulling something out of his pocket.

"Here, your majesty." He extended his hand, offering a handkerchief.

"Thank you," I shook my head politely even though I did want it, but Mitch was already jogging back over with the generals, or the three that were here. "Generals," I greeted as they came close and the soldier fell back in line, putting the handkerchief back in his pocket.

"Princess," General Hathor paused, looking me over. "General Tristan should be here soon. He is leading the troops into the city. Seems the enemy is falling back for the night."

"I'm General Sturm, Princess." One introduced himself.

I nodded in greeting. "Generals, when Tristan does arrive, I need the four of you to come inside so I may speak with you."

"You see, Princess, we are still waiting orders from his Majesty." Hathor answered tersely.

"All of you are to come report to me in the dining hall, and then I will take you to my father. There will be no discussion on the matter," I replied in a like tone before I went back inside.

From the grand entry I rushed into the nearest bathroom and stopped at the closest sink. Soon my face was numb from the cold tap and the bowl was stained with the filth I washed off my face. Now that I recognize myself again, I took stock of the rest of me, which was worse. Mitch said Tristan would be here soon, so I doubted I had time to go to my room and shower and scrounge for fresh clothes. Despite the fact that my Gift still felt like it needed to rest, I sent it out and imagined I was as fresh and clean as I was first thing this morning.

When I felt my mud-encrusted shirt unstuck from my back and air flowing around me again I opened my eyes. While it wasn't the skirt suit that mom would have worn to a meeting with the generals, at least I didn't smell like the battlefield anymore. The lights flickered, something not terribly unusual for King's City when the doorway was sealed. When they resumed their normal state, the room was considerably dimmed, as if the light was no longer reflecting off the mirror. I looked up and screamed.

Instead of looking at myself the entire mirror seemed to have vanished and in place of it was blackness, so dark it seemed to smother the light around me the longer I looked. Only I couldn't look away from the man standing where my reflection was a moment ago. He was just as pale as Lady Death, but with eyes that were dark as the empty depths of space. A black cloak covered everything else but his face.

Without meaning to I had armed myself with my Gift and he just smiled. My heart chilled.

"Hello Celestial. I hear you defeated my servant this afternoon. Algoroth was quite the formidable player in my game, but no matter. Everything I needed in play is done, the only loose end is you."

"Me?" I squeaked.

"Malthor will be returning to your city soon with my latest creation, and they will leave nothing in existence behind them. Come with me, Princess, and I will return you to your home after the desolation is over."

He stretched out his hand, fully into the bathroom, over the sink. The room was getting darker and darker to the point where I could barely see the door and I wouldn't be able to see anything if I weren't using my Gift. I flashed my light just to distract him as I raced to the door and out into the fully lit grand entrance. I hadn't even had the chance to breathe yet before I heard a horrible crumbling noise, and the door was replaced by whatever portal he was looking through.

There he was again and this time I could see his whole frame, draped in long black robes with a longsword hanging from his waist. The only color on him was a bright and highly polished ruby on the hilt of his sword.

"Get away from me!" I screamed and hurled my Gift at him.

He flinched at the light, but my power didn't make it through his portal. Instead of offering his hand to me again tentacles of darkness crept out of the blackness behind him. Wide eyed with terror I screamed without hearing myself. Mitch and the generals, including Tristan, were through the front door I'd left open almost immediately. Tristan came to me without hesitation, but the others were paralyzed at the sight before them. Snarling at the interruption and wincing harder at the new brightness Tristan's Gift brought into the space, he withdrew his power.

"Who are you?" Tristan demanded. "Why have you trespassed here?"

He pushed back his hood and stepped briefly out of his portal. As he did, I recognized what I saw. His portal led to the same place that the witch always left to.

"I am Thorkin. I am King of the Dark. I am the night and every shadow. I am Darkness and rest assured that she will see my Droschuil tear the flesh from every creature in this wretched city before they devour the souls. Only after they've feasted will they deliver her to me."

He stepped back into his portal before he was done speaking and it closed completely on the last word. Nobody moved for several minutes after he and all his power was gone. The bathroom I'd been in before was reduced to rubble, but that was the only evidence of his short appearance. My mind was racing, my chest pounding and nothing going on around me registered. I vaguely noticed Tristan gripping me on the shoulders, the generals and some few soldiers moving within the entrance, and someone was talking by me. It all washed through me, nothing sticking and nothing sinking in.

The rubble was getting farther away and then it was replaced by the dining hall table, but I wasn't sure how I got there. Someone snapped in my ear and slowly senses started coming back to me. I was sitting in one of the polished wooden dining chairs and Tristan was shaking my shoulder as if to wake the dead. My heart was still racing g and I became aware of the fact that I was hyperventilating, breathing too quickly and shallowly to really call it breathing. Tristan's voice finally broke through the shock after probably the five hundredth time of him calling my name.

"Celestial! Look at me and breathe!" I could tell he was getting frantic now.

Pulling myself together I finally looked up and found his eyes bearing into mine. He pulled me in, steadying the trembling as I tried to breathe.

"You're safe now. I'm here and nothing could pull me from you."

"If she needs time, we still have a great deal to tend to for our men tonight."

If anyone else had spoken up I might have considered it, but because I was already cross with General Hathor I stood up and turned to them. Never mind the trauma I just endured, I was their Princess, and technically the highest-ranking person here. The lack of respect brought out my anger, and my determination that I would prove myself more than capable of being everything they needed from me.

"You all might want to take a seat," I stepped away from the chair and Tristan followed me to the head of the table. Hesitant but obedient, the Generals took seats while Mitch bowed out. I let him go and waited for the whispers to cease. "Report," I ordered when I had their attention.

"Our frontline has held out well, though the loss was high. No enemies have made it through the city walls, and at dusk Malthor called them back." Tristan jumped in first, inspiring the others to speak up.

Overall we were defending and maintaining our hold on the city, but it seemed to be a common concern that if we were vastly outnumbered we wouldn't hold our position much longer. I knew more of Malthor's troops were coming, supposedly any day now, not to mention the monsters Thorkin spoke of. "Do we have messengers we can send to find out the position of the reinforcements?" I asked.

"Each of us has a few fairies ready. We had a few volunteers to stay behind instead of following the refugees." Tristan offered when no one else would.

He seemed to be the only one willing to work with me. At least it was a start, but I had to get them all on board or we were doomed.

"I want a messenger sent to check how far out the elfish forces are, and to tell them we are in immediate need. I want another sent south to pull all our troops from the coast. Fangthorn's fleet should be in position by now and I trust them to hold it."

"With all due respect, Princess," General Sturm cleared his throat, "and I'm sure I'm not alone in this." He gestured around at the other generals besides Tristan. "You're not qualified or authorized to give such orders. King Stephen should be here. Where is he?"

At his mention, the lump in my throat threatened to rise, breaking the resolve in my voice when I spoke again. Tristan watched me steadily, offering silent strength as he stood beside me.

"I'm here, because he can't be." I paused, clearing my voice, and grasping at what was left of my composure. "I fought as hard as I could, but he Fell in battle today-" My voice broke again and tears escaped, running down my cheeks before I could wipe them away. "He faced off with Algoroth and did not survive. I finished that battle for him." I stopped there, letting Tristan take my hand and letting the generals understand. "If we're done here, I will take you to see him so you can witness for yourselves."

"We will also perform the Rite of the Passing on of Keys to Princess Celestial and prepare him for transport to the hospital morgue," Tristan added.

When nobody moved or said a word after what felt like forever I stepped away from the table and a little closer to the door.

"If you will all follow me please, I will take you to him."

I didn't wait for them to follow. Tristan and I just started walking and they eventually came and hurried to catch up with us down the hall. The walk back to his chambers was the longest and worst of my life. I paused at the door, fingers almost too unsteady and trembling to grasp the door handle well enough to open it and allow everyone entry. I did open the door and they all followed me in. While all but Tristan and I gathered around the bedside I held myself together enough to whisper to Tristan.

"What is the Passing on of Keys?" I asked in a hush.

"A short ceremony to give you the right to rule independently, and power over the doorway between Eä and Earth. I'm not sure how it works, but the highest-ranking military official is supposed to perform it in the event of the loss of a monarch. You'll have it until your mother returns," He explained.

"I have to give her the news and ask her to look after Levi."

More tears came. I didn't fight Tristan as he pulled me to him, instead I let him hold me together. It seemed like at least half an hour had passed before anyone said anything but when the generals finally turned away from the bedside after draping the black shroud over him, I was almost all cried out. They approached us tentatively on the other side of the room is an area that had been specifically designed as a sitting space. Tristan and I stood from the love seat we were sitting on, comfortably spaced from the recliners on either side and a modern coffee table before it, and the sofa on the other side of the table. After drying my face and one last deep breath, hand in hand Tristan and I moved and met them in the middle of the room.

"So, what next?" I asked, looking up into each one of their faces. "Tristan said something about Passing the Keys? How is that done?"

"If you will bear with us for a few minutes, wait here while I get Caleath's Book of Founding. Hathor, as our head General, will perform the actual passing of the keys." General Sturm left the room without any other explanation and so I looked to Hathor to clarify.

"Let's go into the throne room," he said. "Sturm knows to meet us there."

He led the way and if it weren't for Tristan I wouldn't have been able to follow. It was wrong. Dad should be here, but instead it was me. Tristan kept a firm hold of my hand the entire way and as we entered the throne room, still decorated with white roses everywhere from our wedding.

"Have you done this before?" I asked.

"No, but I was there when your grandfather gave the keys to Stephen after his coronation. It's a simple ceremony, but only those close to the person holding and receiving usually know how to do this."

"Close in rank or close as in relationship?" I asked, stepping onto the dais after him.

"Usually the keys are given either as part of the coronation or before the previous king's passing, and he chooses someone to do it. Stephen unfortunately did not have that opportunity, so in this case, close as in rank." He explained and gestured for me to sit.

I looked back at the throne, made of gold and a white shimmering stone with a massive red diamond. Around it was much smaller purple ones. Dad rarely sat here, but my only memory of my grandpa was of him sitting here in the robe and crown for some kind of ceremony. Dad became King before I was born so I knew it couldn't have been his coronation or anything.

"Please have a seat, Princess. Receiving the keys tends to leave the recipient woozy, so this has become part of the ceremony."

"Alright," I sighed and reluctantly sat.

Nothing about this felt like it was supposed to happen yet, but I couldn't dwell. Sturm was already walking in holding a small gold-plated chest and passed it to Hathor.

"Those who have not been instructed are dismissed, except you two, obviously." Hathor looked at Tristan and I when Tristan hadn't moved.

Everyone but us and Hathor left the throne room and pulled the doors closed after them. Hathor knelt before me and motioned for Tristan to do the same. Side by side they knelt before me, and I felt a bead of anxious heat trickle down the back of my neck. Hathor opened the chest and pulled out a book, bound in leather and velvet and opened to the marked page. The paper wasn't the paper I knew, but more of a very thin leather or cloth, or maybe animal hide. No matter what it was made from, Hathor handled all of it with a feather light touch.

"This book has been in your family since the founding days of Caleath. To my knowledge your father and I alone could read these runes. He learned from his father and so did I. There's more written here than just how to pass on the control of the doorway to Earth, but we keep this passage marked. It's rare to need anything else."

"How does this work?" I asked nervously drumming my fingertips on my knees.

"Both of you close your eyes and I will begin," he said by way of an answer.

When my eyes were closed he began to read. The language was nothing like I'd ever heard. It was even different from whatever language the witch had chanted when she took my soul. It seemed like he'd only said a few sentences when he suddenly went quiet, and the air felt different. I waited and waited but he just sat there. Slowly I cracked an eye open and peaked. He was still there, they both were, but just like when Father Time came to me in Lyonshire, they were both frozen.

"Hello?" I called out, both eyes open and standing, I looked across the empty room. After a moment, a doorway of light appeared behind Hathor and Tristan.

"I see you figured out the amaranth easily." Mother Nature walked through the doorway, followed by Father Time and then it closed again. Father Time whispered something to her and then was gone. "Hello Celestial. Are you sure you are ready to defend the doorways? It's much more than simply learning how to open and shut them. With skill and practice you will be able to feel any time it opens, closes, or any time it changes locations, including summoning."

"If it means protecting my people and my family, then yes." I answered, trying to sound sure.

She stepped up and then around the men to stand right in front of me even though there wasn't much room between Hathor and I for it.

"I see my daughter healed your soul. Try not to dig too deep with your Gift again. There are some kinds of wounds that do not heal. Now, the keys will let you control the doorway, but it is also a power that will open your eyes and understanding of the writings in that book. You may choose one other person to share the understanding with, and after that it must not be shared again until you summon me to pass the keys from you onto another. Is there someone you want to share this knowledge with?"

She seemed to look at Tristan before I did but I nodded.

"Tristan," I confirmed. "Who made that book?" I asked while I had the chance.

"I did. Read the book and it will give you more understanding about these things. Close your eyes. This will be bright. Celestial, Tristan, receive!" her command echoed off the vaulted ceiling.

Even before my eyes were closed, she reached out and touched two fingers over my heart and two on my forehead. Just before my eyes closed there was a flash brighter than anything I'd ever seen before and then it all rushed into me, knocking me back into the chair. When the light normalized again both men were moving again and rubbing their eyes.

"What was that light?" Tristan asked.

"I don't know... I mean, there was a light when Stephen got the keys but not that powerful." Hathor confessed.

"I'm guessing it was because dad got them from grandpa and mine came differently."

"Could be," Hathor mused. "I suppose I should call and arrange his Majesty's transportation. Other than calling for reinforcements, do you have any other orders, Princess?"

"Send a messenger to me. I have to write the Queen... and leave the book. Apparently, I have a lot to learn."

21

Tristan walked with me to the library where he looked through the book and I wrote my mother. By the end of the first draft I knew I would be writing at least one more. It was impossible to keep my eyes dry and so the ink kept running and smudging. After four drafts I finally gave it to the fairy who had been summoned by General Hathor to deliver this tragic message to my family.

The enemy returned to the battlefield at dawn the next morning, and before he rejoined his troops Tristan made me promise to stay inside the palace and not try to be the hero. While I had promised Lady Death I would end Malthor, Tristan's promise was easy to keep for a few days while my Gift fully regenerated. On the eve of the fifth day the enemy rotated forces again after over forty-eight hours of continuous bloodshed with no end in sight. Tristan and General Hathor were the only generals to return that cloudy night from battle and there was still no reply from the messengers we had sent calling for reinforcements, or from my mom.

Alone in the gardens, I watched Malthor flying over the palace on his dragon, its stripes glowing in bright fluorescence in endless circles overhead, highlighted now and again by lightning cutting through the heavy clouds. This wasn't the first time I'd seen him do this. Almost every night he was up there, as if watching to make sure I stayed here. The first of many drops of rain landed, cold on my forehead.

"Celestial," someone called my name from a little way off from the bench I sat on.

"No... No!" I flung myself to my feet and towards my brother. "You shouldn't be here. This is the last place you should be!"

"I came with a couple hundred men who volunteered to come back and fight. Mom demanded I confirm your letter was true. She wouldn't trust anyone else to go when we all restrained her from coming."

Head high, shoulders squared, fists clenched at his sides and face set in hard lines, it was clear to me that his old fears of my betrayal were back. I stayed a short distance away, but let my face speak for me as I briefly met his eyes and motioned for him to follow me. The original plan had been to transport Dad to the hospital morgue, but with so many injured and dying in the fight we were forced to use the small and outdated one beneath the palace grounds. The palace had also become a hospital overflow. Almost the entire first and second floor was occupied.

He followed me down an offshoot from the hall that led down to the dungeon. The morgue wasn't so far beneath the palace as that, but it was cold enough that we both were uncomfortable when we arrived. The two soldiers and doctor on rotation were surprised to see us but gave us access when I asked to see our father. The doctor acting as the mortician led us to the holding area while the two soldiers stood guard at the entrance.

Stainless steel was everywhere, except the linoleum floors, making everything feel even colder. Wordlessly the doctor pulled open a drawer from the wall and a long gurney slowly slid out, revealing an occupant on his back covered by a white sheet. I gripped Zach's hand as the sheet was folded back just below dad's chin.

"I'll wait by the door to give you some privacy," the doctor said as he stepped away.

I let Zach approach first, but I followed and let him take his hand back once we were close. Zach's face was so closed it was impossible for me to tell what he was thinking, but then he turned to me, and the harness returned.

"Why are you at the center of every horrible thing to happen to this family?"

That was all he said before he stormed out. I tried not to make eye contact with anyone as I followed him. I know they all heard him, and the looks on their faces was more than I wanted to deal with. Yes, I was at the center, but none of it was my fault. I'd tried and failed to stop most of the horribleness. It wasn't until we were back on the main level of the palace heading towards the entrance that I finally caught up to him.

"Zachary wait a minute!" I finally raised my voice after the several times I'd called after him.

He paused in front of the doors, and only because I'd caught his arm. Some of the soldiers and nursing staff around us looked our way but just as quickly hurried back to their business.

"Let me go. I have to send someone back to mom to confirm your letter." He didn't even turn to look at me, just stared at the door. "I'm contesting your right and place as successor. If I must, I'll rule Caleath from Parna."

"Zach…" I let my hand fall as he raised his to push the doors open.

To our mutual surprise they swung open before us, revealing a very battle worn and bleeding General Hathor.

"Princess, Prince Zachary, good! Finally, some luck on our side." Hathor seemed oblivious to the tension going on inside and came in with the others.

Putting everything with Zach behind me, I followed Hathor, trying not to panic. He was pale, with almost no color in his face.

"The medic suspects some internal bleeding. We need one of your healing expertise. I would have tried myself, but I couldn't find the source of the bleeding." He went on as the soldiers hung in the entry.

"This way," I guided him to the antechamber of the throne room, where there was just medical surplus being stored. "Right here," I pointed to the empty wall that would have him tucked out of sight from the palace entry. "Will you help me?" I looked at Zach.

He nodded curtly and stood over Hathor who voluntarily laid on the floor. Zach placed his hands gently over the bloodied and shallowly moving belly. I sent my Gift into Hathor at the same time as Zach, both of us searching for anything and everything that needed healing. My eyes were closed, allowing me greater focus. The number and extent of his injuries were greater than we realized, but not as bad as it appeared on the outside.

My hands were shaking when the job was done, but the minute I put my power away I felt it regenerating again. The color returning to his face was the first thing I saw when I opened my eyes. It was then that Tristan walked into the room, freshly showered, and dressed in a clean uniform and looking utterly exhausted.

"I'm ok. I'm fine," he affirmed, seeing the anxiety in my eyes as I went to his side. "Pleasant surprise to see you, man." I could only assume he meant Zachary.

"I came to confirm the facts of her letter. I'll be staying to fill Dad's place, since things seems to be unraveling so quickly with someone *else* in charge." Everyone tensed when Hathor stood and swayed ever so slightly. He caught himself, but we were all still on edge. "Hathor, I brought some men with me, but from the looks of things we need much more. The elves won't return from escorting the refugees up north for at least two more weeks. What's been done to ensure we even make it that long?"

"Princess Celestial sent for reinforcements to come from all who could be spared, but there has been no word. I believe more messengers were sent this morning as well, your Highness. Your men, however many, couldn't have come at a better time. On my way here a fairy intercepted me with news that some sort of Darkness is rapidly approaching."

"I'll ride out with my fresh men to head the battle. Also, the doorway... the keys were with my father. What's been done to secure the doorway to Earth?" He asked, being every bit the responsible prince and future king he was bread and trained to be.

"Celestial has the keys, and secured everything," Hathor confirmed.

Zach didn't hide his distaste at the decision, but held back whatever he was thinking, instead requested a fairy or other messenger to send his message to the queen.

"Now that you're on the road to recovery," Zach nodded to Hathor as he talked, "let's regroup and figure out how we're going to deal with this. Obviously, the current plan isn't cutting it." His glare was pointed directly at me, and heat rose to my cheeks, though not from embarrassment.

"How dare you!" I sprang forward and grabbed his shoulder, forcing him to turn back and face me. "I've done everything I can here! I might not have been able to get to dad in time, but I turned Algoroth to stone. I've called for reinforcements twice now, opened our home to help ease the burden... I secured the doorway and am keeping it from being opened, and someone has been trying very hard. Lady Death made me promise on my own life that Malthor would be stopped, permanently..." I huffed and threw my hands in the air. "It's like... I mean... what more do you want from me? What more do you need from me before you'll trust me again?"

Nobody was able to respond. The entire palace rumbled, walls shaking and windows rattling. Dust and debris from the ceiling flurries down on us. Faintly over the rushing people I could hear Malthor's dragon roaring along with the thunder, almost as if singing a duet. Feeling this was more than a coincidence I ran out of the room and through the open doors to look up at the sky through the now heavy rain. Everyone followed. The dragon roared again, something more like a cracking bark before lightning struck the top of the palace.

"Get everyone out!" I ordered, realizing too late what Malthor and his beast were up to. "He's trying to bring the whole thing down!"

Even as I spoke another bolt struck, this time it hit the palace on the side, collapsing a smaller tower into the second story and smashing through the outer wall. Zach ran inside barking orders at everyone, attempting to control the panic, while I raced towards where the tower hit. There had been patients there who might need help.

"Get everyone out!" I called out as I all but flew down the halls and up the stairs.

People rushed past me, some supporting a wounded patient well enough to walk, while others pushed patients on a gurney. The hall leading to the damage was already mostly clear, only one nurse was still there when I reached the gaping hole in the wall and saw bits of the tower crumbled all over the two rooms it had demolished into one.

"I heard someone in there, but I can't see him!" she grabbed my arm, scared almost senseless.

"Where?" she pointed over towards a wall where a couple beds had been buried. "Wait here."

Lightly I stepped into the room, careful about where I put my weight. The ceiling was quickly cracking above me, but the floor was also starting to give. The closer I got to where she pointed, the more I thought I could see someone slumped against the wall, holding onto something so as not to fall to the ground below.

"Wait!" he called out to me.

Now that I was closer, I could see his uniform and a nasty gash on his head. Upon further inspection I saw a bandage around his hand, revealing only two fingers. The missing digits were no doubt the reason he was here. The small bit of stone flooring he was on looked precarious at best.

"It's not stable!" he warned.

"Just hang tight!" I called back.

I used a little more of my Gift to clear some of the smoke to see a path to him that wasn't showing light from the floor below. Armed with my Gift spreading out under my feet like snowshoes, my weight was dispersed, lightening the burden on the crumbling floor. "Can you walk?" I asked when I was close enough.

My light spread out until it was under him too and without answering he stood, hesitantly inching towards me.

"Hurry, Princess! The ceiling!" The nurse's voice was faint over the sound of falling debris and crumbling.

I looked up, and the ceiling over us was dangerously bowed and cracked. The soldier must have looked to because he was inching just the slightest bit faster. Behind him something sped past my vision. Looking passed him and focusing on where the blur had been, I waited. It passed by again, this time further away but I recognized the dragon instantly.

"Keep coming, maybe take bigger steps. I got you," I encouraged, sending out more of my Gift as a pathway all the way to the nurse. I heard something above us snap. "Run!" I snapped, watching the dragon circling back.

The Soldier took off, clearly expecting me to follow. Staying where I was, I waited until he was safe before I pulled back all my Gift and waited. On the return trip the dragon sprayed the gardens with its fire but stopped as it came lower.

"Come back!" the soldier was yelling at me.

I positioned myself to do just the opposite, backing up and racing to the edge, jumping and reaching out just in time to catch the foothold of Vince's saddle just as that section of the building collapsed. My power coursed through him, and he was plummeting to the ground before either he or the dragon knew what hit them. The dragon roared, spewing fire everywhere and trying to fling me off its back.

Because you killed Algoroth my mate has gone home without me!

Her thoughts invaded my head and left a ringing in my ear. She spun wildly as she soared high and started circling the palace on the way up. Lightning was striking all around us, narrowly missing in some cases.

"Help me kill Malthor and you'll be free to go too!" I screamed, clinging soaking wet to the saddle I wasn't even fully in.

The spinning stopped and she circled around to the front of the palace, descending slower and lighter than I ever imagined she could.

You think you can defeat him? Mere months ago, you were so weak you let the witch summon him. What makes you so strong all of a sudden, little human?

"I made a promise to Lady Death because she believed I could finish the job." I answered boldly as she landed. "He's got to pay for all his wrongdoings and cheating Death." I added when she made no move as Tristan and Zach led soldiers armed with machine guns towards us.

"Celestial, get clear!" Tristan was yelling at me, waving to the men to stand down until I was down.

You're certain you can ensure my freedom? she finally asked, sounding the tiniest bit hopeful.

"Tonight, you will be free." I swore, sitting myself fully in the saddle and sliding both feet into the straps. The reins, while wet, were still plenty enough grip.

Very well. We go on your word.

Locking eyes with Tristan for just a moment I snapped the reins, and she sprang into the sky, pumping her wings and bringing us into the storm above.

There he is. If you fail, I'll kill you instead. She warned.

"Can you get me right under him?"

I let go of the reins, holding myself in place with just my legs and feet. Steadily against the wind ripping around us and the rain in our faces, she positioned herself underneath him. As of yet, they seemed unaware of us, or maybe they didn't care. Either way, they were about to. Digging down deep, I sent out as much of my power at once as I could. The stream went straight up and collided with the belly of the beast. In that instance the entire sky lit up with my light and the inner fire of the beast escaping as my power nearly tore it in half.

"Go! Go!" I screamed as the torrent of fire started coming down to meet us.

She needed no prompting, gracefully rolling out of the way, and fast enough that the momentum kept me from falling until I could grab the reins again.

Get ready. He's preparing to land.

The warning came from nowhere and I didn't get to respond or process before Malthor dropped down on us out of the sky, wrestling me out of the saddle.

"I should have anticipated something like this from you, little Princess. Rest assured. When I'm the new King of Caleath your antics will not go on." His arms and Gift wrapped around me, pinning mine to my sides, and entrapping my power within me. "Don't worry," He crooned into my ear as he brought us lower to the ground, "I'll let you continue to control the doorway, if keeping it closed means that much to you." Beneath us the valley was an angry ocean of confrontation between my army and his, and in the distance a tidal wave of black sped closer and closer. "It's time for my Droschuil to end this."

I watched, and to my surprise I saw a small band of Caleathian soldiers swooping around the battlefield to the front, getting ready to stop the onslaught of monsters. At their head, just like in my vision when I was a little girl, was Zachary, brandishing his sword and his Gift as he led the men to the frontline.

"No," I said calmly, "It's time for me to end this."

Burning hot white light erupted from me, catapulting us both from the dragon's back. While that hadn't been my intention, his grip on me didn't break until we hit the ground. He broke my fall and we both went rolling and struggled to gather ourselves after. I looked up from the ground, if not for the power already burning on his hands and shoulders as he stumbled to his feet, I would have missed him out of all the others fighting and dying around us. He wasn't in the robes he usually wore, but tactical gear. His black cloak lay on the ground, already getting trampled by feet scrambling to get away from him.

Just like when Algoroth fought my dad, both armies gave us a wide birth. The dragon was nowhere to be found, maybe taking her chance at an early escape.

"Give in Celestial. There's nothing you can do. I felt your soul. I know how strong you are, and trust me, your power is far inferior to mine."

I said nothing back, instead focusing on healing myself as I got up just so I could remain standing. By my feet was a sword, abandoned by some now defenseless soul. Knowing I needed to conserve my Gift for when it would count the most, I bent down and gripped the handle.

"I don't need my Gift to stop you," I bluffed.

To my surprise he pulled back his power and instead unsheathed his blade, accepting my challenge. I waited, letting him make the first move. Air rushed past me with each of his swings. He moved in a practiced flow that looked effortless. While I met him stroke for stroke and he hadn't broken my defenses, I knew he was playing with me. I braced myself for another blow and instead of blocking I dived and rolled, slicing him in the ribs with the edge of my sword.

Jumping back to my feet, I backed up a few paces and waited. He was just standing there, looking at the blood on his fingertips as if in awe. Then he turned and lowered his weapon.

"If I try any harder, I will inevitably cut your head off, and my King would prefer not to have to resort to our back up plan."

"I'm sorry to disappoint you, but I'm not backing down." Malthor's face twisted into a malice I knew he enjoyed. Fangs cut through in between his lips as a blood thirsty smile grew and he licked his lips. "Vampire?"

"No, worse," he laughed before crouching as if to pounce. "Your blood might be the purest, princess, but there is one other line that may yet prove fruitful. According to the prophecy, Darkness will rise! I will quench my thirst with your blood."

He crossed the space between us in the blink of an eye to grab my wrist. I had no plan anymore, acting in pure defense. My Gift flooded my veins as he aimed to bite, and he didn't notice until it was too late. Instead of blood his mouth was now full of fire, burning down his throat and down into his stomach. He howled and thrust my arm away from him, but it didn't matter. Still feeling the connection with the fire within him and the power in me, I made the fire grow. Frantic, his hands were aglow with his own power. He dived for me, knocking me to the ground and breaking the connection and extinguishing the fire in him.

I screamed as his power wrapped up my arms from his hands, scorching my flesh as it went. Close enough to feel his breath, I swung back my head and smashed my forehead into the bridge of his nose. While he reeled, I healed myself and slammed him with an endless stream of power. If I couldn't finish this now, then I was done for. His Gift pushed against mine, so I dug deeper, anchored my feet into the earth and pushed that much harder until I could feel it cutting through him to his very soul.

Death had been right. His soul was so dark, twisted and broken it was barely connected to his Gift. He gave a little push, and when I only cut deeper, he exploded in rage, sacrificing himself fully into my power to swallow me up in what was left of his. With the energy of our powers suddenly combined, the air around us combusted, exploding, and abruptly stopping the both of us. I fell to my knees and rolled down into the bottom of the crater the blast created.

Other than an incredible pain all over my body, there wasn't much else I felt. Joints popped as I maneuvered from my back onto my side and looked around. Through the dust I saw Malthor, lying still and unmoving, then came the sound of footfall.

"This part is done. Now come with me to finish the job. Be warned, you're dangerously close to burning yourself out, and I cannot interfere with your battle with Malthor's soul." I recognized

Death's voice. Even as she spoke everything changed around me and I was lying at the base of the first river of death. "He is trapped on the other side of the seventh river, but you must take the journey from here alone. You are to speak to no one, apart from Sagan, my niece, and your father, if you should happen across him, otherwise you may attract too much attention to yourself too soon."

"Sagan?" I repeated, stiffly climbing to my feet, "like Queen Sagan who created the Gift, Sagan?" I asked, but Death was already gone and in her place was a gondola, bobbing in the gentle current as it floated half in and half out of the water.

The mist around me was so thick I couldn't see the field like last time I was here, and the other side of the river was obscured too. With a grunt I swung my legs in and then pushed off into the water. My whole body ached, but not as much as when I first woke, so I figured my Gift could charge while I made my way to the seventh river, and I would see if I needed healing then. The shore came up after only a few strokes. Climbing out of the boat I suddenly felt as if I was in the center of a full stadium with everyone staring at me.

"This one still has a body."

"A perfectly aged body!" another chimed in.

I heard the voices but saw nobody they could belong to. More whispering followed and I did my best to ignore it and to focus on the task at hand. Other than feeling disturbed, I felt tired, as if the very air were draining me. This side of the river was just as seemingly vast and empty as the other, and to make things worse by far it was much colder. Moist, cool air pricked my skin, and the mist made my clothes damp.

"Keep going and keep ignoring the voices. The river is just up ahead."

"Dad?" I couldn't stop myself from calling out and then as I did, he was there by my side.

"Don't stop here. There are spirits that want to take your body and go back to Eä. I can take you across and to the third river, but I can't go further than that yet."

"Thank you."

Without thinking I made to take his hand like I used to do when we would go for walks in the garden back home and felt my heart sink when all I felt was a brisk rush of air as my fingers slipped through his.

"There's the boat. Get in and I will see you when you get out."

Just like when Death left and the boat appeared, so did this one when dad vanished. The rowboat rocked as I stepped in and used one of the ores to launch. Unlike the gondola this required two ores to steer, and the current wasn't as forgiving. After a little bit of time and another drop in temperature I docked on the shore of the other side and saw dad waiting for me a little way off. In the distance I could see a few small shack-like buildings emerging as we came close, and I could also faintly see my breath.

"What are these buildings for?" I asked quietly, noticing that some were bigger than others.

Faintly I could see larger, nicer buildings, if I decided to deviate from the straight line, I was currently traveling in.

"Ancestral dwellings, simply put. The older the family line, the larger the building, though each one is infinite inside." Dad sounded like he didn't really want to talk but answered anyway.

"I'm sorry I wasn't fast enough to help you," I blurted, overwhelmed with guilt.

"As I said before, it's not your fault. Many would have not even been strong enough to try. Celestial," his tone changes from comforting to urgent, "try to hurry. You don't want to be stuck deep in death too long. It will get colder, and the rivers will only get wider and wilder. You're strong, but not invincible. Be careful."

The bank of the third river came up much too quickly for my liking and I almost walked right into the choppy waters.

"I love you dad," I looked back at him one more time.

"And I love you. Hurry, Celestial."

He was gone after that and so I jumped into another rowboat and started across. Because the waters were a little swifter it took me longer to cross and it was impossible for me to go in a straight path. It was more like a zigzagged, diagonal path. When I finally crossed, I couldn't get the boat to stick in the bank and had to wade through water for a few feet. Dad was right. It was much colder, cold enough for frost to form on the wet part of my pant legs.

"Three down, four to go," I breathed out a large thick cloud that joined with the heavy fog.

Setting out, I walked what felt like forever before I found the next river, and a single open kayak. I supposed the quick water warranted a more maneuverable boat, but I still wasn't prepared when I got splashed repeatedly and was nearly soaked through when I got to the other side. The fifth river went almost the same, except I capsized once and was carried downstream quite a way before I could right myself. As I heaved my shivering body out of the river, I decided it was worth it to dry myself with my Gift rather than battling hypothermia.

"I bet that feels better." I startled, bearing my Gift like a two-handed sword. "Hold on, you met me last time you were here. I'm Sagan."

She was nearly impossible to see. With her almost translucent frame and the thick fog, she almost became the fog.

"To what do I owe the pleasure of your company, your Highness?" I bowed my head and averted my gaze, trying to keep my wits about me even though I was completely star struck.

"I'm not a queen anymore. There's no need to do that. I never wanted to be queen, oddly enough. I only did it for Ryan," she mused and floated deeper into the mist, and I followed, hoping she would quickly lead me to the next river.

"I don't want to be Queen either, but it seems inevitable," I confessed, strangely at ease with her.

"Most of the best never asked for the power they obtained and protected. My father forced my hand, and I was a fool to think

I'd gained the balance between him and his brother so easily. Icarius knew exactly what he was doing, and I believe my father did too."

"What do you mean?" I asked, suddenly nervous as I remembered my encounter with Thorkin.

"That's a story for another time. Your ferry is waiting. Oh, and Celestial, before you go, remember: when you get to the other side, don't dawdle. Run!"

She and the fog faded into nothing, revealing a figure in long white hooded robes waiting in a larger rowboat with a lantern, waiting for me. I approached as if it was a hungry wolf waiting within the boat. Black water rushed past, making it extremely difficult to get in. Once I was in, the figure turned its back to me and began taking us across. Expert hands delivered us with an eerie calm and then extended a hand to help me out of the boat.

"Thank you, um…"

I paused and the figure pushed back his hood, revealing long dark hair and a long beard to match. Striking and serious eyes met mine and I felt pulled into another existence centuries and a world away. Tearing my gaze away took more force than I wanted to use, but he didn't fight me and instead broke the gaze himself.

"Hades. Listen to Lady Giltinė and speak to no one else. I will not tell her of this infraction. Now go!"

He was calm until the end when he bellowed this last instruction at me. Remembering Sagan's advice, I turned and sprinted away blindly into the fog, and I didn't stop until I unexpectedly fell headlong into the raging seventh river. As if it had a life of its own it sucked me in and drug me into the current, beneath its frozen surface. Tiny needles of cold stabbed me all over my body, paralyzing my lungs. The water I tried to swim through felt like slurry. The harder I tried to swim the harder the current pulled me through and with such force that the ice broke overhead as I reached the shoreline.

Frigid air filled my lungs as I heaved myself onto frozen but dry land. My Gift came out, wrapping me like a blanket until my body temperature was back to normal and I was dry. For being so deep into death, it looked emptier than the rest. The fog was all but gone, instead a thick frost covered the ground. There were a few ancestral dwellings here and there but all of them looked decrepit and abandoned. I wondered what that meant but tried not to dwell on it. Somewhere in this place was Malthor.

22

Tristan saw the blast in the sky high above and recognized his beloved's light. He stood watching helpless as the dragon she rode flew wildly out of control and towards the battlefield. The other dragon fell from the sky in a fiery inferno, crashing in a new explosion only a few blocks from the palace. More than anything he wanted to go after Celestial, but general Hathor ordered him to manage the situation at the palace. All he could do as he went back to the task at hand was put his faith in her that Zachary's suspicions of her consorting and betrayal were wrong and she was strong and cunning enough to defeat Malthor like she apparently promised. The better he did here, the safer a place she could come home to.

*****

I walked for a while, doing my best to think warm thoughts so I wouldn't waste any more of my power. There was no telling what he could try to do to me here. The Gift and the Soul were inescapably linked, but did a spirit who was Gifted in life retain that same power and the abilities after death? I supposed I would find out soon enough.

I should have asked dad or Sagan, I mused.

"Well, what a surprise," came Malthor's all too familiar voice. I stopped abruptly, spinning in circles looking for where he could have come from. He laughed lightly and appeared before me. "You aimed to end me and ended up killing us both. How priceless. You must have more than a few dirty secrets to have arrived this deep in with me as your welcoming party, Princess."

"Don't flatter yourself," I sneered. "If I was really dead you're the last person I would go looking for."

Through a narrow gaze he studied me and then stood a little taller, back a little straighter and head high, with his chin almost in the air.

"I didn't think the living could come this far. The ferry always sent me away." The jealousy in his voice gave rise to a satisfied smile across my lips. "What do you want?" he asked, calmly waiting for me to explain.

"Our fight isn't over just because you died. Body or no, you still exist, and I've been asked to correct that." Setting my hands ablaze, I put my fists up.

"You have lofty goals, Princess. Maybe we should make this a little more interesting. If you win I cease to exist, and if I win I go back to Eä in your body. Agree to these terms and my allies here won't interfere with our battle."

Out of nowhere thousands of souls appeared behind him, including Algoroth, and all the fallen members of Vince's coup. The eyes staring me down was a seemingly endless sea. My flames flickered and almost went out. Stepping back a little I let his proposal settle in and fully absorbed my situation.

"I would play along." Sagan flickered into sight beside me. "This should only be between the two of you, and other souls don't need to get caught in your crosshairs. Should you fail, Hades won't let him get far with your body."

With those brief reassurances she was gone again, leaving me shivering in front of Malthor and his masses. The air I breathed in deep was frigid and thin, but enough to calm my anxiety about following through. If it were only him I would have a chance.

"No others will interfere, and I walk out of here without their retaliation if I win," I countered, reigniting my fists with a shake, grateful at least my hands were warm.

He clicked his tongue, considering.

"Instead of just your body I want *you*. I won't kill you, but if you can't beat me and I overtake you, you escort me out of here and bind yourself to me forever. The rest I agree to."

I swore under my breath. The idea of such a thing made my stomach curdle. That would be the lowest of the low, the greatest form of necromancy and the most abhorrent sin I could commit. Not only would I trap myself with him, but I would be abandoning Tristan and everything and everyone else I cared about at the same time.

"What do you mean, bind me to you?" I asked, biding my time while my Gift slowly built back up in my heart.

He came up to me, coming much closer than I was comfortable with and leaned into my face. I stayed where I was, refusing to let him intimidate me.

"I think you know what it means. You hold the keys so you must have read the secrets in the ancient text. A ceremony with a more binding agreement than marriage, an unbreakable contract forged between our souls with blood."

"Yes," I consented as he gave a little space between us. "I know of it, but I'm surprised you do, or of the book for that matter."

"My history is a complex tapestry. I agree to these terms. Do you?" he asked, going back to the others.

"Fine. I accept. Send them away. Let me finish what I started."

A crooked lipped smile crept across his face as his supporters all dispersed. While not close enough to get in the way, all were still in sight, watching this like we were gladiators in the arena. Electing not to waste any more time I hurled fire and broke the thin layer of ice on my clothes that accumulated while I was standing still. Floating gracefully away from each attack, I changed tactics, charging him and used the fire in my hands to help me grab ahold of him.

Instead of fighting free he just stood there, grinning at me. My fire wrapped around him and all he did was laugh before he vanished. I stumbled forward, suddenly panicked. I spun around when the crowd's eyes shifted. No sooner than I saw him, than he rushed me, passing into me and trying to take hold. I was on my hands and knees, the fire extinguished, and fighting for control of my own body. Ice spread up my hands, knees, and feet from the ground, stinging and burning as it grew.

"Get *out*," I hissed. "I will not be the victim again!"

Clearly not expecting me to attack myself he screamed inside my head as I filled myself with fire, ignoring the pain until he ejected himself and I felt my control again. His power ripped me off the ground and into the air before I hit the ground rolling onto the frozen surface of the river. Ears ringing, body bruised from the landing and burning from the cold and my self-inflicted injuries, I didn't feel the searing gash on my head until I rolled onto my hands and knees and saw the blood soiling the ice, already frozen.

"Just admit defeat," Malthor stood beside me. "It's a waste to kill you now, just to bring you back to be my bonded later," he mocked. "The first thing I'm going to do once my body is restored is get rid of that General you call your husband. I'm not interested in being the third wheel."

He knelt and invaded, this time anchoring his hold on my nearly numb extremities and bringing me to my feet. Willing my control back only granted me a flinch of the finger while we struck out across the ice, and away from his audience. My control over everything was slipping, even my ability to maintain my sight was a battle. Everything was going numb from the outside in. When we reached the other side, his hold was almost absolute. My only hope was now shallowly flickering against my soul.

Envisioning I was the fire, it grew until I was filled. Knowing he would flee again, my Gift gripped him and trapped him inside the inferno.

You'll destroy us both! He wailed.

So be it, then, I thought in reply as I increased the power.

Now surpassing the intensity that ended his mortality on the battlefield outside King's City, I kept pushing, knowing I was starting to burn out my soul too. His frantic yet futile attempt to escape faded with his and my screams as I felt his presence disappear entirely. The moment he was gone I the snuffed fire, falling to the cold ground just to let the ice soothe the burn.

Outwardly, I looked a little different than when the battle began, aside from the bleeding gash on my head. Inside it was like someone had shoved me through a meat grinder and then tenderized what was left. I spat a mouthful of blood so dark it was almost black and stood on shaking legs, swaying with each step as I stumbled my way back to the ferry. It felt like miles even though I had already gone the actual distance not that long ago.

"Just a little farther," Sagan encouraged from somewhere beside me.

Through the thick fog she was impossible to see, but I didn't spend much time looking. Even slight head movement was agonizing, surely this and the developing halo around everything I looked at meant it was more than just a bump.

"You don't want to have a crack at healing me, do you?" I ventured.

"I sincerely wish I could, but somehow much of who I was did not cross the river with me. Get to the ferry, and Hades will take you back to the first river where Lady Giltinė waits to congratulate you on your victory." She dropped the healing subject, going back to the matter at hand.

"I'm sorry..." I panted, beginning to feel dizzy. "I didn't know."

"Don't be troubled. You stopped a war today, Celestial. Be proud. There's the ferry."

The ferry and Hades slowly appeared out of the fog. I sighed. While it wasn't much, at least I would get to stop moving for a bit.

"Thank you, for everything. It's been an honor to have met you."

Now that the fog was thinner, I could just make out Sagan next to me and so I turned and gave a slight bow, as much as my pitiful state would allow.

"Farewell until we meet again, Celestial." She was gone when I stood back up.

"Lady Giltinė is waiting," Hades called from the boat. "Better not to keep her waiting too long. I already sent Persephone to tell her you're coming."

Getting into the boat was much more challenging than I anticipated on the walk over here, but once I was in I sat tucked in a ball, resting. I listened to the water around us and waited for my Gift to come back enough for a little healing. It wasn't my intention to fall asleep, but Hades knew I was about halfway into our crossing.

"Princess," Hades called, louder than intended, but it didn't seem to matter. "It isn't safe for you to sleep with such injuries."

The boat rocked a little while he shook Celestial's shoulder to no avail. Filled with urgency he went back to his post and took up rowing again, faster than before. He had seen many fall to the same end. If not healed and woken soon, she would succumb to the death sleep.

"My Lady Giltinė," Hades called as they reached the shore. "Celestial is unfit to travel. Her injuries are far to extensive."

"So I see," came her voice as she appeared within the boat. "Give her your cloak. Someone will retrieve her." With that she was gone, and Hades undid the clasp at his neck and draped the shimmering white velvet robe over her.

*****

Zach wandered the battlefield, still not believing what was happening. The shadow monsters came, and it was as though the fates had forsaken them. Then in the blink of an eye they were reduced to little more than dust after a bright light flashed behind them. More than that, the moment those creatures were gone all the other foes turned tail and fled, abandoning their weapons mid swing. Rather than let them off so easy, Zachary and Hathor ordered they be rounded up to be escorted out of Caleath. Hathor headed that endeavor. Choosing to investigate the source of the blast Zach went to the site. A massive crater still smoldered, and only one body lay at the bottom.

Several soldiers swore it was Malthor and that his sister had caused the blast. When he asked where she was, the answer was always the same: after the blast she fell into the crater, and nobody had seen her come out. Zach stood by Malthor's body, he assumed, because it clearly wasn't a woman. There were no footsteps within the crater besides his own, so if she had been here, she didn't walk out. Letting out a frustrated sigh he paused. A little cloud of his breath hung in the air and his skin pricked with a sudden cold.

"Zachary Andavir," came a woman's voice and a thick wall of fog filled the bowl at the same time.

Twin daggers of his light armed each hand as he took a battle-ready stance and waited for the figure to emerge from the fog.

"Who's there?" he called back.

The sound of a river not far off met his ears and the fog lightened to a soft, silvery mist, revealing a changed landscape and an ethereal woman dressed all in white robes.

"I am Death. Your sister fulfilled her promise to me and now needs your help. Go meet her past the fifth river and bring her home. Hurry. She hasn't much time before her body gives up and I am forced to break my promise and keep her. Your father will escort you once you cross this first river." Zach had to do a double take when she left, leaving a boat in her wake.

Left with no other options besides to continue to stand there or get in the boat, he chose the latter. The river was tame enough to traverse, though when he got back out there was nobody there.

"Hello?" he called into the mist.

"Hello, son," came an immediate answer. Stephen materialized by Zach's side. "Why can't any of us seem to keep out of trouble in this family?" he asked, as if a joke.

"Death found me and brought me here, not the other way around," Zach snapped, the fresh hurt ripening again.

"And yet here you still stand. Every Andavir has a tale to tell, it seems." A new voice came from the mist and Stephen bowed his head.

"Lady Sagan, how is she?" Stephen asked, forgoing any introductions.

"She is growing worse. He needs to hurry if he's not just planning on bringing home her body."

Zach searched the mist, but the mysterious Lady Sagan remained out of sight. Stephan walked into the mist and reluctantly Zach followed.

"What is Celeste doing here?" he asked as he caught up with his dad.

"She destroyed Malthor and ended the war. If you're strong enough when we reach her, she will need any healing you can give."

"Wait, what? Dad, come on. You can't destroy a soul. I believe she killed him. She's certainly killed plenty, but you can't expect me to believe-"

"That is *enough* Zachary." Stephen turned and leaned into his son's face, flickering in anger and unable to fully focus on being visible. "I'm sorry I failed you, but she understood what Malthor was truly after. She sacrificed herself to stop it. She paid the cost to save this family because I couldn't. Stop your doubts and animosity towards your sister. Let's go. There isn't much time."

Stunned into silence, Zach followed his father at almost a running pace through the mist. In no time at all they reached the second river, and then the third, and then the fourth and fifth. Zach's fingers and toes burned from the cold, and his entire body ached from the marathon of getting this far so fast. Looking ahead to the shore he saw Lady Death, a hooded woman, and a man holding his sister in his arms as if she were a small child. All three of them were dressed in all white, shimmering robes, and Celestial was wrapped in a matching cloak.

"How is she?" he panted, climbing out of the boat.

"She is very badly wounded, both internally and externally."

"If you're Death, don't you decide when people die?" Zach asked the question before he could stop himself.

"I am not so simple. A body, mind and spirit can only endure so much suffering without consequences. It would be better if I took her before too long, but if you quit chatting and get her out of my realm she might stand a chance."

Admonished, Zach bit his tongue and instead carefully took Celestial from the man. Seeing her face clearly he saw the sudden urgency everyone was talking about. Instead of taking her directly to the boat, he sent out his Gift and flooded her with healing light, feeling for himself the extent of the damage. No organ that should have been connected was, and everything inside was bruised almost beyond recognition. How she was even breathing was an enigma. He started there, reconnecting every organ he could before keeping a small portion of his power just to help them get out.

Initially he had planned to use his Gift to send them back to the first river, but now he knew the damage and how much healing was truly needed. Every ounce of power he had wouldn't be enough. Their only option was to travel as quickly as possible to get to Tristan at the palace. There were other healers closer, but none as skilled or likely willing to give all that would be needed to save her.

Getting passed the next couple rivers took some time but not as long as Zach had expected. Perhaps it was the adrenaline, but he was able to maintain a faster pace than before. Towards the second river, he really began to feel the challenge of endurance. The fog was clinging to him, giving as much resistance as it could to restrain them both. Each footfall felt like he was carrying cement shoes, and soon he felt eyes on him. As if the feeling of being watched weren't enough from time to time he knew spirits were tugging on his arms and shoulders. Whether they were trying to get to him, or Celestial was unclear, but each time he felt something he shrugged it off and picked up the pace.

Second river finally in sight, he gained a sudden burst. Pushing into a full run he was able to reach the boat and deposit Celestial before he heard the voices. Chills raced up his spine, causing the briefest of pauses.

"Don't stop here. Get in the boat." A new voice urged him forward. "They want to take you both. Go!"

It came again and Zach vaulted into the boat and risked the use of his power to get them going even faster. Even the river resisted, but he saw why when he stole a glance back. Spirits clamoring over each other in an avalanche of souls, they dared to cross the river behind him. When the boat crashed into the shore a few moments later it capsized sending them both into the frigid waters. Celestial stirred, barely waking before losing consciousness again. Heaving her over his shoulder Zach sloshed out of the water.

"Keep going. I'll try to hold them off. Your father is back at the first river, guarding the boat."

The voice came again, finally showing himself as Zach completely came out of the water. It took no time at all to recognize the face of the man in the largest portrait in the palace's Hall of Honors. Caleath's first King after the Dark war, King Ryan Andavir stood before them, Gift armed and ready to hold back the mob coming after them.

"Thank you," Zach gave the simple heartfelt thanks and then took off, not willing to risk their lives and waste the opportunity for a safer escape.

The spirits here were fewer in number, but even more determined to hitch a ride in their bodies back to life. Not even mid-way, Zach was forced to cloak them in his light just to keep the souls at bay. Ahead light kept flashing, no doubt his dad's Gift as he guarded the boat. The fog began to thin to the mist and allow a clearer sight of their escape. As they got close, more spirits converged upon Stephen and broke through his power, turning on the boat and turning it on its side and then upside down. Blasting them all away and using up the last of his power, Stephen cleared the way just enough for Zach to splash into the river and try to cross on foot.

"We're almost there, sis," he panted, halfway through and unable to feel the bottom with his feet anymore.

Struggling to keep them both above the water in the ever increasing current they were both trembling with cold, and Zach was completely winded when he dragged them ashore. Celestial was blue lipped and in shock, so Zach used more of his Gift and dried them, warming them a little. Death's realm had chilled them to the bone and was settling in enough to keep them both trembling when every last trace of water was gone.

"Let us out!" Zach looked around hoping a doorway would appear back to Eä.

"Be free. We will meet again when the infirmity of old age settles upon you, Zachary Andavir. Heal her in time and my promise will still extend to her as well."

He heard Lady Death. Instead of seeing her a bright light appeared and wrapped around them and then was gone.

*****

Tristan waited, armed with his long sword and his Gift as he waited for the mysterious mist to clear and reveal who the palace's intruders were. The sword clamored to the floor, and he rushed forward, vision clear.

"We need a doctor, now!" Tristan scooped Celestial out of Zach's arms and both men sunk to their knees.

It was clear how close she was to death. Tristan held her close, flooding her with all the healing he could manage. It wasn't more than a second or two before Zach was doing the same. When both men were completely tapped out, Celestial's breathing was less labored, but they'd only managed to hamper the internal bleeding and hadn't even touched her head wound. Her body was resisting the healing.

"What happened?" Tristan ignored the streaks on his cheeks as they both pulled back their powers and let the doctor get to work when he arrived.

"She kept her promise to Lady Death and destroyed Malthor. She ended the war." Zach spoke softly, anxiously watching the doctor work on his sister.

"The bleeding has stopped for now. There was some swelling of the brain, and a head bleed. I think I've gotten it to stop but she's going to need transfusions and possibly surgery. She's got the fates to thank, I think, that it was you two healing her first instead of lesser Gifted individuals. I'll go myself to the hospital and come back with my team and some supplies to treat her properly. I trust the two of you can prep her for further care and get her in a bed?"

All the men stood, Tristan cradling her as close to him as he could. They nodded and let the doctor rush off without another word.

"I'll take her to her room and get her ready," Tristan said.

"I'll come help. I want to make up for the complete jerk I was when I got here. Dad really laid into me when I went to get her, and after learning everything I feel like trash."

"Let's be honest here, Zach. You've been a complete jerk since I found her on Earth. You never trusted her and looked for reasons to find her guilty. You should feel like garbage. Hathor called me just before you got home. Go help him instead. We can hash this out later."

"... Alright," Zach barely got it out.

Tristan turned a cold shoulder and left Zach standing in the entry way. All he cared about right now was making sure Celestial was alright, and right now she was far from it. Whatever she did, whatever happened to her, it really was in the hands of the fates whether he would be allowed to keep her with him, or if he would be forced to say goodbye. Zach would go to Hathor on his behalf and that would more than make up for his disobedience to a superior officer.

Celestial's old room and the royal sleeping quarters of the palace had been fatefully and blessedly undamaged, and Tristan already had Gifted soldiers working on the repairs while non-

Gifted began cleanup and quick, minor repairs. Celestial remained unconscious as he used the scant amount of his remaining energy and slowly restoring power to clean her up and get her into a hospital gown that one of the remaining nurses brought up to him. After several transfusions and another round of healing for her head from the doctor he seemed satisfied and promised to return a few hours later at dawn.

While he was elsewhere in the palace assisting patients that were unable to be relocated, his nurses remained behind to check her vitals and IVs every hour. Celestial slept soundly, and Tristan eventually drifted off on the bed beside her, waking when the doctor came again and remaining by her side. A day of rest turned into days and then a full week passed, and another, and another, and still she slept.

"I can sit with her if you want to go get some air," Zach offered on the morning of the twenty-eighth day.

"I'm fine here but stay if you want." Tristan barely looked up.

"I think I will. There have been reports that Vince is in the city, but none of the leads have been fruitful. I guess she took that dragon she was on from him."

"She's always been one to go for the gusto. We'll catch him. The entire army is looking for him, the city is basically an army base, and he can't escape to Earth this time." Tristan, sitting on the bed beside her, took her hand and offered a little healing.

"Is she accepting it?" Zach wondered. "The doctor said her body rejected the last couple days of healing sessions."

Zach approached the subject lightly as Tristan still held out hope she would wake up despite the doctor's prognosis. The breathing apparatus strapped to her face hummed a steady constant rhythm along with the IV fluids and monitors she was hooked up to.

"She hasn't, but I noticed her hand flinched when I held it this morning, and occasionally throughout the day today. She's in there."

Tristan watched her with a distant look in his eyes as if thinking of things long ago. Both men remained, quietly pursuing their own thoughts for a while. After about an hour Zach's phone rang, he answered without any more than a greeting and then hung up again.

"Hathor wants to brief us and has a message for us from my mom. Do you want to say, or will you come with? It shouldn't take long," he invited.

"I should go. I need to stretch my legs and I think the nurses will be doing their rounds soon anyway." Tristan got up off the bed and walked around it to the door, following Zach out and to the top floor of the library.

*****

I opened my eyes and saw the mist covered field and a thinly trickling river. With a strange assurance I knew I was on Life's side of the river. I watched the trickle of water flowing at my bare feet and noticed as I looked down the night gown I wore that was reminiscent of something I remember my grandma sleeping in. Deciding that was the least of my worries, I called out.

"Hello? Lady Giltinė?" I stood there waiting for a reply and then she and Sagan appeared next to me.

"Celestial," Death's greeting was cold, per usual, and Sagan just looked at me and smiled.

"So, care to explain why the rivers were miles wide when I was here last and now, I could literally hop over it? Seems a little messed up."

"It's because you're on the verge. The only thing holding you to your body is your desire to be there." Sagan was blunter than I expected, delivering the news I was almost dead.

"But... you promised?" I said lamely looking at Lady Death confused.

"I did, but a body can only take so much before it can't anymore. There's nothing I can do about that. You, however, aren't going to die. You'll be different when you wake up, but nothing will change the quality of life you've known. We're here for a different reason."

"I needed to talk to you about my father, Thorkin." Sagan jumped in. "Things are going to happen in your lifetime and you, and your family will need to prepare. Before I get into that, I think my aunt wanted to say a few things."

I looked to Lady Death again, wondering where this weird conversation was headed.

"First, thank you for your following through instead of stopping when it got too hard. Second, I'm afraid it wasn't enough to deter Thorkin like I thought. Your war *is* over, but a new, different kind is brewing. My father offered me a glimpse into Thorkin's future so we could prepare you. I'll let you and Sagan get into that. This is where I bid you farewell until your time comes. Oh, but first, a gift, from my mother."

A quick touch of her fingertips over my heart and a strange floral smelling power combined with my Gift and sealed itself there with a flash. True to her usual self she was gone again after I blinked. The trickle of water widened slightly, giving maybe three feet across instead of the twenty it had been when I first laid eyes on it. Sagan sighed but motioned for me to walk with her.

"I've learned that part of the reason my father is so interested in you is because you're of our blood line," she said as we began, "and therefore your children and grandchildren will be too. To one of those generations will be the ordeal of restoring the balance. I thought I'd done it, but I only tipped the scales in the wrong direction without even knowing it. Father Time warned me not to say too much, but somehow the One from the prophecy will be born, and Elementals will be born too. I can't say if this is why Thorkin is interested in our blood line but it's as good a hunch as any. Use it wisely and guard the amaranth flowers with your life. You will need them again. While we're pleased they were able to help you, that wasn't the reason my grandmother gave it to you."

"What can I do to at least protect the palace and our home, and the people's homes from Thorkin? I saw him in the palace...

before I went after Malthor. He opened a portal and tried to get me. Are there ways to stop that?"

Sagan stopped and listened intently to me, then looked a little panicked. While she seemed to recover from the news the river widened again and continued until it seemed back to normal.

"There are ways, I think some are in the library, if the scrolls have lasted this long. I can teach you to draw a symbol that will both alert you to his power and should stop him from entering unless invited... Wait... *No!*"

Black mist billowed to us from behind. Sagan made to grab me to pull me out of it as it gathered around me, but her immaterial passed right through my arm. I uselessly swatted the blackness away. Though I could feel my Gift, I was still far too weak, and it was still too painful on my soul to use it. Circling above my head it blocked out all light and I felt my environment change. Sandy riverbank turned to stone. I felt when the black mist let go of me, but there was still no light.

"Hello Celestial Andavir."

Thorkin's deep cold voice rumbled from somewhere ahead of me. Stagnant, heavy air whooshed past me and then torches of green and purple fire lit themselves all along the walls. The dim light revealed a long rectangular reflection pond sprawled out before me in the center of a grand throne room. Beyond that was the dais and an intricately crafted throne. On that throne sat Thorkin.

"You look impressed," he mused casually as he stood and descended the few steps from the dais.

I might have been impressed that literally everything had been carved from the same glass-like, black stone if I wasn't completely terrified. Thorkin held his hand over the pool as he walked by it, coming closer. Flames bubbled out of thick venomous smelling liquid, sending toxic fumes into the air above us.

"It doesn't matter what you do, what you know, or how you prepare. I will face off with 'the One' of the prophecy, and I will win. You are mine. Your loved ones are mine. Your children will be mine and your grandchildren. Everything in Eä will be mine and I cannot be stopped. I am Darkness, and I cannot be destroyed."

He drew closer, almost an arm's reach away now. The entire time he spoke and with each step I grappled with my Gift, trying with all I had to grasp it to escape. He reached out, the same toxic flames appearing in his hand as he extended it out to me. Unbearable heat tickled my face as I finally grasped my light and unfurled it upon him. Deafening screams echoed in my head, his and mine, and then it was all gone.

"Princess Celestial," I heard my name being called.

Turning I suddenly felt heavy and groggy, Gift no longer armed and unattainable. I was on my back but propped up to a semi sitting position. I tried to sit up more, but something on my face and pinching my arms made me think twice.

"Doctor! She's gaining consciousness! Shall I make the call?"

Where am I? I wondered as my anxiety started to pass. Thorkin was gone and that was enough of a blessing. Against filtered light that seemed brighter than it should have been, I cracked my eyes open. A nurse was running out of the room and a military doctor came and leaned over me, shining a light in my eyes, and asking me to look this way and that.

"Let me move this." He said it mostly to himself and reached over me to disassemble the breathing apparatus strapped to my face. "What's your name?" he asked, looking at my eyes again.

"Celestial Andavir Thompson," I rasped, noticing for the first time that my throat was raw.

"Good, good. Now I need you to lift your left arm in the air to the level of your shoulder, then your right."

He waited patiently as I struggled to get them off the bed. His tongue clicked against his teeth, and he put down a few words on his clipboard.

"Any dizziness, altered vision, headache or nausea?"

"No nausea, and yes on the other stuff." Somewhere inside me was my Gift, but it refused to be called to restore me to my good health.

"What is your birthday, and your age?"

He waited while a puzzled expression made its way across my face. I did have a birthday, but for the life of me I couldn't remember the date, or how old I was. After a minute I shook my head.

"That's ok. It'll come to you. We'll try again later. What about your husband? What's his name?"

"Tristan," I didn't hesitate this time.

"How many siblings do you have?" he asked as he scribbled some more.

"Do I have any? My throat hurts. How many more questions?" I whined and worried I wasn't giving the doctor the answers he wanted.

Besides very few tidbits of information, things were blank. It was like most of my brain was still wrapped in Death's fog.

"Just a few more. The soreness is from the feeding tube. We just took it out a few hours ago. I'll get you something to make you more comfortable in a minute."

"Sure," I consented, keeping my voice down so it wouldn't hurt as bad.

"Do you know where you are? Do you recognize this room?"

He gestured around and allowed me to take it all in. At first nothing looked familiar but then I saw the French doors and recognized the view of the gardens and the city from the balcony.

"Hospital?" I tried. "... all the machines..." I added a little breathlessly.

Reaching for the oxygen mask he gently put it on my face and waited for me to catch my breath. In catching it, I began to feel unbelievably tired again and fought to keep my eyes open. Along with this it felt like I was back in one of the boats, rocking and floating while the room took on a glow of its own and my ears started to ring.

"Stay awake if you can. I'll be right back with your meds. They'll all be IV's so as not to further irritate your throat." He said over the ringing.

Instead of answering I just gave a lamely attempted thumbs up and dropped my arm back to the bed. He left without giving me any indication of if my answers were satisfactory or not.

23

"Malthor's army is almost out of our borders. They'll all be funneled out through the Serpent's pass and be on the Dwarves land after that. I already received a message from the Dwarf King that they will be taking Malthor's army Farther south."

General Hathor finally finished his hour-long report and sat down in his chair on Zach's left-hand side. Tristan was on Zach's right, though he wasn't sure why. As prince and the current acting monarch in place of Queen Katherine until her return, Zach sat at the head of the table. In Tristan's mind, General Hathor should have his seat. He was the highest ranked officer here under the prince, after all.

"Did you say, when we first got here, that you had a few messages for us from the Queen?" Zach apparently couldn't restrain himself anymore.

Tristan noticed the prince's foot tapping impatiently towards the end of the General's speech. It was hard not to, with all the impatient fidgeting. Reaching down to grab the case off the floor, Hathor clicked it open and passed two scrolls to Zach and one across the table to Tristan. Before he had even completely unrolled and smoothed it, Zach had already excitedly punched his arm.

"Guess it's official! Welcome and Congratulations!" Zach smiled.

"For what?" Tristan asked.

The last roll of the paper smoothed out, revealing a polished new pin, the same pin that Zach wore on very important, very rare occasions. As if it might disintegrate at his touch Tristan pinched it and held it up.

"It's to be placed on the right breast closest to your heart and before all your other pins and medals," Hathor explained.

"Right," Tristan let out a long breath. "I guess this is why you insisted on the seating arrangement," he said as it sunk in.

"Yes, Prince Tristan." Hathor snickered at Tristan's flinch.

"You knew what came with marrying my sister," Zach said dismissively, "Now you just wait until the next gala, and you're announced *before* Celestial." He laughed, keeping the twinkle in his eye, and fully enjoying just how uncomfortable Tristan looked as he put back the pin and rolled up the parchment.

"If we're finished, I'd like to get back to Celestial."

Zach reached under the table, fishing a buzzing phone out of his pocket. Tristan sighed. He only came because he hadn't been to one of these briefings in weeks and felt guilty. Now all he wanted was to get back to her, where he was most needed. Zach answered the phone, and Tristan stood, preparing to go.

"Hold on, it's her doctor." Zach jumped up. "You're sure? You're without a doubt positive?"

"What's going on?"

"We're coming." Zach hung up and shoved the phone back in his pocket before almost tripping out of his seat. "Get moving! She's waking up!" He couldn't keep the smile off his face or out of his voice and Tristan waited for no one as he began sprinting back to her room.

All the way back to her room Tristan felt like he simply could not move fast enough. His footfall echoed off the walls as he came bounding down the hall and to her door, where the doctor was just leaving, closing the door behind him.

"How is she?" Tristan asked before he even bothered to try and catch his breath.

Tentative hands rubbed course stubble and then found themselves running through thinning hair. The doctor's sigh was heavy, and Tristan's heart felt the weight. Turning the knob again and pushing the door open, the doctor led him into the room, followed by Zach.

"I thought you said she woke up?" Zach's face fell to match the tone of the other two men.

"She did and was able to answer a few questions for an assessment; but her body is still under a massive amount of stress. There was confusion upon her waking, which was not unexpected. With an injury to the brain like she sustained it's common for there to be some confusion. She did remember her name, and yours."

"Isn't that good?" Tristan watched her monitors, now the same as before he left, as if she hadn't woken at all.

"Yes, I am just flabbergasted that she's doing as well as she is. Please don't take this the wrong way. I just mean to be honest. When I started treating her I honestly didn't see a good outcome, but she's a fighter. If she follows the current trend, she should start waking up more and more for longer periods of time until she has a normal schedule again. I'm not sure what to expect with the confusion. Time will tell if it's temporary, or if we're dealing with a deeper issue like amnesia."

"So basically," Zach cleared his throat, choosing his words carefully, "you think she could make a recovery over time."

"Ah... well, I mean... its more complicated than that." He stumbled over his words.

Tristan breathed, clenched, and unclenched his fists just to keep his cool. Supposedly the best in the city, this quack couldn't give a straight answer for anything, and answers were all he wanted.

"Why don't you go home, Dr. Paulson." A woman entered the room dressed in a white lab coat and scrubs and a surgical mask. "I am taking over this patient's care."

"Who are you? You have no authority over me," He retorted.

One handed she removed the mask and crumpled it into a little ball before dropping it into the waste bin by the door. Zach stood tall and made no argument as she strode in with another woman appearing in the doorway and took Celestial's chart from him.

"Prince Zachary, please escort Dr. Paulson out while I review the princess's chart with my assistant and General Tristan."

"You can't just fire me!" He pulled his arm free at Zach's touch.

"Actually, we can and are. I'll write your check in the library for your services. Please follow me." Zach remained calm but the authoritative force in his voice was enough to get the doctor to comply.

"What's going on?" Tristan demanded, watching them leave and the two women proceed to review the chart and take Celestial's vitals.

"I made a promise to your wife that if she took care of Malthor, she would live a long and healthy life. My sister has come to help me follow through on that promise."

"That means…" With realization he trailed off and wondered for a moment if this was really happening.

"My name is Giltinė, and yes. I am Death. This is my sister Laima. She is Life. Your wife is in good hands now. Dr. Paulson is good, but not good enough."

"You should have called me sooner!" her sister interrupted, tucking a loose lock of golden hair out of her sun-kissed face. "Her recovery could have been made smoother."

"Thorkin is meddling again. I had to divert multiple necromantic attempts to enter my realm." Death explained.

"Ugh…" Laima sighed and rubbed her temple as if fending off a headache at the mere mention of Thorkin's name. "I don't think father looked far enough into the future when he adopted those brothers," She complained.

The two worked round the clock making sure Celestial's conditions and care were at their peak for optimal recovery, and every couple of hours Life would take Celestial's hand for a few minutes, infusing her with vitality only offered to newborns. Little by little all the color in her face was back, and everything about her had a healthy glow. By the next morning as Tristan roused himself after nodding off on the sofa in her room, the women were removing all the IV's, all the monitors, and life-assisting machines.

"You woke up just in time!" Life chirped like a morning songbird.

"We're going to wake her up," Death clarified.

Rubbing his eyes to remove the rest of the sleepiness Tristan hurried to sit beside Celestial while the two immortal sisters stood on the other side.

"You might want to close your eyes for this."

Even through closed eyes with his face tucked into his arm, the flash of power seemed brighter than staring at the sun until it's too late. It faded faster than he could conceive, but it still took a few seconds for his eyes to come back to normal when he raised his head.

"I will be back to do physical therapy with her every day until she's back to normal, but for now I have to go. There's a mom about to deliver twins in Ire who could use a helping hand with one of the babies."

She would have left without a trace, but the room definitely felt tired to Tristan without her infectious energy.

"Wake up, Celestial," Death reached out, patting her cheek. She flinched but remained asleep. "Celestial." Death's voice was firm, borderline annoyed and the second pat sounded more like a smack.

Tristan moved back a little, giving her room to breathe as she came to. He didn't notice he'd been holding his breath until he sighed as her eyes fluttered open and then stopped.

Open your eyes and fulfill my prophecy. I heard Thorkin's voice in my head but once it was gone I heard Death calling my name and someone gently speaking in my ear.

"Hey, babe. Can you open your eyes?"

"Come on Celestial," Death urged. "I can only keep my end of the bargain if you let me. You're healed, but you must *want* to live if you're going to. Pick a side of the river to stand on," she added.

I squeezed my eyes shut just to feel my muscles to force them open. The light was bright, making me flinch my face away from it. My body felt much better than all the agony I remembered after I ended Malthor, but any strength that had been left was gone now. Once my eyes adjusted I looked around. Where was I? I looked at both faces looking expectantly down at me, and neither were faces I knew. To make things worse, the thoughts and feelings I had upon waking and before that were lost in the mental fog.

"Good to see you awake." The woman seemed to be speaking to me but was turned away to pick up a clipboard and pen. "Do you know who I am?" She asked.

"Ah..." I hesitated, finding my voice, "a doctor?" I ventured based off her scrubs and the stethoscope hanging from her neck.

Her lips pursed in displeasure, but she didn't correct me.

"Do you know who he is?" She nodded to the man sitting at the edge of my bed, holding my hand.

I just shook my head and searched his face while he hung his head. These were not the answers they wanted, I realized.

"You don't know me?"

He gave my hand a squeeze and I felt something on his finger and mine. I looked down to see a simple wedding band on him, and a gorgeous solitaire diamond ring paired with a diamond studded wedding band on mine. The rings became a weight smashing down on my chest and panic seized my mind. This was something I should know about. I said nothing, just stared at our interlocked fingers in a blind panic and searched my mind for any traces of who he was or maybe how I got here. When nothing surfaced I felt the heat building in my face up to my eyes and trying to spill out.

"It's okay," he soothed, giving my hand a little squeeze. "You just woke up. Give yourself some time."

"What's your name?" The doctor jumped right back in, shifting her weight anxiously from one foot to the other.

Again, my mind went blank. Something whispered in the back of my mind that I was somebody. I had a life. There were people that knew me, and I'd known them. I had a home, and apparently a husband too. There was more whispering, but it wasn't loud enough for me to understand.

"What happened to me? Why can't I remember anything?" I asked.

"You're going to be fine. We'll work with you on your memory. For now, why don't you try and sip some of this broth on the nightstand while I figure out a treatment plan. I'll come back in a little while but call if you need anything."

She mostly said this last part to him but laid her ice-cold hand on my arm before walking out of the room and closing the door.

"I'm so sorry," I let go of his hand to wipe my eyes and cover my face.

"Shhhh, don't worry." He moved up higher on the bed to sit closer and wrapped his arms around me. "Here," he reached over and for a steaming mug. "Sip this. I'm going to step out into the hall and call your brother to tell him you're awake."

"Thank you."

I blushed as he helped me sit upright against the headboard and the pillows and then handed me the mug. I gingerly brought it to my lips, testing the heat and watching him glance back from the doorway before going out. If nothing else, at least his face seemed familiar. I took a few sips, savoring the flavor and grasped for his name teasing me in the back of my mind.

When he returned no more than ten or fifteen minutes later there was a woman with him. Medium length brown hair peppered with age, gentle smile marks lined her mouth and eyes, except when they found me, there was no smile.

"Tristan said you have amnesia," she said by way of a conversation starter.

When I didn't say anything, just shyly sipped more broth, she brought a hand to her lips, as if that would stop the trembling there. Now that she'd said his name I knew that was the one that had been teasing me, the name of my husband. I set the mug in my lap and waited for the tightness in my chest to stop squeezing.

"I'll let you rest," she stood and wiped her eyes before any of the tears could streak her face.

"Wait," I blurted before I could stop myself. She paused, turning a little to see me.

"Yes?" She seemed eager to stay.

"I don't remember your name, but something is reminding me that you, and him," I looked towards Tristan in the doorway, "are people I love very much."

"We love you too, sweetie. Rest now and I'll come to you later. No, soon. In a few hours," she corrected herself.

"Bye," I attempted to wave, and was glad she was already turning away because the mug nearly tipped over in my lap.

"I'll be back in a second, babe."

"Ok," I nodded shyly, watching him close the door behind him as they made their way into the hall.

*****

True to his word Tristan stayed with me. Over several weeks the amnesia passed and my strength started to return with the help of physical therapy. While I was nowhere near my former self, at least I appeared normal to anyone ignorant of what I'd been through. It wasn't until spring that I was deemed healthy and strong enough to stop the physical therapy and constant fussing and resume life as normal again.

Standing in the kitchen with a steaming mug in my hand, I watched Tristan and Levi toss a football back and forth. Them in the present and flickers of them in the future raced up and down the yard and side of the house as if laying down yards and scoring touchdowns against each other. Meanwhile, twin teen boys ran alongside them, flickering in and out of sight, blocking passes that hadn't happened yet. They played and wrestled without a care in the world. It was a comforting sight to see after all that happened. Even better were the glimpses of that peace continuing for many more years.

"You and Tristan settled in together pretty quickly. I love your homey touches. It finally doesn't look like a bachelor pad, or mom and dad's pretend house." Destiny nibbled her chocolate chip cookie, leaning on the counter beside me.

"Eh, there are too many flowers," Zach chimed in from the dining table. "And there's too many pillows on the couch."

"So do you have an update or are you Mr. Negative today?" I asked with a wave of my hand.

"Still no sign of Vince, but everyone is on the lookout."

I sighed, tired of getting the same update over and over. Part of me wondered if Vince didn't survive the fall after I took his dragon, but most of me believed he was still out there, laying low and hiding.

"How about no updates until you have an actual update?" Destiny snipped, seeing my face fall.

"I was trying to be reassuring," he defended but still got up out of his chair and waved his hand, opening the doorway back to Caleath and the palace. "See you at dinner. I have a meeting with Lady Margaret in a little while."

"How is Princess Scarlett and her aunt?" I asked, "They're staying safe from the rebels and protesters? The issues are just in Wilden, right? Nowhere else in Parna?"

"Right, well… for now. Hopefully, it doesn't spread," he affirmed with a nod. "Lady Margaret says they have taken extreme precautions, but that everyone is safe and well."

"Good, good..." I sipped, glad at least that things hadn't escalated since we were there.

"Kay, see you at dinner," He waved, we nodded, and he was gone.

Destiny sighed, "I was afraid he was going to ask me about Fangthorn again."

"Well," I turned back to the window to hide my face. I never had been a good liar. "It's getting serious. Isn't it?"

I already knew it was, and where it was going next. Fangthorn came to me yesterday after having lunch with my parents to ask for help keeping Destiny busy today so he could surprise her at the gala tonight. It was the perfect opportunity to propose. The Elf King and his son, Prince Aeson, would be there, Lady Margaret of Parna, the Steward of Ire and more... all Caleath's allies together in one place to celebrate Malthor's defeat. All were friendships Fangthorn wanted to strengthen for the sake of Lyonshire's future. Not to mention, he and Destiny had great chemistry and it was plain to see that they adored each other.

"Are you ready to be announced as mom and dad's heir tonight?" She asked, changing the subject.

"Yes, I think so. Becka and I were going to get manicures in an hour. Do you want to come? You know, have a little girl time before the gala?"

"No need to ask me twice! Let's go!"

Epilogue

The body crumpled to the ground; head flopped to the side with wide, vacant, unseeing eyes. Thorkin cupped the glowing orb in his bloodied hands, smiling. Vince played his part well enough without even knowing it, even after failing to obtain the princess and the throne of Caleath. His bloodline combined with Celestial's would have been ideal, but the soldier she married had a strong enough tie. The blood bond between each generation and himself was almost strong enough. One more generation to manipulate and he could finally enact his revenge and fulfill the prophecy.

Gently he brought his hands to his lips and opened his mouth. Soul fire scorched him all the way down, but once it was absorbed, he would be that much closer to his former strength. Thorkin was almost strong enough to face his brother again. His sources confirmed Icarius hadn't left his mountain top in hundreds of years, which meant he was still ignorant. Only a few more decades to wait, a few more souls to consume... Then he could leave the darkness of the cave and survive the daylight and crossing to earth. Thorkin walked the halls of his underground dwelling until he reached his throne room, a vast cavern carved from the floor to the mile-high ceilings with his mark and runes infused with ancient, wicked magic.

A reflection pool filled with toxic black poison rippled almost unnoticeably with the soft fall of each step. Standing beside his throne Caoranach stood waiting.

"Bring me Algoroth's soul and raise me a worthy general. It's time to start the next phase."

"Yes, my King," Caoranach grinned, baring teeth she'd filed into sharp points. "But" she stepped down from the dais and kneeled as the Dark King approached, "What about the doorway in Caleath? Because of that child's failure it is still controlled by the Andavir family."

He passed her without so much as a sidewise glance and sat on his polished black stone throne, sighing comfortably. The icy chill of the stone soothed the soul burning away within him.

"We will secure it, but right now our focus must be else-where and you must keep a weather eye open and control your bloodlust. The next generation will be much more troublesome. Now, go. I have a soul to absorb."

A note from the author:

Hi! I am so excited to share these stories and want to say thank you to all my readers and anyone who has shared these books with someone else. It means the world to me to see these in print and as ebooks, a childhood dream come true! Keep your eyes peeled for the third book in the Out of the Shadows series, Shattered Curses. Also soon to come is Serpent Key, an addition to the Out of the Shadows series as a standalone novel!

Want to reach out? You can email Natasha at natasharosesbooks@gmail.com

Made in the USA
Columbia, SC
29 July 2024

326ceb33-e568-45b8-97d6-eca3919cea1eR01